ALAMIR
BLOOD OF KAOS SERIES

To Janet.
Rippy reading!
Roda Miller

ALAMIR

BLOOD OF KAOS SERIES - BOOK ONE

NESA MILLER

Visit the author's website at www.ladyofkaos.com.

Cover Design: Amy Queau – Q Designs

Formatting by Serendipity Formatting:
https://www.facebook.com/SerendipityFormatting/

First Edition

ISBN-13: 978-1548140595
ISBN-10: 1548140597

CONTENTS

ACKNOWLEDGMENTS

Daniel, my incredible husband – I adore you! Thank you for your patience, support, and inexhaustible willingness to confirm the authenticity of certain intimate scenarios.

Meredith, my irreplaceable critique partner – POV! The most valuable lesson you have taught me! Thank you for your friendship and cracking the whip to "show, not tell".

Kim Young, my indomitable editor – thank you for sticking with me and saying it straight. Your hard work makes mine look like I know what I'm doing. Check her out!
     https://www.facebook.com/KimsFictionEditingServices

Amy Queau of Q Design, one helluva cover illustrator – thank you for your beautiful work and wonderful talent. See her work at http://qcoverdesign.com/

Thank you to my beta readers and friends who have advised and provided their invaluable assistance. Special thanks to Anna Johnstone, Ingrid Hall and Derek Barton for your invaluable help along the way!

To Jamie, without you this story would never have come to life. Thank you for your friendship and contribution.

Many years ago, a small group came together in the spirit of community. They called themselves superheroes. Super they were and super they remain — thank you for your super ways, support, and continued friendships.

Long live all you Superdudes!

1

ETAIN

When your big brother yells at you to run, you run.

Scared out of my mind, I dashed across the road and into the park, searching for a place to hide. A copse of trees looked like the perfect spot. Darting into a tangled mass of shrubs, I tried not to cry out at the branches slapping me in the face and tearing at my hair. It was so dark, I could hardly see.

Hearing footsteps, I panicked. They didn't belong to my brother. Too heavy. His one word blazed through my mind. *Run!* I tried, but getting traction wasn't easy. The ground, slick from the rain, made me slip, and my stupid shoes weren't helping. Man, how I wished I'd worn my boots. On hands and knees, spitting mud, I scrambled out of the shrubs, losing a shoe.

Whatever pursued me was close. I heard the rasp of its breath, glimpsed its red eyes searching and veered to the right, hoping it would be the quickest way out. As though growing claws of its own, the brutal darkness grabbed at my favorite dress, ripping it into shreds.

I'd worn it because it made me feel older than I was, even though my brother said I looked more like twelve than fourteen. It didn't matter what he said. The smile on Dad's face made it all worthwhile. Not that I would've admitted it to anyone…especially my mom, who constantly nagged about my usual outfit of jeans and t-shirt. Jeans would've been the better choice tonight. The scratches on my legs were stinging, the lines of blood tickling. Whatever lay ahead scared the hell out of me, but it had to be better than what came after me.

I finally burst out of the trees into the city lights. It was no less alien, but at least I could see. The empty streets, wet and shiny, reflected the monotonous green-yellow-red flickering of the traffic lights.

Where did everyone go?

The city had been busy as hell when we'd driven through on our way to supper.

Behind me, I heard the transition from a muffled step on wet earth to a firm stride on solid asphalt.

Holy shit! Oh. Damn. Sorry, Mom.

Suddenly, reality sank in.

Mom. Gone forever… Stop it! Get a grip, Etain.

I needed to hide, give myself time to think, come up with a plan. A black alley seemed perfect…until I got close. The disgusting smell of trash hit me in the face. *Ugh.* Breathing through my mouth, I pulled the neckline of my dress over my face. The fabric filtered the air a bit, but didn't help much with looking over my shoulder. And I had to look. I had to make sure the red-eyed devil hadn't followed me. However, the dork in me walked straight into a brick wall.

"Oof…"

Flat on my back, stunned, cold, and wet, I wanted to cry, but the footsteps stopped those tears. Then, I heard a man's voice in my head. It wasn't my father or brother, but I knew I should listen. He had a funny way of talking, like he was from a different time and place. His presence calmed me down. He urged me to breathe deeply, calm my heart.

You must move, little one. The shadows will keep you safe.

I knew he was right, but I couldn't move. Fear had me in its grip. That's when my brother's voice spoke to me.

Don't worry about it, little bit. I guess wimping out's your right, being the baby of the family.

Then he laughed.

I'll show you what a baby can do.

Shaking, I rolled onto my side, pushed up on my hands and knees, and crawled into a dark doorway. Seconds later, steps rushed past. The dark figure, reeking worse than the trash, growled a curse. The words were strange, but the tone of voice left no doubt as to their intent. My heart beat so hard, I was certain he could hear it. Hugging my knees to my chest, I squeezed my eyes shut, waiting for his stinking hand to grab me.

I held my breath for what felt like an eternity, listening for a noise, any indication he was near. It was quiet. Good thing, too, because I was ready to pass out. Gulping in a lungful of air, there was a lingering stench, but lighter than before. Thankfully, the night was still.

Relieved, I let go of the tension I'd held onto since this nightmare had started. Then reality hit me again...hard. Hot tears flowed down my cheeks. Tremors shook me to the core, mourning the loss of my family – my mom, my dad, and my brother.

Why? Why me? Why my family? What purpose did their deaths serve? I prayed the soothing voice would return and tell me what to do.

As if in answer, a soft glow reached out from the alley. With a sniffle, I wiped my tears and peered around the corner of the doorway. Suspended just above the ground, a bright orb glowed. Its silver light sparkled and danced, inviting me to come closer. There was no sense of danger. Instead, images of home, safe and warm, drifted through my mind. I felt the love of my family around me. Without a word spoken, I knew what I needed to do. Standing before the orb, I crouched down, its warm blaze enveloping me. Bit by bit, my fear faded, replaced by a sense of purpose and the knowledge my life was just beginning.

The mud and muck lifted from me, leaving my skin clean. Power pulsed through my awkward limbs as my girlish form began to transform into womanly curves and stretched to new heights. My ruined dress fell away, replaced by black leathers that fit like a second skin. I stood up, trying to comprehend what had happened.

From the corner of my eye, I saw something move, and ducked down, afraid the monster had returned. I held my breath, listening, hoping to remain unnoticed, ready to run. Slowly, I stood again then realized what I'd seen was my reflection in a window. A quick look over my shoulder assured me I was still alone.

"Holy crap." Floating above my head, the orb cast just enough light to see my image in the glass. My fingers traced the outline of the woman I had become. "Is that me?" I marveled at the silver hair lying in stark contrast against the black leather. Leather that accented an audacious body. Little did I know at the time that the transformation aged me by five years, taking me from fourteen to nineteen in a matter of moments.

My *body... I have boobs.* Delighted by the prospect, a new thought hit me. *Could Dad's stories be true? The ones he spoke of only when Mom wasn't around? Stories of the Alamir, warriors who lived in the dimension between humans and demons...and worse.* I wondered if what had pursued me was the "worse".

The orb quietly burst into sparkling stars, showering me with their light. It made me smile, something I thought I would never do again. But it didn't last long.

Would this nightmare evaporate by morning? If it turned out to be real, could I do what was required of an Alamir? I wasn't ready. I wasn't prepared. However, revenge burned in my heart, making me look hard at myself. With or without my angel, I would learn how to fight. My family would be avenged.

2

NEW LIFE

Above all things, Etain loved the thrill of the ride. Her little red convertible, weaving through traffic, hummed like a well-oiled machine. Her appreciation for cars came from her father. She would listen to him banter with her brother and his friends, enthralled by their conversations about muscle cars of the past. She'd lost count of the discussions over stroking out a 350.

The car of her dreams was a '68 SS Camaro. She didn't care if it was stroked out or not. Power counted, but wasn't at the top of her list. Nowadays, cars like that were rare, and were usually not in the best shape. Even if she could find one, time would be another factor. Maybe if she'd been able to stay with her first clan, Darth, things would've been different. They had become close to family, teaching her what it meant to be Alamir, helping her move past the tragedy that had brought her into their world. But after a couple years, the chieftain, Master G, had said the time had come for her to move on. She'd never understood the reason for his decision, and he hadn't left room for discussion.

Her newest clan, LOKI, lived by a different structure. Getting approval to transport any sort of machinery into the Alamir realm was hard. Her experience with the LOKI High Council told her it was more than likely the request would be denied. Despite her worries, she smiled, her silver hair whipping in the wind.

Then again, here I am in Texas in the human realm, close to home and on my own. My first real Alamir assignment.

Sudden pangs in her heart made her frown, almost bringing her to tears. *No, Dad. I haven't forgotten. It's only a minor detour. Okay, another minor detour, but I've learned a lot in the past five years. Dar will help me find him.*

Instead of the elusive red Camaro, she'd settled for a slick, two-door Benz that handled like a dream and floated over the road. This little beauty was always ready, no matter how long between visits. Biting her bottom lip, she engaged the clutch and downshifted to pass a truck.

Before she could make her move, a sleek motorcycle pulled up even with her. The boy flipped up the visor and winked as he revved the engine. Flipping the visor down, he popped a wheelie and sped on.

Etain eased off the gas, glancing ahead of the motorcycle, checking to see if the coast was clear to follow. She saw an even bigger truck, traveling much faster, headed straight for the bike. The boy tried to swerve, but the monolith to his right refused to budge. He had nowhere to go.

Etain laid on the horn as she pressed the gas and straddled the center line, hoping the truck driver would see her in his large side mirror. Whether the man was an idiot or just an asshole, he ignored her attempts to catch his attention. The boy held onto the handle bars and jumped to his feet, landing on the seat. Finding the right balance, he stood up then leaped, making a grab for a handle on the side of the trailer van. Just missing his target, his shoulder slammed into the trailer. The driver jerked the wheel enough to throw the boy across the gap into the other truck as it passed. With the oncoming truck having a soft-sided trailer, Etain thought the motorcycle guy just might have a chance of holding on. She suddenly had to veer to the right, barely avoiding the abandoned motorcycle. She saw the boy bounce from one trailer to the other, slamming hard against the metal. Downshifting, she veered to the left, ready for a face-off with the oncoming truck. At the last moment, the driver jerked the steering wheel to the right, colliding with the lone cycle and running it over.

As the trailer of the second truck jack-knifed toward the first, Etain noticed a gap open. Shifting into fourth, she lined up with the biker, then shifted to third, praying she had timed it right. He landed face down over the back of the sports car. With a quick shift to fourth, she grabbed him by the collar and dragged him into the passenger seat. She looked up just as the tail of the trailer hit the first truck, which drifted to the right. Seeing her chance, she floored it.

The churning in his stomach was his first clue. Clinical smells had that effect on him. He opened his eyes and blinked several times. Everything was white. Maybe he was dead and this was hell. He closed his eyes, took in a slow, deep breath, and willed the turmoil in his belly to a mild flutter.

Must be a hospital.

Daring another peek, he noticed bandages over most of his body, including a fresh cast on his right arm, confirming his recent adventure.

It is *hell, but not permanent.*

Struggling to sit up, he felt an IV stuck in one hand, and a call button at the fingertips of the other. In moments, a nurse appeared, accompanied by a man he thought to be a doctor. He certainly had the look – tall, well-groomed, spotless white coat, black-rimmed glasses, and a fancy watch. He ended another conversation as he stepped into the room.

"-as soon as I found out." The doctor smiled at him. "Nice to see you found the call button. I'm Dr. Green." Approaching the bed, he extracted a small pen-like object from his coat pocket. "Can you tell me your name?" He flicked a switch on the pen and flashed a light into the patient's right eye, then his left.

"Joe." His voice was barely above a croak.

"Joe. Good." He nodded, tucked the pen away, and checked Joe's other vitals. "How about a last name?"

Joe was thankful for whatever this doctor had done to save his life, but not enough to get that personal. "Water?"

The doctor raised a brow and looked at the nurse. She eyed the patient, stepped toward the head of the bed, and rolled a table over, a small plastic pitcher and matching cup sitting on top. She filled the cup, but despite her giving Joe instructions to take small sips, he drained it then grabbed the pitcher, emptying it, as well.

"I told you to take small sips," she huffed, narrowing her eyes at him.

"Can't talk with a dry mouth." Joe wiped his lips with the back of a hand and held out the pitcher. "How about a refill?"

Her eyes bulged.

"Nurse Jordan, get our patient more water," said Dr. Green, smiling.

"But, doctor-"

"Just do it, please."

With pursed lips, she stoically walked out of the room. The doctor looked at his patient. "Joe, we'll forego the last name for now. Do you remember what happened?"

"Minor disagreement."

The doctor grunted. "Hmph, you're lucky. Your helmet and bike took the brunt of it. Fortunately, the young lady who brought you in had a compatible blood type."

Joe nodded, as though he knew all this. "How long will I be here?"

"A few days. It depends on how well your injuries are healing."

"My bike?"

"Let's just say I hope it was insured."

Joe frowned. It wasn't. "So, what do I do in the meantime?"

"Rest." The doctor pointed to a television in the corner, then the remote at the side of his bed. "Watch TV. Keep in mind, we only get the basics." Dr. Green jotted a few notes on the chart. "I'll look in before I leave for the night. Maybe you'll have a last name by then."

"Like you'll ever get it," Joe muttered as the doctor left the room.

He reached for the remote and surfed through the channels. From the corner of his eye, he noticed someone come into the room. *Must be the panties-in-a-wad nurse.*

"Thanks for the water," he mumbled, his gaze on the TV screen.

Unimpressed with his limited viewing pleasure, he tossed the remote on the bed and tugged at his hospital gown. "Don't you people have air conditioning in this place?" No response. He was damn sure she hadn't left the room. "Hey, nurse." A strong energy pulsed around him. "What was your name? Oh, yeah…" The temperature continued to rise. "Jordan." Brow cocked, he leaned to his right, grimacing, and moved the white curtain aside. "Nurse Jordan?" A low laugh from his left made him turn. He jumped, seeing a girl clad in black leathers. "You're definitely not Jordan."

"Thanks for noticing." She chuckled and strolled to the foot of the bed, eyeing the baffled young man, and checked his chart.

"Kinda hard not to." He looked her up and down.

"Not bad for near road kill. You do this often?"

Joe smirked, shrugging, as though his acrobatic moves between the two trailers were nothing more than a walk in the park. "Bike riding, yes. Being a puck, no." He glanced at some of his more minor injuries, which appeared to be damn near healed already.

What the hell? The thought faded when he heard her laugh.

"Puck?" Her eyes widened in a mild show of surprise. "More like a rag doll. Good thing I got the big guys to veer off. A few more taps and we'd be at the morgue."

"You…made two eighteen wheelers…*hauling ass* in opposite directions…veer off?" Now it was his turn to laugh. "You got a golden lasso tucked in those leathers somewhere?" Considering the fit of said leathers, he highly doubted it.

A devilish grin on her lips, she darted up to the head of the bed and leaned down into his face, making him jump once more. "A girl has her ways. Don't dwell on it too long." She patted him on the head. "Wouldn't wanna undo the good doctor's work."

Joe cocked his head, brushing her hand away. "Yeah, sure. How about answering one question?"

She smiled, giving no indication whether or not she would.

"You were driving the red convertible. I remember seeing your face before I passed out. Who are you?"

The young woman stepped back with an elaborate bow. "I am Etain. Welcome to *my* world."

He wasn't sure whether to laugh or press the call button again. "*Your* world?"

"You're welcome." She kissed his cheek, then disappeared through the curtains. The soft thump of the door against the jamb confirmed she'd left the room. He shivered from the sudden drop in temperature.

"Weird girl," he muttered, shaking his head.

Needing to pee, he pushed the table away and sat up. Using his left arm as leverage, he twisted, dangling his feet off the side of the bed. As he scooted to the edge, he realized there was no pain. He twisted the bandaged arm. Nothing. At that point, he noticed his bare legs. He was certain there'd been several scratches and cuts. At the least, there should be bruises. Now, there was nothing.

What the hell?

He focused on the bandaged arm, grinning as he removed the dressings. "This is some wicked mojo." The only items left were the IV, the sling around his shoulder, and the cast on his right arm.

Having formed a theory, he ripped off the tape and pulled out the IV. Still sitting at the edge of the bed, he brought the cast up to eye level. "Time for a trial run."

At the door, he discarded the sling, then took a chance with the cast. A couple hard taps against the counter cracked it open, revealing a perfect appendage. Another twist of the arm confirmed all was well. With a satisfied smirk, he remembered the need to pee.

Afterward, he washed his hands, checking out his head and face in the mirror. "You're even better looking now." With a chuckle, he dried his hands and made a beeline for the door, peeked out to make sure the coast was clear, and dashed down the hallway. After a slight detour to switch his hospital gown for scrubs, he raced out of the building.

Forget the bike. Forget Joe. Freeblood ran.

———

Etain stood there, a fresh set of scrubs in her arms, watching who she considered to be a "baby Alamir" pop out of his hospital room and disappear down the hallway. He was gone in seconds.

Sixty seconds. She snorted, laughing at her own joke.

Contemplating whether she should chase him or just let him go, she went into the hospital room, noticed the discarded bandages, the IV dripping its contents onto the floor, and placed the scrubs on the bed.

How do I catch something like that? Should I?

Think back to your first days. You were terrified.

Yeah, but I was also a kid, and my family had just been... She ran a hand through her hair. *He wasn't remotely intimidated.* She shook her head. *No, he'll find his way a lot easier than I did. He'll be-*

Shit! No, no, no! Bad idea, Faux.

The blue of her eyes glowed, spreading out, surrounding her entire body. She had to get to her sister, Faux, before she could go after the new blood. Just as the door opened, Etain faded in a blue shimmer. She heard an intake of breath, but was gone before its release.

Emerging on a remote island, its white sandy beaches drenched in glorious sunshine, palm trees swaying, and white-tipped waves rolling onto the shore, she lifted her mane off her shoulders, enjoying the breeze, cool against her neck. Unable to resist, Etain sat down on the sand, unlaced her boots, threw them to the side, then wiggled out of her leathers, and dashed into the waves, not stopping until she was chest deep in the water. Diving under the surface, the rush invigorated her, clearing her mind, and placed things in a better perspective.

Refreshed, Etain twisted the water from her hair, running her fingers through the silver strands as best she could. Once dressed, she walked toward a lone house set back from the beach. The large deck facing the beach had several lounge chairs but all were empty, which she thought strange. The mornings were usually Faux's favorite time for sun bathing. Shading her eyes with a hand, Etain tried peering into the house through the glass walls but the glare made it difficult to see anything inside. At the door, she knocked. No answer. She knocked again. After her third try, she turned the handle.

A naked young woman walked onto the deck, stretching her arms over head, and turned her face to the sun. Life on a remote island afforded such freedoms. Although modesty was not a virtue she subscribed to, complaining neighbors could make life difficult.

"Still hate clothes, I see," Etain said, stepping out onto the deck.

Faux's tail flicked out, grazing her across the cheek. Etain knew she had recognized her voice, sharing the same blood gave them a unique connection, but Faux feigned surprise as she turned. "Oh, it's you."

Etain swiped at the trickle of blood. "You should get a leash for that thing."

Faux leaned back against the railing, her tail looming over her head like a viper, ready to strike. "You shouldn't sneak up on people."

"I didn't sneak. You chose to ignore my knocks."

Faux smirked. Noticing the cut on Etain's face, she sauntered closer. "Here. Let me get that for you." Her tongue darted out, licking away the blood. "Mmm, Alamir with a touch of taint. Such an exquisite flavor."

Etain frowned. "Stop it," she said, pushing her away.

"Aw, did big sis miss her widdle sis?" Faux laughed.

"Not so much. Just thought I'd pop in and see how you're doing."

Faux walked to the bathroom, working her fingers through her short black hair. She liked styling it to set off the small curved horns on her forehead. "More like making sure I'm still here." She caught Etain's gaze in the mirror. "Which reminds me. I never thanked you for getting me exiled. What a great sister, giving me up to those stupid *Ass*bassadors."

Etain held her gaze. "I guess it's easier to blame me than accept the responsibility for your own actions. I told you to stay out of the conflict brewing in dc2a. There were too many snakes."

Faux shrugged and resumed styling her hair. "I have other plans now. I'd like to visit a few old friends."

"You don't *have* any 'old' friends." Etain looked at her own reflection in the mirror, happy to see the cut healed. "Get some clothes on and let's chat." She jumped back in time to avoid another swish of the malevolent tail as Faux walked out of the room.

"No time for talk." She slipped on leather pants and a slinky black top as Etain walked into the room. "Hmm. Three or five?"

"Excuse me?" Etain watched her standing at the closet, a thoughtful finger to her lips.

Faux laughed to herself, grabbed a pair of ankle boots, and headed for a chair. "Under these circumstances, I suppose three inches will suffice."

"Nice boots, but you aren't going anywhere. We're going to talk."

"You're really getting on my nerves, sis. I have peeps to do and things to see." Standing up, she glared at the blonde annoyance.

"Going after him will only bring you more trouble. Let it go."

Faux smirked. "Do you know he calls himself Freeblood? Isn't that just the best name? Freeblood. I'm going to find out how 'free' he is."

"At the rate he's going, he won't be free for long."

"Your time would be better spent worrying about your own ass, rather than some poor sap you turned. I doubt your new little friends will ever play nice now," she said, giving Etain a smug look. "Why don't you save them the trouble of exiling you and stay here? It's not so bad."

"Neither of us is staying. You're coming with me."

Faux laughed. "Are you fucking serious? Where the hell are we gonna go? After your escapades in the human realm, I'm pretty confident we're both pariahs in the Alamir community."

Etain rolled her eyes. "Like that gives you any grief. But you may be right. This so-called assignment is starting to feel more like a set-up."

Faux raised a brow. "Do you think this Freeblood is part of it?"

Etain blinked, running a hand through her hair.

"Look…" Faux sighed. "Don't drag me into your drama. Whatever's going on between you and the Scooby gang has nothing to do with me. I have my own agenda." She headed toward the front door. "You're on your own."

"You can't go after him. Whether he's part of their plan or not, he's too hot."

Faux's skin glistened, making the tattoos on her shoulders glow. She turned, black eyes targeting her prey, catapulting Etain into the opposite wall. "Don't tell me what to do."

Etain pushed up from the floor. "That was a dirty play. I don't want to hurt you, but-"

Another blast of power shoved her face into the floorboards. An invisible force turned her body, wrapping her in bands of dark fire, squeezing the life out of her. The blonde warrior rippled an electrical blaze of blue light down her sides, detonating the bands.

Faux was on the move, straddling Etain before she could completely break free. "A little hurt works wonders. I've done more than work on my tan while I've been here." Her tail aimed, its tip fanning out into the shape of a notched arrowhead, and thrust down, penetrating Etain's chest. Faux pushed through until the tip hit the floor. "I've been sharpening my skills."

Etain's blue light faded, relinquishing the fight, the electrical pulses dissipating into the air. Faux shivered, altering the tail's tip for an easy release. "Sorry it came to this, but I gotta get busy. I have plans for my new beau," she said, standing. "I'll be damned if I let those Alamir toons get to him first." She frowned, noticing Etain's lack of response. "I guess it comes down to me to train our new protégé. It doesn't look like you're up to it."

3

KINDRED

The castle was a strange place, existing in a different dimension – somewhere beyond the Alamir and the human. He called it Krymeria, his home.

Etain pushed up from the stone altar, feeling only a minor rush of dizziness. A memory floated through her mind.

"Dar."

He was the one and only living Krymerian. His warm scent lingered, but the man with long brown hair, eyes as blue as the ocean, and seven-foot frame of lean, powerful muscle was gone. As an Alamir, she knew him as Lord Darknight, chieftain and High Lord of the LOKI clan…the Lords and Ladies of Kaos. As a friend, he was Dar VonNeshta. He had brought her here once before, after another near fatal attack. His blood had saved her life.

"Faux." She checked her chest for any telltale signs of her sister's assault. Her top was ripped and discolored but her skin beneath was unharmed. She sighed and ran a hand through her hair. Apparently, Dar's blood had saved her again.

A scroll atop a package at the base of the altar caught her eye.

Curious, she slid off the altar and picked it up. The parchment was extremely delicate. Seeing another object tucked under the stone, she kneeled and reached into the darkness. At first touch, it seemed to be nothing but cloth. However, as she pulled it into the light, the weight of it told her it was much more. The fabric fell away, revealing a grand sword, its beauty was captivating. The pommel consisted of precious jewels inlaid in bronze and a sleek, silver hilt and guard forged into the logo of LOKI. The guard, reminiscent of the wings of a dragon spread in flight and its tail curled around the hilt, gleamed like the light of a thousand stars. The blade, polished to a high sheen, was smooth as glass, its honed edges curving gracefully to a sharp point. Its scabbard was made of the finest leather work, bearing the emblem of a sword and shield in grey on a field of red and white…the Warrior Caste symbol.

Resting the prize across her lap, she tore open the other parcel to find a black hooded cloak made of a fabric similar to a fine silk. A sudden gust of wind blew the scroll into the air, causing it to twist and flutter about her head. "Aye, milord, I see it." She recognized the bold handwriting of her chieftain:

Etain,

You are now a Lady of Kaos of the Warrior Caste. Your strength and abilities have increased threefold after this second infusion of my blood. They will serve you well in your search for the spawn and the one she hunts. Keep these mischievous souls in your sight. Do not allow the Bok'Na'Ra to turn them to the dark. More importantly, beware of the Alamir Ambassadors.

I give you my most favored sword, Cheartais. Wield her with honor and in the name of justice. Keep in mind, she will not allow herself to be used in any evil endeavor. Remain pure of heart and strong in spirit.

The cloak, spun from the finest thread created by elven hands, belies its strength and protective properties. Wear it in good faith.

One last thing. Should I hear of you sharing blood again for any reason — and I mean any reason — the anguish your spawn has inflicted will seem like child's play compared with what will befall you.

Leave this place. Remember, I am watching over you always.

Dar

Oh, yeah. She remembered the rag doll. *Freeblood.*

After weeks of chasing the elusive Freeblood, Faux decided her time could be better spent. Wet from the pool, the breeze felt cool against her sun-bronzed skin. This evening, as with every other since coming to her favorite hacienda, consisted of endless margaritas, tequila shots, techno mariachi music, and a lustful stream of gorgeous men and women. Faux's malevolent tail and wicked little horns never failed to intrigue the affluent of the young jet setters, who fell over themselves to party with the kinky demon girl.

Reclined on a bank of oversized pillows, Faux watched her party friends at play. Sensual sensations vibrated around her, the smell of sex scenting the air. It reminded her of the mind-blowing orgasms she'd experienced during an earlier rendezvous. However, despite the pleasurable company, she kept shifting amongst the pillows, trying to focus on the faces around her.

Scenes of the last meeting with Etain continued to push their way into her fantasies. The slash of her tail had left a bloody welt across Etain's cheek.

Teach her to lie to me.

A handsome young man, standing on the other side of the pool, his body sculpted and tanned, stared at her, his dark brown eyes heavy with lust. Blowing him a kiss, a clear sign he was the chosen one…for the moment, she shifted to a more comfortable position, and admired how his muscles tensed and relaxed as he made his way around the pool. Anticipation made her wet.

Another memory flashed in her mind. *Etain flat on her back*. The thrill of the kill sent a flush over her skin.

It was the least she deserved, thinking she could deceive me. Freeblood will be mine…eventually. If I can ever get him to stay in one place longer than a second.

The young man now stood before her. Faux brought her tail up, caressed the line of his jaw, his muscular shoulders, his tight abs, and down to the prize so proudly presented.

Etain's defiant look in the face of defeat…

Faux refused to let the memory ruin the moment. Their foreplay complete, he slid her tiny swimsuit bottoms down, inch by tantalizing inch, tossing them aside. Her tail slithered around her prey, bringing him between her legs. He smirked, sinking the smooth head of his cock into her wet heat. Faux growled her approval. His self-control drove her to near madness, drenching them both in sweat.

"Senorita…," he gasped.

"Finish me."

His body tensed, ready for his final thrust. Throwing her head back, she envisioned her tail poised in the air, ready to penetrate Etain's warm flesh. Her scream of ecstasy melded with the memory of her sister's.

Sated, Faux dismissed her Latin lover, tied a filmy sarong around her hips and left the party, opting for a walk along the shoreline. Able to think more clearly, she concluded her restlessness stemmed from the presence of a kindred spirit. Knowing her mental attempts to reach the cocky little bastard had proven successful, she grinned.

"We'll see who's laughing this time."

Freeblood's explorations of his new powers had been sloppy, but effective. Proof enough he had something, but with it came a large measure of arrogance. Every time she came close, he would laugh, spout a snarky remark, and dash off. Still, she admired the young man. Anyone who could get under the skin of the Alamir *Ass*bassadors like he had was worth the effort of the chase.

Her blood ran hotter than usual as she continued down the

shore, unaware of the moonlight bouncing off the water...or the shadow figure keeping pace with her every step. She stopped and gazed down the beachfront. Not happy, she turned toward the dunes.

There. That's the right path.

As quickly as her pursuit began, it ended.

"What the...?" Her tail whipped out. "Get out of my way." The dark silhouette leaned back as the deadly tip breezed past where a face should've been. Faux let out a surprised gasp when a viselike grip clamped onto her tail. Whipping her around, the dark figure brought her to her knees in a puff of sand. "Hey, that hurts!" she yelled, struggling to get a better look at the bastard.

"Settle down." The dark presence tugged harder.

"What's your deal, man? Let go a'me." Faux funneled all her energy into her tail. The grip loosened at the very moment she pulled away, causing her to spin and fall flat on her backside. "Who the hell do you think you are?"

A sword flashed in the moonlight. "Give me an excuse to pierce that useless heart of yours."

"What do you want?" Her eyes narrowed, trying to identify her assailant. "I have friends waiting."

The specter chuckled. "You don't have friends. You collect toys."

"True," she admitted, thoughtfully. "But, toy or friend, he'll come looking for me." The tip of the sword followed her as she came to her feet. "If for no other reason than curiosity."

"I'm sure he will. He seems to be attracted to train wrecks."

"Hmph." Faux slapped at the blade. "Move this stupid candy sticker and show your face."

Another laugh. "Not much fun when the tables are turned, is it?"

"Who are you?" She knew it wasn't Freeblood, yet she felt...something.

The sword disappeared into the darkness. The next moment, the hood of the cloak fell back, revealing silver locks glowing in the moonlight, framing a set of startling blue eyes.

"No... I would have known." Faux sat heavily on the sand. "You're dead."

"Close." Etain smiled, looking quite satisfied with the situation. "Lord Darknight took a chance with his own life by crossing realms to save mine."

"Darknight? Why would that son of a bitch help you?" Contempt dripped off every word.

Moonlight sparkled along the blade as Etain pointed it at the demon girl's chest again. *"Watch what you say about my lord. He is the only reason either of us is alive."*

"Whatever." She rolled her eyes. "Would you stop waving this stupid thing around?" Faux gestured to the sword. Etain lowered her weapon, keeping it at the ready. "Since you joined his clan, he hasn't paid you any attention. Why now?"

"You ask a good question to which I have no answer. What I *can* tell you is what I said before you tried to take my life. You're coming with me."

"I have plans, and not you or anyone else is gonna change them. Freeblood and me are kindred. Once I turn him to my way of thinking, we'll be gold."

"I think he's already there," Etain muttered. "Faux, I don't know if my assignment in the human realm was a way to get me thrown out of LOKI, or even the Alamir itself. If this whole situation *is* a set-up by the LOKI High Council, you may not be as safe as you think."

Faux came to her feet, dusting the sand off her backside. "Why would they be interested in me?"

"Because of your heritage."

"Heritage?" Faux placed her hands on her hips. "How stupid do you think I am?"

"You are far from stupid," Etain replied. "Merely uneducated."

Faux's skin took on a golden glow. "Are you calling me ignorant?"

"You're what Dar refers to as a spawn. A somewhat unfortunate outcome of a process."

Her dark brows furrowed. "An unfortunate outcome of a process?"

Faux laughed, not amused. "I don't know whether to be insulted or outlandishly proud." Etain shrugged. "Who is Dar?"

"Lord Darknight."

Faux narrowed her eyes. "When did you get on a first-name basis with his lordship? Wait. Isn't he the head of your precious High Council?" Etain nodded. Faux shook her head, thinking although her sister had not lost her life, she had obviously lost her marbles. "And you say *I'm* ignorant. Etain, they don't do anything he doesn't order. Can't you see he's the one who had you thrown out of the clan? You can't believe anything he says. We don't owe him a thing."

"No. He wouldn't do that. We have an..." Etain had no words to explain what lay between herself and the elusive Darknight.

"What? What does someone like you have with someone like him?" Faux stepped up into her face. "You think you have a connection with a man like that? He can have any woman he wants, if that's where his tastes lie. Why would he want you?"

She met the black-eyed glare. "You...are coming with me."

"Like hell I am." Faux turned away. "I have better things-"

Etain grabbed her by the arm, spinning her around. "You have memories of a family, right? A mother, father, and a brother?" She could see the answer in her eyes. "What about me? Your sister? Do any of those memories include me? Think, Faux! Do you see me anywhere in your past?" Her expression confirmed it. "Those are *my* memories. *My* childhood. You were never a child. You came into this world as you are now."

Flames flashed as Faux's tail whipped out at the silver-haired nuisance. "You're trying to confuse me! Maybe you should remember what happened the last time you came to visit."

Etain blocked the attack with the flat side of her blade. At the same time, her other hand, still wrapped around Faux's arm, lit in a blue electrical blaze. "You won't get another shot like last time. Circumstances have changed."

The girl screamed, defiance dancing in her black eyes. "Why didn't I feel you coming?" she asked, teeth clenched against the pain. "Why doesn't my blood boil with you right in front of me?" Etain released her, watching her fall to her knees. Faux lifted her face, tears in her eyes. "How the hell can I be a spawn?"

As Etain opened her mouth, a new voice entered the conversation.

"I see the party's just getting started."

Although the moon was high and the night almost bright as day, the young man didn't appear familiar. However, between his strut and the burn in her blood, Etain knew who the arrogant vexation was, and so did her sister. Faux swiped at her eyes and came to her feet, while Etain kept a blue-eyed glare on his approach.

"Interested in a little *ménage à trois*?" He laughed, dancing a little jig. "You should see your faces." Giggling, he grabbed his sides. "I can't believe I just walked up." More giggles. "*Ménage à trois...* Priceless!"

Etain shifted, her hands on her hips. She couldn't decide whose ass to kick first, Faux, for being a handful, Freeblood, for his audacity, or herself, for not paying attention to the burn. The spinning bottle stopped on the brat. *"You're a riot. A regular Chris Rock."*

"Nah. More like Chris Farley." He tried his best imitation of the comic. "I got a van...down by the river." He trailed off into a fresh string of giggles.

Faux laughed, too, then placed a hand over her mouth at the look from her sister. Etain crossed her arms. "I'm not impressed."

He clutched at his heart. "Oh, lady, thou doth wound me." His lips spread into a big grin as he inched to his right. Faux mirrored his move in the opposite direction.

"What do you want?"

"Me?" He feigned a look of innocence. "Well, since you asked, you didn't give me the chance to thank you for my new powers." His expression turned serious. "Not to mention any explanation of how to control them."

"You ran off before I had the chance," Etain quipped, stepping out of the line of fire. "Besides, something tells me you're a fast learner."

He moved with her, keeping her between him and his newly acquired partner in crime. "The fastest you'll ever know."

"Not to mention destructive." Visions of his expertise in demolition lit in her mind... buildings burnt, cars smashed; buildings smashed, cars burnt; cars smashed into burnt buildings...followed by a silent chastisement for not having the balls to explain the Alamir condition to the boy before she'd left the room, and for not being able to stop him.

Hell, I don't know that I fully understand it, even now.

"Aw, don't hate. I had to try it out."

With hooded eyes, she looked at the boy. He didn't act like someone personally bent on her destruction, but best not take chances. "The Council can deal with you. Me and Faux are out of here." She turned toward the girl, sheathing her sword.

Was this his destiny? Or did I alter his fate? Did the simple act of sharing blood truly bring him into the Alamir realm? Maybe this is why Dar forbade the practice.

"Something else I've learned is how my blood burns when either of you two are near."

Etain whirled around, her hand alight with electrical charges. "There is no connection between you to me."

"That's BS. I've been tracking you for weeks."

It was Etain's turn to laugh. "You've been following *her*." She pointed at Faux with her glowing hand. The girl flinched. "Which has been a waste of your time. Once I get her to a safe place, I can return to whatever life I have left."

He glanced at Faux. "Safe from what?"

"You."

He laughed, back to his jovial self. "I'm a free spirit. You can't stop me."

"Enjoy your freedom while you can. You won't have it much longer."

"They gotta catch me first." Freeblood sent a regretful look to his lost accomplice. "Looks like no party tonight."

Etain watched him take a step into the night, but he did not take another. Puzzled by his sudden change of heart, she saw a green glow creep up from the ground, encompassing him. Stunned, she followed his gaze and gasped, seeing what had made him stop. She backed away, yelling at Faux to run. Etain turned, intending to run after her, but found Faux was also frozen within a green glow.

Etain drew her sword and advanced toward a green-eyed apparition. Shielded by her own blue light, she spoke with an authority she didn't necessarily feel. "Release the girl and be on your way. You have no jurisdiction here."

A thunderous voice blasted her to the ground. "I have jurisdiction wherever I please. What pleases me most is the power with which you have been imbued from our most generous benefactor, Lord Darknight."

Defiance blazed in her blood. "You will release us and leave this place." She came to her feet, sword in hand.

A sudden breeze blew over her, blowing her hair out behind her. She could hear the water rushing against the shore and feel the heat in her blood rising to an uncomfortable level. Freeblood and Faux, each paralyzed within the green glow, hovered inches above the ground. Sand swirled across the beach, licking at her boots, cutting into her like bits of glass. Realizing her sword was useless, she sheathed it and ran toward an outcropping of rocks at the water's edge.

By this time, the wind roared, whipping the sand in its frenzy to overtake her. Etain climbed to the highest point of the rock, jerked the cloak close to her body, and crouched down. Having no idea what to expect, she waited.

Silence. Even the wind had stilled. For some unfathomable reason, she thought of Inferno, the chieftain of the UWS clan. Unusual circumstances had brought them together after she had left Darth. Inferno and his wife, Spirit, had taken her in and treated her like family. His Irish accent rang in her mind. *The Alamir came about to protect the human realm from evils worse than humans.*

Is this one of those evils?

Wary of the stillness, Etain chanced a peek. Raising her head, she realized the protective cloak no longer rested on her shoulders. Her hands went to her hips. Although she wore the scabbard, the sword was no longer in it. Darkness surrounded her – there was no moon, no green glow, nothing. She searched for anything to give her a clue.

Preparing to jump from the rock, she heard a deep voice rumble from the darkness. "No need to leave your perch." Her head snapped up, hoping for a glimpse of something. "Your position is perfect. Thank you for saving me the effort."

It was still too dark. "Where are Faux and Freeblood?"

"Interesting companions, Lady Etain. They are as they were."

"Who are you? It feels…different. Where am I?"

We live a hair outside human perception. Inferno again.

Damn, I wish you were here now.

The man's laughter mocked her. "You were always full of questions. You will have your answers soon enough. I have transported our little band to my realm where I prefer to work. No interruptions, no distractions. I get more done."

How the hell does he know who I am?

She drew in a deep breath, slowly letting it out. "Is your realm always this dark?"

"Dark?" The deep voice chuckled. "Forgive my rudeness. Let me ignite our young friends again."

A faint green light emerged. The man was true to his word. Having glazed expressions, neither had moved. Their sickly glow gave Etain just enough light to assess the situation. Four rock walls materialized from the flickering shadows. "Are we in a dungeon?" Looking up, she figured the ceiling must be very high because there was only blackness above.

"I forget how young you are. How…human." Although she could not see her captor, the smile in his voice was evident. "I imagine it's what *you* would consider a dungeon. We're merely within the deepest confines of my castle." Cloth rustled in what Etain assumed was a bow. "Welcome to my home."

Inferno's words rang in her ears again. *There are those who live with 'em, but only the Alamir know the Alamir.*

"A dungeon," she said. *This guy's definitely not Alamir. But if he's familiar with Dar, he can't be human, either.*

"You will learn to love it," he said, scattering her thoughts.

An unexpected laugh gurgled up from inside her. "Excuse me?" *Crazy, creepy guy. That's who he is.* "Look, whoever you are, as soon as I find a way, we're out of here." She took a step, but was unable to move forward.

"Do not test my patience, *mon petit.*"

She attempted to move in another direction, then another, her hands pressed against the coolness of the invisible walls. "You have no right. I am a Lady of-"

"You are no longer who you once were. Do you not see that your Lord *Dork*night has removed his protection? How else would I have been able to obtain the cloak and the sword? You stand alone, milady."

"It's *Dark*night." Her fingers dragged through her hair. "I still have my powers."

Could he be Bok'Na'Ra?

"The powers entrusted to you remain. No one can interfere with them. What's the saying? Once an Alamir, always an Alamir?" Revulsion rang through his words. "Yet you are more than Alamir. Your blood sings with it."

Her concerns shifted at the mention of her chieftain. "Where is Dar?" She pushed against her prison. "Is he hurt?"

She heard him laugh. "Doubtful," he said. "Were you expecting him to step in and save the day? Poor deluded girl. He knows he's not welcome here and certainly doesn't have the backbone to defy me." Etain followed the voice as it moved through the space. "As I was saying before, I hope you and I can come to a mutual understanding about how to apply your powers." A torch flamed to life from where she last heard the voice, but she still could not make out his features. "With my brother out of the way, I can proceed without hindrance."

"Huh? Wait. What does your brother have to do with this?"

Several torches lit up, their soft illumination allowing her a glimpse of the man. Etain expected a greasy-haired creep with a detestable face and dirty clothing. Instead, she saw a handsome man in his early thirties, about six-two, dressed in an impeccable grey suit, black curls resting on broad shoulders, intense green eyes, and full red lips. Although Dar had blue eyes and brown hair, their resemblance was uncanny.

"Not what you were expecting, I see." He clapped his hands. "I am Midir, *Dork*night's brother. Sorry we had to meet in this manner, but Dar and I don't see eye to eye on most things. I thought it best to wait until he was otherwise engaged." She continued to stare. "Come now. Surely you have something to say."

"*D-Dark*night. He's never mentioned a brother." *There's something in the way he moves.*

"Dar has never mentioned many things, *mon petit*. You will learn that in time, as well. He tells you only what he wants you to know."

"What do you want?"

He walked toward her invisible prison, green eyes dark with intent. "You."

Her heart skipped a beat. "Me? Why? I'm nothing special."

"*We* are going tear the Alamir to shreds." He jumped up on the rock, pressing his hands against her prison. "They will either turn *Bok'Na'Ra* or they will be eliminated."

Crazy town.

The fear she felt earlier passed, replaced with a growing annoyance. She crossed her arms over her chest. "Like you said, once an Alamir... How do you propose to change that?"

Midir flashed a grin and leapt from the rock, walking to Freeblood, then Faux. Seemingly satisfied, he addressed his anticipated accomplice. "Since my dim-witted brother has most graciously shared his blood with you, *we* now share the same blood. Add to that your own generous nature…" He motioned to the suspended puppets. "I also have these two astounding conduits with which to seduce you."

"My generosity does not extend to blackguards like you." *What if he can change me? No way. It's not possible.* She lifted her chin, willing herself to stand tall. "You will not do this."

"I will."

Etain searched for something to incorporate toward their defense. She could not let this happen. She had to fight. *Can my electrical charge break this barrier? Can I shimmer out of here? Damn, I can't leave Faux…or the brat.* As her thoughts tumbled one over the other, a glint of light from below caught her eye. She spied her sword standing tall, plunged into the stone floor, her cloak to its right. *How did that happen?* She ran a hand through her hair. *Who cares? Get to the sword and maybe I can save us all.*

A deep voice spoke in her mind. *I am coming.*

Lord Darknight, chieftain of the LOKI clan, stepped from the shadows. "I have come for what is mine." He walked to the sword, effortlessly pulled it from the floor, and picked up the cloak. "You will release my clanswoman and the others." Dar approached Etain, reaching through the invisible wall in an offer of freedom.

Etain hesitated. "Am I?"

"Give me your hand, Etain." At his command, her delicate hand slipped into his and she stepped from the darkness. "I am sorry for this inconvenience, milady. My brother's interests are usually more… general in nature. However, since he has made his presence known, perhaps I should share our story."

She gave him a look. "Really, there's no reason-"

Midir stepped forward, sword in hand. "You have no right to be here. This is *my* realm. You break the tenets by showing your face."

"Tenets?" Dar turned to the man, shielding Etain with his body. "I see. Rules count when they play to your advantage; otherwise, they're a nuisance." He laughed at his brother's indignant look. "Put the sword away, Midir. This is not the day for us to die."

Dar held his brother's acidic gaze as he talked to Etain. "Many years ago, there was a boy named DarMidirets, eighth in a long line of men who had carried the same name. His life was not that of a normal child. Blessed by the light on one side, yet cursed by the dark on the other." He stepped aside and turned to Etain. "As he grew, the priests recognized the behavior of a troubled soul. Should the boy continue as he was, his mind would surely be lost to lunacy. Not an admirable trait for a future king. So, before the boy reached his third birthday, he was taken to the temple. There, the priests separated the evil from the good. In doing this, they created a brother who became the dark to his light.

"The boys grew up together and were a constant torment to one another. One was called Midir." He waved his hand toward his dark brother. "The other, Dar." He placed a fisted hand on his chest. "You see, we are one and the same. If one dies, so does the other. Such is our curse." He looked at Midir. "I believe that covers the highlights, would you agree?" Not expecting an answer, he turned to Etain. "Forgive me for bringing you into this, milady."

She shrugged, glancing at her sister. "Family is something we have no power over. You're not accountable for his actions. But-"

"There is more to the story, but now is not the time."

Etain raised a brow. "Oh, *now* is not the time? I have a few-"

"You are leaving." Dar faced his angry brother, speaking in his native Krymerian. "*Ní thuigim do leas tobann sa cailín, ach fios agam a fhágann tú í a bheith. Níl sí go mbeadh rud ar bith a cheapann tú de dhíth ort. Níl aon chumhachtaí speisialta nó eolas aici. Fill ar do réimse dubh agus fanacht ann* (I do not understand your sudden interest in the girl, but I suggest you leave her be. She does not possess anything you think you need. She has no special powers or knowledge. Return to your black realm and stay there)."

Midir narrowed his eyes. "*Agus saoire a ar do thrócaire? Tá tú chomh aineolach inniu mar a bhí tú riamh. ní fheicfidh sí a bhaint amach ar a gcumas iomlán má fhágtar a thabhairt duit* (And leave her at *your* mercy? You are as ignorant today as you ever were. She'll never realize her full potential if left to you)."

Hands on hips, Etain glared at the arguing men. "I'm standing right here."

"*Liom, tá sí an rogha a roghnú* (With me, she has the option to choose)," Dar said, unaffected by her statement. "*Ba mhaith leat a dhiúltú di go saoirse, agus go leor eile. Geallaim duit seo, dearthair. Tiocfaidh an lá nuair a beidh muid a bheith saor den chlár seo curse, agus beidh duine againn bás. Idir an dá linn, a fhágáil léi, agus a cairde, ina n-aonar* (You would deny her that freedom, and much more. I promise you this, brother. The day will come when we will be free of this curse and one of us will die. In the meantime, leave her, and her friends, alone)."

She cleared her throat. "I *can* hear you."

Dar suddenly turned, giving her a strange look.

"*Beidh sin an lá rince agam ar do corp* (That will be the day I dance on your corpse)," Midir yelled. "Do you hear me? Dance...on... your...corpse!"

Without further comment, Dar invoked a spell and, within moments, the green glow faded from Faux and Freeblood. Snapped from their trances, they, along with Etain, vanished from the castle. Dar faced his brother then disappeared into the shadows.

Under a bright moon, Faux gawked at the other two, who gawked in return. "What the hell?"

"I'll say." Freeblood stepped back from the circle.

Etain remained silent, considering the position of the moon. *Three-quarters. It was full when we left.* "Time is different," she murmured, bending down to pick up the sword and cloak at her feet.

"What's that about time?" Faux asked loudly. "Did you pull another fast one?"

"Chill, Faux. Give me a minute here." Etain walked away.

"Come on, superhero. One minute, I'm sitting on my ass way over there, and the next, I'm standing here with you two eyeballing me. I want to know what's going on."

"Shut up, superfreak," Freeblood snapped, backing farther away. "I don't care what happened. I'm outta here." He turned, ready to speed off, but a whip of blue light yanked him to the ground.

Etain stood over him. "Before you go, you will heed my words." Her eyes matched the glow of the cord. "You will leave here and not return. Ever. You will forget me. You will forget Faux. The mere thought of this part of the world will make you burn with a black fire." Her authority was absolute, manipulating his memories. The blue cord vanished. "Now, get up and get out."

Freeblood snapped out of his trance. He jumped up and looked at the women, no hint of recognition in his eyes. "Whoa, such beautiful ladies. Sorry I can't stay. I have somewhere else to be. Later." The night swallowed him in an easy gulp.

A tap on the shoulder made Etain turn.

"Hey. Remember me? I sure remember *you,* and I sure as hell won't forget *him*. What is going on?"

"I'll explain, but not here." Etain wrapped the cloak around her shoulders, then took Faux by the arm. No one spoke as the blue shimmer transported them to a safe place... She hoped.

4

MORTAL COIL

The women emerged on the sands of a distant shore as the first rays of morning illuminated the sky. Faux shivered from the cool wind blowing across the estuary, but turned her nose up at Etain's offer of her cloak. "I can warm myself just fine." She glowed in a warming shimmer. Noticing the expression on her sister's face, she said, "Don't worry. I'm not going anywhere. Whatever it is you have to say might be worth a laugh."

Etain noticed lazy, dark clouds rolling over the sea. "We should get moving. Looks like rain." Her boots sank into the light brown sand, but once she reached the green grass, the walking became easier. Realizing she was alone, she turned, finding Faux still standing at the shore.

"What is that?" she asked, pointing past Etain.

All too familiar with the massive stone structure set back from the shoreline, she didn't need to look. "It's Castle Laugharne. Grand, isn't she?"

"I've never seen anything like it."

Five round turrets towered over the lush landscape, serving as sentinels to the front and sides of the grey monolith. A backdrop of green forest softened the hard outlines of the castle.

"Where are we?" Faux asked.

"In the human realm, it's known as South Wales"

"What do the Alamir call it?"

"The chieftain of the UWS clan lives here."

"Someone *lives* here? It looks more like a prison."

Etain laughed, walking back to her. "Don't be so negative. You'll love these people as much as I do." She linked arms with her. "Let down that gruff exterior and try to act at least subhuman for a while"

"This is gonna suck." Faux rolled her eyes, but walked arm in arm with her sister. "Are these the people who took you in after..." She hesitated.

"After I met Dar?"

Etain seemed to be all right with it, so Faux carried on. "Yeah."

"Aye. They have become my family. Now they'll be yours, too."

"What are those?" Faux almost pulled Etain off her feet. Two hairy blurs dashed from the side of the castle at a dead run.

Etain laughed and tried to pull free from the death grip on her arm. "It's Felix and Ruby, come to say *bore da*. Don't tell me you're scared of dogs?"

"Those are *dogs*?" She cringed, keeping a wary eye on the rampaging mutts. "More like the hounds of hell."

"Then you should be right at home." Etain pulled free, waving to the dogs, laughing at their antics of chasing and nipping at each other. "*Shw mae*, me friends!" Hearing her call, they resumed their run, overtaking her within seconds. One muzzle black and the other red, the hounds sniffed and snorted, tongues lapping their long, lost friend. "Easy guys, I'm glad to see you, too." She bent down to accept their kisses.

Faux wrinkled her nose, standing stiff as a board. "Revolting. Never saw a hellhound act like that."

"You've never seen a hellhound, period." Etain laughed. "Felix and Ruby are Irish Wolfhounds. Very friendly and very loyal."

Hearing a new voice, their attentions switched to her. "Get away from me. Ugh, you nasty mutts. Get back!" They chased her hands, pushing against her in their efforts to greet the new acquaintance. "Etain, do something." Jostled back and forth by the enthusiastic welcome, she lost her footing and landed on her backside, tail wrapped around her waist. Felix and Ruby proceeded to smother her with kisses. "*Etain!*"

"I'm sorry, but it *is* quite a sight," she said, trying not to laugh.

"Get these...animals away from me, or I'll-"

"They won't hurt you." Etain took hold of each collar and pulled them away from Faux's heated glimmer. "Come on, guys. Give her a break. She's not really a dog person."

Faux sat up, spitting and wiping her face with hands and arms, trying to remove the desecrations. "Filthy beasts."

"Hallo." A young man, coming from the same direction the dogs had, caught them by surprise. "You all right? Usually me hounds don't-" His inquisitive demeanor broke into a gleaming smile when Etain turned around, still holding the collars. "Crikey!" He rushed up, wrapping her in a rough embrace. "Are ya real? Yer a sight for sore eyes. We thought we'd lost ya, lass."

"Oh! Inferno!" Etain let go of the dogs, hanging on for dear life as he swung her around, both of them laughing. "Okay, okay. You know I'm real. Put me down." She straightened her clothes and smoothed her hair. Giving him a smile to rival his own, she gave a proper greeting. "*Bore da*, Inferno. How y'all doing?"

"*Diwrnod i'r bren.* A memorable day indeed. Damn good to see ya." Felix and Ruby added their sentiments to the mix, barking and tails wagging. A movement from behind the dogs caught Inferno's eye. "Who ya got here?"

Etain purposely stood between them. "Inferno, this is Faux." She turned her head. "Faux, this is Inferno, chieftain of the UWS clan. He and his lovely wife are the proud owners of this breathtaking estate."

"Yeah, great. United we stand. Just what I need." Her tone

mirrored her opinion of the dogs' greeting. "Shouldn't those things be on a leash?"

Etain whispered to Inferno. "I would prefer you keep your distance for now. She can be…difficult."

He smiled, nodding. "We have leashes. We use 'em on trespassing strangers who don't like dogs." Faux's head shot up, eyes full of venom. Inferno guffawed. "This is *their* home, lass. You'd do best to remember that."

Inferno and Etain headed toward the castle. "Come, Felix, Ruby."

Faux eyed the man as she brushed the sand from her clothes. *Another Alamir asshole.* She figured he was in his late twenties, maybe early thirties, and about five-ten. The cropped brown hair with matching goatee didn't do much for her, but his muscular build struck a chord. The well-developed muscles of his legs strained against the fabric of his jeans.

Not a bad backside, despite his smartass disposition. "So… It's Inferno, right?"

He turned his head without missing a step. "Aye… Faux."

She skipped to catch up. "You sound a lot like a leprechaun I met once. I thought you were Welsh."

Inferno chuckled. "*Yer* here now, does that make *you* Welsh?"

Faux gave him an odd look. "No."

"There ya go, then."

Etain laughed. "Be careful, Faux. He may not be Welsh, but he'll have you speaking it in no time."

"I doubt that," she said, rolling her eyes.

"Nothing wrong with learning how the locals speak," Inferno said. "Shows respect for those who came before ya."

Faux snorted, shaking her head. "I'm not planning on sticking around that long." Taking in the landscape as they walked, she asked, "What do you do around here for fun?"

Inferno smiled. He looked at Etain, then back at Faux. "There's a pub or two in the village, but we don't go out much since the wee

ALAMIR
BLOOD OF KAOS SERIES

NESA MILLER

ALAMIR
BLOOD OF KAOS SERIES

Website: https://ladyofkaos.com/

https://www.facebook.com/AuthorNesaMiller

@LadyofKaos

Available on Amazon

ones come along. Bloody hell, they're plenty entertainment for the likes of me."

"Wee ones?"

Inferno grinned. "Aye, four of the little buggers."

Her brows scrunched together in thought. "Oh. You mean…kids?" His laugh was the most outrageous thing she'd ever heard. Giving him a *whatever* look, she swished her tail and marched ahead. On cue, Felix and Ruby ran up to flank her on each side. "Holy hell! Get away from me. Go away!"

Etain chuckled, watching her storm through the grass with entourage in tow. "I was surprised to see Felix and Ruby unescorted by your small horde. Are they out terrorizing the countryside unchaperoned?"

"Aye, they can be wee terrors, but, no. They've gone to visit their gram."

"Really? I thought school was still in session."

He cast a sideways glance at her. "Aye, it is."

"Oh." Etain frowned. They walked a bit farther. "How bad is it?"

He stopped, lowering his voice. "Mostly rumblings and rumors at this point. It's hard to tell with the *Bok*. They can wipe out everything in the blink of an eye. Ya know the bastards don't care about age. I'm not taking chances until our information is more concrete. It's all I can do to keep me head straight with Spirit here."

She placed a comforting hand on his upper arm. "Spirit can take care of herself. Heaven knows, I wouldn't want to meet her in a dark alley." That made him smile. "Besides, me and my new sidekick are here now. We'll keep everyone safe."

Inferno laughed all the way to the castle courtyard.

As Faux got closer to the building, she noticed the stones were not just grey but a mix of colors – shades of grey, red, green and a few others. The immense front doors were at least fifteen feet tall and wide enough to accommodate a good-sized tank. As she approached, a smaller door within one of the larger ones opened, a brown-haired young woman emerging.

"Spirit." Etain brushed past Faux, giving the woman a warm embrace. "How are you?"

"Gob smacked is what I be." Inferno joined his wife as she gave Etain a good once-over. "We thought you were-"

"Yeah, I know. I have so much to tell you." Etain motioned Faux up to the door. "Come over here."

She hung back like a child who wished to be anywhere but in the company of adults and turned her back on the group. *Breathe, Faux. So what if it looks like a prison?* Turning her head slightly, she sneaked another peek at the stone façade. *God, it* is *a prison.* She closed her eyes and focused on her breathing. *But, I have to admit, she's said things that need explanation. Once I hear her out, I'm gone.* She opened her eyes to the grey skies. *As long as I don't have to deal with hellhounds...or kids.*

Etain shrugged. "Don't mind her. She'll warm up eventually."

"Aw, bless, she'll come round." Spirit opened the door wider for everyone to walk in. "It's a pity the kids aren't here. They'd have loved to see you."

"It's okay." Etain cast one more glance toward her sister. "Inferno said they'd gone to visit their grandmother."

Faux kept her eyes on the estuary, acting as though it were the most interesting view she'd ever seen. Much to her dismay, not only did it start to drizzle, the hounds were just as determined to have her join them inside.

Faux stomped through the door, Felix and Ruby happily bouncing behind her. Etain hid a smile behind her hand. Spirit chuckled, watching them parade in. Once the coast was clear, she linked arms with Etain. "Aye, it wasn't easy letting 'em go, but it was either that or kill me husband, and I didn't much care to be a widow...yet."

Within the castle, his home since birth, Dar crossed a great chamber toward a set of silver doors, the scrape of his black armor rubbing against itself echoing through the hall. A whispered spell made the doors crumble into pieces. Stepping over the rubble, he entered the outside courtyard and faced the building.

Using the tip of his sword, he traced an ancient symbol of destruction in the dirt, murmuring a powerful incantation. Once complete, he crouched and laid his hand on the symbol. The ground shook. Glass shattered. Walls of stone cracked and crumbled.

"It is time I moved forward. Leave the past where it belongs."

Forcing more of his power into the spell, the walls collapsed. Small explosions ignited fires, spreading through what was left of the castle.

Dar turned away from the destruction and raised his hand. A thin line rippled, splitting the air. He peered through the portal, finding a land of rolling hills covered with green grasses and lush trees, framed by waters of the deepest blues. He stepped through into the Alamir realm, standing on a precipice overlooking the sea.

"Perfect."

Dar moved inland, counting his steps as he walked. Several hundred feet from the edge of the cliffs, he turned, drew his sword, and surveyed the distance. He marked an *x* on the ground with the tip of his blade, then searched for a good-sized stone. Being at the cliff's edge, it did not take long. Stone in the desired spot, he walked toward the southwestern side of the cliffs. Once again, he counted his steps and marked the spot. He returned to the center mark, turned to his right, and counted his steps to the southeast. With *x* and stone in place, he returned to the center. Raising his sword, he spotted each mark down the length of the blade. Satisfied, he lowered the tip to the ground and scratched a power symbol into the earth, this one larger than its predecessor. This one was for protection.

"Let no man, woman, or demon destroy what I build here."

Energy centralized, he pushed the life force out from his core. The ground shifted, giving way for a wall of stone the color of heavy cream streaked with veins of gold to rise. It curved from the southeastern shore to the southwest. Massive gates of black agate split the wall at its northwest point. The outer barrier in place, Dar raised a great manor house…two stories above ground, one below. An elegant structure of quiet beauty and strength, it was constructed of the same warm stone as the outer wall, minus the gold veins. The southern and southeastern sides of the massive house extended to the cliffs, overlooking the blue water of the sea.

Taking a step, a road emerged before him, winding to the main gates. He followed the road into the courtyard, and approached the entrance of the house. Once inside, he moved into the largest room of the first floor and called upon his powers again. In the center, a dais rose to a height of four feet. Upon it sat a throne created from a rare Krymerian mineral, its high, arched back in the shape of a great winged serpent, its arms made of skulls from long-dead demons. The feet were shaped like griffins, while the whole of the throne boasted flames of black and blue. Dar climbed the stairs and sat on the great throne. "Today, I start anew." He scanned the room, a slight smile coming to his lips. "Not bad, but far from complete." He stood, descended the throne, and left the room.

With a mere thought, his second-skin armor retracted into itself and disappeared, revealing his black leathers and thigh high boots with tops finished in silver. Appropriately dressed as the lord of the manor, he strolled through his new abode, doing his best to see it as a home instead of a base of operations.

It is set well from an offensive point of view, but lacks a certain touch.

In the great courtyard, he viewed the tops of the walls imagining where the roofline would be. "A reconnaissance mission should do the trick." Decision made, Dar enjoyed the long walk to the north side of the island, taking note of the rise and fall of the land, the thick forests, the richness of the earth, and the beauty of his surroundings.

When the town came into view, he canvased its comings and goings, the various ins and outs, the distance of the port from the town center, and how easy or difficult it would be to defend should the need arise.

"*Akureyri*, time to meet your new master."

Once in the bustling harbor town, he spent the day with local shop owners, as well as their patrons, and made inquiries as to the best craftsmen and women who could turn his fortress into a home. The people welcomed the handsome stranger with smiles and warm handshakes, as though they had known him all their lives. Dar tasted the fresh bread, sipped local wines, tested the balance of new steel, and went out to the docks to view the latest innovations in boat construction. Within a few hours, tradesmen had been contracted to begin work. The people knew his face and name. The town was his. Mission accomplished. Now, he could concentrate on more personal business.

Upon his return, Dar opened a portal and stepped into the Hall of Memories, a room lined with Krymerian memorabilia left by those long gone. He passed the displays of weaponry, drawings, pottery, and art, walking toward the far end of the hall. A table and chair, both carved from a rare red hardwood, similar to mahogany, stood apart from the other displays. On the table sat a skull carved from a single crystal. The cavernous eye hollows lined with black diamonds contrasted with the teeth of red rubies. Upon its brow sat an opal crown.

At Dar's approach, the skull spoke. "What is it you seek, young traveler? Future, past, or present?" As if reading the Krymerian's mind, the skull faced north. "The past, is it? Sit, and all shall be answered."

Dar obeyed. "Tell me of the death of my family."

After a long silence, the skull began. "A sad day it was. The morning dawned bright and happy, like most of the days during King Dari's reign. His son, the High Lord, was away on patrol in the western reaches of his father's kingdom." The skull quieted for a moment, as though taking a breath. "The High Lord's wife and children were in the garden when they came, a vast hoard of demons and soldiers of the *Bok'Na'Ra*. The heads of the men, placed on pikes, were displayed in the courtyard. The women and children ruthlessly massacred. Even when tortured and asked the whereabouts of the High Lord, none would tell."

After a slight pause, the skull continued. "King Dari's head was removed and placed on the throne, his eyes plucked from their sockets and placed on each armrest. The High Lord's wife and children suffered the most, skinned alive, the children forced to watch as the monsters chained their mother to a table and peeled away shallow lines of flesh, one at a time. Before she could pass to the nether world of our ancestors, they did the same to her children.

"If not for a wandering priest, their bodies would have been food for wild animals. He set a great funeral pyre and said prayers for everyone as their remains disintegrated into ash."

Dar wept for his children, his wife, and his people.

Wiping at the tears, his gaze returned to the soothsayer, his voice thick with grief. "Tell me who gave the orders."

Black diamond eyes glittered. "It was a dark day indeed. He knew to kill his brother was to kill himself, but to kill those his brother loved would surely destroy his will."

Dar felt the color drain from his face. "Are you telling me my own brother destroyed everything I held dear?"

Turning to the south, the oracle looked to the future. "One will die by the hand of the other. If the dark brother is the victor, all will be lost for there will be none to stop him." Dar stared, his thoughts on his brother. He had always suspected Midir's involvement in the slaughter, but had convinced himself it was not true. How could the man be so brutal? They had been Midir's family as much as they had been his. The skull faced him. "King of Krymeria, High Lord of Kaos, you must be victorious in this endeavor."

The last words jarred him from his thoughts. "How am I to do that, Skull of Memories? You know the legacy. If one dies, so goes the other." This was all ancient history. He had not come all this way to hear the same old story. It had been his life. *What a waste of precious time!* He pushed out of the chair.

"The birth of a child ends one legacy and begins a new one." A hairline crack appeared at the base of the skull. "Therein lay the path to his demise."

Dar stopped his pacing. His anger felt like a wild stallion, waiting to break its bonds. He was not sure how much longer he could contain it. "What in the name of Krymeria are you talking about? What child?"

"A dragon warrior of Lyoness will lighten the dark…," the skull counseled, another crack inching toward the first, "or darken the light."

"Lyoness died in battle!" He paced again, lost in thought. "She has no line, nor would she have sullied herself with a Draconian. Stop talking in riddles. Tell me what I need to know."

The two cracks merged, traveling up the back of the skull, meeting at what was once the forehead, splitting again. The diamond eyes fell away.

Hearing the fracture, Dar rushed to the skull, grappling with the pieces, hoping to keep it together a little longer. "Wait. There must be more."

"Lothous knows the way." The words floated eerily through the hall as the skull crumbled.

Dar felt as though his brain would explode. "A dead priest?" He stared at the pile of dust. "A dead priest. For the love of…" Scrubbing his hands over his face, he left the great hall.

Dar roamed the hallways of his new home, mentally assessing the completion of each room. Work on the house had progressed far beyond his expectations during his absence. His time in the Hall of Memories had lasted longer than anticipated, mainly attributed to the altering time flows between the dimensions.

Inspection of the roof reinforced his choice in utilizing tradesmen from the small town. The workmanship was impeccable, exquisite. *These Alamir work fast, but the quality is beyond reproach.* A few more days would see the house finished.

Eventually, he returned to the throne, collapsing into it, drifting off to sleep.

A battle fought. Alamir against Alamir – or who were once Alamir. How had it come to this? They were given a gift as protectors of the human realm, to rise above the frailties of being human, to keep their brothers and sisters safe from atrocities. However, these Alamir became more human than humans, fighting one another or, worse, siding with the Bok'Na'Ra. Scattered across the ground, corpses of fallen heroes lay among dead Bok. Moans of pain carried for miles, the air thick, smelling of metal. Bloody and tired, the faithful managed to push the dark soldiers back once again. Still, the losses were great and, in time, would take their toll on the heroes. Assessing the carnage, Dar searched for survivors to help in any way he could...a healing spell here, a prayer for the dead there.

Having just completed a prayer for a fallen warrior, he stood, seeing a body suspended on the outer wall of a building. As he neared, he realized it was a young woman, her silver hair dirty and tangled, her body held in place by a sword thrust through her mid-section and deeply embedded in the wall. He checked for a pulse. It was faint, thready. He had to act fast.

At the sight of the hilt, he froze. "This cannot be." Recognizing it as his, he gently cupped the dirty face. "Just keep breathing." With great effort, he pulled out the blade, dropping it so he could catch the woman in his arms. Shifting her to one side, he barked a single command, raising the sword to his hand. He placed it in its scabbard. "Hold on, young one. I will right this wrong."

Dar jerked awake. Shaken, he closed his eyes again and conjured up the last time he had seen Etain, locating her current position. Through her eyes, he saw a man, woman, and another strange creature who could only be her spawn. "Where is this, and to whom have you run?" He watched, listening for a clue. "Hmmm, UWS." *What is his name? Inferno. That's right. It was to you she fled when she left me.*

He vanished, reappearing on a hill overlooking a grey castle framed by full autumn splendor. Something in the air gave him pause and, for a moment, he was not quite sure why he had come here.

After what I have discovered, despite the task set before me, why are you foremost in my thoughts? Is it instinct, or intuition, or something deeper?

"It is my hope to remove Midir's taint from this world, but should I not be successful…" He drew a deep breath, gazing down on Castle Laugharne. "I leave you this." The skies blackened, lightning flashed, and a wicked wind whirled around him. "A gift for you, sweet lady. I pray it will be enough."

Walking into the lounge, Inferno got straight to business. "Yer new clan hasn't done much for yer manners, girl. Ya been gone a long time with no word on yer whereabouts."

"Love, give her a chance to sit down and catch her breath," Spirit chastised her husband. "Why don't you get us something to drink while she gets settled?"

He eyed his wife, then Etain. "Don't start without me."

"Aye, I'll wait." Etain took a seat on the brown leather sofa in front of a great stone fireplace. She was happy to see nothing had changed since her departure over a year ago. Back then, she decided to make a change in clans and left to join LOKI, a choice Inferno had taken as a personal affront. Her need to "spread her wings", the excuse she used at the time, made no sense to the UWS chieftain. If she had told him her real reasons, of her plans to use LOKI for their resources and Dar's links to the demon world to track down her family's killer, he would have raised holy hell. Then he'd have insisted she stay put and use UWS instead. As much as she loved Inferno, Spirit and the UWS clan, their influence could not match that of LOKI's.

Spirit sat in an easy chair, facing her. "You look good, lass, despite what he says. But I do wonder why you've been away for so long with no word."

"I want you to know how much I appreciate you two." She ran a hand through her hair. "A lot has happened."

Spirit leaned over and patted her on the knee. "No need for that, but it's good to hear."

Inferno returned, three mugs filled with home brewed ale in hand,

and sat down next to Etain. After a tap of mugs and a hearty "Cheers," he took a drink, then looked at her. "Right. Tell us what's been so important ya've not had a second thought for the likes of us."

She refrained from her signature eye roll, knowing it would set him off. Instead, she enjoyed another sip, noting the mix of concern and doubt on both faces. "I was given my first assignment in the human realm." She watched Inferno, waiting for a reaction. When none came, she continued. "Nothing too heavy. There'd been some strange happenings back home, so they sent me to check 'em out."

"Strange happenings, ya say?" Inferno cocked his head. "And what would be considered 'strange' by LOKI standards?"

"Well..." She swallowed, her heart beating a little faster. "That's why they sent me. To see if they were truly strange, or if they could be explained."

"And what did ya find?"

Etain tittered. "There's where the story takes a turn." She glanced around the room. "Where's Faux?"

"Last I saw of her, Ruby and Felix were escortin' her about the place. She's not going anywhere."

Etain took a deep breath, looking at this man who had given her so much, drawing strength from his protective gaze. "It's a long story." She told of the events leading up to her visit. How she had come across Freeblood and felt compelled to save his life, meaning she had to donate blood. She included her visit to Faux and her merciless attack. How Lord Darknight stepped in, saving her life, his gifts, and her pursuit of Faux. She detailed the encounter with Midir and how, once again, the High Lord had saved the day.

They listened, never interrupting, which agitated her further. Keeping his opinions to himself was not one of Inferno's attributes. She was well aware of his opinions about Dar and his clan. He'd taken every opportunity to share his thoughts since learning of her decision to leave.

"I know a thing or two about how LOKI works. It's the High Council what gives out the assignments."

Etain nodded. "With the High Lord's approval, aye."

"Why didn't he send ya back to your original assignment, especially knowing the bad blood between you and the girl roaming through me house?"

She shrugged. "I figured correcting my mistake took precedence."

Inferno leaned back. "Is that how ya see it? Since when is saving a boy's life a mistake? Darknight, just like every other chieftain, knows any goings-on in the human realm take precedence over Alamir business." He raised a hand when Etain opened her mouth. "Once that boy turned, he became Alamir business. Ya should've gone back and completed yer mission."

He possessed an innate ability of making her feel like a child. "It wasn't the saving of his life. It was the blood. Dar, er...Lord Darknight had forbidden the sharing of it. I guess I now know why. I did the deed, so it was my responsibility-"

His eyebrows shot up. "On a first name basis, are we?"

The man knew how to push her buttons. Nothing with Inferno was ever easy when it came to one of his own. Never mind the implications of what her sharing the blood meant to this boy, or how it had forever changed his life...and hers. Etain rolled her eyes, running a hand through her hair. "Inferno..."

"It's *his* soddin' blood, isn't it?" He pushed out of his chair. "Makes no sense to me. Makes the rules and breaks 'em when it suits. That's a bloody Krymerian for ya." He paced to the window, staring out, muttering to himself.

Etain sent Spirit a silent plea. She answered with a shake of her head and a shrug.

Inferno stormed back, standing in front of Etain. "Tell me it's at least knocked some sense into ya and yer coming home. That lot doesn't deserve ya and neither does the blackguard who leads 'em."

"That's the thing. With Freeblood on the loose, Faux'll definitely keep tracking him, which will end badly for her. He's on his own, but I can't leave her unprotected."

Spirit stood next to her husband. "Leave? Are you going back to the human realm?"

"No. I have to go back to LOKI-"

A disgusted snort from Inferno made her stop. He looked at his wife. "She's lost her soddin' mind! Going back to the wanker what put her in this bleedin' position." He turned on Etain. "Ya don't need him, or his bloody clan, or that silly girl with the tail. I know what yer after. We'll do what needs doing."

"Inferno, they're one of the oldest clans. They have connections everywhere."

"Doesn't mean they're the ones ya need. We have resources. We'll find the bastard who murdered yer family."

Spirit placed a hand on his arm. "Please, love. We'll get it sorted. Why don't you get us a refill, give us all a chance to calm down?"

He grabbed each of their mugs. "As long as that son of a bitch is in the picture, there'll be no calm." He glared at Etain. "Be right back."

Spirit waited until he was gone, then sat next to her. "What's on your mind, lass?"

She tried to smile, failing miserably, and took Spirit's hand in hers. "It was my first assignment. I did the training. I served my time and waited, watching as every newbie who joined the clan was sent out. Some had joined at the same time I did, and some came later. At that point, I knew something was going on, so I started asking questions. Not long after, I received an assignment. I was so excited."

"But now?"

"Nothing makes sense. Midir provided irrefutable proof I'd been ousted from the clan, but Dar had just promoted me into the Warrior Caste. He gave me his sword, his *personal* sword, and his cloak. He told me I was a Lady of Kaos. You know what an honor it is. And that was *after* Freeblood. Why go to all that trouble only to kick me out?"

Spirit squeezed her hand. "Sounds like Lord Darknight has a few problems of his own."

"Perhaps, but it comes down to me to find out why I've been ousted from the clan. Once that's done, I'm hoping Dar will open some doors to the demon realm, find me a lead. While I do that, I need Faux tucked away with a clan who will protect her, as well as keep her out of trouble." Inferno came into the room, quietly handing out the refilled mugs. She held his concerned gaze. "I could think of no safer place, no more caring a clan than UWS. I hate to ask for such a huge favor, but I didn't know where else to turn."

"Take her to Darknight and be done with both of 'em," he said. "Ya have no business messin' with demons, her included."

"Everything I've done since turning Alamir has been for my family. I won't stop until I find the one who murdered them."

"Not had yer fill of the dark side, have ya?"

Etain came to her feet, needing to move. "A lot depends on what happens with LOKI. At least I wouldn't have to worry about Faux."

Spirit went to Etain and wrapped her in a loving hug. "If you're that determined, we'll help any way we can."

Inferno seemed to sense the importance of the moment and joined in, holding both women in a protective embrace. "At least she'll be one less worry on yer mind, lass. Whatever happens, ya have a home here...and so will she until ya come back."

"Not that I don't appreciate it, Inferno, but-"

"Hey! An orgy, and I wasn't invited?" Faux sauntered around the room, tail swishing, a smirk on her face. "You people are full of surprises." She picked up Etain's mug, sniffed it, and downed the contents.

Etain's gaze stayed Inferno's sharp retort. "There you are, Faux. Have a seat." She gave the couple one last reassuring hug, then turned. "Let's talk."

"I'm not in the mood." Faux walked to the window, watching Inferno and Spirit exit through the front doors.

Etain joined her. "There are things you need to know."

Her lethal tail swished. "I know more than you think I do. One, you're a pain in my ass." She turned, looking her in the eye. "Two-"

"Aye, I know. You won't be told what to do." Etain swallowed a flash of temper. Losing it wouldn't save this demon from her impulsive nature. She remembered something her dad would do when a client proved difficult. Shrugging, she sauntered back to the sofa. "Okay, I see your point." She leaned back into the cushions and propped her arms along the back. "So, you'll be ready when he shows up."

Faux turned her head. "When who shows up?"

"You don't know?" she asked, eyes wide in innocent surprise.

Faux shifted, placing her hands on her hips. "Why are you fucking with me?"

Their eyes locked in a childish power game Etain hoped would give her an edge.

"Fine. I'll bite." Faux plopped down in the chair across from the sofa. "Is this about Dar?" She crossed her legs and wrapped her tail over a shoulder, twirling a strand of hair around a forefinger. "Is he coming to this boring little party?"

Etain leaned forward, hands in front of her. "He'll show up if there's a need for it. But there's a few things you should know first."

"If this is another discourse on the pros and cons of who I am and how I live, I'd prefer to do it while intoxicated." Pushing out of the chair, she left the room.

Having no choice, Etain followed. She breathed in the warm scents of the Welsh country kitchen. "I love this room."

"Well, maybe when you grow up, you can have one, too." Faux topped off two mugs and slid one across the granite-topped island. "Here's to that little bitch called fate."

Etain raised her mug in salute and drank. The elixir had a stout bite, settling her nerves and boosting her resolve. "Basically, you're here because of Dar and me."

Faux eyed her over the rim of her mug. "Sounds like you lost more than just your marbles."

Etain gave her a strange look. "I met Dar a couple years after coming to the Alamir...after Darth. There wasn't a Council of Ambassadors then, and battles between clans were ugly." She took another drink. "Darth taught me how to work the streets, what to avoid, what to capitalize on, how to survive."

Faux lowered her mug. "You? Lived on the streets?" She sat on a barstool. "You *worked* the streets? Hell, Etain." She snorted a laugh. "What was the worst you had to do? Dance on a street corner, sing a little song?" She shook her head, swallowing another mouthful of ale.

Faux had always treated her as though she were a princess who relied on others to do everything, and maybe that were true when she had had a real family. But at fourteen, she had no idea how the real world worked. Her education since becoming Alamir had been unrelenting and tough. Her life as a princess was long gone.

"Nevertheless, I was pretty good at avoiding clashes, clearing out before things got too heated, but sometimes my sense of timing..." Biting her bottom lip, she said, "That needed some work. You know the story. The day I was on the wrong street at the wrong time, and ended up with a sword through my gut." She cast a caustic gaze at the demon girl. "Kinda like your tail."

Faux avoided her gaze and busied herself refilling her mug. "Yeah, yeah. You lost a lot of blood. He gave a lot of blood. You almost died. He almost died. What does all that have to do with me?"

She could see through her blasé attitude. "Well, once we both recovered, we spent the night in conversation...debate, really. He has a rather different view of the Alamir world."

"Conversation? That's it?" Faux seemed disappointed.

"He was a perfect gentleman."

"Ha! No such thing as a *perfect* gentleman." Faux smirked. "Not if he's any good in bed anyway."

"Not everyone indulges in...whatever it is *you* indulge in."

Faux gave her a genuine laugh. "Trust me. One way or another, they do. You'll learn that someday. How long were you there?"

She shrugged. "I'm not sure. A few days maybe?"

"Something had to have happened."

Etain gave her a long look. "This is a brutal world we live in. Battles are fought blade to flesh, hand to bow, brawn versus brains. Dar explained how the Alamir live in a modern time, yet modern weapons have no power against the magic they wield." It was her effective avoidance of other avenues of discussion. "In the days after, he taught me the warrior ways of his people and how to wield a sword."

"His people? You mean his clan?"

"No. LOKI is Alamir. Dar is Krymerian."

"What the hell is that?" Faux appeared amused by the new word, pronouncing it in different ways. "Kry-*mer*-ian. Krymer-*ian*. *Kry*-merian."

"Krymerian," Etain repeated. "Inferno told me they're a race as old as time. Warriors born of Kaos, created to face some great evil."

"That's where he gets it. Lords and Ladies of Kaos. I guess evil won. I've never heard of Krymerians."

"Dar's the last."

"Seriously?"

She ran a hand through her hair. "By nightfall, what little energy I had left was spent on a quick supper and collapsing into bed. Mornings came early at Dar's, and the days were long."

Faux stared at her. "A man like that, and he never *tried* anything?" Etain confirmed it with a nod. "Men of strength usually take what they want, to hell with whatever your wishes may be. But, then again, maybe women don't interest him…in that way." She shrugged. "Okay, he kept his hands to himself, yet he's the reason I'm here?" Her brows raised in question.

"My last night there, we argued. He was so angry with me, saying I wasn't ready. I told him if I was going to be a part of the Alamir world, I needed to be *in* it. Drained, I went to bed. My only thought was to find some semblance of peace. The next thing I knew, a rude, dark-haired woman with horns and a tail was shaking me. Morning had come, bringing with it the promise of a controversial day."

"Are you making this up?"

"Absolutely not."

"I don't remember any of it." Faux stood up. "How could I be there and not run into him?"

"We looked for him, but what we found was a note. He'd gone to avert further bloodshed in another skirmish between clans."

"I just appeared...like hocus pocus?"

"I believe you're a direct result of Dar and me sharing blood."

"I still don't get it."

Etain recounted the events in Mexico, including the visit from Midir and the struggle between the brothers. Faux stared at her.

"What?" Etain asked.

"Am I brain-damaged or something?"

"I don't think so. Why?"

"I don't remember Dar. I don't remember Midir. I *do* remember you, me, and Freeblood staring at each other like idiots before you chased him off."

Etain shrugged. "You and Freeblood were trapped within some kind of green glow. It looked like you were in a trance."

"Ugh, green? I was glowing *green*?"

"Midir's trick. It's probably best you don't remember."

Faux became thoughtful. "So, Dar's *not* the last."

"Hmm, I guess not."

"Have you ever thought about what that could mean?"

Etain rolled her eyes, anxious to get on with her story. "What?"

"All this time, you've never known about Midir, right? Well, what if there are others...living among us, lying low?"

"For what purpose?"

Faux shrugged. "I don't know, but what if?"

Etain sighed. "When you figure it out, let me know." She ran a hand through her hair. "Anyway, listening to Dar and Midir's story, I saw similarities with ours. I figured, with the changes in me and the power of his blood..."

"I'm, like, your dark side?"

"Kinda, but nothing even close to Midir."

She narrowed her eyes. "What caused his sudden interest?"

"I don't know."

Inferno walked in, stopping at the door. He looked at Etain, then Faux, and back. "Everything all right in here?"

"Aye. We're good."

"There's something ya need to see." He jerked a thumb over his shoulder.

"What is it?" Etain asked.

"Ya just need to see it."

Once outside, the unusual stone formation in the center of the courtyard was the first thing they saw. Etain frowned. "I don't remember this being here."

"Aye, it wasn't," Inferno said, circling the rock. "It's a strange sort."

Etain recognized the stone. It resembled obsidian, smooth with a rainbow sheen. At first glance, the stone seemed opaque, but if one continued to gaze into its depths, a secret horde of crystal shards appeared. "I've seen it before. It has to be from Dar."

"Whoever it's from, there's a ring on top." Faux reached for the bauble. "What the...?" She tried again. "It's all shimmery. I can't touch it."

Spirit looked at Etain. "If it comes from him, I can't imagine it being for anyone but you."

"Come read the inscription, lass," Inferno cut in, "and Bob's yer uncle."

"Inscription?" She walked around to Inferno.

Etain, this is the last of my gifts. Use it wisely and it can come to save you. Be ye well and forever a dear friend.

She warily peered at the ring on top of the stone. "How am I to use it wisely when I don't even know what it is?" As Etain effortlessly picked up the ring, a loud *humph* came from Faux.

"Let me have a look at it." Spirit scrutinized it closely, pointing out the lavender glow and dark metal veins. "It reminds me of a Tiffany stone."

"What's that?" Etain took the ring from her outstretched hand.

"We use it to help with psychic communication. A Tiffany is lavender, like this one, but it doesn't glow. It's said to give the wearer strength to face change."

"Let's hope this one does the same." Etain placed the ring on the middle finger of her right hand. "I have a feeling we're gonna see a few soon."

Several days later, Etain received a request she knew would not sit well with her family. "Spirit, Inferno, we have to leave."

Relaxing in the grounds, Inferno looked up from his newspaper. "Already?" He glanced at Spirit. "We thought ya were gonna stay a wee bit longer."

Etain sat across from the couple. "It won't be for long." He raised a curious brow. "It's Dar. He's asked I...we come see him."

"Asked, my ass. It was a summons," Faux said, rubbing her temples.

He leaned back, set the paper aside, and crossed his arms. "He says come, and ya go runnin'?"

"That's what *I* said." Faux plopped down in the chair next to Etain, tail swishing back and forth.

"It's only out of respect for my chieftain."

"I thought ya were out of that den of snakes." At the look on her face, he said, "Tell me ya have the sense to meet him at the LOKI castle."

"That's not where he is," she said, pushing her hair from her face.

"Bloody hell, Etain." Inferno came to his feet. "Yer not going alone. He doesn't have the right to demand ya do."

"I won't be alone. Faux's coming with me."

"For fuck's sake." He threw his hands in the air. "Have ya not learnt anything from all this?"

"Etain, are you sure you should go?" Spirit asked.

She looked down at the ring on her right hand, twirling it on her finger. "He wouldn't ask if it weren't important." Her gaze met Spirit's. "It could have to do with my status in the clan. I need to find out."

"The bloody wanker could come here. I don't like it, Etain."

"Don't worry, folks." Faux attempted to ease their minds. "I may look small, but I pack a serious wallop." A fireball lit in one hand as she stroked the tail languishing over her shoulder. "And our little Etain has learned a few things in her travels. Between the two of us, we can handle an overstuffed Krymerian."

5

SÓLSKIN

ppearing in Dar's home world, Etain and Faux were surrounded by total devastation. The once beautiful land smoldered amongst the ruins of the old castle, scorched and blackened, green trees now ash, rose gardens destroyed.

"Ouch. Someone was pissed off." When Faux noticed tears in her sister's eyes, she experienced an emotion she'd never felt before. Compassion. Feeling awkward, she draped an arm over Etain's shoulders. "Maybe he's dead." The pointed tail patted her on the back in a show of consolation.

Etain swiped at her tears, pulling away. "Look around. Tell me what you see."

"A bunch of rubble and burnt stuff."

"What do you *not* see?"

"Uh, well... Dar?"

"How long do you figure it's been like this?"

"I don't know. I'd guess it just happened. Surprise attack?"

"Look closer." She kicked at a burnt portion of wall. "See? Weeds have already begun to sprout. This didn't just happen. And there aren't any body parts or blood. Dar wouldn't have gone down without taking a few with him."

"Oh, okay. Now you mention it..." Faux kicked at a few stones. "But if they were demons, would there be any bodies to find?"

"Maybe not. Can you feel Dar's presence?"

Faux shook her head. "Even if I did, I wouldn't know it was him."

"Let's see if there's anything that can tell us what happened here. You take the area over there. I'll take this section."

During her investigation, Faux stumbled across what must have been the armory. Remnants were everywhere, some were gold-colored, others silver. A few pieces were of a metal she had never seen. Moving on, her next find was a pair of black gloves finished in silver and decorated with two unusual stones… One in the palm, another on the back. There was also a strange writing etched into the leather. Their relevance unknown, she tucked them in her belt. *Maybe it'll mean something to Etain.*

The sisters met where the great hall once stood. Faux held the gloves out to Etain. "Any idea who these belonged to?"

"No." Etain held her hand out. "Let me have a look." After a close inspection, she said, "They must've been dearly loved. You see the writing here around the cuff? It says, *To the light of my heart.*" Turning the gloves over, she pointed to the underside of the cuff. "They were created for a certain person." She then pointed to the rune in the palm of the glove. "This stone has the rune of power carved into it. The rune of the burning light. It can cast a powerful spell that allows the caster to burn anything. Now, this one on top… I think it's a naming rune. It's so the gloves know their owner." She gave them another good look. "Judging by their size, they probably belonged to a woman. The name is strange and I can't read it fully, but the last part says *'goddess.'*" Etain handed the gloves back to Faux. "If I were you, I'd leave them here."

"How do you know?" she asked, eyeing Etain with a new respect.

"I told you me and Dar talked."

"Yeah, for a long time. Does this Dar wear a pocket protector?"

Etain's eyebrows puckered, giving Faux a strange look. "Why would he need one?"

Faux placed an imaginary pen in her imaginary shirt front pocket. "To protect his pocket."

Etain rolled her eyes. "I think you're the one missing the marbles."

Faux sighed and let it go. "Did you find anything?"

"Maybe. I believe he's still alive and that Dar-"

Etain vanished.

"Very funny." Faux placed her hands on her hips. "Now come back."

"Was the one who..." Etain trailed off. Shielding her eyes from a single spotlight aimed in her direction, she turned, trying to make out the rest of the room. There were no windows or furniture, other than a raised throne currently occupied by a dark figure.

"Welcome to *Sólskin*, milady."

Watching him descend the stairs, she reached for a hilt that wasn't there. "Damn," she murmured. Taking a defiant stance, she said, "I told you I would not play your game." When the man came into the light, she recognized his face, the black leathers, and the great sword strapped across his back. "Oh, it's you."

"Somewhat." He lifted a hand and stroked her cheek. "I think you are the most beautiful woman I have ever laid eyes on, Lady Etain."

"What?"

Running his fingers along the silky length of her hair, his blue-eyed gaze held hers. "I wonder..."

"Dar, are you okay?" He wrapped an arm around her waist, pulling her close, his hand delving into the silvered mass on her head. Etain stiffened, pushing away from him. "What the hell are you doing?"

Tilting her head to the side, he extended a talon and cut the leather of her top. Her flesh was warm against his lips, her scent intoxicating. Her body pressed into his, struggling against his hold, encouraged the darkness within him, the need to taste, consuming. His sharp incisors sank deep into her shoulder, the rush of the blooding taking him by surprise. He staggered and withdrew, staring at her beautiful face as he gently laid her on the floor. *After all this time.* Yet, he had to make perfectly sure.

The demon girl appeared in the great hall, the sudden change in scenery making her uneasy. "Etain?" Seeing her sister on the floor, unconscious, she crouched, checking if she was okay.

"Usually I would say I didn't do it." The deep voice made her jump. She looked up, watching the dark figure come down from his perch. "But I so obviously did."

A fire-induced sheen glowed from the tattoos on her shoulders. Her tail loomed overhead, ready to strike. "What did you do to her?"

"She will be fine."

She took a defensive stance over Etain. "You'd better hope so."

He chuckled, looking her up and down. "Ironic."

Faux's eyes narrowed. "What?"

"It wasn't so long ago I stood over her, fighting to bring her back from a lethal wound…" He walked around the vigilant demon, "inflicted, I'm sure, by that intriguing tail."

"We made up." She turned her head, following him.

This made the big man laugh. "She deserves better than either of us."

"Who the hell are *you*?"

He flashed a toothy grin. "Lord Darknight, at your service," he said, bowing his head. "You may call me Dar."

"If you're Dar," she eyed him from head to toe, "why didn't Etain just bring us here?"

"Because this…" He spread his arms wide, "is my *new* home. She has not had the pleasure."

She looked down at her sister. "I doubt *pleasure* would be how she'd describe it. What happened to the old place?"

"The time had come for a fresh start." His hand shot out, but Faux dodged it. "I won't hurt you. I promise."

"Come any closer, I promise *you'll* get all kinds of hurt."

A fireball flew from her outstretched hand, exploding against the wall where Dar had been.

"Back here." Turning, she came face-to-face with the leather-clad lord. "Good moves, but not fast enough. Let me teach you better ones."

"Let *me* teach *you* not to mess with us," she hissed, intensifying the flames. In the next instant, his deep blue eyes had her mesmerized long enough for him to grab her by the throat, her feet dangling. "Let me go," she rasped, astonished he was unaffected by her fire. Her tail swung forward, but he caught it mid-strike. "What do you want?"

"First things first," he said, turning her head to the side. "Just a little pinprick." Again, his teeth sank into soft flesh. This time, he drank until the blood ran down his chin. Swiping the back of his hand across his mouth, he dropped her to the floor. Seeing the gloves tucked into her pants, he smirked, confiscating the gift meant for another. "These are not for you. But she no longer has a use for them, either." The gloves disintegrated in a puff of smoke.

A delicious aroma drifted into the room, rousing the women. Disoriented, both sat up, and looked at each other.

"Are you okay?" Faux asked, rubbing her neck.

"Aye. Except for a tender shoulder, I'm fine." Etain noticed the bite marks on her sister. "You?"

"Are you sure that's *your* Dar?"

"He's not *my* Dar."

The man walked into the room. "Good evening, ladies. I am glad you're awake. You must be hungry."

Etain scrambled to her feet, fire in her eyes. "That's all you have to say? Good evening and let's eat?"

"So, you're *not* hungry?"

Oh, how she wanted to slap the grin from his face. He caught her by the wrist before her raised hand made contact, but she was ready with a counterstrike. Her dagger came at him from the other side, its sharp edge breezing past his cheek. Releasing the one, he made a successful play for the other, spinning her around and pulling her arm behind her back. She held onto the blade until Dar yanked to the point she felt her shoulder would pop from its socket.

"Bastard," she grunted.

He clucked his tongue, keeping an eye on Faux. "Such language from a member of my Warrior Caste." He placed his lips to her ear. "I'll have you know, my mother and father were married long before I was conceived. Watch your words, or I shall make you eat *them* instead of the delicious meal I've prepared." His abrupt release made her stagger into Faux. Dar picked up the blade and handed it to her, hilt first. "Now, as I said, you must be hungry."

Etain rolled her shoulder, watching him leave. "I don't care if his parents were married a thousand years before his birth. He's a bastard." She sighed and returned the dagger to her boot. "And he's ruined a perfectly good shirt."

"Let me see if I can mend it." Faux held the leather in place and fired a single finger.

"That won't fix it," Etain said, rolling her eyes. "Maybe we could find something to pin it together."

"Then can we eat?"

"Faux, don't be fooled by his false courtesy. This is a side of Dar I've never seen before."

"Would that be the forgetful side? Looks like he forgot you're not in the clan anymore." Faux looked around the room. "And it looks like we're not gonna find any pins in here."

Etain sighed. "The man doesn't forget anything. Ever."

"Well, maybe he doesn't know." Etain gave her a sharp look. "Wouldn't be the first time a chieftain's most trusted stabbed him in the back. But we're here, and I'm hungry. How about we make the most of a weird situation?" The grumbling of her stomach seconded her remark. "Maybe we can get to the bottom of his dastardly behavior *and* ask for something to fix your shirt."

"Fine. We'll eat, but then we go."

They wandered down the hallway, unsure of which door belonged to the dining room.

"In here," Dar called out.

They found him standing at the head of a large table set for three. "Please, come and enjoy."

Etain remained at the doorway, watching as Faux walked in and took the seat to his left. Giving her food a quick inspection, she looked at Etain and shrugged, then placed the napkin in her lap. Fork in hand, she dared a taste, smiled, and dug in. Etain's gaze moved to Dar, standing behind his chair, his eyes on her.

"You can glare at me all night, but it won't fill your belly," he said.

"You ruined my shirt."

He almost grinned. "I could loan you one of mine."

"I like this one."

Dar considered her for a moment then turned toward a sideboard sitting along the wall behind Faux. Etain exchanged a glance with her sister. Faux mouthed, "What's he doing?" Etain shrugged. She heard the scrape of a drawer as it was pulled out, but couldn't see past Dar's body.

He turned and walked toward her, stopping in front of her. His hand came up, holding a small metal skewer. She flinched when he reached for her shoulder. "Be still," he said. Placing the skewer between his teeth, he pulled the two cut ends together then weaved it through the leather, bending the ends to keep it in place. With a cock of his brow, he returned to his chair and sat down.

Rumblings from Etain's stomach forced a resentful submission, but she took her time, almost dragging her feet as she walked. Her hand on the chair to Dar's right, she scraped it across the stone floor with as irritating a sound as nails on a chalkboard, sat with the grace of an aristocrat, and scooted up to the table like a sullen child. Ignoring Dar, who was obviously ignoring her, she looked at Faux, who didn't appear to be suffering from any harmful side effects. After a few cautious bites, Etain found the fare edible.

Faux ventured into conversation. "This is good."

"Glad you like it." Dar smiled, wiping his mouth with a napkin. "It's a family recipe I prepared myself. I hope you enjoy the wine, as well."

"I'm no connoisseur, but it's going down pretty good." She nodded toward his chosen glassware. "Do you usually drink wine from a mug?"

"Not usually." He sat back, mug in hand. "I've chosen a rare Krymerian grog instead of wine."

Etain set down her knife and fork. "No victimized minions to serve their lord and master tonight?"

His blue eyes sparkled. "A night off."

She dabbed at her lips with her napkin. "Just because we've accepted your hospitality, don't think we've forgotten what you did."

He leaned forward, placing his mug on the table. She could feel his eyes on her, but refused to look at him. "Etain, where is the boy?"

"Huh?" She blinked and met his gaze. "What boy?" Hearing Faux cough and sputter, she looked across the table.

Dar turned his head, as well. "Aye. *That* boy." He looked back at Etain. "I believe you called him…Freeblood?"

Her heart skipped a beat. She'd effectively written him off. "Oh…him." Etain emitted a not so humorous laugh at his raised brow, chewing the inside of her lip, wondering what the hell she should say. "Well…"

"She erased his memory, then told him to go away and never come back," Faux blurted. Etain gave her a scathing wide-eyed look. She shrugged, returning the glare. "He's going to find out anyway."

Dar leaned back. "I see. And to where did you send him?"

"I didn't *send* him anywhere. He just…took off. I had Faux, so the trouble was averted."

"Tell me, Etain." His fingers drummed on the table. "What were you doing in the human realm?"

Her mouth opened. She was torn between being a snitch and telling him how his High Council had obviously given orders without his approval, or taking the brunt of his anger now and dealing with the Council herself later.

Dar cleared his throat. "Let's try an easier question. Who is responsible for him coming to the Alamir?"

She didn't like his tone of voice. However, she could answer this question with a clear conscience. "At least he's *in* the Alamir realm now. I figured the Ambassadors would catch him eventually. Let them deal with him."

"That does not answer my question."

She stared at Faux, willing the girl to look at her, but she wouldn't bite. Etain rolled her eyes and looked at Dar. "I was trying to save his life, not turn him Alamir. How was I supposed to know my blood was so…so powerful?" She grabbed her glass, downing the wine.

His lips pressed tight together, he closed his eyes, and inhaled. "It is forbidden-"

"I couldn't let him die!" She slammed down the glass, breaking it at the stem, and came up fast, her chair crashing to the floor. "Is that what you would've preferred? Letting an innocent die when I had it in my power to save him?" Tears of frustration brimmed in her eyes. "I felt his life force pulsing, flowing through him, flowing *out* of him. He was so full of life. Bloody hell, he glowed with it! But within moments, he was fading. All I could think was what a waste it would be." Swiping at her eyes, she gave her hair a proud toss, lifting her chin. "So, I saved him."

Dar opened his eyes. "And left him to the *Bok*."

"No!" she yelled. "He will not go that way."

His blue-eyed gaze penetrated hers. "Etain, he has not been trained. He does not know anything about the Alamir world."

Faux snorted. "From what I saw, he looked pretty clued in to me." A sharp look from Dar made her shrink in her chair. "Just saying…"

Etain shook her head. "No. After the transfusion, I felt more than just his life force. He doesn't tolerate evil." She ran a hand through her hair. "Okay, he's a bit mischievous and he *did* cause *some* trouble, but…" Her eyes went to Dar. "He isn't evil. He won't turn."

Dar came to his feet, causing both women to start. "I shall hold you to your word, milady. For your sake, I hope you are right. For now, it is time to retire. I have rooms I think each of you will find to your liking." He walked to the door. Faux popped up from her seat, hot on his heels.

Etain hesitated. "We are *not* staying. We'll go back to Laugharne." Her vexation stopped at the doorway, causing his shadow to bump into him.

A corner of his lips twitched. "Do you have any idea where you are?"

She blinked, a rosy glow blooming on her cheeks.

"It is late, Etain. I know you're tired, and I have plenty of rooms." The doubt in her eyes obliged him to extend the one assurance she would accept. "I give you my word as the chieftain of LOKI. No harm will come to either of you this night."

Faux piped up. "Come on, Etain. I'm beat."

Her gaze narrowed. "Does your word extend to tomorrow's light?"

"Tomorrow is a new day. Who knows what it will bring?" Without another word, he turned and left the room. Shrugging, Faux dutifully tagged along.

Etain lagged behind for a short time, but soon caught them up in the south wing of the manor. Dar stopped before three nondescript doors.

"If you need anything, please let me know," he said, pointing at the middle door. "I will be in my room." Turning to Faux, he bowed, gently taking her hand. "It was a pleasure to meet you, milady." Leaving a light kiss on it, his eyes lit on Etain's disapproving glare. "Good night, ladies. Sleep well, and pleasant dreams."

The sisters looked at each other. "It doesn't look like it matters who sleeps where." Etain motioned to the door on the right. "I suppose you can take that one and I'll take the other."

Faux swished her tail. "I *suppose* we can check it out before we make any decisions. This place is heavy on the man's touch, but you never know…" Opening the door, she sucked in a breath. "Wow!" She ran to the black lacquered bed, diving into covers of deep purple. "What a great room."

Etain turned in circles, taking everything in. The walls and ceiling, lined with alternating folds of crimson and violet silk, gave the exotic appearance of a sultan's tent. Tiffany lamps of black and red added an erotic touch.

A dark hearth, surrounded by black stone, pulsed with energy. Although a fire had not been lit, heat emanated from its surface. With her fingertips millimeters from the mantel, a huge fire came to life in the grate. She snatched her hand back, staring at the sudden flames.

Laughter filled the room. "You're such a sucker, Etain."

She smiled to herself and turned, narrowing her eyes at Faux. "*I'm* a sucker? Easy to say from way over there."

Maybe it was the wine or the exotic surroundings, but she felt carefree for a change. It felt good. She dashed across the room, grabbed a pillow, and proceeded to bash Faux about the head and shoulders. Her sister returned the volleys with equal exuberance. Finally collapsing, they lay across the covers, chatting, taking in the splendor of the room.

To their left, an expanse of bronze-colored velvet drapes lined the wall. Curious, Etain rolled off the bed and went to investigate. After an involved search, she located a split in the draperies, glanced back at Faux on the bed, and reached through the opening. Her fingers touched the smooth, cool surface of glass. "It's a window." She disappeared behind the curtains. "A *big* window." Her voice muffled. "I think it spans the entire wall."

"Can you see anything?"

"There's something out there. It's too dark to see, but it sounds like waves." Etain emerged through the opening. "We must be by the sea."

She glanced around the room and noticed something she'd not seen earlier. "Hello. What have we here?" Just to the right of the bed was a black door.

Faux joined her and bent down, peering through the keyhole. "Maybe it's a secret room where he performs ritual sacrifices." She gave Etain a knowing look, eyebrows raised. Seeing the expression on her sister's face, she laughed, turning her back on the mysterious door. "You know, it's like this room was made especially for me. Do you think…?"

They hurried to the room on the other side of Dar's. Paneled walls of sage surrounded an enormous bed of amethyst. An oversized Persian rug covered creamy travertine, adding to the warmth of the elegant room. Near the bed was a similar black door.

Faux peeked again. "Hmph."

Etain waved her over to chairs upholstered in dark bronze sitting in front of a roaring fire. "Someone's done their homework. It's…" She shivered, "creepy."

Faux, sitting in the other chair, slipped off her boots, curling her legs under her. "It *is* kinda spooky. On another note, he totally called you out on the Freeblood thing."

"Yeah. Thanks for your support on that one."

Faux shrugged. "Even *I* know you can't hide anything from that man. He's so…"

Etain blew out a breath. "Overbearing."

"Um, not the word I was going for, but…" She shrugged.

"It doesn't matter. When we leave here, I guess I'll have to go looking for the arrogant brat and drag him back."

"Want some help?"

"Oh no…" Etain pushed out of her chair. "You're not going anywhere near that troublemaker. Once I find him, I'll take him to the Ambassadors. Job over. Then I'll have a think about how to deal with my former clan and this new Dar."

"What am I supposed to do while you're playing bounty hunter? There's no way I'm going back to that stupid island. No fucking way."

"I didn't expect you would. We'll figure something out... tomorrow. Right now, I could use a good night's sleep."

"As long as I'm free of the island and the clans." Faux stretched her legs, grabbed her boots, and headed to the door. "Think about the Freeblood thing, and I wouldn't mind having a shot at those LOKI people. They mess with you, they mess with me. With Dar, though, you're on your own. See ya in the morning."

Etain stretched, the effects of the day heavy on her shoulders. The bed was more inviting than she wanted to admit. Slipping under the covers, she sighed. Just as sleep threatened to steal her away, she came awake, snaked a hand down to her boots, grabbed the dirk, and placed it under her pillow. A small comfort. She dimmed the lamp closest to her instead of turning it off. Time would tell if she could trust this new Dar.

Faux's mind ruminated over recent events, floating in and out of dreams, tumbling, twisting. People, places, and things appeared, then disappeared - Freeblood in the distance, an air of Etain circling her head like a bothersome fly, Dar rising from the ground wearing black, red eyes aglow.

She turned onto her side, her body twitching. Flopping onto her back, she shook her head. She flipped to the right, then rolled onto her back again. A low groan melted into a laugh.

Walking through a dark cavern, she searched for something...or was it someone? A faint light ahead confirmed she moved in the right direction. Entering a large room, she sensed a light, but the source wasn't apparent. Steps came from behind. Spinning, tail ready to strike, she stumbled back, a low "Oh" escaping her lips. The form resembled Dar, yet he didn't look like the man she'd recently met. This one stood well over eight feet tall, dark hair flowing, red eyes, and black shiny wings spanning farther than the walls could accommodate.

"Are you afraid of me?" His deep voice resonated throughout the enclosure. Too shocked to talk, she slowly shook her head. "Then why do you run?"

Another step back found her against the wall. She looked to her left, then her right, having nowhere to go. "I-I'm not running."

"You and I will be friends. Very good friends."

"If you say so."

"But you must bear my mark first."

No sooner did the words leave his mouth than Freeblood and Etain appeared on either side of her. Each took hold of an arm, securing her in cuffs mounted to the wall.

"Etain? What're you doing here? Where'd these come from?" Once cuffed, she was alone with Dar again. Intrigue replaced her fear. "I hope this is a game we'll both enjoy."

The dark form moved closer. She looked up with a seductive gleam in her eye, thinking to charm her captor, but the form in front of her was no longer Dar. His smile, if it could be considered as such, was not one of friendship. Two rows of sharpened fangs gleamed in the flickering light. It was then she realized the light in the room came from the flames atop his head. A large hand clutched her throat, dragging her up the wall. Blood-curdling screams filled the cavern as the beast rammed a red-hot branding iron into her belly.

Tangled in the sheets, Faux woke, a sheen of sweat covering her skin. Throwing off the covers, she slapped at the bedside lamp, fumbling for the switch. She checked her stomach in the dim light. "Just a dream," she breathed, collapsing back onto the pillows. A small noise made her look up. "Who's there?"

Dar awakened in the dark hours of the morning. Not yet accustomed to his new surroundings, he found it difficult to sleep for any length of time. Dressed in only leather pants, he padded out of his room in search of a small distraction.

Etain was his first thought. He found her sprawled face down across the bed, naked, pillows askew, the comforter in a puddle on the floor. He started to close the door, to leave her in peace, but changed his mind.

Her pale skin appeared golden in the soft light, warming the coolness of her silver hair. The seductive curve of a hip and swell of a rounded breast made his fingers twitch. Tremors ran through him, imagining her breath against his ear. The promise spoken earlier in the night came back to haunt him. *No harm will come to either of you this night.* Harm was not his intent, but she might not agree. Inhaling a deep breath, his traitorous hands curled into fists at his sides. He picked up the comforter and covered the fair angel asleep in innocent abandonment.

Watching the spawn sleep brought on a different mix of emotions. This creature invoked a burn in his blood. It felt as familiar as the burn he experienced with Etain, yet it was not the same. The desire, the need was there, a song that was music to his soul; however, there were underlying notes…offbeat, sour. He attributed it to a lack of sleep.

He sat in a shadowed corner, contemplating the jumbled sensations. Closing his eyes, he entered her mind. Not as he was now, but in demon form, taking great liberties to interact with her. He was pleased when she woke and tossed off the covers, exposing her naked body, frantically checking for the mark. A delighted chuckle escaped his lips.

"Who's there?" Faux called out, scrambling to retrieve the covers so hastily thrown off.

"Modesty doesn't become you." He came out of the darkness, naked, a playful grin on his face. Eyes dark with desire drank her in. "I thought I would look in to see if you were comfortable and decided to have a rest."

"I didn't know watching someone sleep was so exhausting. What do you want?"

"This is *my* home. I go where I want, when I want."

Faux edged away. "Does that include *taking* what you want?"

"I will do only what you want me to do. Nothing more, nothing less." He watched her, waiting. "Or I can leave you to your dreams..." Dar sat on the edge of the bed, "if you wish." Caught up in her black gaze, he reached out, rolling a stiff nipple between his fingers.

Faux blew out a hot breath and shivered. "You better be all go and not just show." She pulled him on top of her, challenging his passion.

Between exquisite pain and pleasure, Dar found the distraction that helped him set aside the torment of the past, temporarily forgetting the agonies of the future. He had forgotten how consuming the act of passion could be, letting himself drown in it.

When the skies began to brighten, he pulled away from the heated hellcat, leaving her in bed. Walking to the door with no handle, he opened it with a single word.

"Would you care to bathe?" he called out, stepping through the doorway. Not hearing a response, he returned to the opening. "Come now, before Etain wakes."

She sighed, gathered the comforter around her, and scooted out of bed. "The door with no handle leads to a bathroom?" she asked, leaning against the doorframe, entertained by the sight of his firm, round ass. "Privacy issues?"

Bent over the copper bath, Dar looked over his shoulder. "This is my personal bath. No one enters unless invited." He turned off the water and eased into the tub, flinching from the scratches across his lower back.

"Aren't I the lucky one." Faux ventured farther into the room. Polished black marble lined the walls and ceiling. The floor was of the same stone, but left in its natural state. "Mmm, warm floor." Dropping the comforter, she approached the large copper tub, admiring its shiny bright outer skin. She stopped, staring into the reflective surface, and screamed.

6

EMISSARY

Etain jerked awake. Disoriented, she dragged a hand through her ragged mass of hair, listening for whatever had disturbed her sleep. It was quiet. She dismissed the interruption as one of those dreams that jars you awake, disappearing as soon as you open your eyes. She turned her head, already drifting off again.

A subsequent scream set the Alamir into motion, dagger in hand. She rolled off the bed and grabbed the robe lying on the chest next to the footboard. In her race to get to Faux, it didn't register that the robe hadn't been there the night before.

Running into her room, she found the bed in disarray, no sign of the girl. Then she spied the open black door.

Etain charged through, tripping over Faux, who was sitting on the floor. "Faux, what's happened? Are you hurt?" A splash drew her attention to the bath. The deep scratches over Dar's shoulders told her plenty. "What have you done?" Her grip tightened on the hilt of the dagger.

"Nothing she didn't welcome with open legs." He smirked. "It's the mark that's upset her."

Etain noticed the bite marks on the girl's neck. She crouched down for a closer look, careful to keep Dar in her sights. "Not too bad, certainly not worth screaming bloody hell over."

"Farther down," he said.

Faux twisted away, trying to escape. Etain grabbed an ankle. "Hold on a sec." Sight of the brand on her belly set her teeth on edge. Her eyes cut to the bathing animal. "Holy shit. Is this your doing?" She stormed up to him. "What in the name of Kaos-"

"Be careful, Etain!" Faux screamed. "He's not who-"

Dar waved his fingers, his eyes on the angry vixen standing over him. "Be silent." Etain looked back at Faux, who was now slumped over.

"You are despicable. Is this why we were summoned? To satisfy your lust?"

His blue eyes darkened. "My house, my rules. You would be well advised to remember your place."

She bent over the edge of the tub, getting in his face, challenging the savage with every word. "*You* would be well advised to remember *your* place, High Lord. Play your games with some other depraved subject."

"Is that an invitation?"

Light flashed off the blade digging into the flesh below his chin. "You will *never* touch me *or* my sister again. Aye?" She held his amused gaze for a long moment. "You are disgusting." She turned, silk robe billowing behind her.

Dar seized the smooth fabric. Mid-step, she halted, grasping the front of the robe as it slid off her shoulders and down her back. She heard water splash onto the floor.

"You will not deny me, milady."

She did not deign to look at him. "I am not *your* lady." She turned sharply, careful to keep the robe tightly clasped in her hand. "Or a lady of the..." Her mouth dropped open at the glistening form in front of her, the well-defined, rippling muscles across his bare chest and shoulders. She blinked, trying to concentrate on what she meant to say rather than the tight abs stacked above a chiseled pelvis that led to… Her head swam. Realizing her mouth was still open, she closed her eyes and managed to get out a single word, "clan."

"Time to play."

Massive wings arced and swept round, encasing her within their black walls. His blue eyes morphed into slits of red. A soft breath crossed the demon's lips, blowing the silver strands from the translucent skin of her neck. Her dagger fell to the floor.

His prize, so close, so intoxicating. Mesmerized by the beating of her heart, the demon closed his eyes, basking in their effects. The lavender glow of the Tiffany stone went unnoticed.

To mar the slender neck would be a violation even he could not endure. Instead, he followed the curve of the delicate flesh to the shoulder, breathing in her scent. Ready to pierce the white skin with sharp incisors, a blast repelled the unwanted kiss. Demon eyes widened, seeing the outline of a lavender dragon at the base of her neck.

"What is this?"

His eyes returned to their normal state, meeting a piercing lavender gaze. He tried to push away, but an unseen force bound them together.

She spoke, but it was not her voice. "This one you shall not have, brother. You will honor my domain."

"Midir. She is not yours to have."

An evil laugh filled the room. "The same fool, as always."

"Show yourself. Let's end this." Dar ceased his efforts to break free, deciding the wiser course was to conserve his energy.

"You know I cannot physically enter your castle. You've made sure of that. Nonetheless, I can extend my will through my emissary."

75

"How can she be your emissary? She was in your realm for only a short time. I made sure of it."

"Yes, so you did. So you did. As a precaution, I made the preparations during transport to my castle. All you interrupted was the final step. Although I was annoyed at the nuisance and quite perplexed on how to complete her transformation, I was most pleased when you gave her the ring." The joy was evident in his voice. "It gave birth to a most devious plan."

Dar remembered the ring he had left in the castle courtyard, given with the intent to protect, including from him. A terrible oversight at this stage of the game. The lavender glow made perfect sense. He closed his eyes in acceptance of the wrong nearly perpetrated against a woman he held dear.

"Forgive me, milady." Put in his place, Dar engaged his brother. "Yet she is here with me."

"The lady *denies* you," Midir stated, more as an insult than fact. "Before your interference, I placed the mark of the dragon on the lowest part of her neck. I marked the other, as well."

"There was no dragon. I was quite thorough in my attentions."

"I know well your appetites. I marked both women. Whichever one you took would simultaneously activate the mark on the other. It didn't matter which one because I knew I had a backup."

"Etain carried no mark when she arrived."

"But she did." Midir's delight sparkled in Etain's eyes. "It remained invisible until you fraternized with the other. The taste you enjoyed upon their arrival started the process. Your interaction with the demon girl solidified it."

Dar couldn't resist asking. "The ring... What part does it play?"

"It's actually quite interesting." Midir raised Etain's hand, eying the ring. "The stone comes from inside the dwelling of dragons. Its properties come to life when combined with a mark placed on the body. It doesn't have to be a dragon," Midir chuckled, "but I thought it appropriate. Your assault on Etain provoked its protective qualities, thereby repudiating your advances. You have played your part most admirably, *brother*."

"The ring is a family heirloom, not a relic of a dead race."

Midir's laughter grated on Dar's raw nerves. "How little you know of our family…or hers, for that matter. The ring was a gift from an old Draconian king."

"Enough. You speak nothing but lies. Get out." Dar shook Etain by the shoulders. "Wake up, milady. Wake up. You are safe."

The lavender glow faded. Her gaze held his for a moment, then moved up over his head. Her eyes rolled back and she fainted, collapsing in his arms. "Damn." He drew in his wings, reverting to his Krymerian form, and carried her to her room.

With Etain safely tucked in, he returned to the bathroom, wrapped Faux in the comforter, and put her back to bed.

He strolled to his room, deep in thought. *Draconians were not a generous people. Why would they gift a Krymerian? Then there was the ridiculous prophecy. Lyoness and Draconians? Insanity, is what it is.* Standing at the wall of windows, Dar gazed out at the clouds shifting lazily through the morning sky. *I must find a way to protect Etain from Midir. Thanks to my idiotic lack of judgment, the ring is of no use where he is concerned. Although he is right about her potential, his interest in her does not make sense, other than as another way to torture me. Be that as it may, if he turns her to the dark, it could mean serious consequences for the Alamir…and myself.*

Just past noon, Dar rose, revitalized and ready to attempt a fresh start with the ladies in the house. Once dressed, he ventured to Etain's room. His knock going unanswered, he poked his head around the door and found her still asleep. Her warm scent invaded his senses and, for one crazy moment, he considered joining her under the covers. However, an innate appreciation for his manly parts made him think better of it.

At Faux's room, he considered erasing her memory of the night's events, but decided against it. He would have to cleanse Etain's memory too, and memory cleanses were dangerous.

You are alike in some ways, but you are demon where she is not. She is a warrior who has a job to complete. You are not, which makes you far better equipped to carry out my plans.

He laid a hand over her belly, reaching out with his mind. At first, he sensed nothing and had to delve deeper. In time, an impression touched his heart, bringing a faint smile to his lips. "There you are."

Thoughts drifted to the encounter with Etain, bringing him back to the reality of their situation. "Let's keep this between us for now, little spawn. Etain's connection with Midir is too strong. I will not risk our futures." Regret stabbed at his heart. "If only I had been there to protect her as promised…" He sighed. "But that is in the past." His attention returned to the girl. "Remember what I say." Dar weaved a flow of power into his words, his breath glowing with its strength. "We must keep Etain here a while longer. Use any excuse you can, but she must stay here." When the flow of power subsided, Dar left her to her dreams.

Etain moaned, her body aching. She remembered Faux crying out. Dar had done something unsavory. How she'd gotten back to bed, she had no idea, adding to her uneasiness. After dressing, she made her way down the hall, ready to have a conversation with her sister. She found Faux standing in front of the dressing table, hand circling over her belly.

Etain charged into the room. "I need to know what happened last night." Sight of the mark confirmed it hadn't been a dream.

Faux started at the intrusion, quickly slipping into a robe. "A knock would be nice." With brush in hand, she sat at the dressing table, catching Etain's gaze in the mirror. "Please tell me you aren't *that* naïve. Surely you've noticed."

She snatched the hairbrush from Faux's hand. "I noticed the scratches on his back and the marks he left on you." Dragging it through her sister's short black hair, her thoughts went to the object of their conversation. *How do you* not *notice a force of nature?*

Faux smirked, admiring the bruises on her neck. "Love bites. They don't hurt. He's such a tasty treat. You should give him a try."

"You weren't singing his praises last night."

"The mark on my stomach took me by surprise, that's all. He didn't do anything I didn't want." She rubbed her hands over her breasts and down her belly. "If he fights as passionately as he..." Mischievous black eyes mocked her, "fucks, well..."

"Shut up, Faux," Etain barked, throwing the brush onto the dressing table. "We both know you're just another conquest added to his collection."

With a dark laugh, she stood and pushed past Etain. "Don't underestimate me, you sanctimonious bitch. *He's* been added to *mine.*" She paused at the door. "I need to eat."

I remember the terror in your eyes, she thought, following Faux down the hall.

The dining table was set for two. Enticing aromas floated from a row of warming trays on a sideboard. Faux filled her plate with eggs, bacon, sausage, and waffles, then poured herself a cup of coffee. Etain kept it simple - eggs, toast, and fruit.

Sipping a glass of juice, Etain broke the silence. "Yesterday, you had no use for Dar and couldn't care less if he lived or died. This morning, he's your shining knight of the bedroom?"

Faux seemed to be oblivious to her nagging sister. Moments passed.

Etain slammed her hand on the table. "Damn it, Faux. Answer me."

"I am *not* just another conquest." She raised her head. "He's given me his trust. No one has ever done that. He sees me as a person, not some stupid demon girl who's nothing more than trouble."

Etain sat back. "Maybe if you wouldn't *act* like a stupid demon girl, people would treat you differently. Why the hell would he trust you?"

"Me-ow. Jealous?"

The sisters stared at each other, neither ready to answer questions about their relationship with the Krymerian.

The ring of steel on steel broke the silence of the afternoon. Etain pushed from the table, her chair falling to the floor, and ran out to the courtyard, Faux close behind. She found Dar surrounded by four ugly demons. Bound by honor to come to the aid of her chieftain, she drew her dagger, ready to fight.

Faux grabbed her by the shoulder. "Stop."

She shrugged away. "I can't leave him to be slaughtered by those demons."

"He doesn't need your help." She motioned to the practice ring. "Watch."

Etain held her dagger close. Questions raced through her mind. *How the hell does she know?* She stole a glance at Faux, who was preoccupied with adoring her new champion. *Did he share blood with her, too?*

Four Geryon gladiators – ugly, mean, and big – circled the Krymerian. One came from his right side with a mighty slash. Dar easily ducked under the blow, disemboweling the creature with lightning speed. Its guts spilled onto the ground as it scrambled to hold them in. Unsuccessful, it collapsed into dust.

Of course, he didn't share his blood.

From the left, another demon charged in with a low thrust, which he blocked with a double cross down. As the blades connected, Dar kicked out, catching the demon in the face, busting its snout, spraying black blood over his bare chest. With a reversed grip on the blades, the Krymerian came up, cutting deep into the demon's torso. In the same motion, he spun and severed the head from its body. It also fell to dust.

She's of his blood. And mine.

The remaining two charged at the same time. Dar blocked the attack of the first, and parried the thrust of the second. He dropped to the ground and rolled, coming up inches away. His blades in motion, he soon dispatched one. The other immediately launched a new attack, proving to be faster and more cunning. Dar dodged, blocking some blows, but several hit their mark. Blood showed on his arms and back. The demon turned, his blade in the lead, opening a gash in Dar's side. A second slash left a deep cut across his chest. Dar answered with a frenzy of blows, driving the demon back. His blade ultimately scored the fatal blow, piercing into the chest of his foe.

So why is she acting so weird?

"You see. I told you he didn't need your help," Faux said, a smirk on her face.

"And I told you he's changed too much to be trusted."

"If you'd have a civil conversation with the man, you'd understand why he does some of the things he does."

"He's a *demon*, Faux," Etain argued, tucking her dagger away.

"Some of the best people are," she snapped, waving her tail.

"What I mean is he was never cruel. You were right when you said he's not the Dar I once knew."

"Sounds like a personal problem to me. I don't know what he was like before, but I like what I see now." She sauntered toward the house. "Maybe he's just what you need."

"What the hell has gotten into you?"

Faux stopped and turned. "Keep watching."

"Huh?" Etain turned in time to see the man transform.

Deep blue eyes morphed into red vertical slits, like those of a serpent. Black, leather-like wings emerged from his back. A bone-like substance extended from his knuckles, elongating into sharp claws. Spreading his wings, he took flight with one flap.

"Holy hell," she whispered, feeling an odd sense of, well... She wasn't sure what she felt, but it was definitely odd.

He circled the grounds, gliding easily through the sky, as though born to such a thing. Faux beamed with pride. Etain shielded her eyes from the brightness of the day, watching him fly over the cliffs. Banking a turn, he headed toward the courtyard.

Something felt wrong to Etain.

Dar's massive wings went limp.

She watched, certain he was merely showing off.

Buffeted by the wind, his wings jerked him back. It appeared as if he were in control, but when his head lolled to the side and his arms flopped, she knew he was not. Another gust of wind pushed him into a nosedive. Watching, Etain felt helpless, unable to stop what was happening. She took off in the direction he headed. When he hit the ground, Etain stumbled from the resulting sonic boom, but managed to stay on her feet. Faux screamed, coming up behind her. She ran to her fallen lover, slid to her knees, and tenderly cradled his head in her lap.

Etain stared at the winged creature, his blood staining the pebbles of the courtyard. She thought she knew these people. *People? Not now. This thing is…is… What?*

"You have to help him." Faux smoothed the hair from his face. "Don't worry, lover," she cooed. Noticing her sister's lack of action, Faux hit her in the stomach with a small fire blast. "Etain! I don't know what to do."

The jolt snapped the blonde warrior out of her paralysis. *Whatever he is now, he's bleeding.* Shaken, she knelt and placed a hand on his forehead. "He's cold." Her eyes traveled down to the slash across his chest. She ascertained it as superficial and lightly ran her finger over the wound while releasing an electrical charge. The wound cauterized, she turned to the larger one. "Help me roll him onto his side. Careful of his wings. Fold that one under gently." Faux carefully wrapped the wing toward his body as Etain eased the injured warrior onto his side. She bit her bottom lip. "This one is much deeper. He's lost so much blood."

"Can you do anything?" Faux searched her face. "You have to save him."

"I've never dealt with such a deep wound." She ran a hand through her hair, tingeing the silver strands red.

"There's no one else. You gotta do whatever it takes."

"I only know one way."

"Then do it!"

"But he threatened me with my life if I shared blood again."

"Etain, he's dying!"

She highly doubted the man would die, but his loss of blood was undeniable. Etain swiped at her tears and shifted, taking the dagger from her boot. A slash to her forearm released a warm flow of blood into his wound. It brought back the night she met this man, the night he saved her life, the chant used.

Remember the words. She linked her mind with his. *Dar, you must hear me. You have to help me. Tell me the words, Dar. Tell me the words to heal your wounds and save your life. You have a reason to live. Give me the words.*

Images drifted like smoke in her mind's eye, the words taking shape. Etain quietly repeated the healing chant. "*Beannaigh an fhuil gur féidir le do sheirbhíseach a chur ar ais. Líon isteach an soitheach leis an saol, a thabhairt ar ais chugam* (Bless this blood that your servant may be restored. Fill this vessel with life, bring him back to me)." She continued until each layer sealed. To bless his restoration, she placed her hands on the repaired flesh. "*Beidh mé saol fada agus rathúnas a roinnt le leat mo cheann chothaímid* (Long life and prosperity I share with you, my cherished one)."

They eased Dar onto his back. Etain straddled his hips. "Get behind him. We've got to get him into a sitting position."

Faux scrambled, doing as she was told. Etain clawed at the neckline of her top, but the leather refused to give. Grabbing the hem, she lifted it over her head. "Move him closer to me."

Faux grunted, pushing the dead weight up as her sister pulled. "I don't know what you hope to accomplish by stripping in front of him. He's not conscious."

"You'll see. Push a little more. Make sure to keep him propped up. I can't hold him on my own."

They maneuvered him into position. Etain grabbed her dirk and dragged it across the upper part of her shoulder, unaware she sliced the dragon mark in two. She heaved Dar up to her chest, his head lolling onto her shoulder. "Help me keep him in this position."

The two locked arms to hold him fast. Etain whispered in his ear. *"Fuil mo chuid fola, ar ais duit féin mar a bhfuil tú ar ais dom* (Blood of my blood, restore yourself as you have restored me)." She rubbed her cheek against his. "You must drink, milord." With a nudge of her shoulder, she tried to angle his head so the blood would trickle onto his lips. "Dar, wake up. You have to drink." She let go of her sister's arm for a moment, taking hold of a handful of his hair.

Faux grunted again, her nails digging into Etain's flesh. "I can't hold him much longer."

Etain shifted her hips, getting as close as she could, forcing his face into the bloodied crevice of her shoulder.

"Dar!"

She felt his head jerk and his tongue dip into the fresh blood. A deep vibration rumbled from his chest, rising into a growl as his mouth clamped onto the irresistible fount. The effects of the blood were immediate. His arms came to life, crushing the source of his resurrection to his chest. Etain moaned and let go of Faux. The demon girl fell back as Dar's great wings arced. Locked in a blood embrace, the couple lifted into the sky, airborne within seconds.

Satiated at last, his eyes opened, realizing what he had done. He veered northwest to the mountains. After an effortless landing, he hugged his wings close as he eased her against a tree. Kneeling before her, he studied the sleeping savior. Dark lashes against pale skin, the curve of her cheek, lips daring him to taste, the rise and fall of pink-tipped breasts...blood trailing down her shoulder. "*Tartarus.*"

He reached for the wound. Her skin was electric, the blood vibrant. Images reeled through his head, telling him of her efforts to save his life. A song enflamed his blood, consuming him with...desire?

Not quite right. Desire was in the mix, it was all he could do to keep himself in check, but it wasn't the driving force behind what he felt.

He healed her wound, unable to resist lapping up the long line of blood from her breast to shoulder. Breathless, he rested his forehead in the curve of her neck.

What is this between us?

Senses somewhat reclaimed, he shifted to her side and leaned against the tree. As a distraction, his mind wandered to the gladiator foes dispatched before his short flight. *I know the last one hit me hard.* A curious finger traced over a faint scar across his chest. He twisted, taking a good look at his side. Except for minor stiffness, there was no mark.

He glanced at Etain. "Do you never do as you're told?"

Dar pulled her into his lap. With an extended talon, he made a small incision in his forearm and pressed the line of dark blood to her lips, murmuring the reviving spell.

Heavy eyes opened. "Hey, you," she said, lips ruby red with blood. *Just one kiss.*

"You've been a naughty girl." His expression was stern, but his heart swelled knowing she was well. "Did I not tell you never to share blood, no matter the circumstances?"

She groaned and closed her eyes. "Rules were never my forte."

"A fact I should have remembered. I have no idea why I waste my breath."

"Neither do I."

A slight smile formed on his lips. "Someone has to do it."

This made her laugh. Her eyes sparkled, looking up at him. "You enjoy brick walls, do you?"

"Some more than others." His authoritative air crumbled into an easy grin.

"Well…" She tried to sit up. "Oh." Her hand going to her head, she realized her state of undress. "Oh!" The other hand made a valiant effort to cover her breasts.

Dar cradled her in his arms, ignoring her attempt at modesty. "Not so fast. Even brick walls must rest, especially when faced with another. And you need to replenish the blood you have lost." He offered his arm. "It's your turn to drink."

"But you just said-"

"Never mind what I said. Drink."

"But I've never-"

His stern look quieted her. Without another word, she did as he commanded.

Swept up in the blooding, Dar tightened his arm around her supple form, increasingly conscious of the bare skin, warm and solid, pressed to his. His nose burrowed into the mass of silver locks, inhaling her scent. No one had ever affected him this way. Not his wife. Not even the demon girl. It was a revelation, one that extended back to his first encounter with this unusual young woman, a revelation which demanded further investigation.

"That's quite enough," he moaned, pushing her away. Seeing the look in her eyes, he tilted his head. "What?"

"You bring out the strangest feelings in me." She pulled his head to hers, kissing him full on the mouth.

It felt natural, right. He returned the kiss, then abruptly ended it, shifting her from his lap, uncertain of their relationship.

"I'm sorry," she said, watching him get to his feet. "I didn't mean to make you uncomfortable."

"I am not...uncomfortable." *Quite the opposite, milady.* "You need to rest."

"So do you." She reached for his hand. "Sit with me. Let's just be together...as friends."

"If you think you can control yourself." Dar smiled, happy to sit.

In quiet reflection, they enjoyed the panoramic views of the valley below. A light breeze brought the freshness of the sea up to the mountaintop. From this vantage point, the great manor house looked ethereal, its white stone pristine against the blue of the water. Dar felt at peace, something he had not felt in a very long time.

"It's beautiful," Etain said. "How did you find this place?"

Purely by chance, a roll of the portal dice. He liked what he had seen and decided it was perfect for a new start. He told her of his introduction to the town, hiring of local tradesmen, and their impressive work.

"Do you like my new home?"

"I do. With the right décor, it could be quite cozy."

"I find the den rather homey."

"A bit masculine, but aye, it's a good start. I was thinking more along the lines of the throne room."

"What man doesn't have his own throne room?"

"Well, most men do. They just aren't so big…or made of skulls…or on a dais."

Dar shook his head. "This one is rather understated compared to my last. How is a man expected to rule his kingdom from a small, insignificant…" He searched for the right word, "stool?"

Etain pressed her lips together, trying not to smile, and blinked several times. "I don't know, milord. It baffles the mind."

More in control of his thoughts, and his body, he stood up, offering her his hand. "We should get back. I'm sure Faux is worried."

"It's never a good thing to leave her alone for too long."

Coming to her feet, she stumbled into him.

"I have you, milady." Safe in his embrace, they gazed into one another's eyes, frozen for a heartbeat. Dar broke the moment, spreading his wings, and gliding off the mountaintop.

As the tips of the manor turrets came into view, he descended until they were only a few feet from the ground. With a few beats of his wings, they landed softly. He picked up her shirt.

Leather back in place, Etain pulled him close. "Can we talk later?"

Her breath was soft, hot. *You are a temptation.* He nodded, unable to speak.

She turned, prepared for a frantic Faux, who ran up to Dar and grabbed him in a tight embrace. "Are you okay? You look like hell." She looked him over. "I don't know what I would've done if I'd lost you."

Etain cleared her throat, pushing the hair from her face. "I am fine. You need not have worried for me, but I do thank you for asking." Her ice gaze traveled from Faux to Dar. "I need a bath." She left the couple in the courtyard.

Dar placed a kiss on the dark beauty's head, but his eyes followed the blonde warrior. "It has been an eventful day. Let's go inside." They casually strolled into the house. "Shall we have a bite to eat?"

Foraging through the leftovers from breakfast, he soon had a small feast set out in the kitchen. Faux blew out a breath, eying it all. "You must've worked up some appetite while you were gone. What were you doing?"

"Resting, and talking." Dar took a swig of ale.

"Talking? About what?"

"This place," he said, waving a hand. "And her inability to do as she is told."

Faux snorted. "A little advice, slick. Ask, don't tell. You'd be amazed at the results."

"I shall try to remember your words of wisdom the next time I lead my clan into battle."

She rolled her eyes. "She isn't afraid of you...or me." She ran a hand over his muscular arm. "I suggest you be careful."

Having left Faux at rest in her room, Dar returned to his to wash away the residue of his time in the practice ring, inspecting his injuries. Impressed with the results of Etain's ministrations, he dressed and went to meet with the young woman who had become the proverbial fly in his ointment. He puzzled over how he could take her blood. What had changed since the early hours of that morning? After an uncharacteristic knock, he waited for her invitation to enter.

She opened the door. "Thank you for knocking." Tying the sash on her robe, a blush colored her cheeks. "Shall we sit by the fire?"

Dar smiled and followed her into the room. Fresh from the bath, her clean scent was as enticing as the silk robe flowing over her curves. He reminded himself he was here to talk, nothing more. "There are many things that need to be said."

Taking a seat, she said, "Let's start with your sudden interest in Faux."

Not what he expected. "We can start there." The connection was strong, and even though Etain broke the initial link, he watched the beautiful face, willing her eyes back to him. "I admit, I paid little attention to her escapades…until her attempt to murder you, but your determination to protect her intrigued me. I felt I should learn more of your unusual bond."

She rewarded his efforts with a raised brow. "Interesting technique. Despite being at odds most of the time, she *is* my responsibility. Were it not for me, she wouldn't exist."

"I believe I played a part, as well." She accepted his response with a weak smile. "Upon our introduction last night, I was strongly attracted to her. Her smell and taste are so like yours." He took her hand in his, raising it to his lips. "However, they do not satisfy."

She cleared her throat, snatching her hand away. "Don't patronize me, Lord Darknight. You knew what you were doing."

"Aye. I knew what I was doing." By the gods, he enjoyed seeing the spark in her eyes.

"Faux likes variety. She thrives on it. She's always been for Faux and Faux alone. Whatever you've done to invoke her new devotion to you won't last long."

"A point you seem to have forgotten in your own relationship with her."

She leaned back, her gaze holding his. "It won't happen again."

"I do not doubt it." He looked away, needing to break the connection, if only for a moment. Considering recent revelations, what he had to say did not come easy. "I thought Faux could better… accommodate what I had to give. You made it clear you were not interested in my attentions."

"I was not interested in being *forced*."

His eyes came back to hers. "I was not referring to what happened here." He felt somewhat heartened when he saw the color drain from her face. "I am close to two hundred in human years and, for the most part, have spent them alone. It is not a long time by Krymerian standards, but I do not live with Krymerians. Believe me when I say living with the Alamir has been a lonely existence."

"That makes no sense. You've always been surrounded by people, plenty of them women."

Dare he trust this woman with his soul? For him, there was no other choice. "As I have told you, Midir and I are one and the same. We have been at each other's mercy all our lives." The need to move forced him to his feet. He could not watch her face at what he next had to say. "What you don't know is I once had a wife and children." He dared to look. She seemed interested. Encouraged, he continued. "Alexia was a loving wife and wonderful mother. Victoria and Henrí, our children, adored her, and I adored them all."

"Something happened to them." It was not a question.

"They were slaughtered." An intense sadness came over him. "To say I was devastated would be an understatement. One morning, as I was on patrol, the *Bok* attacked. No one was spared." She remained silent as he walked to the bank of windows. "We hunted the murderers for months, but their deaths did nothing to satisfy my hunger for revenge. I wanted the one who ordered the massacre." He gazed out at a sea turned gold by the setting sun. "But the name has constantly eluded me. His men opted to die by my hand rather than reveal his name." He clenched his jaw, his stomach churning. "It was Midir. My own brother." He turned to her. "Because of his hatred for me, I lost my family and the people of my house. He could not kill me and live, so he destroyed my life instead."

"I'm sorry for your loss," she murmured. "Betrayal and losing your family in such a violent way..." A tear slid down her cheek. "The desire for revenge. It all changes a person." She crossed her arms over her chest, as though she were shielding herself from an unseen evil.

"Have I changed?" He walked back to her, stopping before her.

She looked up at him. "Aye. The Dar I knew was not a demon."

"Etain, it will take the strength of a demon to defeat his evil."

"This demon drinks blood for pleasure and takes any woman he pleases."

He crouched, coming face-to-face with the beauty who haunted his dreams.

"Since the death of my family, I have not allowed myself to feel anything. I cannot explain what I feel at this moment. So much has happened." He hesitated, searching for the right words. "The day you stepped into my life challenged me to believe in a different future. To dream again." Watching her face, he hoped for a glimmer of acceptance. "Because of that belief, I am determined to make Midir pay for his sins."

"None of this explains why we were summoned."

"I abused my authority to bring you here. I knew you would not ignore a summons." She lowered her head, obviously uncomfortable with the admission. "Etain, I have worn my past as a shield to avoid living, to punish myself for not being there to protect my family, for trusting a man I thought..." He closed his eyes, dismissing the thought with a shake of his head. "The destruction you saw was the demolition of a past that has held me back. I do not know what the future holds, but I am ready to face it." Dar sat back on his heels. "I see now I have made a mess of it. At the end of the day, it comes down to what *you* want."

A passion only he could stir enflamed her heart, his heat an enticement to surrender to the fire. However, that small voice within reminded her of his betrayal. With the cock of a brow, she leaned back and brought a bare foot up, pushing him away.

"What do you mean by accommodate?"

Dar breathed deep. "I gave her a child. My child." He stoically absorbed the electrical current.

The foot pushed him onto the floor and she loomed over him. "I never thought you a fool. Her body may well accommodate your seed, but I guarantee her character will be the death of it, and possibly you."

Eyeing the curve of her bare leg, he pushed up on his elbows, a smirk on his lips. "You don't approve?"

She stared at him in silence, her emotions at war. *The audacity of the man. Tells me about the loss of his family, revealing what I thought was a secret part of himself. Surely, it's all lies to lower my guard. How many bastard children live today because of him?*

Amidst all the doubts, she could not deny the burn in her blood or how all else faded when he was near.

No! He is a scoundrel. He brought us here to satisfy his own desire. Ha! I'll use him to my advantage.

"Would it make any difference?" She turned, walking away.

Dar was quick to his feet, catching the hem of her robe. "Not at this point." His hands rested lightly on her hips. "Will you forgive my error in judgment with Faux? Can we start over?"

"I..." Her eyes closed as Dar brushed her hair aside, kissing her neck. His breath was warm, raising gooseflesh over her skin. "There may be something you can help me with." Breathless, she faced him. "A token gesture to jump-start the rebuilding of my faith in you. But first, you need to hear of *my* past."

"I know your story, Etain."

"No. You've only known me as an Alamir. I'm talking about the time when I was human...er...a regular human."

"Then tell me."

He took her by the hand and led her back to the chairs. She pulled away, choosing to sit on the floor instead, safe from his touch. Her mind traveled back to the days before the Alamir and their strange world.

"I had a family. Not a husband and children." She shook her head. "I had a loving father, a doting mother, and a big brother. I had just turned fourteen." Dar's brows lifted. "My father was a businessman. Mom did volunteer work, mostly with local museums, fundraisers, stuff like that." She shrugged, her thoughts in another time. "My brother was a typical big brother, picked on me as brothers do, but protected me from anyone, including my parents." Her legs shifted to the side. "My dad worked with different people, important people. Many of his contacts weren't of an honorable sort and I'm pretty sure some weren't even human."

"Being so young, how would you know?"

"I didn't *know*, but I sensed something wasn't right. It wasn't until I became an Alamir that it began to make sense."

She cocked her head, gathering her hair over one shoulder, combing it with her fingers. "We'd gone out for pizza and a movie. It was a rare treat for dad to be free. I remember my brother and me in the back seat, competing for his attention."

It had been years, but it felt like yesterday. "We were driving past the park on our way home. Suddenly, Dad slammed on the brakes. I couldn't see anything, but I felt the energy pulsing around us." Her monologue grew in animation, using her hands to emphasize the enormity of what they had encountered. "A wall of darkness blocked the road. Dad wanted to check it out. Mom wanted to leave, which sounded pretty good to me, especially when he opened his door."

Dar listened, intent on her story.

Etain pressed her hands to her head. "My head hurt so bad." She looked at Dar. "Dad walked up to the wall and stuck his hand right into it." She waved her hand through the air. "Mom looked back at me. She *knew*." *I remember her blonde hair, sweeping out when she turned and opened the door.* The sadness in Etain's voice matched the expression on her face. "She jumped out of the car, but stopped when a dark figure came out of the wall. My dad looked at my mom, then at me."

She trembled, tears shining in her eyes. "The top part of his body went in one direction." She waved to the left, "His legs the other," and to the right, tears sliding down her cheeks. "My mind couldn't process what was happening. I watched the dark figure turn toward Mom, making a Z formation in front of her." A sad smile touched her lips.

"It's weird how the mind works sometimes. The motion reminded me of an old TV show where two funny men would give snaps in a Z formation." The smile faded. "He was big. Bigger than you, his eyes red, like a demon's." Her hands dragged through her hair. "My mom…" She choked on her words, struggling for composure. "My mom fell into pieces."

In need of a reassuring touch, an anchor to the present, she let Dar pull her onto his lap. Curling up to him, she rested her head on his broad shoulder. "Blood was everywhere. My brother made me look at him as he dragged me across the seat. I couldn't think. I couldn't cry. I couldn't move. I just stared at his mouth forming words I didn't understand."

Dar's jaw was warm against her forehead. "He slapped me, yelling at me to run." Etain rubbed her cheek in remembrance. "I ran. We ran. We got as far as the park, but once I went into the woods, I lost him.

"That night, I went from being a kid to this…" She gestured to herself, "warrior woman. Only I didn't feel like one." She took a breath. "The only thing that's kept me going was the promise I made to avenge my family." She sat up and looked him in the eye. "I've learned a lot since becoming an Alamir. How to survive, how to fight. But there are other things I've yet to learn. What I look like on the outside doesn't reflect what I am on the inside." Her gaze bore into his, willing him to comprehend what she meant without having to say the words. "Do you understand what I'm telling you?"

Dar pressed his lips together, pursing his brows. "Etain, your strength of character and integrity make you all the more beautiful."

"No, not that." She bit her bottom lip. "Just because I *look* like a woman doesn't *make* me a woman."

His eyes widened. "You're not a woman?"

She growled, baring her teeth. "I was fourteen, Dar. *Fourteen*. An *innocent* fourteen."

He looked her up and down. "Fourteen?"

"I was, but after the silver orb-"

"Etain, what are you talking about?"

She narrowed her eyes. "A silver orb brought me to the Alamir." He nodded, a doubtful look on his face. "It did."

"I'm sorry, Etain, but you do not look fourteen to me."

"I'm not, that's what I'm trying to tell you. The orb aged me by five years."

Dar rested his chin in his hand. "So, you're nineteen?"

"No." Her story had sounded much more credible in her head. She turned away. "I've been Alamir for about five years now." Hearing his sigh, her gaze came back to him. "Whether I'm nineteen or twenty-four doesn't matter, the innocent part has not changed."

It was clear the wheels turned behind his blue gaze. "Are you telling me you're a virgin?" he asked, hiding his amusement behind a hand.

She pushed away from him, wanting to escape. "How could I expect such a cretin to understand?"

"I'm sorry. Please forgive me. I am surprised, that's all," he said, refusing to let her go. "I never thought-"

"Of course not, considering who you keep company with. Let me go." She pushed against his chest. Not expecting his sudden release, she ended up sprawled on the floor, face down. She flipped over, a scowl on her face.

"Oops." His eyes sparkled at the disheveled robe revealing a pair of long, bare legs.

She picked herself up, slapping away non-existent dust. "My mistake."

"Etain, you ran with one of the roughest clans in the Alamir. They weren't known for their civilized ways."

"We survived any way we could." Her body vibrated with indignation. "Nobody wanted us. We weren't good enough for their precious clans, so we created our own. Just because we *looked* filthy did not *make* us filthy. We watched out for one another, protected our brothers and sisters. We didn't use them or throw them away. Master G was adamant about loyalty."

"On that we can agree. He was loyal to his own, if no one else." He leaned back in the chair. "It explains much that happened, or did not happen, those first days we were together, but you've had plenty of opportunities since then. Why didn't you tell me when you joined LOKI?"

She lifted her chin, her blood cold. "My virginity is *my* business, not yours. It doesn't matter anyway. You have my demon sister to keep you company. This isn't a package deal."

A scowl darkened his features. "This has nothing to do with her."

"I said I was innocent, not stupid."

"You overestimate the relationship," he snapped.

Etain backed away, glaring at the insufferable man. "She carries your bastard."

Dar came to his feet. She sidestepped his advance, her eyes lighting upon the fireplace poker within easy reach. Making a grab for it, she waved it in his face. "Get out."

He leaned back, avoiding the makeshift weapon, then crossed his arms over his chest. "No."

"I *will* hurt you."

A deft hand took hold of the poker, pulling it, and an angry Etain, to him. He easily removed the tool from her death grip and pinned her against him. "You do entertain, but my patience wears thin. I would prefer another form of entertainment that requires no more than my flesh to yours."

"No," she said, a desperate panic rising. She hated the feeling and hated him more for causing it. "You said it was up to me."

Shot down by his own words.

Etain saw it in his eyes. He loosened his hold, setting off a different panic within her heart. His body was hard, strong, hot. She wanted to melt into him, have his hands moving over her skin.

Damn. What's happening to me?

She gripped his arms. Set afire by his questioning gaze, her lips met his in a fiery clash. Everything else disappeared. He held her tight, her body molding to his chiseled curves. Whatever betrayal she had felt was forgotten. He was her angel, her savior, her tormentor.

Dar abruptly let go, staggering back, uncertainty on his face. He opened his mouth, then closed it without a sound.

Shaken, Etain watched him leave, her emotions a jumble of rampant insanities. Dragging her hands through her hair, she stumbled to the bed and collapsed.

7

AN UNDERSTANDING

Sleep eluded the silent warrior. Sitting on the edge of the bed, head in his hands, Dar went over what had happened. Thinly veiled breasts against his chest, the taste of red lips, mixed with a red-hot passion on the verge of explosion.

What in Tartarus am I doing? She's barely more than a child and a virgin.

He needed a distraction, something physical, violent. Dar made his way to the far wall, placed a hand upon a small rune, and pressed. The wall opened far enough to reach in and pull out an object encased in black silk. He carried it to a table in the corner, uncovering a black-bladed sword. Its blade alone was a meter in length, the gold handguard inlaid with rubies. The handle, forged into the head of a griffon, was made of a rare metal and wrapped in gold wire. Runes on the blade revealed the sword's true name.

"*Ba'alzamon*, my old, dark-hearted friend. A long time it has been since we worked as one. But with the passage of time comes many changes and I find your services are once again required."

Its name spoken aloud, *Ba'alzamon* awakened, sucking light from the room. The runes engraved on the blade burned bright red. *It has been far too long since our last adventure,* the blade spoke in Dar's mind. *I sense you mean to end things with your brother.*

"Not yet. I have other things to settle first." Dar slid the dark blade into its scabbard and strapped it onto his back. "His time will soon come."

The warrior strode down dark hallways to the armory and headed to the back of the room. Enclosed in a glass case stood another old friend...the Armor of Kaos. Infused with powerful Krymerian magic, the black armor had served him well in his previous life and would do so again. He opened the door of the glass case. "United once more." With head bowed, he chanted the words of transference.

Black bands appeared around his neck, hips, and each wrist. From the band around his hips, a string of bands, sliding out from one another, advanced down his legs and over his boots. Bands from the neck covered his torso, meeting those from his wrists at his shoulders, spanning over his head, forming the helmet. The VonNeshta family crest, a sun encircled by a crown of swords, adorned the breastplate. The High Lord of Kaos was ready.

Standing at the foot of Etain's bed, Dar linked his mind with hers, searching for the past. Delving deeper into her memories, what he found gave him pause. He stared long and hard at the woman, peaceful in her sleep. He could see the fourteen-year-old girl in her face, could imagine the light in her eyes, then the fading of it. He knew the demon responsible for the death of her family. Worse, he had seen something Etain's mind had evidently hidden away. Intent in his mission, he chanted a location spell, and disappeared.

There was one other piece of business he needed to complete before going after the assassin. Wandering through the Plains of Time, Dar hunted for a particular dimension...the Realm of the Dead. After a time, it came into view, the priest's temple of white stone being the noticeable landmark.

"At last, the resting place of the High Priest of Kaos."

Only those with the right passphrase could enter its enchanted gold doors. Fortunately, he was privy to those words.

"From chaos comes clarity. From clarity comes enlightenment. Thus, I seek the knowledge that will set me free." The doors opened, revealing a great white hall, at its center stood an altar of black stone.

Memories from his own childhood flooded him. A small body on the altar, a figure dressed in the red robes of a Krymerian High Priest standing over it. The priest held a dagger in his hand, suspended over the boy. Dar could not hear the words spoken, but he did not need to. He remembered them as if it were yesterday as he watched the path of the dagger, cringing when it plunged into boy's chest.

When the priest turned, the vision evaporated. "Why are you here?"

Dar stopped, surprised by the priest's reaction. Then he remembered his armor.

"Apologies, Father," he said, releasing the helm and breastplate of his armor. "I did not intend to startle you. Forgive me for disturbing your eternal rest."

"High Lord..." The priest cleared his throat. "Tell me why you have come to this place."

"I am here on the advice of the Skull of Memories." He lowered his head in a show of respect. "You are my last hope of being free of Midir."

Lothous threw his hands in the air. "Do not speak that name here. I despise the fact you remain connected to him." Seeing the blanched look on Dar's face, the priest softened. "Apologies, High Lord, I spoke out of turn. You are most welcome." He held out his arm, inviting Dar to join him. "There is a way to be done with the blackguard, but I fear you may not like it."

"Whatever it takes, I will do."

"Walk with me." As they strolled through the great hall, Lothous reiterated the tale. "We are all created with light and dark in our soul. You were different from others, destined to serve the light. However, you inherited the capacity to do great evil from your mother's family.

Although she was not an evil woman, she could not alter her heritage. Thus, her son took on the curse of her bloodline.

"The light and dark were at constant war within you. So much so, your father feared for your sanity, as well as your life. In desperation for his only son's future, the king came to us and asked we separate the darkness from the light. We agreed and prepared for the ceremony, knowing what the cost could be. The darkness was so powerful, it created another being.

"Seven priests and seven apprentices lost their lives that day." Lothous shook his head. "A great loss to our order, but..." He gave Dar a faint smile, "a great blessing to our world." His demeanor turned sour. "That Midir is pure evil. Since that day, I have done all I can to watch over you, but it is time for a new order. To conquer the dark, one will require a strong magic. To sever the connection, you will need the Jewel of Life."

"How do I obtain this jewel?"

"To possess it, you must defeat its protector to prove you are ready to do what must be done."

"Show me the way, Lothous. It does not matter how far I must go to meet this protector. I am ready to put an end to this."

Suddenly, Lothous took the form of King Dari. Dar staggered back at the sight of his long-dead father. "I am its champion." The old Krymerian king appeared untouched by the ravages of death. Standing face-to-face, father and son were a mirror image, except for the king's burial leathers and the silver streaks in his brown hair. "All you have to do is slay me, my son. Prove you have the strength to strike down your family. Although Midir is evil, he remains your brother."

"I cannot take your life, Father."

Seeing his son's hesitation, the king attacked with his great sword, opening several wounds across the warrior's chest and arms. "My *life*? You cannot make me anymore dead than I already am."

"You are in front of me, just as Lothous stood before me." Dar dodged what could have been a fatal blow, hissing from a burn along his side. "I will not condemn my soul by slaying my father – apparition or not."

"You will…" His next move pinned Dar against the altar, "if you expect to leave this place." His blade slashed down.

Dar's powerful claymore appeared in his hand, blocking the king's move. Blades locked, Dar pressed against the stone and lifted a foot, pushing his father back. "Killing Midir does not compare to this. You've done me no injustice."

"Have I not?" The king swept out, grazing Dar across the abdomen. "Were you not told what happened the day he came with his horde?" He slashed back, his son jumping to the side to avoid the blow.

"Everyone was dead, including you. We could only surmise how it had gone down." Dar blocked another strike. "I thought I saw Midir's influence, but…"

King Dari looked him in the eye. "But you let him live. Did you not believe your family worth avenging?"

"No! Yes!" Dar felt as though his heart had stopped. "For years, I lived with a vengeful heart, searching for confirmation of who led the attack." He closed his eyes and turned away. "I could not fathom my own brother doing such a thing. I knew he hated me, but not you or my innocent wife and children. I could not accept it."

"You knew it in your heart, but did nothing."

Dar heard his father's disappointment, felt it in his bones. He had wandered for so long, searching, blaming himself for the death of his family. "I found the others. Those involved in the slaughter. I would not allow my men to touch them. I killed them myself." Afterward, he had left his men, wandering to new lands, becoming the mercenary known as Darknight. Kill after kill to forget, to atone for his cowardice. Many called him a savior. More called him a reaper.

His shoulders drooped, the tip of his sword dipping to the floor. "I was a fool.

King Dari squared his shoulders, sword ready, and spoke in a commanding voice, jarring Dar from his self-pity. "Indeed. I wonder what you would do if I said *I*, to save my own skin, told him where your family hid." He stepped forward on one foot. "He promised I would live if I gave them up."

Dar struggled to breathe. Everything he believed in...honor, loyalty, love...came into question. "You loved them more than your own life."

"I had a kingdom to rule, to protect."

Nothing made sense. Surely, he had not been wrong about his father. He was not a coward. Never had he run from a fight or hidden behind an innocent.

"Three versus thousands..." The king raised his blade higher, a smirk on his lips. "A small sacrifice by any standard."

"*Small sacrifice?*" The words lit a fire in Dar's belly, blinding him to the consequences of his actions. "Not by *my* standards!" He swung up with his mighty blade. "They were my *future*." The honed edge sliced the king from hip to shoulder. "They were the future of our people." Using the momentum of the move, a twist brought the blade across his father's lower abdomen, finishing the job. "You had no right. They were my life."

The king collapsed at his feet. "As you were mine..."

Dar dropped to his knees, his shirt bloodied and torn. "Why do you punish me? Have I not suffered enough?"

The apparition faded, along with Dar's injuries. The old priest stood before him and placed a consoling hand on the young man's head. "You have done well, High Lord. Understand, *you* must be the victor in the fight with your brother."

"Midir has already won. My memories are poison. I have murdered my father."

Lothous removed an object from a pocket in his robe and held it out. "I give you this."

The High Lord eyed a red gem the size and shape of a peach seed. "What is it?"

"It is what will free you from your murderous brother. The Jewel of Life."

"This small thing?" Dar emitted a growl, coming to his feet. "You must think me an idiot."

"Small it may be, my boy, but it contains great power. Come." Lothous guided him toward the altar. "It was given as a gift of peace to your great-great-grandfather, Dareios."

Dar eyed the stone with greater interest. "Dareios? Am I to slay him, too?"

Lothous chuckled. "Not today, young one. Not today."

"Dareios brought the clans together, made the Krymerians a united force." Dar held the stone up in the faint light. "Was it from another chieftain?"

The eyes of the old priest gleamed. "A king."

Dar's brows lifted. "What king?"

"The Draconian king, Saki." Lothous caught the red gem before it hit the floor. "The young Saki, of course, not his grandfather. The old dragon never understood his grandson's acceptance of Krymerians."

"Draconian?" Dar rubbed his hand on his leathers. "Why would a king of Krymeria make peace with scum?"

"Dareios was wise. He knew when to fight and when to negotiate."

"I will not carry such a stone. There must be another way."

"Boy, if you wish to be victorious over your dark brother, you will honor the wisdom of your ancestors. Lay upon the stone."

For a Draconian stone to become part of him left him apprehensive. The idea of Krymerians associating with Draconians made his blood run cold. Every story he heard as a child painted the Dragon people as ruthless and cunning with no sense of loyalty to any but their immediate kin…and even that had been questionable. They had no allies, becoming extinct long before Dar's birth. Yet, this was the second gift supposedly given in friendship.

Despite his personal feelings, he knew it was important to trust the old priest. Loyal and faithful, Lothous had been an avid supporter of his family. Dar stretched out on the altar. It felt as rough today as it had all those years ago. The sight of the dagger positioned over his heart brought back a small boy's terror. He lay helpless, unable to defend himself. In one swift motion, the priest buried the blade deep into the young man's chest.

Dar grunted, trying not to cry out.

Lothous murmured a chant as he withdrew the dagger. "To do what is necessary comes with sacrifice." He held the stone before him, its light the color of blood. "Jewel of Life, bind your strength and power with that of the light." His voice grew more powerful as he raised the stone high into the air. "Protect him from the dark." He plunged the jewel deep within Dar's chest, forcing it into his heart, chanting over the screams of his victim. "Protect him from evil, and give him life over death. May you be victorious, High Lord. Long live the king!" He removed his hand and sealed the wound with a healing chant.

Dar lay still, sweat trickling off his brow. He breathed in, concentrating on the rise and fall of his chest. The pain was gone. "There can be no greater sacrifice than the one made long ago." He accepted the priest's hand and slid off the altar.

"With new power comes new sacrifice."

"Thank you, Father Lothous." He rolled his left shoulder and stretched the arm. "Am I truly free of my brother?"

The priest nodded. "It was foretold before you were born. 'A child will carry the light of salvation and the death of worlds, destined to be both, fated to end his own life.' I have given you a way to overpower the darkness and live. I pray you win this fight for I have one last duty to perform before I can complete my journey. Your victory will make my eternal rest all the sweeter." Lothous faded into the shadows.

"Father, wait. What of the legacy child the skull spoke of? Is it the one Faux carries?" Turning in search of the priest, he yelled into the darkness. "What is the sacrifice?" The riddles and clandestine messages had pushed him to his limit. At the lack of response, he slammed his fist on the altar, breaking the stone into pieces. "Give me an answer!"

Unable to raise the priest a second time, Dar stormed from the temple, concentrating on his next task for the evening.

In the back of a crowded nightclub, at the fringe of pulsing lights and gyrating dancers, a group of men sat on a semi-circular, black velvet sofa around a table, engrossed in the mumblings of a large man in their midst. His gaze drifted over each man. "What's the take this week?" he asked one to his left.

The five men were similar in size, shape, and coloring. Dar was not sure which was the one he sought, but the chatty man spoke with authority and appeared to have the others cowed. Dar was confident this was his man.

"I call you out, demon."

The malcontents around the table looked up in unison. The leader laughed, followed by the others, eying Dar with lethal intent. "You are a long way from home, little man. You should run along before you get hurt."

"A life for a life. Or in this case, your excuse of a life for four." His gaze roamed over the others. "Unless your friends want to sacrifice their lives, as well."

The man rose slowly, discarding the human façade. His form, freed of its forced confinement, towered over Dar. Dancers shuffled from the dance floor. The music stopped, but the colored lights continued their chaotic ripples over the two factions.

Dar recognized his kind. The jagged arch over the left eye, a mark given to survivors of the Battle of Azeroth, confirmed his alliance with an elite sect of hired assassins. It was not a battle of war but of initiation, where recruits fought for their lives against other recruits. Only the most brutal earned the privilege of displaying the self-inflicted scar. Dar mused that his target, close to nine feet tall with eyes as red as the fires of hell, should prove a worthy adversary, providing a welcome release from his conflicted emotions.

The demon's voice boomed through the nightclub as he reached for his great sword. "If you were smart, you'd turn that puny ass around and leave while you can. But, then again, your kind isn't known for their intellect."

Laughter surrounded the Krymerian. A squatty demon with pitted brown flesh waddled from table to table, accepting bets on various aspects of the night's unexpected entertainment. Who would move first? Who would draw first blood? Some bet on the origins of the rogue challenger. Others wagered on his soundness of mind. Those less adventurous with their cash bet the assassin as a sure win.

"Hurry up and finish him, Zagan. We have business needs tending," said one of the cronies at the table.

"I do my best work when I take my time. Sit back and enjoy while I slice this one down to size."

Dar rolled his shoulders. "It's time you paid for your crimes." He stepped back onto the dance floor and drew his blade, watching the demon come toward him.

A female voice squealed. "I knew it! Taly, come here and pay me."

"No pay until the game is played," he yelled over the din.

Another demon growled and slapped a six-digit hand on a table at Dar's first move. Taly jotted a note.

"Tell me of the four. There have been so many, I doubt I will remember, but let's give it a try…for kicks."

"A family. A father…" Dar twirled his blade to one side, "a mother…" He twirled to the other, "a brother." He held his blade aloft.

The assassin came in with a slash Dar easily blocked. Zagan landed a ferocious kick, sending Dar flying across the room. Demons and their human pets screamed and scattered to avoid the Krymerian. Dar was certain he felt at least one rib, maybe two, give way when he hit the far wall.

"You're a fool to think you can defeat me," the demon yelled, stalking around the dance floor. Cheers from the crowd ushered him on. "DJ!" His red eyes stayed on his prey. "Play us a killer tune." He laughed, watching the Krymerian struggle to stand. "That shit armor won't protect you from *my* sword."

Back on his feet, Dar took a defensive stance. A barrage of bruising blows rained down. One jab slipped through a gap, opening a gash behind Dar's left arm. Another laid open a slash across the side of his face.

"You're fast, but it won't be enough to save you." The demon slapped the flat side of his blade against Dar's cracked ribs.

Dar grunted and blew out a breath. "But I have not told you about the girl." He sidestepped the next attack, dropped to the floor, and rolled past his assailant. Determined, he charged in from behind. Too late, the demon found himself on the defensive, receiving a slash across his own back. Dar channeled the pain from his ribs into a series of well-placed hits.

Zagan danced away, bleeding but otherwise unfazed by the blows. "By all means, tell me about the girl." He laughed, grabbing his crotch. "Did I split her in two with my monstrous cock?" Laughter broke out around them.

"She was young, smart." Dar attacked like a man possessed. "Smart enough to outwit you. She lives amongst the Alamir now. I am sure a failure like that did not go unnoticed by your benefactor." He faked a low cut.

"Your shit talk means nothing to me." The demon slashed down to block the hit, lowering his guard. The tip of his sword slammed into the floor.

"Etain." Judging by the look on his face, Zagan clearly remembered. Dar's black blade ran up the length of the great sword, striking the demon's exposed neck. *Ba'alzamon* sliced through the bone, neat and clean. "This is for her." An inky trail of blood, made black by the flashing colored lights, streaked across the dance floor. Shocked by the suddenness of the move, the body held its position, supported by the demon's blade stuck into the wooden floor.

Bruised and battered, Dar collapsed to one knee and inventoried his wounds, keeping a keen eye on the other patrons of the bar. He was not sure if they would come for him or let it be. Faces turned to one another. Some smiled. Some frowned. Others had no expression at all. The cronies at the assassin's table stared at Dar, their faces like stone. He held his breath, his grip tight on the hilt of his sword.

The show over, the demon bookie waddled up to the table. "Pay up, boys. You lost."

One flashed a menacing grin at Dar then looked at the bookie. "Not me, Taly. Zagan never wins at anything. You owe *me*."

Everyone at the table turned their stony expressions on the winner. One closest to him, punched him in the arm. "Bastard! I should've done the same."

The others broke into laughter, paying their bets from the pot in the center of the table, the Krymerian warrior forgotten.

Dar released his breath and struggled to his feet, straining to sheath Ba'alzamon, doing his best to keep the broken ribs in place. Ready to be on his way, he kicked the inert body over onto the floor, and dragged the dagger from his boot. With the precision of a seasoned hunter, he opened the chest and plunged his hand into the bloody mass, removing the black heart. Dark liquid oozed from the useless organ in its final rhythmic beats. He moved across the floor and retrieved the head, its eyes forever frozen in a shocked glare.

Chanting a spell, he vanished, reappearing in Etain's room. He left the trophies of his kill on the chest at the foot of the bed.

"A debt is paid."

The first rays of morning light peeked through a gap in the drapes. Stiff muscles demanded a wakening stretch in preparation of the day. Twisting and turning, Etain noticed the open door and sat up, now fully awake. The gruesome sight at the foot of the bed gave her a start, clouded red eyes staring at her.

What the hell?

She shivered, scanning the room, her gaze coming back to the ugly head. At its side sat a chunk of coal. Upon closer inspection, she realized it was a heart. It was then she saw the bloody footprints leading out of the room. She dressed and followed the trail to Dar's room.

Dark smears of red covered the open door and frame. Without knocking, she walked in, seeing a black sword on the floor. Its master was on the bed, dressed in blood-soaked armor, his back to her.

"Dar," she called softly, coming closer. "What's happened? *Dar*, are you awake?"

"I am now," he said, irritation in his voice. "What do you want?"

"Why are you dressed like that?"

She stepped back as he turned and pushed up, his jaw clenched. Weariness showed in his eyes. With a grunt, he stood and picked up the sword, clearly favoring one shoulder, swaying as he faced her. "Hold this." He placed the hilt in her hand. When she tentatively grabbed it, he commanded, "Recede." The armored breastplate tucked into itself. Dar shivered as each piece vanished into the next, revealing his battered torso. Taking hold of the blade, he placed the tip at his heart. "We can end it right now. Push it in. That is all you have to do. One good push and all this will come to an end."

The audacity of his request outweighed the shock of his lacerated appearance. "What are you talking about?" Etain tugged on the hilt, but it wouldn't move.

He pulled the tip hard against his chest, cutting into the bruised skin. "A single thrust and the bad man will go away forever," he said, daring her with his eyes. "Is it not what you want? Me gone?"

"I'm perfectly willing to leave. There's no need for this."

"Your leaving will not solve the problem. Use this blade to end it."

She knew the pain reflected in his face wasn't from the blade digging into his flesh. "Is this a test?"

"This is the only way to release both of us from this hell. If you want me out of your life, drive it in. If not, tell me why."

"Don't be stupid. I will not take your life."

"Why?" Anger flickered in his eyes. "We circle each other, taking pieces here and there, never accepting what the other offers, yet never letting go. End this agony for both of us."

"Do *not* tell me what to do." She jerked the blade from his flesh, pacing in exasperation. "Don't tell me what I feel." She stopped, pointing the sword at him. "And do *not* expect me to give you an easy way out. A flash of your boyish grin, the flex of a muscle, and a few pretty words aren't going to spread my legs."

Dar grit his teeth. "Do not insult me with your jealous taunts."

The sword returned to his bruised chest. "It was *you* who summoned *us*. We came, thinking you needed our help. Instead, you abused our naïveté, then took Faux to your bed with no regard to how it may affect *me*." Electrical charges crackled along her form. "You far outdo me with the insults."

"Let me assure you, there was nothing naïve in Faux's performance. She knows what she does, and does it damn well."

"Then you're well-suited for each other. Each contemptuous word you speak makes killing you a temptation that's hard to resist."

"Before you end my miserable existence, let me clarify one thing." Dar wheezed another breath, holding his ribs. "I did not take her to *my* bed."

"It doesn't matter. You fucked my sister and thought to do the same with me." Her voice was low, close to menacing. "All on the same bloody night."

"It *does* matter. Since the death of my wife, taking a woman to *my* bed is an intimacy I have never shared."

Etain recognized the red tint around his blue eyes. To keep the situation from escalating to a level she couldn't handle, she released an electrical charge, hitting his bruised ribs. Dar hissed and dropped to his knees, the red glow disappearing.

"Guaranteed, you won't be sharing it tonight." The sword hovered over his heart, ready for a quick dispatch.

Life would be much simpler.

A trickle of fresh blood oozed down his chest.

Her gaze came up, ready to challenge his arrogance. What she found was not what she expected. His earlier aplomb had dissolved into misery.

Bloody hell.

She tossed the blade aside.

"What have you done?" He groaned, allowing her to help him to the bed. "Let me have a look. Sit as still as you can." Light fingers ran over his side, determining the damage, trying not to hurt him further. "I'm no healer, but Spirit's taught me a thing or two." After a quick inspection and a few grunts from her patient, she confirmed the cracked ribs. "There's not much I can do about it other than wrap you up and wait for them to mend by themselves. Do you have bandages?"

"I have no need of an infirmary."

She placed her hands on her hips. "I hate to burst your macho bubble, darlin', but you have a need now. Where are your linens? I'll have to make my own."

"Linens? Good question. I believe there is a closet of some sort at the end of the hall." Etain disappeared from the room. "But I do not know if there are linens."

Gone for only a few moments, she returned with sheets and towels in hand. "I'm happy to say you have plenty of linens." She tore one sheet into strips, setting them aside. Seeing the door to the en suite ajar, she slipped inside, dampening several towels. His shirt removed, she set to the chore of washing away the sweat and blood. "Don't worry, big man. You're in good hands."

"I have no doubt in your abilities, milady."

With his chest and upper abdomen firmly wrapped, she stepped back, admiring her work. "I believe I can put off piercing that black heart for a few more days. You won't be charming any lasses in your bed...or otherwise." He grunted in response. "Care to tell me what caused these injuries?"

"I did it for you and the family you lost, milady." The truth in his eyes caught her off- guard. "I have avenged their deaths. The head and heart are from the demon who killed your family, trophies to be dispatched of as you see fit."

His admission set her emotions into turmoil. Sadness for a family forever lost clashed with the satisfaction the assassin had paid with his life. Her only regret was that he had not died by her hand. "I will see them burned." She refused to consider what that meant in regards to her humanity. It seemed as though it was fast becoming a lost commodity in the Alamir world.

To keep it could get me killed, but to lose it would certainly turn me into a... Her gaze met his, *demon.*

"I would choose better protection next time, Lord Darknight. This one nearly cost you an arm."

"It is the armor of my forefathers," he defended. "It has served me well in the past. I thought it appropriate for the battle."

"Do you not like having all your body parts?"

He grinned. "Some more than others."

Etain reached for the blade in her boot, positioning it over her forearm. "Shall I administer our special elixir?"

"No," he said, shaking his head. "You need to recover from yesterday. Just wrap me up."

She cleaned and bandaged his shoulder, then helped him relax into the pillows. "You are to rest."

"Will you stay with me?" he whispered.

"Me? I'd think Faux would be more to your liking."

His face, a mix of weariness and frustration, made her relent. "Thank you for what you've done." She sat on the edge of the bed and encased his hand in hers. "Did he happen to mention why he murdered my family, before you took his head?"

"No. But he *did* remember them...and you."

"I guess that's something." She sighed. "I just wish it had been my blade."

Her fingers traced along his forearm in admiration of the well-defined muscles flowing into elegant hands. She thought how unusual it was to see such hands on a warrior. Their elegance belied their capacity for destruction. What would it feel like to have those hands moving over her body, caressing her skin, driving her to an ecstasy of destruction? She smiled, lost in the thought.

"Does this mean you don't hate me?"

Jarred from her thoughts, she shrugged. "Hate is such a strong word." Etain looked him in the eye. "I heard what you said. You need to give me time to sort out what it means."

"I don't think that will be a problem." He flinched with the laugh.

"I *should* hate you."

"I have made mistakes, hurting you in the process, milady. For that, I cannot apologize enough."

She dropped his hand on the bed. "Yes, yes. Sorry is as sorry does."

He grabbed her thigh before she could get away. "I speak the truth." Something in his voice made her listen. "My time with Faux was not planned. Contrary to what you may believe, I did not bring either of you here for that purpose." He waited for another inevitable eye roll. When it did not come, he decided it might have been easier than the ice-cold gaze he presently endured. The contrite man ventured further into the fray with a brave outlook, thinking a common-sense approach would help. "There is *some* good that has come from it." A blonde brow lifted. "We can breathe easier knowing the mark on Faux's belly will deter any sway Midir might have over her. He can no longer use her as a tool to get to you."

She nodded thoughtfully, giving him a sideways glance. "I see."

He watched her twist off the bed and look down at him, an unearthly smile on her lips. He felt the hairs on the back of his neck rise.

"You fucked *her* to keep *me* safe? You almost had me believing you and your patheticness."

He had not seen that one coming. "Etain..." He reached for her, but she dodged him.

"Then with her fucked and me fucked, everyone would be fucked...except Midir. All this fucking has dulled your senses. Have you forgotten what he did to your first family? Mark or no mark, he won't use her to get to *me*. He'll use her to get to *you*. Thank you for convincing me I don't belong here."

"This is exactly where you belong," he blustered, groaning as he shifted to the edge of the bed. "I thought we were past all that."

She turned and walked away. "I suggest you heal fast. You're gonna need everything you got to keep the likes of her safe." At the door, she stopped. "I'll be gone before morning.

"You *will not* leave," he roared, standing, doing his best to come to his full height.

"You're not my chieftain, or my lord. I am no longer under your command. You are nothing to me."

"There's nowhere you can hide, Etain. Wherever you go, Midir will find you."

"You two have a lot in common, don't you?" she quipped, turning her back to him. "Don't be concerned. He will never use me against you. *I* won't allow it."

Dar swayed, bracing himself with a hand to the wall, watching her walk away, the needed words unspoken. For the second time in his life, he felt unhinged. He'd not felt this way since the brutal death of his family. His brute strength, which had served him well in so many instances, was as useless now as it had been then. What was it about this young woman that affected him so strongly?

He was amid a tragedy he had no idea how to stop. His experience in dealing with women was limited. As a youth, he had played his fair share of games with the young Krymerian maids, but nothing serious. With Alexia, he had only just begun to learn that intimacy with a woman went beyond the physical.

"You must stay," he said with less vigor, his world starting to spin out of control. Tumbled thoughts slammed into one another.

She said you were nothing to her.

If I were nothing, she would not be so angry.

Are you certain? Do you truly know her heart?

Aye, I do.

He had to make her stay, wanted her to stay, *needed* her to stay. Not the warrior or the chieftain, but the man.

"It has always been you, Etain. Since that day at the wall, the moment I held you in my arms, I knew." His heart felt on fire, his stomach turning inside out.

How do I tell her?

The truth shall set you free.

Or seal my coffin.

"Coming to your defense is the excuse I used to stay close." He rested his forehead on the cool stone of the wall. "Etain..." He had to speak the words, lest she leave and never know. "I am in love with you."

Dar waited, watching the door, hoping she had heard him and would return. Several minutes passed. It was obvious he had pushed too far, his words inadequate. Collapsing back onto the bed, he released a long, hard breath, believing she was lost to him forever.

Ever the warrior, a plan to confront his brother began to take shape. Better to take the offensive in this situation, find a way to lure Midir to his realm and fight him on familiar turf.

On the other hand, Midir's castle is as familiar to me as my own. I will not let him take her. He will destroy everything good in her, and heaven help us should she turn to the darkness.

Out of the corner of his eye, there was a sudden movement in the doorway. Etain was there, staring at him. He sat up, watching her walk toward him.

"Do you know what love is?" she asked, standing over him.

"I loved my family with all my heart, but there was a void. One they could not fill, no matter how much I longed for it. Meeting you changed my life. I do not know how it happened, or exactly when, but having you in my life, no matter how small, fills the void. A look, a smile..." He blinked, unshed tears hot in his eyes. "I love you, Etain."

She kneeled in front of him, covering his hands with hers. "That first night we spent together, talking..." She reached up, pushing a lock of hair from his face, "you stole my heart. I think it's why I've been so angry with you. I've not been able to get it back."

He ignored the pull of his ribs and brought her up between his legs. "I am sorry I have been so thickheaded." His deep blue gaze held hers, allowing one last search. Any hint of treachery and he knew she would be gone. "It appears I have a lot to learn, as well."

A soft smile touched her lips. "Good thing I'm so patient and understanding."

He raised a brow. "Ahem... Aye. Were you not, I suppose we would be less one Krymerian." Now was the time to take the risk, to ask the damning question he had avoided for fear of her rejection. "Etain, will you be my lady? Can we work as one?"

She held his face in her hands, tracing a thumb over his lips. "I have been your lady since we first met." She kissed him. "As for the other... Give me time."

8

CASTLE LAUGHARNE

Etain knocked on Faux's door and, not waiting for a response, entered. A small figurine flew past her ear, just missing its target. "You lying bitch!" Another figurine sailed past.

Etain ducked. "What's *your* problem?"

Faux stormed up to her, eyes full of fire, tail ready to strike. "I wasn't serious when I said give him a try." Etain stepped back. "He is *mine*. Do you hear me? He gave *me* his gift. *Me!*" The deadly tail darted out, intent on piercing her imagined adversary.

"Faux, calm down!" she hollered, diving across the bed to keep the angry demon at a safe distance. "No one is questioning the gift he gave you."

"Where have you been?" Her eyes flashed. "Is he still in your bed?"

"You know I'm not like that," she countered. "I was alone last night...*all* night."

"So was I, locked in this room with no way out. How is it you just walk in? Where the hell is he?" She charged the bed. "Where was he if he wasn't with you?" Unable to get to her prey, she picked up another object, prepared to launch.

"Stop throwing things at me," Etain said. "If you'll calm down and listen, I'll tell you where he's been." Faux fell silent, murder on her face, arms crossed, foot tapping, and solid object in hand. With a shrug, Etain sat on the side of the bed. "Dar went to great lengths last night to right the wrong done to my family."

"What *great* lengths?"

"He avenged their deaths. Suffice it to say, there's one less demon tormenting this world."

"He actually found the bastard?" She returned the crystal bobble to its spot on the nightstand. Etain nodded, relieved she had chosen to listen. "How do you know he killed him?"

She walked around the bed and took her by the hand. "Come with me." She led her to the abomination perched on the chest in her room.

Faux stared at the head and heart. "Ug...ly. Are you sure he got the right one?"

Etain shivered. "I will never forget those red eyes."

She noticed the bloody footprints. "What's all this?"

"Leftovers from last night. Don't worry about it. We need to get back to Laugharne."

Faux walked around the footprints. "Whose blood is this?"

Etain didn't hear her questions. For her, the present faded into a vision of two boys.

"Come on, brother. It will be fun. You know you want to." The taller of the two pulled the other toward a river.

"Stop. You know it is not allowed."

"If you don't, I will tell father about the other night."

"What are you talking about?"

"You know what I'm talking about." Pulling his brother again, he worked him closer to the water. "The lady you killed. You did things to her that would make the darkest heart proud." He ran and jumped into the river.

Years pass, and the brothers stand facing the river yet again. Etain recognized them as Dar and Midir. They turned to face each other, both surrounded by bright light, storms brewing in their eyes.

"A test," she whispered.

Midir released a blast of energy, striking Dar, dropping him to one knee. Dar retaliated with a blast of golden light, knocking Midir unconscious.

"Etain."

The earth shook.

"Snap out of it."

Etain did, rubbing her cheek. "Why'd you hit me?"

"It was a slap. You were lost in space, rambling about a test."

"Seriously, we have to get out of here."

"You didn't answer my question. Whose blood is this?"

Disoriented by the vision and angered by Faux's insistent demands, she blurted, "Dar's a little banged up from last night."

"Why? Where is he?"

"He's in his room, resting."

Faux headed toward the door. "What did you do to him, Etain? Is that why you're in such a hurry to leave? Afraid of retaliation?"

"*I* didn't do anything." She followed her to the door. "Besides, he's coming with us. Someone with experience needs to look him over to make sure I didn't miss anything."

The demon girl followed the footprints into Dar's room, Etain behind her. "Damn, girl. You *didn't* miss a thing. Is there any part of him you didn't bruise?"

"*I* didn't do this." Etain frowned, not happy with the amount of blood seeping through his bandages. With a light touch to his battered body, her voice was soft. "Dar, wake up. I need to change your dressings."

He stirred and tried to rise. "Ouch!" Falling back, he smiled, seeing her face. "Hello, beautiful." Her eyes shifted across the bed. Turning his head, he encountered watchful black eyes. "Not just one beautiful lady, but two. I am a fortunate man." They helped him sit up.

"Etain told me what you did," Faux said, sitting on the side of the bed. "It must've been a magnificent battle. I'm glad you won."

"As am I," he managed to answer between groans.

Etain motioned for Faux to help her remove the bloodied bandage. Eager to change the subject, she told him of her vision. "Were they real?"

"Aye. You saw a part of my past I wish had never happened."

"Is that the test you mentioned?" Faux asked her.

Etain wasn't in the mood to answer questions. "Get your things together, Faux. It's time to go. I'll make sure everything else is ready." Faux gave her a long look, then Dar, before she left the two alone.

With several gasps and groans by the patient, Etain helped him to his feet.

"Where are you going?" he asked, his voice a little too loud. "We agreed to work as one. You know I cannot protect you if you leave."

"We're going to Laugharne, you included. You aren't in any shape to defend anyone at the moment, and I need to make sure you heal right. And, I didn't agree to anything."

"And if I choose not to accompany you?"

The arrogant glint in his eye proved to be too much. Etain poked him in the ribs. He groaned, dropping onto the bed. "Point made."

"Between Inferno and Spirit, we'll have you fixed in no time." She went to the chest of drawers and gathered a few of his things.

"Okay, I'm ready." Faux rushed in and flopped down beside Dar. "So, you're coming with us, huh?"

He hissed, clenching his jaw. "It appears so." His attention went back to Etain. "Laugharne. Interesting choice. Tell me. Do you know how to get there from here?"

The realization made her stop. *Bloody fucking hell.* She turned. "Well, I guess you're gonna have to show me the way."

Eyeing the two handfuls sitting side by side on the bed, something her dad used to say came through to Etain. *The choices you make in life decide your destiny. You are in control. Never give someone else power over you by casting blame. You always have a choice.*

"That should be enough," she said, bestowing a beautiful smile on her charges. "Help me get him to his feet and we'll get out of here."

Sorry, Dad. I didn't choose to fall in love. I just...did.

"I doubt your friends will be pleased to see me," Dar said, which degraded into a coughing fit. Etain became more concerned when blood darkened his lips, but he continued to ramble. "I think you punctured one of my lungs. We should have a serious talk about your...patience."

"My patience didn't crack your ribs."

"Hmph," he responded, returning her insolent look. "Before we leave, I need a few more things."

After a slow breath, he bent down to pick up the black sword. A sharp pain ripped through his side, sending him head first to the floor. The women tried to catch him, but his size and dead weight proved too much. They fell to the floor in a mass of tangled arms and legs. Etain scrambled to disentangle herself, running her hands over his chest and abdomen, checking his bandages. On his stomach, he turned his head, watching her. Satisfied all was well, she caught his roving eye and pushed back the errant strands of hair over his face.

"Thank you," he said.

"For what?"

"For caring."

"If I'd known it was going to be a full-time job..." She and Faux helped him up. Etain bent over, reaching for his blade. "Is this what you were after, warrior man?"

Dar grabbed her outstretched hand and yanked her back. "Don't touch it," he growled. Seeing her appalled look, he let go. "It's a powerful weapon, drenched in magic. Just a touch can change a person."

Etain rubbed her hand as she listened, refusing to look at him. He cupped her chin. "Only I can wield its power and not be affected by its influence. I'm sorry if I hurt you."

"Like I said..." She pulled free of his touch, "a full-time job."

"I wish I didn't have to bring this along, but I may have need of it." With help from the girls, he strapped it across his back. "I am ready."

Etain leaned toward Faux. "Get on the other side. We don't want him to fall again."

He waved them off. "Ladies, I am touched by your concern, but please afford me my dignity. I would prefer to show up on my feet."

"There'll be plenty of time for your dignity once we arrive. For now, we have to be close so I can transport us." Flashes of blue surrounded the three. "Show me the way."

Within moments, they stood in the courtyard of Castle Laugharne.

Dar smiled, taking in the view. "Such a lovely place. Reminds me of ho-"

The big man swayed and his eyes rolled back. Faux and Etain missed catching him by mere inches. He landed in the gravel, flat on his back.

"At least he can't complain about his dignity," Etain said, hands on her hips. "Let's get him up to the house." They grabbed his legs and attempted to drag him to the door.

"Damn, he's heavy," Faux complained, tugging with all her might. "Why don't we shimmer inside?"

"Unannounced? I don't think so."

After considerable effort, Etain decided to leave him and, with Faux at her side, approached the steps.

Spirit opened the door just as Etain raised her hand to knock. The two women shared a look of surprise. "What're you knocking for, lass? This is your home as much as it is-" Etain and Faux stepped apart, giving her a view of the bundle lying in the courtyard. Spirit's smile faded. "Blimey, he's not gonna like this. Hold on. I'll get help."

After a minute or two, Inferno came storming down the hall, followed by his four-legged sentinels, Felix and Ruby.

Faux side-stepped toward Etain, using her as a shield. "Keep them away from me."

The hounds bounced past the girls and toward the new intrigue passed out in their territory, sniffing and nuzzling into his hair.

"For fuck's sake, girl," Inferno said, giving her a look that would make a lesser woman quake. "Felix! Ruby! Off with ya!"

The two had one last sniff, whining their concern for the man, then ran up to Etain and Faux for a quick hello. With the niceties out of the way, Ruby returned to Dar, licking his face. Felix stayed with Etain, enjoying a good scratch behind the ears.

"Ruby, girl, what'd I say? Off with the two of ya!"

Felix licked Etain's hand and joined his counterpart, but Ruby had different plans. She sat next to the comatose man. When Inferno yelled again, she huffed and lay over Dar's chest. Felix barked and nipped at her, receiving a low growl for his efforts. Felix looked at his master, then sat down next to Ruby.

"Bloody fucking hell. If any trouble comes from this..." Inferno left it at that. "Shimmer him to the goddamned lounge and we'll have a look."

With Dar on the sofa, Spirit checked his bandages and general physical condition, all under the close scrutiny of his red-haired champion. "Would you mind, Ruby, love? He's in good hands," Spirit said, giving the hound a nudge.

Inferno snapped his fingers, a stern expression on his face. Felix padded over to Ruby, gave her a snort, and left the room. She sniffed at Dar, licked Spirit's face, and followed Felix, stopping at the door for one last glance and a growl directed at Inferno.

"Trouble already and the man's not even awake," he said, watching Spirit's ministrations.

"Inferno..." Etain felt it the perfect opportunity to ask about the relationship between the two men. "Why do you hate him?"

"That's me own business."

Spirit looked over her shoulder. "You should tell her, love." He gave her an annoyed look. "She'd not brought him here unless something's changed. She needs to know what she's in for."

Faux settled in, a cocky grin on her face.

"Inferno." Etain placed a gentle hand on his arm. He tried to avoid eye contact, but she followed his every move until he relented. The look on his face twisted her heart. "What could've possibly happened to make you hate him so?"

He pulled away, crossing his arms over his chest. "I was there the day this one…" He nodded at Dar, "took ya down from that wall." Etain's eyes widened. "Aye." He walked to the window, but it was clear he looked on a different landscape. "The clans were on a rampage. There was no Council, and everone was tryin' to figger it out. There weren't much in the way of order. The *Bok* reared its ugly head, taking advantage of the confusion. Me and me clan were on patrol when we happened upon a nasty battle. It was total chaos, and being as that one there is the Lord of Kaos, he was in his element."

"Was he for or against you?"

He turned his head, looking her in the eye. "I don't know, lass. It weren't easy to tell."

"It must've been really bad."

He nodded. "There are no words."

"But that's not all, is it? I know you better than to think you'd pass judgment so easily."

Silence permeated the room. Inferno stiffened, the struggle to find the right words evident on his face. His gaze returned to the window.

Faux exploded out of her seat. "Then what the hell is it? Stop with all the dramatics and spill." Etain and Spirit looked daggers in her direction. Inferno turned.

"Ya'd do well t'keep yer mouth shut, girlie," he fired at her. "This is none of yer concern."

"Is that so?" She strutted toward Inferno, tail whipping left to right. "I may have come into this soap opera during the second season, but I'm part of the main cast now. I have as much to lose here as anyone."

Etain noted the flickering flames at his fingertips, warning signs of the Alamir chieftain losing his temper. "Inferno, she *is* a part of all this."

"Hmph, not that I would know. Don't see or hear from ya for

months, then ya show up with this one." He turned a caustic eye on Faux. "Ya disappear again, then come back with…with…"

Spirit moved to her husband's side, placing a hand on his chest. "Be still, love. We're family here." Accosted by his glare of disbelief, she stepped back.

"That monster is *not* family," he shouted, his body shaking, pointing a finger in Dar's direction. "And this one here…" He was back to Faux. "Who the hell knows how this one fits in."

Laugharne had been Etain's safe zone, a place she had found love, support, and acceptance. His judgment, suspicion, and accusations pushed her beyond her endurance. Electrical charges exploded around her, shattering every piece of glass in the room. Faux fell to the floor. Inferno pushed Spirit into a corner, shielding her with his body. A rumble resounded throughout the room. Faux shuffled away on hands and knees, tail between her legs. Spirit and Inferno leaned into each other to stay on their feet.

In a voice that would give demons in hell reason to quake, she decreed, "Dar was Lord and Master long before your great-grandparents were even conceived, and he will be here long after your great-grandchildren are dust in their graves." She turned her glowing eyes on Faux. "Faux is my sister by the blood of Kaos. She and Dar are as much my family as you."

Light as bright as the sun filled the room. Faux raised an arm, shielding her eyes. Inferno and Spirit ducked their heads into each other.

Just as the scorching heat threatened to engulf the room, it disappeared. Cautious, the three opened their eyes and took a quick inventory, ensuring they weren't injured. Finding no damage, they dared to look in Etain's direction. Instead of the blonde beauty, they saw a span of black wings arced around a solar firebrand, beaming bright. Eventually, the light dissipated.

Inferno and Spirit stood frozen in each other's arms. Faux, keeping her eye on the winged being, crawled to a chair and pulled herself up.

Her movement snapped Inferno from his fascination. Looking in her direction, he spied the empty sofa.

"Ya bleedin' bastard! Get away from her." He released his wife and marched toward the creature. Spirit screamed for him to stop. Faux shot out of her chair, headed for Inferno.

Dar turned, his eyes red, Etain safe within his protective wings. "She is not hurt." His attention returned to his beloved, stroking her face, whispering reassurances to abate the demon blood raging in her veins. "*Tá mé anseo, mo ghrá. Calma do chroí. A bheith fós* (I am here, my love. Calm your heart. Be still)."

Faux stopped, her tail stiff, and released a disgusted gasp.

Inferno stopped. "Yer havin' a laugh. Are those words of love comin' from yer vile mouth?" He paced a wide circle around the two, shimmering from the heat he held just below the surface, glowering at the demon. "What the bloody hell have ya done to our lass? I knew ya weren't right. I could feel it in me bones. A full-fledged demon, ya are."

He threw a fireball, hitting his target just below the ribs. Dar roared in pain and retaliated with a winged slap, sending the chieftain flying across the room.

Inferno slammed into the stone wall and fell to his knees. Scrambling to his feet, he spun a web of fire. "*Rhyddhau tanau* (Fires release)."

As soon as it left his hand, the fire web changed from brilliant reds and yellows to icy whites and blues, falling to the floor in tinkling shards. Inferno turned his glare on his wife.

Etain, now back in control of herself, placed her hands on Dar's face, bringing his attention to her.

At the same time, Spirit marched over to her husband, ice in her eyes. "Keep your fires to yourself, boyo." She stood between her husband and the demon. "Have you not heard a word been said? Do you not see they share a connection?" She surveyed the damage. "Me house can't take your oversized egos, and neither can I. Or shall I weave an icy prison for you to cool off in?"

Faux laughed. "You're all pathetic. How any of you became Alamir is beyond me." She headed for the door. "Anyone for a beer?"

Etain held Dar's gaze. "You must rest." Seeing her back to herself, his wings retracted and the demon eyes returned to blue. He slumped against her. She grunted from the sudden weight, but held him up long enough to get him situated on the sofa.

Faux returned with a fresh round. With everyone in apparent agreement, each grabbed a tankard, scrutinized one another, and drank.

Running fingers through her hair, Etain spoke first. "I'm sorry, Spirit. I don't know where that came from. It's never happened before."

Inferno took a seat, still out of sorts. "Someone's been tampering with yer blood again." He shot a steely-eyed glare at Dar. "Can ya not find someone else to curse with yer taint?"

Etain was ready with a retort, but Dar held up a hand. "I can speak for myself, milady." He turned to Inferno. "I did what was necessary."

"Necessary, ya say. By whose standards?" he said, each word drenched in sarcasm. "Like when yer sorry excuse for a Council sent her on a wild goose chase in the human realm? Or is it more like when yer sword pierced her gut all those years ago?"

Spirit shook her head. "Goddess of us all."

Faux sauntered closer to the sofa, standing over Dar, evil amusement in her eyes. "Sounds like that priest missed a bit a something." She poked him in the ribs and plopped down beside him.

Etain, sitting on his other side, stood. "*Your* sword?"

Having lost the support of her body, he slumped to his side. "*Tartarus*," Dar muttered. "At this rate, these ribs will be broken for eternity."

The delighted Faux placed a playful hand on his thigh. "You'll be lucky if she doesn't break the ones on the other side." Laughing, she helped him straighten.

"Hmph, no doubt," he agreed, struggling to catch sight of Etain.

Standing at one of the shattered windows, she stared at the shards of glass twinkling in the sunlight, wondering at the beauty emerging from such destruction. How the sun sparkled through the jagged edges, making them appear as diamonds, never giving a hint to the danger they possessed if touched by bare skin. She reached out to the sparkling edge. Just as a fingertip neared the jagged glass, a small gnat flittered in front of her face. She batted it away, saving the defenseless finger, but the annoyance refused to be ignored.

"Go away, little gnat." She swatted again, just missing it. The small creature disappeared for a moment, only to return in duplicate, then a third and fourth. They continued to multiply until there was a small army of gnat-like creatures, buzzing around her head. "What the...? Spirit, you really must do something about these pests."

She laughed from across the room. "Take another gander at what pesters you."

One of the little buggers landed on Etain's nose. Looking cross-eyed at the minute creature, she recognized it for what it truly was. "Oh." The tiny faerie stuck out her tongue, then darted away. Their giggles sounded like glass chimes, tinkling in the wind as they flew away. Etain laughed, running a finger down her nose. "I forget how close you are to the wee folk, Spirit."

Meandering back to the circle, she chose to sit on the arm of Inferno's chair. She gave the Krymerian a nonchalant look. "So, it was *your* sword, was it?"

Inferno and Spirit exchanged glances. Dar shifted in his seat, watching Spirit take Faux by the hand. "Come along, lass. This is one of those private moments."

Faux glared at her. "I don't think so. I have as much right to hear this as she does."

Inferno walked over to take her by the other arm, catching her tail before it could come to her rescue. The two dragged her from the sofa, forcing her to leave with them. Her protests echoed all the way down the hallway, followed by Inferno's bellows over her squawks. "I'll tell ya the whole story in the kitchen, girl. Now, off with ya before I put ya over me knee like one of me own wee folk."

Her melancholy smile fading to a frown, Etain slipped into the chair recently abandoned by Inferno. "I'm waiting."

"I...," Dar began, stalling for time by taking a swig from his mug. "I didn't do it." His attempt at humor died a quick death. "Right. Unlike what some would like to think..." He held her gaze, "I was there to help, not fight." For an instant, she broke eye contact, but came back to him. "Aye. I heard your conversation." He shifted, trying to get comfortable. "I was searching for those still alive, giving help where needed, saying prayers for those lost. My sword was at my side." He took another drink, knowing all he could do was be honest and hope she believed him. "An old, abandoned building stood at the edge of the field. I cannot say what made me look there, but halfway up one side of the building I saw a body hanging. It was worth investigating, not only because of the poor soul left to die, but because the body had not been there when I arrived...*after* the fight." He shifted again. "As I approached, I realized it was a woman impaled by a large sword. I checked for a pulse. It was faint, but at least she was still alive." A sudden pain caused him to blow out a breath. "Aaah." Hand to his side, he breathed in slowly. "Then I noticed the blade." The vivid remembrance showed on his face. "I was horrified to see my own sword. To this day, I do not know how it left my side. I swear to you, Etain. I don't know."

Her eyes narrowed. "Maybe you've forgotten some part of the battle. Are you sure it wasn't in your hand?"

"I was not involved in the battle in any way. My sword was sheathed at my side. Once I stepped onto the field, my hands were too busy moving bodies to hold a sword."

"Could one of those you were helping have grabbed it?"

"No. Many were already dead. Those left alive were too weak to raise their heads, much less a sword. Even if someone could have grabbed it, they could not have thrown it with such force."

She sighed with an unconscious touch to her abdomen. "I remember slamming into the wall. I was sure my back was broken. The next thing I remember was waking up and seeing you."

He nodded. "Please tell me you believe me. I would not take an innocent life. I knew nothing of you until I saw you on that wall."

Her gaze locked with his for a long moment before she spoke. "I suppose it was Lady Fate who brought us together that day." She pushed out of her seat and settled next to Dar. "We are kindred souls, bound together. Not only by blood, but by spirit." She wrapped him in her arms and rested her head against his. "I'm glad we met, but I wish it had been under different circumstances."

"Aye," Dar agreed, leaning into her. He felt light, content, and...happy.

They enjoyed the rare moment alone, at peace in one another's arms. After a short time, Dar's soft snores attested to his complete submission to sleep. Etain smiled, stroking his hair, and joined him in the dream world.

9

MIDIR'S TAINT

The seething lord stormed about his castle, sparks of green light exploding around him. He, too, knew the heart and soul of Dar and, unbeknownst to his brother, knew the same of Etain.

"I have spent too many years laying out this plan to have you ruin it, you selfish pig. It's not enough for you to have the demon girl. You have to take what is rightfully mine, as well? Not this time!" Midir slammed his fist into the wall. "Not this time."

Small objects exploded as he passed, furniture burst into flame in his presence, and servants cowered in corners. The furious lord donned the twin to Dar's black blade. Sliding on black leather gloves, he chanted the words, which would take him to Etain.

The dark figure loomed over the sleeping couple, a smirk on his lips. "Dar, you are a fool if you think you can keep such a woman. Her warrior spirit far outweighs your abilities. You have no idea of what she is capable, and she will never learn if she stays with you." With a light touch, he stroked her silver hair. "Stick with the dark one. She's better suited to you. This beauty deserves more than you can ever hope to offer." He turned her face to his, touching his lips to hers.

Blue eyes opened. "Get away from me," she hissed, jerking her chin from his hand.

Midir felt a thrill run through him. "You feel it, don't you?" he whispered. "Come with me and I will teach you how to harness it."

"I will not."

"A fire burns in your veins, Etain. A fire *I* placed there…not this poor excuse who sleeps in your presence. He is no match for you. I alone know what you need."

Her body shimmered from barely contained electrical charges. "We will not do this here."

Midir followed her through the main doors. Once outside the courtyard gate, Etain turned, throwing an electric current at his heart. Taken by surprise, he staggered back. She threw another. This time, his head fell forward. Encouraged, she blasted him again, hoping this one would be his undoing. His body convulsed and his head lolled on his shoulders. Etain felt the beats of her heart in her chest. She licked her lips, waiting for the man to collapse.

Instead, he inhaled, straightening his shoulders. His head came up, eyes filled with a blue glow, a smile on his lips.

Disarmed, she ran. Midir raised a hand, but his magic had no effect on the fleeing girl. He considered the useless appendage, baffled by its inability to subdue his target, then tried again.

Etain ran to the estuary. Taking swift inventory of her options, she wrote off the sword left at Laugharne and dismissed the dagger in her boot, knowing it to be inadequate. She didn't want to get close enough to make it effective. Obviously, her electric charge had no impact on him.

"He's so strong," she whispered, her mind racing in its search to prevail over the sinister lord.

Despite their difficult past, every fiber of her being knew she belonged with Dar. This stalking menace had miscalculated. *There is one thing I have the power to control.* As much as leaving Dar pained her, she found some comfort in knowing he wouldn't be alone. Hopefully. Maybe. She shrugged. *If not Faux, then the child.* She looked behind her one last time.

Midir screamed a command, ordering her to stop.

"You're wrong about the fire in my veins. It will never burn for you."

The warrior faced the estuary and walked into the water.

Shaken to its core, the castle tossed its inhabitants to the floor. Spirit called out to Inferno and Faux, asking if they were all right. They could hear the hounds barking outside. Fortunately, no one from the clan was present, having duties elsewhere.

"What in the hell was that?" Faux asked, pulling herself up.

Inferno jumped to his feet and ran to the front of the house, Faux and Spirit close behind. Coming to what was once the lounge, they stepped into rubble, the outer walls in ruins. All eyes went to the sofa, crushed by several large stones. Spirit gasped.

Inferno pushed her behind him. "Let me have a look." The stones were too heavy to budge. He turned to his wife. "There'd be blood-"

"They aren't here." Faux pointed toward the shore. "They went down there."

Water erupted into the sky, showering down like a great rain in Dar's search for her. His powerful wings wrapped tight around his body, he dove into the murky waters, reaching out with his mind in a frantic attempt to link with Etain's. He had her only moments ago, but now all was silent. Dashing to-and-fro, he felt something tickle his fingers.

The light was dim at this depth, making it hard to see. Was it the tendrils of a plant…or hair? He latched onto it, going deeper. He touched on something solid. A drifting hand. Grabbing hold, he pulled her into his arms and surged up to the surface, landing at the water's edge. He cradled her cold body, trying to warm her.

"No, no, no. We had…have an understanding. Why would you do this?"

Gently, he laid her on the sand, doing all he could to expel the water from her lungs. "Come back, Etain. Give me the chance to prove we belong together. Come back to me." He would not give up. Even if it she had changed her mind, he still had a chance as long as she lived.

In time, water bubbled from between her blue lips. Dar rolled her onto her side. "Cough it up. Good. Get it all out."

Etain pulled his head down to hers. Her voice was ragged, barely audible, but he understood.

The blade slid along Dar's back. "I'm here for what's mine-"

Midir flew through the air, his jaw bruised. He landed face down in the sand, but was quick to his feet. Sensing someone behind him, he held the hilt of his blade with both hands and blindly stabbed back. Satisfaction thrilled his blood when he felt the flesh yield to his blade. Midir turned, eager to see his brother's face twisted in death.

Black eyes full of hate met his gaze. Faux gave him a bloody sneer, a foot of the black blade protruding from her back. "You will not hurt him," she seethed, grabbing hold of the blade.

Anxious to get to his intended victim, he pushed her with his foot, pulling the blade free. "Idiot woman." Midir looked up into the face of an enraged demon. His laugh covered his surprise. "You're no match for me, demon or not." He attacked. Dar deflected the move with his talons, the blade skipping across the sand. Midir screamed when his brother grabbed him by the forearm. "You won't kill me. You *can't*."

A stone-faced expression met his. "Watch me." Dar retracted his deadly talons, pulled back a fist, and punched him. A series of brutal kicks to his abdomen pushed Midir to the water's edge. "Before you die, I want to feel the crack of every bone in your body." He kicked again. "And bask in every scream." He jabbed a hand into his hair, closing his fist around a handful, and lifted his head. "You took my first family. You will not take this one." Two quick jabs shattered his nose.

Dragged across the sand, Midir gulped for air just as Dar shoved his head into the water. He sputtered and flailed, fighting against the strong hand holding him under, but his mind separated from the threat of death. Never had he experienced such rage from his brother. He had witnessed his brutality directed at another, but never toward him. Had he finally pushed Dar over the edge? Did Dar have the capacity to kill him? Midir laughed at the thought. If he was so determined, he must have found a way. So be it. But it was Dar's life on the line not his.

Suddenly, he was on his back, spitting water, gasping for air. Another punch to the face snapped his head to the side.

Dar ground a boot into his chest. "This ends here...today." His talons snapped out.

Midir heard a moan. Turning his head, he saw by the look in Dar's eyes that he heard it too. He drew in a ragged breath, watching his brother turn and go to the dark-haired girl.

Swiping a forearm over his face, Midir spit blood onto the sand. How dare he lay her next to Lady Etain. No one could be her equal. To him, it was further proof that Dar didn't deserve her.

Taking advantage of Dar's distraction, Midir reached for the dagger in his belt, seeing the two women disappear. *Always the boy scout.* He lurched forward, driving the blade deep into Dar, scraping the edge of a rib. Dar yelled out, arching his back, and staggered forward.

"I don't know how you did it, but if you're willing to kill me, it means we're finally free of each other." He circled around, swinging a strong left into his brother's jaw, slashing with the dagger. "You've always called *me* your curse." The light did his best to avoid the relentless stabs from the dark. "When, in fact, the real curse is that you're too weak to do what needs doing. I did you a favor when I finished them off. You wouldn't have lasted a month as king."

Despite Dar's efforts, the blade hit its mark several more times. He collapsed onto the mud, chest heaving. Midir towered over his fallen brother. "Our father was blind when it came to you. In the end, I made him see. He learned the error of his ways...before I cut out his eyes."

Dar lashed out. Midir felt a sudden warmth bloom over his lower body. His gaze dropped to the bloodied hands of his brother.

"You should learn to keep your mouth shut," Dar growled, flat on his back.

Midir fell to his knees, holding his gut. "I won't die so easily."

Dar rolled onto his side and grabbed him by the neck, cutting off his breath. "Neither will I."

Midir summoned what little strength he had left and dragged his blade across Dar's chest, deep enough for his brother to loosen his grip on his throat. He coughed, gasping for air. "Next time, you won't be so lucky." On hands and knees, Midir croaked a chant, then crawled through an open portal.

Footsteps crunched on the sand.

"Come to finish me off?" Dar opened his eyes, meeting Inferno's gaze.

"Temptin'. Wouldn't be hard to do."

"Are they safe?" He winced, taking in a breath.

"Aye. We got them to the house. Etain walked on her own. Spirit's seeing to the other."

A faint smile on his lips, Dar nodded. *That's my lady.* His gaze returned to Inferno. "You think all I do is bring her pain."

"Don't need to think. That show was proof enough."

Dar slowly pushed himself up. "If you truly believe she's better off without me, let's end it now." He offered the hilt of the bloodied dagger.

Inferno challenged his gaze, discovering something he never expected to find in the eyes of a demon – sadness. His willingness to keep Etain safe spoke to Inferno's fatherly heart. "You'd let me do it too, wouldn't ya?" he asked, taking the dagger. Dar nodded, watching the blade twirl through Inferno's fingers. With a quick move of his wrist, Inferno aimed the blade at the demon's throat. "Whether I like it or not, there's someone dependin' on ya. Someone I care for." He jabbed the blade into the ground and held out a helping hand. "Let's get back home."

Once on his feet, Dar released his demon and picked up the blade. The two slowly inched their way back to the castle.

"Who the hell was that?"

"Midir, my brother."

"Piss poor reunion, I'd say."

Dar shrugged. "Better than others we've had."

"Must not be dead if he's standing." Spirit took Dar's face in her hands. "But not in such good shape, either. Let's get him inside." She and Inferno helped the exhausted warrior into the kitchen, sitting him down on a stool next to the sink. "Let's see about these wounds."

"How is Etain?" Dar asked as he stood, grimacing, determined to find her.

Inferno placed a hand on his shoulder. "Keep yer bum where it is and let me wife look ya over. The girls aren't going anywhere."

Dar lowered back onto the stool.

Spirt looked from one man to the other. "Love, would you check on them? Just to be sure?"

"Wait, Inferno. There's something I want to say." Dar noticed Spirit's concerned look. "Don't worry, milady. There will be no trouble." He turned to Inferno. "Thank you for your help today." He offered his hand.

Inferno accepted. "*Efallai y byddwn fod yn ffrindiau* (May we be friends)."

Dar smiled. "*Efallai y byddwn yn parhau i fod yn ffrindiau* (May we remain friends)."

Inferno suddenly smiled, impressed by Dar's command of the Welsh. He glanced over his shoulder as he walked out of the room, sending an *I'll tell you later* look to his wife.

Spirit returned to her patient's injuries. "Is he dead? Your brother, I mean."

"You know my brother?"

"I know of him. Etain told me about the trouble he's caused." She pulled out a drawer, grabbing a large pair of scissors and a few dishcloths, then started snipping away the remnants of his shirt.

"He is a hard one to kill, but he won't be back any time soon. His wounds may not be fatal, but they are significant. I should be healed long before he is, so we can move on and not put you in further danger."

She gave him a serious look. "Etain told me something else."

"Did she?"

"Aye. She says the girl upstairs is pregnant. Having met her before they went to your place, I noticed a change when she came back, but couldn't put me finger on it. Is it yours?"

Dar met her gaze. "How is she?"

She dropped the last bit of fabric on the floor, but the scissors remained in her hand, the sharp tips waving dangerously close to his flesh. "She's alive. That's all I can say right now."

"And the child?"

"Hard to tell just yet. But now I know, I'll keep a closer watch."

Dar took hold of her hand, judiciously removing the possible weapon from her grip and placing it on the counter. "You have my every gratitude, milady. These women mean everything to me."

She eyed the scissors. Dar considered grabbing them himself, but thought it could prove a decisive moment in his relationship with this woman. He gripped his thighs, gritting his teeth. If everything went sour, he would be ready. He sucked in a breath as her hand neared the sharp instrument.

"I don't understand one bit of it, and I have to say I like it even less." She picked up a cloth, flipped on the tap, and swished it through the running water, then dabbed away what blood she could. "But if Etain's all right with it, I'll find a way to deal with it."

He let go of the breath, thankful for her support of Etain. "What about Inferno?"

"No." She shook her head, removing more of the grime from his chest. "You'll deal with that hornet's nest on your own when the time comes...and it will. Mark my words. Hell won't come near paying *that* debt."

"I'll find a way, milady, although I don't fully understand it myself."

"At least you've not kept her in the dark about *that*." Spirit gave him the eye again. "What do you hope to gain with this other deception?"

"Other deception?" Dar's face was blank.

"I don't know a lot about Krymerians, but I have learned you're quick to heal." Spirit rinsed the cloth again and set to work on his back. "Etain's been around you long enough to know it, too. Maybe her head's all a dither with the change between you two and she hasn't noticed..." She rinsed one more time, making a final sweep over his skin, "or she chooses to ignore the fact. Either way, whether by choice or not, it's up to me and me husband to make sure she's safe, and stays that way."

Dar answered with utmost sincerity. "It is not to take advantage of her. Please believe me." He lowered his voice. "I trust this will be kept between us."

"Depends on your reasons."

"Fair enough." He winced as she cut through the linen bandage to get to the nasty gash beneath his ribs. "Although our introduction was extraordinary, the time we shared afterward was as if we had known each other all our lives. Conversation was easy. It was..." He thought for a moment, "comfortable." He said it as if the word was a delicious treat saved for a special occasion. "I told her things I've not told anyone, and I believe she did the same. There was no judgment, no façade. The friendship we shared then, and share now, is genuine."

"Then why do you deceive her?"

"That happened before she knew me as the chieftain of a powerful clan. As a clanswoman, she was distant, content to avoid my company. If we spoke, it was stiff and uncomfortable. I came to believe what I felt that first night was mine alone, and she had set her sights elsewhere."

"But you know different now?" Spirit carefully layered new bandages around his torso.

"Aye. I've come to realize what we shared was real. Etain did not place the distance between us. It was me. She was new to an organized clan life, er... No disrespect to UWS."

"None taken. Every clan has their ways."

"True, true. There I was, bigger than life, huffing and puffing my clan edicts, traipsing off into battle to return in a mood, wanting only to be alone to shake off the dregs of war. It's no wonder she left." He looked at Spirit, his expression open and unguarded, hand to his chest. "I need her to see *me* again. Not a chieftain. Not a warrior. I need her to remember the Dar from that night. To see me vulnerable and not so in control. Approachable, if you will. Do you understand?"

"The girl's not daft. She has a compassionate heart, but it only goes so far. I'd say what you have upstairs is pushing her to her limits."

"As long as she understands what she means to me."

Having done all she could for his wounds, she offered him a mug of ale. "Just be careful, lest your work be wasted." Standing over the man, she asked, "What was that between you and me husband?"

He enjoyed a long drink, then came to his feet. "Better from his lips."

She placed a hand on his shoulder. "I don't know what happened whilst she was away, but Etain's not the girl she was. I see a new maturity in the lass that wasn't there before her little trip to your place. You best tread carefully."

"I would go to hell and back for her, milady. Thank you. I owe you both."

Spirit took him by the chin, looking him in the eye. "Just take care of our girl. That'll be your debt paid. Heed my warning, Lord Darknight. Any harm comes to our lass, you'll wish you *could* go to hell for it'll be far more pleasant than here."

He bowed his head in acknowledgment, then took her hand in his and placed a kiss on her knuckles. "She is my life, dear lady. I will gladly give my own to keep her safe."

Etain watched Inferno walk into the room. His grim expression and silent stroll did not bode good news. He didn't speak until they stood face-to-face.

"He is safe." Her knees buckled, but Inferno's strong arms gave her support. "Only hell knows how. It was a mean and dirty fight, lass. By all rights, they should both be dead."

"But Dar is alive?" she asked.

"Aye."

She wrapped him in a tight hug. "Oh, Inferno. Thank you."

"It's not like *I* saved the man," he blustered, but the sparkle in her eyes made him smile. "Last I saw, his bleedin' brother crawled back to his hellhole."

"Hopefully for good this time," she sniffled.

Although not old enough to be a parent to one her age, Inferno donned a fatherly demeanor. "I saw a side of Dar I'd not seen before today." He held up a hand at her hopeful expression. "It doesn't mean I've changed me mind about him. How's the lass?"

"I don't know. She's been sleeping ever since Spirit stopped the bleeding. It's gonna take a while, I'm afraid." Etain bit her lip. "I was hoping you'd allow her to stay here until she's recovered." Not hearing the expected negative grunt, she pushed on, knowing she and Dar were chalk and cheese in Inferno's opinion. "And Dar needs a safe place to recuperate, at least for a little while. Will you give us your blessing to stay?"

He kept his eyes on the sleeping girl. "No need to ask. Yer welcome to stay." He suddenly turned. "Why did she take the blade, Etain? Ya said she didn't give a toss about anyone but herself."

She shrugged. "Somehow, Dar has awakened a thread of humanity in her. I have no idea if it's a permanent or temporary change, but I think we should enjoy it while we can."

He nodded, sitting on the side of the bed. "What about you? Ya never let a man so much as touch ya before. Why this one? Has he bewitched ya with one of his spells?"

She smiled and pulled up a chair. "I love you and Spirit. You've taught me so much, giving me more than I can ever repay. Darth taught me how to survive, but you gave me back my heart. Making me a part of your family, believing in me and loving me, has helped me heal." She reached for his hand, holding his gaze with hers. "I am so thankful we're family." His hand still in hers, she looked away, thinking of how to explain Dar. "When I was little, there was a song I would sing with my mom." Her eyes came back to him as she started to sing. "This little light of mine…" Tears glistened, making her eyes bright. "I'm gonna let it shine." Her voice faltered. "Do you know it?"

His hands covered hers. "Aye," he said, his voice thick. "Ya don't have four wee sprites without singing it a time or two."

"As wonderful as your love and acceptance is…" She knew her next words would be hard for her to say…and for him to hear. "Since he's come into my life…" Her breath caught in her throat. "I shine… hell, I burn…" She blew out a breath, running a hand through her hair, and tried again. "My life before him was missing something. Not to take away from what I have with you and Spirit. It's just…different. It sounds crazy, but his chaos brings me peace."

Inferno pulled her into an embrace, singing softly. "Let it shine. Let it shine. Let it shine."

Dar walked through the door. "Inferno, Spirit's asking questions I..." He stopped, realizing he had walked in on an intimate moment. "I am interrupting." Without a word, Inferno stood and walked out of the room. Dar looked at Etain. "I didn't do it."

She gave him a tender hug. "My sweet man, you have saved me."

With a sigh of relief, he engulfed her within his arms. "No more than what you have done for me." Unexpectedly, he pushed her back to arm's length. "Promise me you will never try to take your life again," he scolded, crushing her to his chest. "You are my life. It is you and I, my sweet Etain. We belong together."

She clung to him. "Midir scares me. My blood was on fire. I could feel him slithering through me." Terror deepened her voice. "I was ready to fight. I *did* fight. But it didn't do me any good." Her expression touched his heart. "I took control the only way I knew how. I won't be used as a weapon against you."

His heart felt like it may burst. Whether from her fierce conviction to protect him or from the fear of losing her, he was not sure. She was here and, by the Krymerian gods, he would not let her go. "Forget about him. Let's take advantage of his weakened state and prepare. He won't stay down forever," he said, holding her close for a quiet moment.

A growl from Etain's stomach broke the silence. "Well, there *is* one other thing."

"So I hear."

"Will ye feast with me, my dark knight?" She pecked a playful kiss on his lips.

"I will, milady."

"You sit here and keep watch over Faux. I'll go see what's in the kitchen." After making sure he was comfortable, she headed to the door, then stopped. Dar raised a curious brow, watching her walk back to him. She crouched down before him, took his hands in hers, and placed one over her heart, the other to her cheek. "Thank you for risking your life for me."

He swallowed and leaned his forehead to hers, his voice thick with emotion. "Lady Etain, I was dead inside until I found you. I had not thought I could love again, or would want to. You have given my life back to me."

"Oh, please," a voice croaked from the bed. "Get a room."

"Faux." Etain smiled up at Dar. He held out a hand, helping her to her feet, not letting go as she sat on the side of the bed. "It's good to see you awake."

Faux attempted to sit up, but fell back onto the pillows. "Ow! What the...?" She looked down at the bandage around her midsection. "Damn. I did something stupid, didn't I?"

"You saved Dar's life. You were very brave."

She rolled her eyes. "Yep. Stupid."

Dar helped her sit up. "Call it what you wish, demon girl, but you acted in a most Alamir manner. I thank you for your sacrifice."

"Never."

"I told you it was in there," Etain chided, trying not to smile. "It just took an extreme situation to pull it out. No telling what other good deeds you'll be doing now."

Her eyes expressed a *go to hell* sentiment. "Is the baby okay?"

Etain exchanged a look with Dar. "As far as we know, the baby is fine."

Faux sighed, closing her eyes. "Did I hear something about food?"

Her sister chuckled. "Can't keep a good woman down. I'll be back in a minute."

After watching her walk to the door, Dar sat in the chair next to the bed. He and Faux eyed one another in a silent standoff.

"You think you got it right this time, slick?"

He gauged her temper, deciding she deserved the truth. "Aye. She is the one."

"No big surprise," she said, tilting her head to the side. "She's always been drawn to big, pathetic louts. I think they bring out her maternal instincts."

He smiled, amused by her dig at his ego. "Pathetic lout, is it? Are you saying I'm not her first?"

"They're drawn to her." A sudden pain made her gasp. "I don't claim to understand what they see, but she's never lacked for male company. That's for sure."

Always a fan of a good cat and mouse game, he decided to play. "Hmmm… Well, perhaps it has to do with her methods of pleasing a man."

Faux's eyes darted up to his. "What does that mean?"

He spread his hands in front of him and spoke matter-of-factly. "I'm merely saying she does not lack for…how should I word this… Creativity."

"What's *that* supposed to mean?" She snorted, clearly agitated.

"You know what it means."

"But Etain's never…" She bit her lip.

Dar forced a concerned look. "She's never what?"

"Never mind." With a roll of her eyes, she dismissed the subject. "Tell me about your nasty brother. Is he single?"

Etain floated into the kitchen, finding Inferno and Spirit in a discussion over the remains of their lounge. "A bit of a mess, huh?"

Inferno grunted a laugh. "We always wanted to remodel."

"The demolition's done," Spirit said. "What brings you down here so soon? I thought you would want more time with your beau."

"That'd be nice, but something more important has come up."

"What would that be?" Spirit asked.

"Food! We haven't eaten since yesterday." She laughed, rubbing her stomach. "And me belly's been a'hollerin for satisfaction."

"Oh, lass, you had me worried there."

Inferno joined in. "It's been a busy day, love. I could handle a few of yer ham butties myself."

"Sounds a plan." Spirit got up from her seat. "Let's see what we can put together for this hungry crew."

"Faux's awake and wants something, too."

"Awake *and* hungry?" Spirit shrugged and set to work, grabbing the needed ingredients from the refrigerator. Etain opened a fresh loaf of bread, laying the slices on the countertop.

"I've never understood why you call them butties. Maybe because you butt the bread up to each other?" Etain giggled, slathering the pieces of bread with margarine.

Spirit gave her one of those motherly looks as she put a pan of soup on the stove. "I would think it has more to do with the butter."

"Except we're using margarine. To be politically correct, shouldn't we call them margies?"

"When have you ever been politically correct?" she joked in return. "For your information, that's butter made by me own hands. Those old margarine tubs come in handy."

Etain grinned. "Oh, well, excuse me, Mrs. Butterfield."

Spirit's smile faded. "Tell me, Etain."

Noting the serious tone in her voice, she looked up. "Aye?"

"What changed your mind about Darknight?"

Inferno scooted to the back door. "Sounds like girl talk to me. Think I'll go see where me mutts have gotten to."

Done with the bread, Etain watched him walk out, then turned to the soup. "I guess I have to thank Faux for that."

"Faux?"

"Well, you remember I told you about her attempt to kill me?" Spirit nodded. "And how Dar showed up and brought me back?"

"Aye, I remember. She tried to kill you, yet you fight to save her life."

"Weird, huh?"

"Why would she want you dead?"

"She blamed me for her exile."

"Exile?" Spirit was more than a little surprised. "What the bloody hell did she do?"

"Her first mistake was joining the dc2a clan." Etain poured the warm soup into a bowl. "I told her they were trouble."

"They weren't in the early days," Spirit said, popping a piece of ham into her mouth. "What was the second?"

Etain placed the bowl on a tray. "She stayed when it kicked off."

Eyes wide, Spirit stared at her. "That was her?"

"She didn't start it. Faux was being Faux, which intimidated the... less confident members. I told her to get out. Somehow, in her twisted mind, it became *my* fault she was blamed for splitting the clan."

"Did she?" Spirit cut a sandwich in two. "Split the clan?"

"No." Etain added a spoon and napkins to her tray. "I'm not saying she was completely innocent. The true culprits were the ones who envied her position and influence."

"You never mentioned how you two met. Is she a friend of Dar's?"

"Uh, not exactly." Avoiding eye contact, she fiddled with the dishes on the tray, positioning each one just so. "That was part of the reason for his invite. Dar wanted to meet her."

"Hmmm," Spirit gave her a long, hard look. "She wasn't part of the clan?"

"Since dc2a, she's never aligned with another clan."

"Then why would she now?"

"Huh?" Etain appeared lost.

"Your first day back, you said you wanted us to watch over her. It'll be fair easy whilst she's down, but once the lass is back to herself, I doubt she'll agree to it."

"Well, yeah. I don't know what I was thinking."

The butties done, Spirit set a kettle on for tea. "What about the man?"

Etain placed a few sandwiches on the tray, her voice quiet, almost reverent. "He avenged my family, Spirit. He tracked down the demon and killed him...for me. He profited nothing from it but broken ribs and a sleepless night."

"Uh-huh. Let me tell you something, lass. I know he's a Krymerian, but from what I've heard about this one, he's a man like any other when it comes to motivation. I've seen the way he looks at you. A man doesn't do what he's done without a reason, Etain."

She grabbed the tray, the color draining from her face. "I've got some hungry people to feed. Thanks, Spirit."

Spirit muttered to herself as the girl walked out. "Ah, lass, meeting Faux was an excuse."

10

MISTS OF PROTECTION

Later that evening, Spirit stopped by Faux's room to check on her patients. Happy to see the girl resting comfortably, she directed Dar and Etain to their rooms down the hall and bid them good night. The couple stacked the dirty dishes on the tray and tidied up until Faux fell asleep.

Dar pulled Etain to him. "Let us go to bed. I am dead tired."

"You look exhausted. You should've been in bed hours ago," she said, happy to be in his arms again.

Walking down the hall, they came to the first open door, peeking inside. A room of magnolia walls and mahogany furniture invited them in. Stripping in his usual manner, Dar headed straight for the bed, which was already turned down, and slipped between the sheets. Standing just inside the doorway, Etain admired the ripple of muscle as he moved. At the glimpse of a beautiful backside, she turned to inspect the wall coverings in depth. It wasn't that she'd never seen a naked man before, living in close quarters with them made it impossible to ignore, but this man was so alive, so full of passion. Passionate about her, no less, and…he was hers. Having that knowledge, she wasn't sure what to do with him, but she knew she would never let him go.

Please give him patience.

Dar patted the covers. "Etain, come here."

"Spirit said *rooms*. I'll just be across the hall."

"Come here."

"Dar." Her voice was barely audible.

"All we will do tonight is sleep. I am too tired and too sore to think about anything else." A sly grin came to his lips. "Well, I may think about it, but I promise that's all. Come here, *mo chuisle*."

Unable to resist, she closed the door and walked to the bed, the emotions obvious on her face. He took her hand in his. "I meant what I said. I will not force you to do anything you're not ready to do, but I want you by my side…always."

Still unsure of what he expected from her, she delayed a little longer. "What is *mo chuisle*?"

"It means 'my heart'." His hand slid up her arm and gently pulled her down to sit next to him. "I'm not able to put what I feel for you into words just yet. But you *are* my heart, Etain. *Mo chuisle*." A shared kiss convinced her to trust his words. She turned, removed her boots, and carefully rolled over, settling in on the other side of the bed. Dar laughed. "Surely you're not comfortable."

She looked over her shoulder at him. "No, but it *is* safe."

"But nothing. Take off your clothes and wrap that luscious body around mine. You've nothing I haven't seen before."

Her eyes widened. "Such a thing for a gentleman to say to a lady."

"*My* lady, and who said I was a gentleman? I'll have their head." Laughing at her indignant look, he said, "It is a little late for modesty, Etain."

Seeing the glint in his eye, she shifted on the bed, facing him. "I believe it's my *lack* of modesty that's gotten us here."

"You could be right. When you removed your shirt at the practice ring at *Sólskin*…"

She grabbed a pillow. He lifted his arms, deflecting her playful swat.

"Dar VonNeshta! You were awake the whole time?"

"*Tartarus,* help me. It was all I could do not to crush those beautiful breasts against me and-"

"You cheeky little-" Another swat of her pillow found him defending with his own.

"This is going to hurt." He pushed up, tackling her onto the bed with a definitive grunt, pinning her beneath him. Her scream of surprise was lost in their shared laughter.

"That didn't hurt at all," she said.

"I wasn't talking to you," he groaned, rolling over and lying next to her.

"Are you okay?" She automatically began inspecting his bandaged body.

He caught her hand in his and lifted it to his lips. "It was worth it, milady." His breath was warm against her flesh, his mouth soft and suggestive. "Take off your worldly façade and be my sweet Etain."

Her trust in this man had grown considerably in such a short time. She held his gaze. His love and appreciation easy to see, she discarded the leather top. Shedding her inhibitions, she wiggled out of the rest of her clothes, throwing them onto the floor. Dar drew her close and rested her head on his bandaged chest. Exhaling a contented sigh, he fell into an immediate sleep. She yawned, relaxed by the beat of his strong heart.

Inferno isn't going to like this one bit.

By sunrise, Spirit was up and dressed, and lightly knocking on Dar's door. A lack of response had her entering the room. It was no surprise to find Etain there…naked, no less. If Inferno found out she had shared Dar's bed, the Krymerian would be out the door, if not dead, no questions asked.

Moving to Etain's side of the bed, she placed a hand on her back. "Wake up, my lovely. It's time to rise and shine." She smiled when the blue eyes opened. "Dar's made a good start of bridging the gap with

Inferno, but let's not burn the bridge before it's built. Aye? Hurry up. We'll have a woman to woman chat while we fix breakfast. I expect you downstairs in five."

"Yes, mummy," she muttered. Waiting until she heard the click of the closing door, Etain rolled over and ran her fingers lightly down Dar's face. "I gotta go," she whispered, placing a kiss on his earlobe.

A smile turned up the corners of his mouth. "Where you going?" he murmured, rolling toward her.

She escaped his grasp, tossing the covers over his head. "Clean-up detail."

Dar peeked out from under the duvet. "I should join you since I helped make the mess." He threw back the covers.

She stopped him with a hand to his chest, doing her best to keep her eyes on his face. "No. You'll stay here and rest, give Inferno time to adjust to our new alliance."

"All alone?" He pouted, puppy dog eyes in full force. Etain ignored his attempt and turned away, picking up her shirt. Noting his ploy to stay close to her had failed, he frowned. "All right. Then here I shall remain all day, all alone, resting." Before leaving, she stopped by the bed and caressed his cheek. He pulled her down for a thorough kiss. "Make sure you wake me for supper."

"What about lunch?" she asked, breathless.

"I think you are right. A nice long rest is exactly what I need." He settled back. "Don't work too hard."

As soon as the door closed, Dar got up and carefully removed his bandages, laying them on the bed. He placed his pillows on top of them and pulled the covers up. Admiring his handiwork, he dressed in black jeans and t-shirt. Anyone deciding to peek in would find the High Lord resting, as instructed. He opened a portal to his homeland.

Standing amongst the ruins, he surveyed the horizon from right to left, then turned around, doing the same. He counted out ten paces, stopped, and surveyed the area again. Not much had changed during his absence. The grass had grown, decorated by various flowers and the odd weed. Happy with his findings, he turned left, counting five paces. An old Krymerian chant revealed a massive metal door set in the ground. Its surface smooth as glass, it boasted no visible handle, lock, or decoration. He could hear the tumblers clicking into place. Opening the door, he followed the stairs down into the family vault full of dust-covered heirlooms.

Time to earn your keep.

He gathered items of the finest silver, including a cherished goblet of his mother's, made of a rare metal found only on Krymeria. Its strength rivaled that of the human metal titanium, but was easier to shape once heated and much lighter.

Arms full, he headed to where the smithy once plied his trade. A simple command brought the forge together. Dar dumped the metals into a large smelting pot, then returned to the vault. In a far corner was a bag tied off at the top. Hefting it over his shoulder, he carried it to the forge, untied the rope, and dumped the contents into the pot. A flash of his solar ultima set the forge ablaze. While the fire heated, he located an anvil, hammers, pliers, and chisels, setting them within easy reach. Satisfied with the fire's progression, he set the smelting pot over it.

Back at the metal door, he ventured deeper into the vault. *"Doras nochtann."* Another hidden door opened. A wave of his hand lit several torches, illuminating the room with a soft glow. Going to a large crevice in the farthest corner, he reached into the dark opening, his arm disappearing up to the shoulder. A few seconds later, he pulled out three pouches - diamond dust, crushed blood rubies, and powdered onyx. Setting them to the side, he reached in again. This time, he brought out a long gold rod and several smaller ones of silver, a heavy onyx block, and a long crystal shard. He returned to the forge, taking his time to assemble and inspect his assorted equipment.

Once the metal had reached the perfect molten consistency, he poured the concoction into several large forms and set them aside.

Grabbing a nearby bucket, he walked to the nearby stream. The air smelled of early spring, fresh, green, and floral, so different from the oncoming autumn at Laugharne. Dar lay on his belly at the edge and dipped his face into the cold, clear water, taking a refreshing gulp. Afterward, he filled the bucket and doused himself. Bucket refilled, he returned to the cooling blocks of metal. Rooting around the base of the forge, he found a trough of wood, filled it halfway with water, and carefully set the metal blocks into it.

Once cooled, Dar began working one block. Strikes of his hammer, assisted by magical Krymerian words, flattened the block into a thin sheet. At first, it was difficult to wield the heavy hammer. His ribs ached. His wounds burned from the sweat rolling off his body. As time passed, though, the pain subsided and his movements became more fluid. The rough metal transformed into a smooth, curved skin, fashioning into a breastplate. Using a similar technique, albeit more magic than sweat due to the passage of time, he worked the next block into the shape of a helm, setting the pieces side by side.

He poured a handful of crushed blood rubies and a handful of the powered onyx onto the anvil. One hand dipped into the rubies and the other into the onyx. Chanting a spell, he cast them into the air.

"*Cumhachtaí a ceangal tú dom* (Powers that be, bind you to me)."

The deep red rubies sparkled and the onyx set off flashes of reflected light. They twisted and turned, rising into the air, as Dar directed the gems toward the armor. Repeating the spell, he cast the diamond dust in the shape of a dragon. Satisfied, he turned to the gold rod, softened the metal until it was easy to manipulate, then shaped it into a pattern to complement the diamond dust. At that point, he used the silver, working it into the helm.

With the pieces decorated to his satisfaction, Dar stepped back for the finishing spell. "*Bandia an dragan, a chosaint mo chroí, a choinneáil slán aici* (Goddess of the dragon, protect my heart, keep her safe)."

Last was the long shard of crystal. The warrior struck a fine edge along each side. Fashioning a hand-guard and hilt from the final block, he inserted the crystal through the hollowed-out center. Holding it in his hands, he closed his eyes and concentrated on his core, raising his inner heat. Channeling the heat into his hands, the hand-guard forged around the crystal. "*Criostail de mo athair a bheith fíor* (Crystal of my father be true)." A quick slash across a palm added his blood to the remaining crushed rubies before he cast them into the air. "I name thee *Nim'Na'Sharr*, the Righteous Hand of Fate." Scarlet dust cascaded over the sword, bonding with it in an instant, the runes of strength, courage, and wisdom emblazoned on the face of the blade.

Exhausted, the High Lord took a well-deserved rest, admiring his work.

A short time later, he gathered up the tools, returned them to the underground vault, and locked the door with a murmured spell. Collecting the armor and sword, he reopened a portal to his room at Laugharne, placing the armor so it would be the first thing Etain saw when she came into the room.

Refreshed by a hot shower, he strapped the bandages back on as best he could and crawled into bed.

In the early afternoon, the demolition trio stopped work for a light lunch. While Spirit and Inferno made a bite to eat in the kitchen, Etain went upstairs to check on the patients.

Coming to Dar's room, she quietly opened the door and poked her head in. The covered mound in the bed told her he was resting. She longed to touch him, to make sure he was real. She stepped into the room and walked quietly toward the bed. Reaching out, her hand hovering over the covers, she remembered the last time she had interrupted his sleep. Curling her hand into a fist, she left him to his dreams.

At the stairs, she remembered Faux, rolled her eyes, and made a quick turnaround, heading back down the hall. She peeked inside and found her sound asleep, but felt the hairs on her arms raise. Stepping inside, eyes sharp for anything out of the ordinary, she walked around the room. Everything seemed to be in its proper place. She went to Faux's side, touched her forehead, and chuckled, finding it cool.

"Get it together, Etain."

Satisfied both were well on their way to recovery, she joined Inferno and Spirit for a lunch of beef sarnies and potato salad. Their conversation flowed from plans for the lounge and possible additions, to future travels. Inferno shared stories of past excursions he and Spirit had taken. Etain didn't think it important to mention the strange feeling she'd experienced in Faux's room, chalking it up to her overprotective nature.

She brought the talk around to the children. "Are the kids coming home soon?"

"They're not due back for a while. Little ones underfoot with all this construction would be another disaster," Spirit said.

"I guess so, but I'd love to see them."

Spirit smiled, patting her hand. "Let's get things back to normal, whatever that is…" She winked, "then we'll see about bringing the wee sprites home."

Etain nodded, content with her reasoning. "What about the rest of the clan? I haven't seen anyone else since we got here."

Spirit cleared the dishes while Inferno explained. "I sent Zorn out to round 'em up. Most'll be here tomorrow."

"Okay, but *where* have they been all this time?"

"Out doing what clan members should be doing…patrolling the perimeter, making sure there's no creepy crawlies making themselves at home and thinking to give us a nasty surprise. I sent Wolfe and Elfin, ya haven't met them yet, off to UKElyte with a few breeding mares in exchange for a new stud. They ought to be back late today or tomorrow."

"Will any of them have a problem with Dar being here?"

Inferno gave her a thoughtful eye. "If they do, they'll keep it zipped and not say a word." He rose from his seat. "Unless something gives 'em reason to unzip it." He finished off his tea and took the cup to the sink. "Let's get back to work."

After a long day, Inferno decided nothing else could be done without more help. They parted company for a rest before a late tea. Etain offered to check on Faux, but Spirit waved her off, saying she would have a peek on the way.

Upon entering Dar's room, Etain noticed the unusual armor and sheathed sword. She walked toward the bed, her eyes on the strange pieces. "Dar, you up?" The armor looked like it would fit her perfectly.

A dragoness of gold, holding a demon by its throat, graced the right shoulder and chest of the breastplate. *Why does it strike me as female?* She eyed the dragon a little closer. *Perhaps the delicate curves and her size allude to a feminine aspect.* She noted the glittering of rubies and onyx. Her fingertips ran along the muscles of the dragon, which seemed to ripple as the light danced over its surface. The helm, shaped as the head of a great dragon, held bared, silver teeth and gleaming crimson eyes, served as a backdrop.

"I made it especially for you, *mo chuisle.* Try it on."

She looked at Dar. His confirmation made her suddenly shy. "I don't know. It's spectacular. Are you sure-"

"It should fit you better than what you're wearing."

"These old things aren't meant to fit." She looked down at her attire and laughed. "Inferno's shirt and an old pair of highwaters from Spirit."

"Was there a leak?"

"No," she said, wondering why he asked. Then realized and laughed. "When your pants are too short, you call them highwaters." He raised a questioning brow. She dismissed the topic with a shake of her head. "Where did all this come from?" Her question sounded more like an accusation.

"It is time you had your own armor."

"Perhaps...but that doesn't answer my question."

"It was crafted especially for you."

She sauntered closer to the bed. "It *is* a thoughtful gesture. The workmanship is exquisite."

A nimble hand slid up her thigh, cupping a rounded cheek. "It took me most of the day."

She smiled, leaning down as though to caress his cheek. Instead, her hand diverted down, poking him in the ribs. "Bad boy."

Dar flinched, grabbing the offensive hand. "Ouch."

"Not quite one hundred percent, but better than this morning."

Holding her hand, he swept out with his other arm and pulled her down on top of him. "Much better. The exercise was exactly what I needed." He slipped a hand underneath her blouse, caressing her bare back. "I love the way you smell," he whispered. "The taste of your skin." His lips grazed her flesh, his tongue warm and wet.

"Dar," she sighed into his ear. Her heart pounded, his hands moving over her, his body pressed to hers. Out of nowhere, her morning chat with Spirit came to mind.

"I need a shower."

His eyes were heavy with desire, but he drew his hands back. "I'm sorry."

"Don't be." She kissed him sweetly. "I really do need a shower. It was hard work clearing out the rubble, but we made a good start."

"Tomorrow, I shall join in the effort."

"We shall talk about it in the morning. It's nearly suppertime, so you get up and dress while I get cleaned up."

"It best be a feast. I believe I could eat an entire Velnoxtica on my own." He grinned, throwing back the covers.

Etain stopped at the door. "Velnoxtica? Sounds disgusting."

"They are, and dangerous. But if you're clever and quick enough to kill one, then roast it slowly over an open flame..." His eyes rolled back in a show of ecstasy. "Heavenly. Well worth risking the acid drool."

Etain felt her stomach lurch. "Ten minutes."

Refreshed, she returned to Dar, her new sword in his hand. "Before we go down, I want you to try it." He watched her draw it clear of the sheath. "Its balance is perfect."

She held the sword before her, moving it easily through the air. "Why a dragon?"

"A moment of inspiration," he said, a smile on his lips.

A single word inscribed on the handguard caught her attention. "What's this here?"

"It is the sword's true name. *Nim'Na'Sharr*, Righteous Hand of Fate. If ever you're lost, call to her. She will come to you and guide you home. I will teach you how to wield her properly." Standing behind her, he wrapped his arms around her waist. "For now, I think I will show you how to wield a knife and fork."

***

A horrible scream shattered the comfortable ambiance. Etain was the first out of her seat. "Faux!" Rushing up the stairs, she burst into the bedroom, finding the girl thrashing about, clawing at her stomach.

"Make it stop!" she screamed. "It burns."

"Faux, what is it? What burns?" Etain reached for her hands.

"My stomach. Oh shit. It hurts!"

"Faux," Etain tried to talk over the screams. "You've got to stop. You'll make it worse."

Spirit came in, followed by Inferno, who carried a small case. She instructed him to place it on the bedside table. "I was hoping this wouldn't happen."

"What's happening to her?" Etain asked.

"Poison from his blade. It's slow to start, but once it does, heaven help the victim." She opened the case, pulling out a small pestle and mortar. Sprinkling several different herbs into the small bowl, she crushed the fragrant plants, chanting as she worked.

"If you knew she was poisoned, why didn't you do something earlier?" Etain tried to soothe the frantic girl. "Faux, you've got to relax."

Covered in sweat, Dar stumbled through the door. The trek up the stairs had proven difficult. He climbed onto the bed, taking hold of

Faux's flailing hands, holding her down. It only served to heighten her panic. "*No!* Get away! Don't touch me. It hurts."

Dar clenched his teeth. "Damn my brother. I should have known he would pull something like this."

Inferno answered Etain's question on Spirit's behalf. "She has her reasons for waiting. She can't talk because she's enchanting the poultice, making it strong. Once she starts, she can't stop or it'll fail. When it's ready, she'll put it to the wound. It should draw out the poison."

"Should?" Etain asked.

He shrugged. "Ya never know with these things."

Straining to hold the girl, Etain gave Dar a nervous look. His calm demeanor reassured her. "Spirit knows what she's doing. It will work. She will save her."

Concoction complete, Spirit straddled her patient, asking Inferno to cut away the remnants of the bandage. The edges of the wound pulsated with a green glow. She scooped the poultice into her hands, spreading it over the opening. "Goddess of the life-giving force, fill me with your power. Strengthen my blood, strengthen my spirit, strengthen my faith. Give me health in abundance that I may save an innocent. Take the poison from her veins, banish all evil within. With the blessing of the Goddess, I heal thee now."

She continued the chant, motioning Dar and Etain to raise the girl up. Faux screamed when the salve touched the wound in her back. Eyes aflame, she tried to head-butt the mage. Dar stopped her with his free hand, pulling her close to him. "My precious girl, don't fight. It makes the pain worse and the poison work more quickly. Be still. Shhh."

Etain caught Dar's eye, giving a supportive smile. "Is there anything that will put her to sleep? Dar is fading fast." She wasn't happy with the pallor of his skin or that his shirt was soaked with sweat.

Spirit barked instructions at her husband. "Break up some valerian root, love. Mix it with water. Quickly."

Inferno moved fast, crumbling the root, crushing it in the mortar. Adding just enough water to make a liquid, he poured it into a vial and handed it to Spirit. Etain shifted, getting a better hold on Faux, hoping to relieve Dar to some degree. The mage pushed the vial between the demon girl's lips, tipping the liquid into her mouth and forcing her to swallow. Faux went limp within seconds.

The three sat back, breathing hard. Etain kept an eye on Dar, but her question was for Spirit. "How long before we know it worked?"

"The glow is subsiding. We'll know more come morning."

"Dar!"

All the color had drained from his face. Etain made a grab for him, but couldn't hold on. Inferno caught him before he fell off the bed.

Spirit went to where he slumped against the headboard, touched his forehead, and frowned. "Let me have a look at your wounds, love."

"No, I am fine. Just a little-"

"Too big for your britches," Etain finished. "Relax and let someone help you for a change." His eyes narrowed, but she cut him off. "You don't have to be the hero *all* the time."

Spirit turned his head, checking his eyes. "You're burning up. Whether it's from the fight or the poison, I'd not take any chances. There's some poultice left." She didn't wait for his acquiescence. "Etain, remove those bandages. Inferno, hand me the mortar."

She used every drop on his wounds. "The valerian root will help with the pain." Tying off the last bandage, she said, "Get back to bed and rest."

"That's it for you, mate." Inferno helped Dar off the bed, draping the Krymerian's arm over his shoulder, holding him around the waist.

Etain slipped under his other arm, giving support. "He can't walk, Inferno."

"Then how the hell do ya expect to get this lump of a demon to his bed?"

"Hold on." Lighting in a blue shimmer, electrical charges flashed around her body, extending out and engulfing the men.

Transported to the High Lord's bedroom, they maneuvered him

onto the bed. Etain wet a washcloth, dabbing it over Dar's face and chest. "Thank you, Inferno. You have a truly kind heart."

"No reason to kick a man when he's down." He placed a hand on her shoulder. "Looks like you have it in hand. I'll leave ya to it then."

She noticed Dar watching her. "You will keep to your bed. No getting up. No more making armor. No slaying demons." He opened his mouth. "No. You'll do as you're told." Her fingers ran across his forehead, over his cheek, and down his neck. Lightly caressing his chest, her touch moved to his belly, stopping just above the band of his pants. She lingered, cutting her eyes up to his. "I need you healthy and strong," she said, her voice husky with emotion.

He brushed her hair back over her shoulder. "Aye, milady." Closing her eyes, she leaned back as he traced the bones at the base of her neck, trailing down the center of her chest. When her eyes opened, he pulled back. "I won't."

She took his hand in hers, placing it over her heart. "Soon."

With Dar settled, Etain left, walking down the hall into Faux's room. "Any change?"

Sitting on the side of the bed, Spirit smiled at her. "None yet. Whatever he used was strong, but mine is stronger. She'll be better by morning." She came to her feet, taking hold of Etain's hand. "You asked why I didn't treat the poison earlier." Spirit appreciated the blush in the girl's cheeks. "I thought there was a possibility, but wasn't one hundred percent sure until the symptoms manifested. It would've been a risk either way it went. Not knowing the poison used, I could've given her the wrong antidote. That would've killed her as effectively as the poison."

"I should know better than to doubt you. I'm sorry."

"We're not out of the woods yet." She guided Etain toward the window, motioning to Inferno to join them. "How's Dar?"

"He's resting okay."

Spirit nodded, confident the man would fare better than Faux. "We must cast a protection spell around the house."

Etain looked around the room. "You really think we need a protection spell? Dar said-"

"Makes no difference. When it comes to Dar's brother, I'll not take any chances."

"What do you need me to do?" Etain asked.

"There's a few items I'll need. Love, come with me." She took hold of Inferno's hand. "Meet us downstairs, lass."

Casting staff in hand, Spirit walked out the front doors, followed by Inferno, who carried a bowl of what looked to be silver glitter. A light breeze lifted the silver ribbons tied to the staff. The mage motioned Etain closer, then cast a sacred circle around them. She turned to each direction, tapping her staff while chanting. "I call those who guard the watchtowers of the (West, South, East, North), to guide me through the darkness and ensure my safety."

The watchtowers invoked, she modified the chant, naming each direction as she turned. To the North… "Hear me knights of the ancient laws." To the East… "Hear me knights who have passed this way." To the South… "Hear me knights who fought for good." To the West… "Hear me knights whose blades were sure."

She stepped into the center of the circle. "I summon you this day to the aid of the true. I invoke thee to the protection of the innocent. As you fought in life, now fight in spirit. Hear me, dead knights. Present your mighty blades. I invoke thee to the protection of our house. Surround this place with your spiritual armor. Envelop these walls with your sacred honor. Inundate these grounds with your power. I invoke you, dead knights. Hear me and come to my aid. Fight the evils we cannot see. Protect us from the dark. Protect us from the heinous spirits." Once again, she faced each direction and chanted, "I invoke thee. I invoke thee. I invoke thee. I invoke thee. Let my will be done. Let it be. Let it be. Let it be. Let it be." She cast the glitter to close the circle.

Inferno unwrapped a chocolate bar. Spirit caught Etain's curious look and chuckled. "Got to keep my strength up."

They shared a light supper, rather than reheat the earlier meal, then retired for the night. The couple escorted Etain to her room, reminding her the clan would be there in the morning. She gave each a hug and slipped into her room. Waiting just inside the door, she listened to their footsteps recede. When all was quiet, she peered into the hallway. Placing a foot outside the door, Felix and Ruby came out of nowhere, tails wagging, whining for her attention.

"Shh…" She spoke in a loud whisper. "Please be quiet." Ruby slipped past her and through the open door. As she made a grab for her collar, Felix also darted into the room. "For fuck's sake," she said, running a hand through her hair. "Come on y'all. You can't stay in here."

Ruby licked her hand and seemed to be smiling. Felix made himself at home on the bed. Sighing, Etain closed the door.

"Fine. But don't think for a second either of you are sleeping in the bed with me." Ruby barked and joined Felix. Etain rolled her eyes. "I'm taking a bath. You two enjoy it while you can."

The quick shower earlier had been invigorating, but hadn't done much to ease the tensions of the day. In the bath, her thoughts drifted to the man in the room across the hall. Visions of his muscular body pressed to hers intertwined with fantasies of him whispering in her ear. The memory of his laugh brought a smile to her lips. Slipping further into the water, her visions turned in another direction.

Two young men stood at the water's edge, facing each other, eyes full of venomous fire… One shining in a golden light, the other surrounded by darkness. The dark attacked first with a ball of black fire. The light staggered back several feet. Recovering, he released a golden orb, hitting the other in the chest. The dark stomped into the river, raising his hands, arcing the waters toward the golden warrior on the other side. She screamed a warning.

In the next moment, she was floating below the sparkling surface, confused. Am I a fish? The light watched through the shimmering curtain as the dark pushed her deeper with his staff. She fought to avoid the offensive stick, but it continued to push. Why didn't the golden warrior save her? "I thought you loved me," she cried. Her vision darkened as she sank to the river's bottom. I thought you loved me. I thought you loved me. I thought...you...loved...me.

Feeling a viselike grip on her arms, her eyes flew open, water cascading down her naked body.

"*Tartarus*, woman! What has gotten into you?"

"W-what? I-I was taking a bath," she said, gasping for air.

Felix and Ruby, standing on either side of Dar, added their opinions to the situation.

"Hush, you two, before you wake the house." The dogs quieted, keeping an eye on him, as well as his charge. Dar wrapped an oversized towel around her shivering body. "You have a strange way of going about it." He moved to pick her up.

"No, you shouldn't be out of bed. I can get out myself."

Nonetheless, he offered a hand as she stepped over the edge of the bath, but her foot slipped on the wet floor. Ignoring her protests, he scooped her into his arms and walked into the bedroom. He dumped his package onto the bed, whipping away the towel.

"Damn, ribs," he said, grabbing his side. After sucking in a slow breath, he gave her a stern look. "What the devil were you doing, Etain?"

She pulled the covers over her body. "I told you. I was taking a bath. What're you doing in here? You should be asleep."

"Felix woke me. Wouldn't leave me alone until I followed him."

She cast an eye on the black scoundrel. "The door was closed. How'd he get out?"

Dar carefully sat on the side of the bed. "The how does not matter. What does matter is this new obsession of yours."

"What? Bathing?"

"Drowning."

"I wasn't *trying* to drown..." The look in his eye made her add, "this time."

"Then tell me what you were doing...besides bathing."

Although safely ensconced in layers of bedding, she felt more exposed now than when naked. "I-I was…thinking…dreaming…"

"Etain, for this to work between us, we must be honest with one another. Aye?"

"Aye."

Dar slipped off the bed, twisting and stretching out the stiffness from his torso. The effectiveness of the poultice was impressive. His fever was gone, and he felt almost normal. At the balcony doors, along with admiring the evening's beauty, he sensed the magic surrounding the castle, quietly appreciating the mage's ingenuity. "What did you see?"

She ran a hand through her hair. "I-I saw you and Midir as boys standing by a river, fighting."

"And?"

"Midir was drowning me," her voice quivered, "a-and you watched as he did it, ignoring my screams."

"It was not you. You were not born yet." He turned, facing her. "The truth is she was already dead. Midir was covering up something that should not have happened." He returned to the bed and took her hand in his. "I need you to do something before I can carry on with the story."

"What is it?"

"I'm not strong enough right now or I would do it. Take us to the river and I will make everything clear."

She shook her head. "If I've never been there, I can't shimmer to it."

"The only way to understand is to see it as it was."

"Give me a minute to get dressed."

Once Etain was dressed, Dar reached into one of her boots, coming up with her dagger. He carved a holy charm in the palm of his hand, then poked six tiny holes in the tender skin of hers - five forming a perfect circle with the last in the very center. Clasping her hand in his, he closed his eyes, showing her the spot in his mind's eye. "Shimmer now."

Side by side, they appeared at the river in her vision. Dar pointed to a tree on the other side. "Watch."

Beneath the tree sat two boys and a young woman. A peaceful scene, it appeared she was teaching them something. In the blink of an eye, the dark-haired boy emitted an agonizing scream, writhing on the ground as if in great pain. "Make her stop! It hurts!"

The other boy lunged at the woman, demanding she leave his brother alone, but she pushed him off. He yelled for his father to help.

"Dar," she said. "I have done nothing. He's playing one of his tricks."

The younger one looked back at his screaming brother. Something inside the boy snapped. His eyes turned an evil shade of red and razor-sharp claws formed from his knuckles. "You lie." The demon charged the woman, ripping into her flesh. Her screams drowned out those of his brother. In time, the demon loomed over the body, blood dripping from his claws. He turned his face to the sky and released an unearthly howl.

Midir quieted, shocked by what he saw. He went to his brother, speaking soft words, soothing the demon's fury. Gradually, the beast returned to the form of the boy.

Dar, the man, turned away. All this time, he thought he had killed the woman with a knife in a fit of rage. Etain watched, unaware of his shame.

Midir retrieved a dagger hidden within the folds of his clothes, covered it in the blood of the woman, and placed it in his brother's hand. With a violent shake, he roused him. "Dar! Wake up."

The man looked back, watching the blood-drenched boy acknowledge the gruesome sight.

Midir played his part well.

"We must hide the body before someone finds it. Father will never hear about this. I promise."

It was the first in a long life of false promises.

The boys grabbed the arms of the dead woman, dragging the body to the river. Using a large branch, Midir prodded the body deep into the water until there was no sign of it.

"Carry us back," the older Dar whispered to Etain.

Once in the room, she pulled away. "That poor woman. You tore her to pieces."

The distaste in her voice crushed his hopes of her understanding. "I was not aware of the game Midir played."

"It was *you* who turned demon, and…and…"

He recognized the accusation in her eyes. "I did not know, Etain."

"What didn't you know? That you killed her, or that you've been a demon all your life?"

"I have never harmed an innocent since that day."

"Oh, Dar." Hands over her face, she turned her back.

He thought it best to leave, give her time to absorb this horrid part of his past. Maybe he could come to understand the events, as well. Until tonight, he was not aware of his transformation so early in life. Knowing Midir was involved pushed him closer to his brother's end. At the door, he stopped long enough to look over his shoulder at Etain. Seeing her back still turned, he walked out.

Etain tried to make sense of what she had seen. Dar had transformed. And he was just a boy. She ran a hand through her hair. But… anything involving his bastard of a brother never boded well for anyone. Her gut told her Midir had manipulated the whole affair, a ploy to get his brother to commit murder. "Dar…," she said, ready to talk. Turning, she found herself alone.

She made her way down the stairs, walking into the kitchen.

"He's in the garden," a voice said from behind her.

She turned to see Spirit sitting in the shadows. "What are you doing up so late?"

"I couldn't sleep. Something wasn't right. I checked on Faux. She was fine, but as I left her room, I saw Dar." She nodded toward the back garden. "He's been out there, talking to himself. What happened?"

"I would tell you…" She looked at the door. "I can't let him leave. You understand, right?"

"He doesn't want to lose you, lass." Spirit reached for her hand. "I'm going to give you a simple piece of advice. Love him for who he is *now*. Leave the past where it belongs. He loves you more than life itself. Even Inferno can see that."

Sitting on the ground, Etain pressed her back to his. "Let's talk."

His intake of breath pushed against her. "Talking only gets me in trouble."

"A lot has happened in the past few weeks. So many changes, everything moving so fast. I haven't had time to make sense of it. Midir…you and Faux…the demon blood." She paused. "The rush of that blood flowing through me, the power…"

"I-"

"Then to find out it was *your* sword…" Her voice quivered. "Now to see that poor woman torn apart by your own hands. Oh, Dar…"

Hopelessness crept into his heart. How could he ever make amends with his past, with this precious woman? At last, he had found one equal to him, a woman who would stand up to him, stand *with* him. He was sure he had lost her due to his ignorant mistakes. Could he walk away? Could he go on without her? He had lived alone for so long, never daring to consider a life with someone new.

Life always found a way to throw her into his path. Wherever he turned, there she would be. Not by his license, but by life's twisted sense of amusement. Constantly drawn to her incessant need of rescue, or perhaps he merely interpreted the circumstances that way due to his attraction to her. He realized none of it mattered now.

I've lost her. Without a sound, he stood. He had to leave before his nerve faded completely.

Etain looked up into his anguished face. His deep blue eyes transformed into the red orbs of the demon, his wings ready for flight. "What?" He drank in every nuance of her beautiful features. "What're you doing?" She jumped up. "No! It was him! Midir set you up. I don't know how, I don't know why, but I do know you would never hurt an innocent. Not like that. Not on purpose. He tricked you. I saw it." She reached out to him, tears of frustration spilling down her cheeks. "You cannot leave. I will not allow it."

"My love…," he began.

"Have you no faith in me?" She moved close, placing a hand on his chest.

His gaze softened. "I have caused you too much pain already."

"Just give me a little time to sort it out in my head." She wrapped her arms around his waist, pressing her body into his. "If you leave me, I will die."

A melancholy smile crossed his lips. "You will be fine."

She pushed him away. "You obviously don't know my heart, although I have willingly opened it to your abuses." He saw violet streaks of light transform her pupils into slits of black fire. Dar stepped back to avoid the electrical charges arcing around her form. She advanced as he retreated. "I confess my fears and desires, and your answer is to run away? Perhaps Midir was right. Maybe you're *not* the man I thought you to be. Perhaps you're not a man at all." A flash of electric fire whizzed past his head.

Astonished by her fury, his anger flashed, meeting the challenge. "Do not threaten me." His black wings fanned out, talons flashing in the dim light.

"Or what? Will you cut me to shreds and throw my body in the sea? Your twisted brother can't help you this time. The dirty work will be left for you to do all by yourself."

Stricken by her reaction, his wings flapped, lifting him into the darkness, muttering words she was not meant to hear.

Etain raised her arms. "I heard what you said! If you believe I should die, then make it so."

He dove past, grazing her side with outstretched talons. She accepted the retaliation with a grunt and sank to her knees, her head hanging. "The thought of you leaving scares the hell out of me. I would rather be dead than live without you."

Ever proud, Dar dove back down, pulling up at the last moment, landing lightly in front of her. "What do you want from me?"

One minute, she was sweet and gentle; the next angry and full of fire. Now she was on her knees, her face stained with tears…for him. His blood cooled and his wings retracted. He fell to his knees, taking her into his arms.

She buried her head in his shoulder. "Please forgive me for doubting you."

Dar relished in the rapid beat of her heart against his chest. He knew the time had come to remove the façade and allow his body to heal. He was of no use to her in this state. Spirit was right about the deception. Either Etain loved him for who he was, or she did not. She deserved better than what he had offered. She deserved the same honesty from him that he demanded from her.

"I have done so many things." He kissed the top of her head. "It is me who asks for forgiveness."

"What are we doing, Dar?" She looked up into his eyes. "You are my heart, not my enemy."

His fingers trailed along the silver strands of her hair. "I heard a human once say that love is a battlefield. As long as we work together, *mo chuisle*, I will gladly suffer the wounds of love."

"Bless your heart," she said, patting his cheek. "How about we start with a healing spell?"

11

THE DEMON YOU KNOW

reakfast trays in hand, Spirit tapped on Dar's bedroom door. Inferno opened it without waiting for a response. Chastising him with a look, she stepped inside, surprised at finding an empty bed. One looked at the other, both shrugging. "Etain's room?" Spirit suggested.

"After last night's row, maybe she's sent him packing," Inferno said, a hopeful smirk on his face. "Don't give me the evil eye. It could happen."

Stepping across the hall, she was relieved to find them fully clothed and sound asleep on top of the covers. Spirit and Inferno deposited their trays on the bedside tables.

Inferno clapped his hands. "*Bore da*, ya dirty stop ins. The day's not gettin' any longer by ya lazing in bed." Dar popped up, dirk in hand. Inferno jumped back. "Whoa, big man. It's only me and me lovely wife with brekkies."

Spirit laughed. "I'd say you're feeling better this morning."

"A person could lose an important body part." Dar's voice

scratched in his throat, but the breakfast aromas made his mouth water. "What time is it?"

"Well past eight," Inferno said. "The clan's here, already working on the repairs. Surprised the noise didn't wake ya."

Spirit tried waking Etain, who was apparently unaffected by Inferno's announcement. "Wake up, lass. We have breakfast." One blue eye opened, rolled, and closed again. "No, you don't, lovey. It's your job to watch over this strapping patient and keep him entertained." Spirit looked at Dar. "Between the noise and the dust, you won't get any proper rest. It's fresh air for the two of you today."

Dar slapped Etain on the rump, laughing at her indignant grunt. "Excellent entertainment she will be, too." He chuckled and delved into the hot food.

Inferno gave the man a skeptical eye. "Just be sure to keep it clean, laddie."

He responded with a boyish grin, mouth full of food. "As you wish, milord."

"Get your lazy bones up." Dar placed his tray on the nightstand and leaned over her inert form. "If you're not gonna partake of this outstanding fare, I guess it's up to me to make sure it doesn't go to waste."

A shapely arm blocked his play for her plate. "Not so fast, buster." She opened an eye. "You'll not be taking what's not rightfully yours."

Laughing, he surrounded her with his body, his hair cascading around her face. "*You* are rightfully mine."

"We shall see, ya wee devil." She smiled, doing her best to ignore the desire burning in her belly. "Now, remove yourself from my personage so I may taste this outstanding fare you've so valiantly endorsed." Dar sat back, indulging in his tray of treats as Etain reached for hers, facing him as they ate. "Are they not the most wonderful people in the world?" She gobbled down a forkful of egg. "What would you like to do today, my good sir?" He eyed her with wicked intent but she ignored his gaze, biting into a piece of toast. "Spirit's right. You need some fresh air and a change of scenery. Let's go into town. The walk will do you good, work the stiffness from your muscles." This elicited a lecherous lift of a brow. "You know what I mean."

"A walk into town. The great outdoors. I think I shall enjoy such a venture."

"Good. I'll check on our other patient and take the trays down while you change. Back in a sec."

Finding Faux's door open, she placed the trays on the floor and walked in. The girl still slept, despite Spirit having applied a fresh poultice.

"Do you need some help, Spirit? I thought she would've been awake by now."

"I'm all right, but thanks. Sometimes they wake up quick. Sometimes it takes days. She's been through a fair bit and lost a lot of blood." Etain's face brightened, certain she had the answer to their problem. "No. The girl needs time to heal on her own. She and the babe'll be stronger for it."

Shot down, Etain changed the subject. "I need a new shirt. Do you have anything I can borrow? We're going into town and I don't want to go looking like a homeless person."

"Let's have a nosey in me wardrobe." Done with administering the poultice, they headed to Spirit's room. "Have a seat while I have a dig round." She rifled through her wardrobe, shifting one hanger, then another. Pulling out a blouse, she held it up toward Etain and shook her head. "No, that won't do." The shifting of clothes continued. "Ah, I know what will. Where is it? I only tried it on the once."

"All I need is a shirt, Spirit."

She emerged with a blouse in one hand and skirt in the other. "I think this will look stunnin' on you. Try it on."

Etain stared in silent consternation. "Spirit, I don't need an entire outfit. My leathers-"

"Pffft," she scolded, bustling over to the tall blonde. "You're a beautiful young woman and it's high time you dressed like one." She pulled her up by the arm. "You can't tell me he won't appreciate seeing you in a skirt for a change."

Etain relinquished her well-worn clothes and let Spirit slip the top over her head. The fine texture of the silk elicited an appreciative sigh. The smooth deep violet material set off her fair skin, and made her feel like a pampered princess. Long sleeves were gathered just above the elbow and cascaded into a full slant cut at the cuff. An elasticized hem came in just below her breasts, accentuating their fullness. The skirt, in the same vibrant violet fabric, had layer upon layer of sheer chiffon with a short overskirt in matching silk. It sat perfectly on her hips, leaving her firm midriff exposed. She stared at the unrecognizable image in the full-length mirror.

Spirit laughed in appreciation. "I knew it'd be perfect. The skirt was too long for me, and the top a wee bit too big." Etain's bare feet posed a problem. "We can't have that." Going back to the wardrobe, she reappeared with a pair of strappy sandals. "Good thing your feet aren't the same size as the rest of you. These should do fine." She grabbed the girl's hand and pulled her to the dressing table. "Let's see if I can tame that mane." After some considerable effort, and several expletives, she put down the brush. "Look there, lass. An honest-to-goodness young lady. No more pagan…at least on the outside."

Etain stared at her reflection. She had never been concerned with her looks, but this vision looking back at her was hard to believe. She caught Spirit's eye in the mirror. "Thank you," she whispered.

"Go have a grand day with your beau." She laughed, seeing the pink flush on the girl's cheeks. "If you can avoid Inferno before you go…" She winked, leaving the rest unsaid.

At the door, Etain turned. "Just so you know, nothing has happened."

"Lass, there's plenty happening. You remember what we talked about."

Hand in hand, Dar and Etain walked out of Laugharne without running into Inferno, his hounds, or any of the clan which was a feat in itself. The sun bright and the temperature mild, they opted for a leisurely walk.

"Please stop looking at me like that."

Dar smiled, the admiration clear on his face. "Like you're the most beautiful woman in all the kingdoms?"

"Like I'm naked."

He caught her around the waist and pulled her close. "That, milady, can be arranged." He placed a suggestive kiss on her lips. Distracted for the moment, she surrendered to his affections, savoring the sweet taste of his lips.

Well into the kiss, curiosity got the best of her, wanting to steal a glimpse of this man who had turned her world upside down. She opened her eyes into an intense blue gaze. Taken aback, she pushed away. "What're you doing?"

Was that a smirk on his face?

"I could ask the same."

"I…well… You were already… Your eyes…were open and…"

He reached for her hand. "I am merely in awe you are here with me. I was afraid it might be a dream."

She let out a nervous laugh. "Seriously? Me, too."

"You seem rather…accomplished with kissing."

A grin came to her lips. "Even virgins get kissed."

Dar laughed. "Aye, I suppose they do." He took in the rolling landscape around them. "Tell me about this place while we walk. Do you know its history?"

Etain pointed out different landmarks, telling their stories as she'd been told them. Of the push and pull between the Welsh and the English in the human realm. Dar listened, rapt in her presence. In return, he entertained her with stories of past conquests, sometimes acting out a particular part for emphasis. His talk moved to his dreams of their future. She wasn't quite sure how she felt about it. Their history had been as tumultuous as any had by a Welshman and their English nemesis.

Once in town, they found a market fair in full swing. Moving stall to stall, they tasted various cheeses and breads, sipped wines of red, white, and rosé, and sampled local beers. There were cakes, pies, and pasties for sale. Farmers had brought their best produce to market and appeared to be doing well. Music and the aroma of roasting meat filled the air.

Dar came across a stall with a variety of weapons on display, succumbing to its irresistible siren song. It was a virtual treasure trove. He moved from one sword to the next. Etain, temporarily forgotten, watched his reverent caress of the blades, lifting each one, testing its weight and balance. Showing special interest in a matching sword and dirk, he called the owner over. They shared a short conversation before the man nodded toward the back. Dar grinned, weapons in hand, and set off in the direction indicated. Curious, Etain followed him to a roped off section behind the stall.

Dar moved to the center, sliding the dirk into his belt. With a seasoned eye, he inspected the blade of the sword, gazing down its length to confirm the workmanship. He extended it out, twisting and turning his wrist to get familiar with the weight of the blade. Tucking the same arm to his body, he lunged. The warrior appeared pleased as he sliced the blade through the air. Increasing the span, he whipped the sword down to his left. With a graceful twist of his wrist, he slashed down to the right, bringing it around, clasping the hilt with both hands at waist height. He rolled his shoulders and stretched to each side, testing his ribs. Stepping forward, he pivoted to the left, brandishing the sword overhead, bringing it down into the same double-handed clasp. The grace he exuded throughout his routine held Etain mesmerized. It had never occurred to her how much swordplay resembled a dance.

Sword in his right hand, he removed the dirk from his belt with his left and extended the sword at an angle, keeping the dirk close. His body twisted, ducked, and weaved, slicing his blade through the air. With a turn, the sword flew from his hand, as though forced by an unseen foe. Dar ducked his head and rolled over in a tumble, coming up on a knee. The dirk came up in a swift, savage jab, stopping just short of Etain's abdomen. She stepped back.

"Etain."

"Dar."

"Your reaction is not one I would expect from an Alamir." He twirled the dirk, slipping it back in his belt as he stood.

"What exactly did you expect?"

"Anything other than what I just witnessed. What if I had followed through with my move?"

She shifted beneath his blue-eyed gaze like a schoolgirl caught not paying attention to the lesson. A feeling she did not like. She cleared her throat, tossing her hair back. "Then I guess I would be left in a rather compromised position."

He cocked an authoritative brow. "Dead, most likely."

"Well, possibly. Had it been so, it would have proven rather inopportune for me...and you."

His other brow joined the first. "Inopportune for me?"

"Oh, aye." She nodded. "Not only would you have to deal with an incensed Inferno and his clan, I'm pretty sure Master G and his crew would not be too happy to hear of my demise. By a Krymerian, no less."

He stroked his chin. "Aye, well, good fighters they are, all of them, but not enough to make me shake in my boots."

"Then, of course, there's Spirit."

His eyes widened and he shivered. "*Tartarus*, I had not thought of that one. It's the small ones who will get you every time." He winked, flashing a grin.

It made her weak in the knees and stirred those blasted butterflies in her belly.

"You're very good," she breathed. "Who taught you how to fight?"

His expression took on a melancholy air. "My father taught me most, but I've learned a thing or two along the way." He picked up the sword. "I do what I can to stay sharp." Arm in arm, they walked back to the stall.

"I find it rather interesting how easily you move after all that's happened to you over the past few days," she said, watching as he reverently wiped down both weapons before laying them on the table.

"Did I see a pub down the road? I'm thirsty." He grabbed her hand and pulled her away from the hubbub of the fair. "I think it's this way," he said, dragging her down the road to a set of heavy oak doors. Once his eyes adjusted to the dim interior, he headed to the bar, ordered two pints, and dragged her to a secluded booth.

Etain dropped onto the cushioned seat. "Beer. Yum."

"Does it not suit you, *mo chuisle*?"

His innocent confusion made her smile. "There's nothing better than a cold beer after a workout, aye?"

He grinned. "Aye!" Returning to the bar, he paid the bartender and whisked away both mugs.

"It *does* feel good to sit. I hadn't realized how late it was. Watching you was captivating." A bluesy ballad began to play on the jukebox.

"I could work with the blades for days." Dar downed half his pint. "Ah, that's better."

She relaxed back. "You are a marvel."

"Am I?" he said, basking in her attention. "What makes you say that?"

"All the things you've suffered, the heartache and broken promises. Yet you still find wonder in this world." She took his hands, turned them palms up, and ran her fingers out to his fingertips. He shivered from the intimate touch. Eyes on his face, she lifted his hands to her lips, kissing each one.

The Krymerian lord was speechless. He held his breath, waiting for the words he longed to hear from her lips. Her touch, her actions told him of her affections, but he needed her to say the words, wash away all doubt. Here was his future, bright and full of promise. Her eyes brightened.

"Come dance with me."

"Beg pardon?" Not what he expected. "I'm no dancer," he said, shaking his head.

"Don't give me that," she laughed, sliding out of the booth, his hands still in hers. "After the way you moved with those swords? Not only can you dance, you have made a miraculous recovery, too." He begrudgingly obliged, letting her lead him to the small dance floor. "I love this song," she said, placing his arms around her waist.

The sensuous music amplified her charms. He found himself hypnotized by her scent as she moved against him. In a flash of inspiration, Dar spun her around, bringing her in close again. His hands firm on her waist, he pulled her in as close as he could. Etain snaked her arms around his neck.

She arched her back, following the rhythm of the song. He liked how this newly awakened passion seemed to have set her free. He yearned to run his hand down her bare midriff, but was afraid he may break the spell. Her moves drove him to the edge. His hand slid up her back, guiding her up to him. Dar dipped his head, catching her lip gently in his teeth and breathing in her gasp.

Sliding his tongue against her lips, he whispered, "*Mo chuisle*, sing for me."

She pulled back. "I'm no singer," she said, giving him a look that clearly questioned his sanity.

"I'm no dancer, yet here I am, dancing with my beautiful lady. You sang to me our first night." His hips moved against hers. "Please."

"That was different."

Another familiar song played on the jukebox. With a growl of satisfaction, he brought her even closer, their bodies moving as one, her voice soft in his ear.

"Perfect," he whispered.

Breaking their embrace, they realized everyone in the bar had turned to watch their seduction. Etain cleared her throat, grabbed Dar's hand, and pulled him off the dance floor.

Boyish grin in place, he waved to the onlookers. "We're here every other Friday night."

Etain giggled, collapsing into her seat. "Except this isn't Friday."

Dar slid in next to her. Her laugh and smile warmed his heart. *If only it could always be this way.* Not happy with the distance between them, he pulled her onto his lap, wrapping his arms around her waist.

"What's wrong?" she asked, stroking his hair.

"You were too far away." He nuzzled into her warmth, soothed by the steady beat of her heart. "I cannot lose you."

"I'm not going anywhere, darlin'." She tipped his head back and kissed him sweetly. "Let's go home. I want you all to myself."

In a moment, they were gone in a blue shimmer.

At the castle, they ignored the looks from the clan, practically running up the stairs to Dar's room. The door closed and the lock turned, Dar pulled her hips to his, leaning in for a kiss.

She placed her hands on his chest. "I want you to rest. I know you're feeling better, but we don't need a relapse now."

"I thought you wanted me all to yourself."

"I'm going to take a quick shower." She ran her fingers through his soft hair. "I won't be long."

"I could shower with you. Then you wouldn't be deprived of my inspirational company."

"You've already done more than you should. Let's not push it." She wriggled from his grasp and dashed into the bathroom.

Dar leaned against the closed door. "I'm beginning to wonder about your obsession with bathing. Is there something I should know?"

He heard her laugh. "I guess it comes from my days with Darth. Bathing was a luxury we couldn't afford."

Dar chuckled, turning from the door. "How can I deny you such a

184

simple pleasure?" Sitting on the bed, he removed his boots and sighed, wiggling his toes. Content to wait for his lady fair, he noticed the bathroom door slowly creep open. Curiosity winning over conscience, he was drawn to the widening gap.

Preoccupied with setting the shower temperature, Etain was obviously not aware of Dar's perfect view of her in the mirror. The rhythm of his heart challenged the throb in his loins as he watched the water run through her silver hair, down the soft curves of her body, flowing over rounded hips, and down long, shapely legs. Beguiled by her unconscious sensuality, he removed his shirt, dropping it on the floor. His pants soon followed.

Etain turned, washing the shampoo from her hair. He held his breath, admiring how the movement emphasized the fullness of her beautiful breasts. Her hair rinsed, she reached for the bottle of conditioner, just missing it. One eye opened. She yelped, sputtering in the rush of water.

"Dar!"

He waited. He knew her heart was ready, but what of her mind?

"It's only me, *mo chuisle.*"

What was she getting herself into? She barely knew this man. The pronounced pounding of her heart, accompanied by flutters in her belly, told her he would demand more from her. More than she had ever given before. Perhaps more than she was willing to give.

Having jarred the bottle of conditioner with her fingertips, it fell onto the floor, breaking her trance. She looked away for a split second. When her eyes came back to him, she wondered why she'd never consciously appreciated the beauty of this man, the curve of well-defined muscles flowing from shoulder and chest to a flat belly and powerful thighs. Her heart skipped, noting the soft brown thatch around his well-endowed maleness. His brows lifted at her curious scrutiny. Her gaze traveling to his face, she blinked the water from her eyes and opened the shower door.

"Etain, I must tell you one thing-"

"Shhh." She took his mouth, her teeth tugging gently on his bottom lip as her arms slid around his neck, pulling him into the shower. "Spirit is a very good friend." Curious hands explored, as though checking the balance of a new sword...shoulders, breasts, bellies, down to those parts yearning for discovery. Tensions of one sort evaporated while others escalated beneath the falling water. He growled in response to her hot mouth on his skin. She reveled in the freedom of letting go, the scratch of stubble against her flesh, and the delicious intensity of his teeth as they raked sensitive peaks.

An overwhelming passion fed an unfamiliar hunger. She looked into his eyes, panting with the need to feel him inside, and froze.

"Etain?"

She began to shake. "I'm sorry. I can't..." *What is wrong with me?* She pushed past him, leaving him alone in the shower. "I'm sorry, Dar."

Etain felt embarrassed about letting things go that far, then running away to her room across the hall. How could she look him in the eye? But she did, opening the door to his knock. Not surprisingly, he didn't smile.

"Come in," she said, clutching the towel around her.

Dar stepped in, her clothes in his hand. "I thought you may need these."

She closed the door quietly. "Thank you." Turning, she didn't know what to say. Her stomach churned, wishing she could shrug it off and move on. It would be so much easier if she didn't care. She looked at him and found him watching her. "Dar-"

"Etain, I am sorry."

"*You're* sorry? For what?"

"I lost control. It's obvious you are not ready. I should not have pushed myself on you."

"You think what happened was *your* fault?"

"I took advantage of your inexperience. What I thought was burning passion-"

"*Was* burning passion." She ran a hand through her hair. "I'm bloody well ready. Holy hell, am I ready," she muttered, taking a deep breath, pacing back and forth in front of him. "I want you. I've wanted you for a long, long time. Granted, it's taken some time to admit it to myself. But once I got past that, I was ready."

Dar opened his mouth to speak, but she kept talking. "I was excited when you summoned us. I thought it would be my chance to find out if you felt the same." She stopped long enough to catch his eye. "When you chose Faux…" She continued pacing, "I figured I had miscalculated. It didn't make sense to me, given our history. But, as you say, I'm inexperienced." She came to a standstill before him. "It's my conscience. That's the problem."

"You're worried about Faux?"

She shrugged. "Of course, you'd think of her." Dar clenched his jaw, holding her gaze. "Inferno is like a father to me. This is his house and he wouldn't approve of this. As much as I want to be with you, crazy as that sounds given our *recent* history, I will not take advantage of his trust. I cannot betray him under his own roof."

His face fell. "You see making love with me as a *betrayal?*"

With those few words, he managed to knock the steam from her engines. It made her realize she had as much power over him as he did her. Seeing him this way, vulnerable and unsure, softened her heart, and made him sexy as hell.

"No, I do not." She felt the air lift between them. "You have to remember we're talking about Inferno here. You and me are still on shaky ground where he's concerned. I want his blessing, but he won't give it if he thinks he's been betrayed. Can you see it from his point of view?"

He put his hands together and bowed his head, looking as though he were deep in prayer. Etain stayed patient, chewing the inside of her bottom lip, hoping he would be able to give in return. Several minutes passed before he raised his head, a somber expression on his face.

Please be the man I think you are.

"Inferno is an honorable man who deserves to be treated with respect in his own house. Thank you for saving us both from making a critical error." His formality threw her a curve. Had she pushed him too far? "It is up to me to prove myself worthy of his trust." He shrugged. "I have *no* idea how I'm going to achieve this massive task, but…" He gave her a grin, "I will find a way."

She flung her arms around his neck and kissed him on the mouth, losing her towel in the process. "You are a saint!"

He groaned. "I won't be for long if we stay like this." He retrieved the towel and wrapped it around her. "I know I said I would not be without you by my side, but I think it would be best if you stayed here tonight. Get your sleep. Tomorrow, we will re-evaluate your swordsmanship and work with your new blade."

After leaving Etain, Dar went to Faux's room, not yet ready to retire. Finding her alone, he pulled the chair close to the bed, then gently smoothed the hair from her face. She opened one eye. He placed a finger over her lips. "I wanted to say thank you again for saving my life."

The door creaked, announcing Spirit's arrival for the evening ritual. "What are you doing in here?" She was quick to inspect her charge, then turned a sharp eye on Dar, further inspecting his arms, turning each one over for any telltale sign of interference.

"I didn't," he said, submitting to her investigations. "I merely wanted to check on her."

Satisfied, she released him and went about her business. "Provided that's all you do. Let the lass heal on her own."

"Aye, milady." He lingered, watching the mage at work.

"Was there something else?" she asked.

"I have forged a new blade for Etain. Tomorrow will be a day of training, teaching her how to wield it in concert with the magic she now possesses." Compelled by the protective nature of the woman, he gave her fair warning. "It won't be easy for her to do, or you to watch."

She stopped what she was doing, considering him for a few uneasy seconds. "I'm not sure how it is you're able to move, let alone train anyone, even for a Krymerian." With an authoritative finger in his face, she gave her two pence worth. "You make sure whatever knocks she gets are lessons well-learned. I know what you speak of, and yes, she has much to learn, but…" Her finger became more of a menace, "I see or hear of any unneeded brutality, I'll not only put Inferno after your arse, I'll make sure his powers are enhanced three times over and he makes a barbeque of your bloody carcass."

Dar muttered, "Yes, ma'am." Then made a quick escape.

The next morning, Dar made his way downstairs and headed outdoors. Walking past the living room, although aware of Inferno and his clansmen busy at work within the room, he did not acknowledge their presence. At the front doors, he realized he needed Inferno's help after all. Taking a deep breath, he backtracked and was surprised by the number of people milling about, a testament to the clan's recruiter. He'd not realized the clan had grown this much.

It might be good business to…

He spotted the scowling face in the crowd. "Inferno, where do you keep your weapons? I have need of a few items, if you don't mind."

"What for?"

"Etain's training. I would prefer four scimitars, if you have them."

"Training, huh? Ya may be right. She's a fair arm with the sword, but could use the guidance of a master. Aye, I have what ya need. Give me a minute." Dar followed him outside, but remained in the courtyard. Eventually, Inferno returned with the blades. "When yer done, hand 'em to me alone."

"Understood." He inspected the scimitars with a critical eye. "I have one more request."

"Cocky bastard this morning."

"I ask you respect my position as a sword master and not interfere with our exercises." An intense look passed between them. Dar leaned in, lowering his voice. "I will take great care with her."

With a grunt, Inferno watched him leave. "I'll take great care to lop yer bloody head off if ya hurt the lass."

Dressed in her old leathers and hair pulled back into a ponytail, Etain met Dar at the estuary. He greeted her with a glorious smile. "There you are, my love. Pick your blades."

She eyed the four weapons on the ground. "I thought we were training with my sword."

"Let's start with the basics. It has been some time since I last saw you move with a blade. We will come back to your *Nim*."

She shrugged, unbuckled the scabbard, placed *Nim* at the edge of the grass, and picked up the first two blades.

The other two in hand, Dar stepped back. "Watch closely. You will do this after me." In slow motion, he swung the blades in a figure eight. "You try."

"I've never worked with two blades at once." After a few clumsy attempts, she had them moving in fluid motion. "Not as hard as it looks. Whatcha got for me next, big boy?"

"Remind me of your ability." His swords snapped out in a whirlwind, straight for her head. She dropped one scimitar and gripped the hilt of the other with both hands, swinging up to meet the strike. "Pick up the other. Learn to use them together."

"You said to remind you of my skills. Didn't I just say I've never used two blades?"

"It's time you learned. Pick it up."

She rolled her eyes, dutifully bending over to do just that. Dar took advantage of her compromised position, slapping her backside with the flat of his blade. She yelped, standing up. "What the hell was that for?"

"I am teaching you to use these swords. Remember to keep your eyes on the one you are fighting, but also anticipate their next move. Let's try again."

"I don't see how slapping me on the ass has anything to do with learning how to use these blasted things." She set her feet in a defensive stance, blades at her sides. Dar came at her, cutting in from the left and right. This time, she blocked his attacks. However, he surprised her with a quick turn and kick to the stomach, knocking her back several steps.

"Good job that time." He charged again, knowing she couldn't move in time, but she held her stance. Apparently, she knew it, too. A smile crossed his face, spotting a slight shift in her eyes. At the last second, he leaped into the air, somersaulting over her head. His feet hit the ground resulting in a puff of dirt. She started to turn, her blade in the lead, just as his elbow connected with the back of her head.

Dar dropped his blades, catching her before she hit the ground. He gently smoothed her hair back, an expression of wonder on his face. "This new development changes everything. We have a long road ahead of us, *mo chuisle*."

Ignoring the varied degrees of animosity aimed at him as he passed through the house, he carried her to her room and laid her on the bed. With great care, he unlaced her boots, setting them on the floor, then wet a cloth and washed her face and neck. "I'll leave you in peace, sweet lady. Let you rest." He left a parting kiss on her cheek.

Going downstairs, again ignoring the evil looks, he went out to retrieve the borrowed blades, returning them personally to Inferno, careful to keep his expression neutral. "If I may, I would like to use them tomorrow."

Inferno glared. "Wasn't much of a lesson if you ask me." He grabbed the swords from Dar's outstretched hands. "Ya didn't have to be so rough on the lass. I wonder how ya'd hold up against one who's yer equal."

"Don't worry about Etain. I believe our late night has thrown her off-kilter. She'll be better by tomorrow."

Inferno looked him over with an enflamed eye. "What the hell happened last night?"

Spirit made an untimely appearance, purposely stepping between the two men. "Did I hear voices raised in me house?"

Dar had one more thing to say before he walked off. "Let me know when you find my equal. It will be my pleasure to put him in his place." He could hear Inferno's heated opinion all the way up the stairs.

———

Hand to her head, Etain sat up just as Dar entered the room.

"How are you?" he asked.

"I've felt better."

"It will soon pass. After our session today, I think we should concentrate on a few other things before working with your sword."

"Like how to use the eyes in the back of my head?"

He sat next to her, intertwining his arm with hers, taking her hand in his. "Like how to control the demon within and use it to your advantage."

She shot him a sideways glance. "Hmph. I know I can be a stinker at times, but isn't *demon* a bit strong?"

"I don't understand why it has taken so long to manifest. Now we know I've had the ability to change since I was a boy, I would have thought by sharing my blood-"

"Please, no more thinking today." She laid her head on his shoulder.

"Today's lesson was a good start." Leaning his head on hers, he rubbed her thumb with his. "Inferno's upset."

"Can't imagine why."

"It may come down to no more than a split second that will determine whether you live or die. You have to think smart, and be quick about it." He raised his head, looking her in the eye. "I have seen too many rough characters come into this world. They won't be easy on you. Because of them, neither will I. You must be able to handle yourself whether I'm around or not."

"Okay, I get it. But did you have to be so brutal on the first day?"

"Etain, I don't pretend to understand how it's happening, but the signs are there. You *will* turn eventually. It's my responsibility to teach you how to control it."

She sighed. "Does that mean more training today?"

He pulled her toward him. "Training, aye." A kiss of apology became a burning desire for more. She brought herself up and straddled his hips, his hands roaming underneath her top. "Perhaps this training will be more to your liking, my vixen warrior."

His exquisite touch felt like velvet on her skin. Her eyes closed, fingers curling, nails digging into his back. She couldn't think of anything but this magical moment.

"No more training today, poppets," Spirit said, peeking around the door. "How goes it in here?"

Etain's eyes popped open as she scrambled off Dar's lap. "Uh, fine. We're…fine."

Spirit grinned. "You look a bit flushed, but I imagine it has more to do with what's going on in here than the assault this morning."

Etain silenced Dar's retort with a look. "You could've knocked."

"And miss the look on your faces?" She laughed, coming into the room and closing the door. "I *did* knock…several times. You best watch yourselves. I understand how it is between you, but Inferno, well… He's a different kettle of fish." Spirit reached for the knob. "I've had a pig roasting most of the morning. Isn't often the whole clan gets together, so we're making a do of it. Get yourselves straight, and behave."

After Spirit left, Dar asked, "Make a *do* of it?"

Etain ran a hand through her hair. "A party, my love."

He pulled her onto his lap. "Let's make a *do* here, just you and me." Sliding his hands to her backside, he jerked her close, taking her mouth with his.

She groaned, breathless, but pulled away. "What did we talk about last night? We can *do* later." She winked and wriggled from his grasp. "Besides, I'm hungry. Plus, it's the perfect opportunity to show off my handsome warrior love."

Dar casually laid his hands over his lap. "You go ahead. I'll be down in a few minutes."

"Don't be too long," she said, leaving him with a kiss.

Grabbing her boots, she took a quick look in the mirror. In moments, she was across the hall, slipped out of her leathers, and into the violet top and skirt.

Let's see what you do *with this, mister.*

12

DISTRACTION

Etain breathed in the sweet aroma of roasting pork, wondering how she had missed such a delicious smell. She walked through an empty kitchen and out to the rear grounds. Aromatic smoke billowed from a huge barbeque pit and a huge pig rotating over a fire. Several long tables held an assortment of treats, while others were set up for dining. And not too far from the barbeque lurked Felix and Ruby.

People were scattered throughout the garden...some in conversation, a few playing horseshoes, and two engaged in swordplay a distance away. Inferno slipped up next to her and wrapped an arm around her waist. "If I'd a'known we'd invited a goddess, I'd a'worn me besties."

Etain playfully elbowed him in the ribs. "Ha, ha. Aren't we the comedian tonight?"

Laughing, Inferno gave her a squeeze. "Let me introduce ya to a few of the newer clansmen." He dragged her to the first group. "Ya know Bad Man. Sakai and Vipercat are fair new. This is our Etain.

Damn near like a daughter to me." No sooner had they exchanged hellos when Inferno led her away.

They crossed the garden toward the two men making a show of their skill with a blade. One had the unruliest hair she'd ever seen, and the other was a dark-skinned elf. "Wolfe, Elfin, I'd like to introduce you to someone." The two stopped their practice, lowering their swords, sighed at one another, and turned to their chieftain. Upon seeing the beauty on his arm, their annoyance at having their practice interrupted melted into admiration. "This is Etain. She's family ya haven't met."

Each bowed with a flourish, speaking in unison. "It's a great honor to meet such a lovely lady." Deep in their bows, they looked at each other and laughed.

Wolfe punched Elfin in the arm. "You dog! You know I'm the gentleman of the clan. My thunder shall not be stolen."

Elfin punched him back. "Gentleman? All I see is a lecher looking for a good tumble." With a snort, he skipped back a few steps when Wolfe presented his sword.

"*En guard*, ye swine."

Inferno laughed. "A mischievous lot they are, but I'd have them watch me back any day."

"Such delightful people," she said, hearing the provocative strains of an Irish jig. Her eyes lit up. "Oh, Inferno, you remembered." She rewarded his thoughtfulness with a kiss on the cheek. A young man of around six-two, brown hair curling about a face that was almost handsome but for a nose too long for his face, weaved through the crowd. Inferno draped an arm across her shoulders, beckoning the fiddler closer. Eyes as deep as the early evening sky extended his greetings with a wink.

"Etain, I don't think ya've been formally introduced to me right-hand man and part-time recruiter, ZornKetahl. Don't let his fiddlin' fool ya. He's a right terror with a sword, and shows no mercy in a game of chess."

ZornKetahl dipped his head, circling around the group without missing a note. Some got up to dance. Etain grabbed Inferno's hand and dragged him toward the dancers. "Let's be pagans, milord, and invite the spirits to celebrate with us," she said, laughing, twirling about, hands overhead.

Dar stepped out the back door just as Etain met the fiddler. He frowned, sidling up to Spirit, his eyes on the stranger. "Who's that?"

"Who, love?"

"The fiddler."

"That's Zorn." With a laugh, she jabbed him in the ribs. "He's nothing to fret about."

With a discernible "hmph", Dar strolled over to the dancing couple, nodding to those he passed along the way, and tapped Inferno on the shoulder. "May I?"

"She's all yours, mate. I'm knackered," Inferno gasped.

Etain twirled into Dar's arms, a brilliant smile on her lips.

"You are a vision," he said.

With a gleam in her eye, she left him breathless with a saucy kiss. "I thought I was a vixen."

"Aye," he laughed, spinning her around and bringing her close again. "That you are."

When the tune ended, Spirit called everyone to eat. Filling their plates with delicious treats, the guests settled in various places around the garden. Dar and Etain chose a perfect spot underneath a large oak. Sitting comfortably, she remembered. "Dar, we need drinks."

"I'll fetch them," he said, handing his plate over.

"No need, Lord Dar. I just happen to have an extra tankard or two of the best ale in the kingdom." An unusual blonde-haired elf grinned at the couple. "I hope you don't mind my escorts. They seem rather *dogged* in their duties."

Felix slinked round, taking a seat at Etain's side, while Ruby sniffed at the elf. Giving him a tentative snort of approval, she sidled over to Dar, positioning herself between the two men.

Dar looked up into a familiar face. "Linq." The elf handed mugs to Etain and Dar, then held out a hand to the Krymerian. Jumping to his feet, Dar gave the elf a sound slap on the back. "*Tartarus*, man. How long has it been?"

Etain considered the ferocious look of the elf. He was as tall as Dar. His fair hair, skin, and blue eyes marked him as a golden elf, but he wore his mane in a single thick strip across the top of his head and plaited down his back. On his otherwise shaved head were remarkable markings.

The men shared a warm handshake. "Too long, I'd say." His eyes moved to Dar's companion.

"Linq, this is my lady, Etain." Dar held out a hand, helping her to her feet. "My love, this is Linq. He may not look it, but he's a very old friend."

Etain stuck out her hand for a solid Texas handshake, but Linq drew it to his lips, placing a respectful kiss on her knuckles. "It's an honor to meet you, milady. By the sea and stars, how did this ugly brute win the attentions of such a beautiful woman?"

Dar nudged his friend. "I'm not so much the brute nowadays."

"He's not so bad once the lights go dim," she teased. "Hi, Linq. Nice to meet you."

"Join us," Dar said.

"I'll catch up later. I must speak with Inferno before he's too far in the drink. Etain…" He bowed his head, "it was a pleasure."

The couple settled in, enjoying their meal. "How old a friend?"

Having just shoved a piece of pork into his mouth, she had to wait until he swallowed the morsel, followed by a gulp of ale. "It was before I joined the Alamir. Sometime after that, he joined UWS, but he and Inferno had a falling out and he left the clan. Never said why. We would get together now and then, teaching each other new techniques. He taught me the somersault move I used on you earlier."

She ripped a piece of bread in half, a steely-eyed gaze on the elf. "Remind me to thank him."

"Would you mind if I leave you for a minute or two? I want to ask of his plans," Dar asked with a hopeful raise of a brow.

Etain shooed him away, Ruby in tow, and relaxed against the tree. Felix inched closer, laying his head in her lap. She laughed. "Wrangling your way into my good graces, are you? Sorry, bud. There's nothing left." Scratching his ears, she watched the merriment around her. For the first time in her life as an Alamir, she felt truly happy.

The clearing of a throat roused her from her thoughts. "May I sit with you?" The young fiddler accepted her slight shrug as assent and sat down. "Hello, Felix," he said, giving the hound a pat. "So, you're the Lady Etain. I've heard stories but I wonder that we didn't meet when you were with the clan."

"There's no wonder, really, when you know Inferno."

He nodded, grinning. "Something we have in common."

She relaxed and smiled in return. "Then you know how protective he is, ZornKetahl."

"Please, call me Zorn."

"Zorn." Etain stroked Felix's head. "Inferno found me at a clan gathering, one where they were campaigning for new members. He was determined to have me join UWS. At the time, I had no idea why he was so adamant, but I found it very hard to say no."

Zorn laughed. "Inferno is definitely a determined man."

"He mentioned you're an impressive warrior, as well as an accomplished violinist."

"I'm just good with strategy." He shrugged. "And I spend a lot of time sparring with Wolfe and Elfin."

Etain grinned at the memory of their introduction. "Aye, a charming pair."

"They disguise their knowledge with charm. It seems to give them an edge."

"So, Zorn, how did one so young become Inferno's right-hand man?"

"He took me under his wing when I first came to the Alamir. We came up against each other one day during a battle. It was actually a case of mistaken identity. He thought I was fighting for the *Bok* and made every attempt to run me through, but I was able to fend off his advances and got a few hits in myself. He finally stepped back and began yelling at me. Such profanity I'd never heard."

Etain laughed. "Aye. If he can't slash it to death, he'll bloody well try to shout it to death."

With the sun setting, Inferno, Dar, and Linq set to building a bonfire at Spirit's request. "She likes a fire, no matter the size," Inferno informed the two men.

"Sounds like a match made in heaven." Dar laughed and winked. "Let's not disappoint the lady."

Etain's laughter drifting across the garden gave Dar more reason to smile. Spying his lady in conversation with the young fiddler, the smile dissolved. He tossed a handful of logs onto the fire with one heave. Ruby barked, shying away from the flying sparks.

"Blast it, man. Watch what yer doing," Inferno shouted.

"I am." Dar stormed off.

The fine art of stealth can only become second nature through experience, requiring a patient heart. Years spent tracking the *Bok* and hunting demons had supplied the Krymerian with more than his fair share of experience. Where Etain was concerned, though, the patience part was still a work in progress. He silently approached the two, who were deep in conversation.

Zorn noticed his presence before Etain, which did not sit well with the warrior. "Lord Dar, forgive me. I'm afraid I've monopolized too much of your lady's time." Zorn came to his feet, fiddle in hand. "She is most engaging."

"So it would seem."

Etain held out her hand. Dar didn't notice, his focus on the fiddler. Instead, Zorn helped her to her feet. Felix followed suit, standing next to Etain.

"Thank you for a lovely conversation," she said, smiling. "I hope you'll play more for us this evening."

"As you wish, milady." He bowed, gave Felix a pat on the head, and walked away, unaware of the dangerous gaze on his back.

Dar waited until he was out of earshot, then cut his eyes to Etain. "You'll not be around to hear any more music."

"Oh?" Her hands went to her hips. "What exactly will I be doing?"

"You won't be talking to him. That's for sure."

"Contrary to what you believe, Mr. Machismo, you will not tell me what I can do or to whom I can speak."

"Etain…"

Caught between the big man and the tree, she sidestepped his warning. "Do not treat me like your possession. Either trust me, or-"

He made a grab for her arm. "There is no 'or' for us."

Felix growled.

"Or you can go back to Faux."

Inferno and Spirit arrived just in time. "How about another dance, lass?"

"Not now, Inferno," Dar grumbled.

Spirit placed a hand on Dar's chest. "This is a celebration. You will *not* ruin it." His steely gaze was met with one of ice. "Calm yourself, or they'll be carting you off."

"Keep that fiddling pup clear of her and we'll be fine." His glare touched each of them in turn. Noting the defiance in Etain's eyes, he turned, spied Linq at the bonfire, and walked away.

From across the garden, the Krymerian watched the women walk into the house. Inferno approached, his expression saying everything without uttering a word.

"Stay out of it." Dar started to follow the women, but the chieftain grabbed his arm.

"I'll bloody jump in the middle of anything that involves me family."

Dar shrugged him off. "She's mine now and no longer your burden."

"Burden, ya say?" His eyes burned.

Linq made an effort to intervene. "Gentlemen, let's have another brew and enjoy the evening." Two sets of glowing eyes turned on him. "As you wish." He stepped back, and made a beeline for the house.

Inferno's attention returned to the Krymerian. "If ya don't like the company we keep, yer free to leave."

"Happy to oblige," Dar sneered in return. "After I gather what belongs to me."

Inferno blocked his path. "No need to put yerself out. I'll send Zorn to fetch yer sword."

"It's not my blade I'm going for."

"She has a home here. Be on yer way and leave her be." Flames licked off Inferno's fingertips.

His words rang familiar. It wasn't long ago Dar had said the same thing to his brother. He took a breath. "She looked to be in pain."

"It's a wonder she has a head at all after that stunt you pulled today."

He let the comment slide. "I should check on her. I can help."

Inferno let him pass, but said over his shoulder, "Ya best think twice before pulling yer shenanigans again." He turned to face his opponent, crossing his arms.

"Or what?" Dar stopped. "You should consider to whom you speak."

"Are ya threatening me now?" The chieftain dropped his arms. "Yer not talking to a wee lass now. I can handle meself a damn site better 'n her."

"I do not make threats," Dar said, his voice even.

"Right. Ya do what's necessary, don't ya? I've seen it with me own eyes. Got one girl with a hole in her gut, and another with a bashed in head."

"Etain must learn to protect herself."

"Who's gonna protect her from you?"

"Inferno…" He lowered his voice to an angry whisper. "There are worse things in this world."

The Alamir chieftain laughed. "The only thing I've seen worse than you, so far, is yer wanker of a brother. Who, I might add, we wouldn't be bothered with if ya weren't around. Do her a favor. Stay out of her life. She'll get over you soon enough."

"You underestimate her." Dar's eyes slipped to demon red. "She came to me of her own volition."

"What's that?" Inferno's eyes bulged. "Ya best not be telling me what I think yer telling me."

Spirit's timing was spot-on. "Goddess of us all, must I get the muzzles out? I can hear you clear upstairs. Faux needs her rest, and Etain has a banging head." She glared at Dar. "No thanks to you. If I could get a guarantee you old hens wouldn't blast each other into oblivion, I'd leave you to it and not give a whit." She turned an evil eye on her husband. "You were to *prevent* a fight, not cause one." She turned on Dar. "I don't know what's got your knickers in a twist, but you've better things to do than abuse me husband." She took him by the arm and guided him toward the back door, lowering her voice. "Get upstairs and tell her g'nite. And none of your fiddling. She needs to rest."

Dar stepped inside and tapped an ale, stalling for time.

It will not do any good going to her in a fury.

Once in the bedroom, he found her asleep. Still wired from the argument, he set the mug on the bedside table and walked out onto the balcony. A flight should help clear his mind. His massive wings fanned out, lifting him airborne in a single flap. He circled around, pleased to see the partiers still at it.

Free from the tethers of the world, he allowed his mind to drift. In time, his thoughts came back to the evening's events.

I almost lost it tonight. Too many would have been hurt if Spirit had not been there. Is Inferno right? Am I to blame for all that has befallen Etain? Had I avoided this realm, would Midir have let her be?

After circling the estuary, he landed on the shore, watching the moonlight dance on the rippling water.

I doubt it. I could end this tonight. "But she isn't ready," he said to himself. *If I fail, it will come down to her to defeat him.* He resolved to endure whatever Inferno or his clansmen threw at him. "For you, *mo chuisle*, I will suffer anything."

"Bloody hell." Inferno cursed at the knock on the bedroom door. Rising from his warm, comfortable bed, and padding barefoot across the room, he opened the door. His angered look softened seeing her face. "What's wrong, lass?"

"I've looked everywhere. There's no sign of him." Etain looked from Inferno to Spirit, who had joined them at the door. "Did he say anything?"

"I take it yer talking about that bleedin' demon. Maybe he's not as stupid as I thought," Inferno mumbled, heading back to bed.

Spirit sighed. "Short-lived truce. No, love. Last we saw, he was on his way up to you."

Etain slipped past Spirit, going after Inferno. She grabbed his upper arm. "What did you say to him?"

"What did *I* say to *him*?" he echoed. "Ya should be worried about what *he* said to *me*."

She blinked, unsure of what he meant, tightening her grip. "Inferno, this is the man I love."

"Ya should let that one go, lass. I told him to get the hell out."

"He would never leave me. Not now, not ever." She released him and turned away.

"You answer me something," he demanded, rubbing his arm. "Have you been with him?"

"How could you do this to me? Why?" she muttered on her way to the door.

"You didn't answer me, girl," he bellowed. "Have you been with him?"

She turned, a dangerous glint in her eye. "I am no girl. What I do with the man I love is none of your business. If he's gone, I will *never* forgive you." She slammed the door with her exit.

Spirit spied the bruises already forming on her husband's arm. "You're pushing too hard." Upon closer examination, she found four tiny punctures on the underside. "I'll not have her disappearing on us like the last time because of your bull head. Let it be, love."

The fire in his eyes burned bright. "Ya heard it as well as I did. She damn well admitted it. Let him come back." His hatred for Dar was clear in his voice. "I'm gonna kill him before his bastard brother has the chance."

A hard slap across his face silenced the rant. "Do you care nothing for anything other than your infuriating pride? Have you thought about what it would mean for me or Etain if you two should cross swords? What about the children, the clan? One of you would end up dead. It pains me to say, but I'm of a mind it wouldn't be Dar. *That* would start a bloody war amongst the Alamir. Something none of us needs, especially with the *Bok* lurking about."

She took a deep breath, closing her eyes, then opened them. "Etain's a woman now. Respect the choices she makes, even if you don't agree." She walked to her side of the bed, slipping between the covers. "In the morning, you will apologize to Dar and talk as civilized men…if either of you know what civilized is."

Dar quietly touched down on the balcony, then shifted back to his Krymerian form. As he walked into the room, a stern voice surprised him. "Where have you been?"

He looked up, further surprised by her nakedness.

By the gods, she is beautiful.

"I could not sleep."

"And?" she asked, hands on her hips, sauntering closer.

He licked his lips, his eyes taking in the whole of her...the perfect breasts, the sway of her hips and graceful curve into muscular thighs, the triangle of soft hair in unexpected silver. His gaze came back to her altered violet eyes. "I needed to clear my head."

"Clear your head?" She stood before him, luscious and irresistible, flushed with anger

There were no accusations made, but he felt something had come between them. "I didn't do it."

"There was an argument." Her hands glided over his torso to his shoulders. "I want to know what happened."

He submitted to her authority, dropping to his knees. With the face of a chastised child, he gazed into her beautiful demon eyes and told her of the heated exchange with Inferno.

"There is no excuse for my actions. Can you forgive me?"

One hand traveled along his shoulder into his thick, brown hair. Gripping a handful, she pulled his head back. "I thought you'd left me."

"You know me better than that."

"I thought I knew Inferno, too." She pulled his head back farther. "He thinks I've given myself to you." She leaned over him, bringing her face close to his. "How shall I punish you for such behavior?"

Despite his best efforts, a smirk came to his lips. "Any way you wish, milady." His balls tightened in expectation, his cock straining for release. Her touch was electric. "I am at your mercy."

She straightened, looking down at him as he caressed the curve of her thighs up to her hips. Holding her gaze, he explored the firmness of her bare bottom, squeezing each rounded cheek, loving the suppleness of her flesh. Encouraged, he placed soft kisses over her lower belly, moving down to the sensuous nexus between her thighs, his tongue exploring the outer lips before slipping between, teasing, savoring the salty taste of her. He held her fast, enjoying her shivers, her fingers tangled in his hair.

Standing, his body close to hers, he unbuttoned his shirt from the top as she worked from the bottom, letting it fall to the floor, all the while maneuvering toward the bed. A playful push had her on her back. The admiration in her eyes encouraged him as he opened his pants, revealing his desire. She lifted a shapely leg, running a toe down his muscular frame. Dar caught her by the ankle and engaged in an assault of feathery kisses down the length of her leg to the inside of her thigh. Her sighs told him of her enjoyment, but he would hear her giggle now and then when he found a ticklish spot.

Ready for more, he leaned over, a hand on either side of her, suspended for a moment, and peered into the windows of her soul. What he saw changed his outlook. He rolled onto his side, lying next to her.

She faced him, confused. "I'm supposed to be punishing *you*, not the other way around."

"What are you up to, Etain?"

"I'm trying to have a pleasant tryst with my lover." She smiled, tossing her hair back.

He smiled briefly. "Is this little stunt for my benefit…" He raised a brow, "or Inferno's?"

"It's not a stunt," she said, trailing her hand down his torso. "I'm taking control of my life."

"I see." He caught her hand in his. "Control."

She didn't seem deterred by his hesitation. "Is that going to be a problem?"

"It could be."

"How so?" she asked, moving her body closer to his.

"After our conversation about Inferno and betrayal…" Her warmth intoxicated him, the brush of irresistible nipples across his flesh and her musky scent was all the more distracting. His body was clearly not concerned about her reasons for the change of heart, and his mind was not far behind. He lifted her hand to his lips, whispering kisses along her knuckles, looking into her eyes. "Have you come to an understanding with him?"

Her seductive gaze hardened as she snatched her hand from his grip and sat up.

The impact of the loss of their connection made him close his eyes, clenching his bottom lip between his teeth.

"Brick walls understand nothing, and there's no reasoning with one, either," she said, her back to him. "He treats me like a child." She pushed at her hair. "It'd be nice if he'd show a little faith in me and trust I know what I'm doing."

Dar came up, his passions cooled, his pants securely buttoned. Not that he did not want her. By the stars, he wanted her, but not like this, the defiant child. It was no wonder Inferno felt protective of her. In some ways, she was still a child, but best not put it to her in those words.

"Perhaps, with a little more time, he will see the woman you have become, *mo chuisle*," he said, tracing a finger along her shoulder and down her arm.

She shrugged the same shoulder and sighed. "A little more time, says the Krymerian who's over two hundred years old. But you're right. Being impetuous isn't going to win his blessings." She gave him a sideways glance. "Picking fights doesn't help, either."

"Aye, but I do love a good fight," he said in an effort to lighten the mood.

"Bloody man," she said in jest.

Hearing her laugh was music to his ears. "Let's not worry about Inferno tonight. You have a busy day tomorrow and should get some sleep."

"Oh, well… Okay," she said, looking rather uncertain of what to do. "You should, too. I guess I'll go."

His arm went around her waist and he pushed her into the covers. "Sleep will be impossible if you are not here with me."

"Dar, it's rather apparent it'll be impossible *with* me here," she said, glancing down.

He grinned, wrapping his arms around her. "Do not underestimate the power of a Krymerian lord. We can be fierce in our convictions."

"For both our sakes, I hope you and your…Southern lord share the same convictions."

Up hours before sunrise and dressed for the day's training, Dar took Etain into his arms. "I have a surprise for you this morning." He laughed. "Don't look at me like that. I promise, you will not regret it. First, you must make a choice."

"Really, Dar? This early in the morning?" She tried to stifle a yawn, failing miserably.

He continued to smile. "We either go to my home world…or wake Spirit."

She rolled her eyes. "Great. A choice between hell," she said, drawing a raised brow from the Krymerian, which she purposely ignored, "or disturbing a sleeping mage. Between the two, I'd just as soon not go back to your place…ever."

"Then Spirit it is. As a powerful mage, she should have plenty of blood rubies on hand. We will need three before the sun rises." Dar nudged her toward the door. "Can you get them now, so we can be ready in time? Tell her they will be replaced once I have a chance to return home."

"She may not appreciate having her sleep interrupted after a late night." Undaunted, his smile shined even brighter. She ran a hand through her hair. "Fine. If I'm not back by sunrise…run."

Her first destination was Faux's room, where Spirit usually started her days. Quietly opening the door, she peeked in, finding her right where she knew she would. "*Bore da*, Spirit. After yesterday's party, I can't believe you're up."

"*Bore da*, lass." She smiled, busy smoothing the covers around the sleeping girl. "Old habits… You've a rosy glow about you this fine morning. I'd say the rest did you good."

Etain felt a flush in her cheeks. "Oh, yes. Yes, a very good rest indeed."

"Glad to know Dar heeded my warning."

She lifted a hand to run through her hair, but thought better of it and let it drop to her side. "I have a favor to ask. Do you have three blood rubies we can use? Dar says he'll replace them as soon as he can."

Done with her patient, she gave her a long look. "Three blood rubies? What're you planning to conjure?"

"I don't know," she shrugged. "Dar says it's a surprise, and he needs them before sunrise."

"I do happen to have three such stones, but I must know what they'll be used for," Spirit said. "You stay here with Faux while I have a chat with the man. Is he in his room?"

"No. Mine."

She raised a brow. "Hmph. Stay here until I get back."

Coming to Etain's bedroom door, which was slightly ajar, she heard something fall to the floor, followed by words in a language she didn't recognize, but was certain they were of a profane nature. His tone was unmistakable. She tapped lightly on the door.

"Come in, *mo chuisle*. We must get going," he said, his back to her.

"Sorry, love. It's only me."

He turned. "Oh, Spirit. I thought you were Etain. Good morning."

"Morning. I asked her to stay with Faux while we have a private word."

"Please allow me to apologize for last night. It is not my habit to show such disregard to those who have been nothing but generous with their friendship and home."

"Apology accepted. No great harm done, aye? The day was anything but normal. Now, these rubies you're wanting… What's to be done with them?"

"I plan to crush them." At the look on her face, he held out the golden scabbard and motioned for her to draw the sword. "Tell me what you think of it. The crystal has been in my family for many generations."

Her eyes widened. "This has to be the biggest crystal I've ever seen in me life."

"What you hold in your hands is very old…and powerful. There's not another like it. I made it for her as proof of my love." Her eyes glistened as he continued. "The rubies will bond the sword to her. Once bound, she will have access to generations of VonNeshta knowledge, and after she has learned how to tap into it, she will have no equal."

"Heavens, Dar. All you have to do is tell her your feelings. There's no need for fancy gifts. If I thought it'd make a difference with me husband, I'd tell you to give it to *him*." She slid the sword back into its sheath. "There's a fine line between protection and possession."

"Faults I seem to share with your husband. It is not my intent to be an overbearing oaf," he said, giving her a smile. "Our new relationship has me acting like a schoolboy. I'll try to keep myself in check."

"I'd think twice about your training tactics, too. Inferno went mental yesterday."

"Spirit, I have felt protective of her since we first met, and I will protect her with my life, if necessary. None of you truly appreciates what my brother is capable of. I pushed her hard, and I intend to push harder. She has to know how to fight him. I cannot…*we* cannot lose her to him."

She gave him a thoughtful nod. "Just remember to treat her with the respect she deserves; otherwise, it won't be just your brother you have to worry about." At the door, she said, "I'll get the stones and have Etain bring them to you. Oh, and do me a favor today. Stay out of Inferno's path. Give him time to cool off."

"I shall, milady. Thank you."

"Between you and me, Inferno would have done the same in your place."

A curious Etain returned to Dar. "The rubies are crushed, so you don't have to waste any ti…" She saw the great sword strapped across his back. "What's that for?"

He picked up the crystal sword and tossed it to her. "Let's go." Dar whisked her into his arms and transported them to the inlet shore. As the skies lightened, he cast the ruby dust into the air, chanting, "*Ghrian mór, solas ár paidreacha le do ghlóir* (Great sun, light our prayers with your glory)." The rich red dust swirled above their heads.

"Come here, Etain. Point your blade into the sun." Drawing the crystal sword, she faced the oncoming light, keenly aware of Dar's body pressed to hers. "Keep your eyes to the east as the sun rises and repeat what I say." He took one of her hands and turned it over, opening a shallow cut along the palm. "*M'fhuil a thabhairt mé dhuit* (My blood I give thee)." Repeating his words, she watched her blood drift up, mingling with the ruby dust.

He whispered in her ear. "The next thing I say will only be in your mind, but you must say it out loud." They waited for the sun to peek over the horizon. "Be warned. Afterward, your mind may be flooded with images. Do not be alarmed if it happens. It is all part of the spell. I will be here to catch you."

As the first rays of the new morning sparked on the blade, Dar mentally recited the words. Etain called out. "*Nim'Na'Sharr, ceangal mé dhuit dom* (*Nim'Na'Sharr*, I bind thee to me)." The blood and rubies swirled together, flowing down, circling around her. At last, the mix settled on the blade from tip to hilt. "What is this?"

He placed a finger to her lips and spoke to her mind. *You are now one with Nim'Na'Sharr, my love. Her knowledge is your knowledge. My family is your family.*

Hundreds of images poured into her mind… Krymerian lore,

family histories, battles fought, how the Krymerians wielded a sword, effective attacks and appropriate defenses, the history of the crystal. So much information came so fast, Etain used his body as support until she could absorb it. Once satisfied she could stand alone, he backed away, presenting his blade.

"Let's test your newfound knowledge, shall we?" His first moves were slow, a volley of attacks she blocked, scoring a hit or two of her own. "Well done," he said, proud of her accomplishment. Switching hands, he attacked with another series of slashes and thrusts. Once again, she blocked the moves, his last being a low jab she countered with ease.

Beaming with pride, she looked up in time to see his fist just before it slammed into her jaw, snapping her head to the side. "Good block, but you took your eyes off me. Never take your eyes off your opponent. It leaves you open."

She swiped the blood from her lip, planting her feet. "Got it."

He moved in with a new sequence of attacks. Defeated at each turn, he swung around with a great slash of his sword, which she blocked. Anticipating his next move, she deflected the fist from the side, but was too slow in dodging the boot in the chest, knocking her to the ground. Dar charged, not giving her time to recover, scoring hits here and there, but receiving several in return.

As she managed to work her feet underneath her, he slipped up from behind and whispered in her ear. "You let them die."

"What?" Unnerved, she watched him spin and come back with another strike.

"You ran like a scared little girl," he growled. "You did *nothing* to save them."

His breath was heavy against her skin. Anger blasted through her like a red-hot flame, her senses honing-in on his position. She snapped her head back, connecting with his nose. The bone snapped, pouring blood over his mouth and chin.

He laughed, spitting blood. "Much better." Leading her through a new array of moves, his taunts continued. "All you had to do was say yes to the darkness."

Something snapped inside her. All cylinders were ablaze in her brain, and her vision sharpened. Her strength and speed increased, matching Dar blow for blow.

"Shut up!" Electrical charges rolled over her skin.

He matched her attacks with perfect blocks. Ducking one slash, he moved behind her, opening a straight cut down each shoulder.

"Such a loving daughter you were, leaving them to their fate. You ran like a coward."

"I ran because they were dead." Electrical charges united into a blue glow surrounding her form, her eyes piercing into his.

Seeing her reaction to his words, he threw his last taunt. "As for your sister, Faux... I have special plans for her."

"If you go near her, I will cut out your bloody fucking heart," she spat, swinging out with her blade.

She felt a surge in her blood. Great leather wings extended from her back, their fleshy membrane a deep crimson, darkening into black. Razor-sharp talons extended from her knuckles, forcing her to drop *Nim*. She staggered back, trying to take it all in.

Dar advanced again, setting his blade to work, opening cut after cut over her arms and legs to slow her movements before she could adjust. Dropping his sword, he engaged his own demon. Her first attempts at warding off his attacks proved clumsy, but her hit ratio improved with every move. Matching him blow for blow, long gashes appeared on his body. They were evenly matched, but for one exception. Dar was in control. As Etain reached for his throat, he grabbed her wrist, slammed her face down on the ground, and jabbed a foot into her back. The demon grasped each wing, pushing and pulling at the same time. With a quick jerk, bones in both wings snapped, accompanied by a howling screech.

Her broken wings crumpled to the ground. Dar grabbed a handful of silver hair and pulled hard, a rapid double punch knocking her unconscious. Stepping away, he transformed back to his Krymerian form and bent over her. A gentle touch to each wing, combined with a healing chant, mended the broken bones and repaired the damage. Another chant calmed the demon within her. He carried her to the water's edge and with her safe within his arms, he splashed the cool liquid on her face. She awoke.

"Not a bad start, *mo chuisle*. You did well your first time as a demon, but you were not in control."

"Huh? Demon?"

"Aye. You can call on the demon at will, but you must be in control…of the demon and your anger."

"Maybe if you wouldn't piss me off…," she said, pushing away. "Your words were cruel and unnecessary."

"It was the only way to bring it out completely. I've seen the stirring behind your eyes for days now. I had to be sure."

"Being a demon was never part of the plan. I suppose I have you to thank for this exciting bit of news."

"The blood of Kaos is strong. I can teach you how to use it."

"Good, then I can rip your throat out if you ever speak to me that way again."

Acknowledging the threat with a nod, he returned *Nim'Na'Sharr* to her mistress. They resumed their sparring, trading sword strikes for the rest of the day with no further insults or cruel remarks.

As darkness fell, Dar called it a day. "Shall we go for a swim?" He put away his blade, stripped, and ran into the water.

She watched from the shore, considering whether to join him or take his clothes and leave him bare ass naked. Knowing he would have no qualms about walking back to the castle in all his glory, she wriggled out of her leathers and swam out to him. The refreshing water cooled her skin and, in turn, helped quiet her emotions.

"Teach me to turn."

"Close your eyes," he said, intertwining his fingers with hers. "Envision your anger."

She peeked out from one eye. "Why?"

He gave her a stern look. "Keep your eyes closed. Listen to my words. Do as I say. The demon comes from deep inside, much like your anger."

She tried again. Her mind went in different directions, not settling on any one thing, constantly on the move, flitting from one thing to the next. She sighed. "It's no use, Dar. I can't get it to-"

"Think on the dark thing that took your family, left you alone, cold, hungry."

A spark…small, yet bright.

"See your anger for what it is, feed it, give it what it needs to grow."

A weekend camping in the woods came to her. Her dad teaching her how to build a fire, dried grass, bits of sticks, striking a match, then blowing gently, fanning the infant flame, feeding it, watching it grow until it was ready for the larger pieces of wood that would keep it going.

"Think of your father, dying before your eyes. Your mother, cut down without a care. Your brother, lost forever."

Etain turned her thoughts to the one moment in her life that always stirred the hate and anger she kept hidden away. In her mind's eye, she relived their murders, watched their blood darkening the ground. The red eyes of the assassin glowed bright in her memory. She felt the anger rise inside her, hot and undeniable.

"Let it rise up, fill you with its heated glory. Embrace it. Give it life, but do not let it take control."

She fanned the flame, its fiery fingertips licking at the tree branches in her head. The hate soon flushed her skin. Reminding herself to keep control, she brought it down.

"When it feels right, envision your demon. Violet eyes of fire. Crimson wings ready to take flight. Talons…long, white, and lethal. These are your gifts. Keep them in check." Heeding his words, she swallowed hard, slowing the beat of her angry heart. "Command the demon, make it obey."

Her wings extended, arcing over the water, her frame growing to six feet. Lifting her hands from the water, she admired the sharp talons with her amplified vision. Fascinated, she looked at Dar.

"Now you."

He shifted into his demonic form. "Is that bet-"

Her lips crushed to his, cutting off his words. Long legs wrapped around him, her talons retracting. She pulled back, a seductive smile on her lips.

"I am not Etain."

"Are you not?" he asked, his wings hovering above the water, keeping them afloat.

"No," she said, a pulse between her legs throbbing in time with her heart. "You are not Dar."

"Then who are we, my love?"

She slid a hand beneath the water, running her fingers down his side and cupping a firm butt cheek. She sighed with devilish intent. "We are Krymerian demons, destined for an eternity of lust, love, and decadence. We share our blood..." She gave him a long, heated kiss, "and our bodies in celebration of the fight we face tomorrow."

"Etain-"

"No," she said, placing a finger over his lips. "I am a goddess and you are my god. We are not of this earth." Her hand came between them, taking a firm hold of his cock. "In this moment, we are free to be who we want to be. I want to be yours...heart, soul, and body."

"*Mo chuisle*, demon or not, it is your first time. It may not be-"

"Shhhh," she whispered. "It will be what we wish it to be."

His arm went around her, holding her tight. She moaned as his fingers slipped through her wetness, stroking the spot that ached for his touch.

"It will hurt, but only for a moment."

She didn't care. She wanted him, needed to be one with him. Her body vibrated with desire, aching to feel him inside. Safe within his gaze, she welcomed him into her fevered sanctuary, their wings fluttering with every thrust.

13

CROSSFIRE

Night had fallen before the lovers made their way back to the castle. Dar and Etain heard the shouting long before they came within sight of the house. He was reluctant to leave her alone, but agreed she had more practice at handling Inferno. They parted with a kiss.

"Call me if he gets out of hand."

"Don't worry," she said, confident.

He watched her until she opened the back door to the kitchen. It went quiet with her first step inside.

He moved toward the door with every intention of following her, but made himself stop.

Give her a chance. This is her family. She's not in danger.

Dar imagined the scene. Etain's comforting smile. Her patient explanation of how things had changed. Inferno's quiet acceptance of their newfound love. He thought it must be going well. There were no explosions or loud denunciations. He smiled to himself.

Well done, mo-

Never underestimate your opponent.

Inferno's voice boomed through the back door, demanding the whereabouts of the "bleedin' demon", spouting his intention of putting "the bastard in his place".

Taking it as his cue, Dar burst through the door. "That's enough. All this yelling will not solve anything," he said, going to Etain and acting as her shield.

Seeing Dar shirtless, Inferno's eyes widened. He flashed a scornful look at Etain. "Bloody fucking wanker!" Flames lit in his eyes. "I'll be sending ya back to the hell ya came from."

Dar held up both hands, ready to push back if things escalated. "Inferno, think about what you're doing. Etain or Spirit could get caught in the crossfire."

"By the looks of things…" He pointed a flaming finger at Etain, "I'd say our girl's been caught up in yer lustful crossfire already." The decibel level rose, his enflamed gaze on Dar. "What the bloody hell gave you the right? This ends right now. Let's take it-"

Etain stepped from behind Dar. Her wings rustled, settling on her back. She waited, obviously affected by Spirit and Inferno's shocked reactions. Dar smiled, his expression a mix of pride and satisfaction. "There will be no crossfire," she said, breaking the silence. "This is who I am now. There's nothing you or anyone else can do to change it."

Although he had witnessed her transformation earlier, Inferno stood with his mouth open, staring first at Etain, then Dar.

"Yer takin' the mick!" His flames subdued, but didn't extinguish. "Nothing can be done, my arse. Once this bloody bastard's dead, you'll be our girl again." He turned and stormed out of the room.

Etain looked at Spirit. "I'm sorry." A tear ran down her cheek as she and Dar returned to their regular forms. Without a word, Spirit eyed Etain, shot Dar a contemptuous look, then followed her husband.

Dar brought Etain close. "Don't cry, my love. Let's go for an evening flight. Give him time to cool down. Come…" He tugged her out the back door. "You'll find it cathartic." In a matter of moments, the demon couple was airborne, sweeping out over the sea, the moon their only witness.

***

Just after sunrise, she woke to find Dar nestled in her arms. A sudden flush filled her heart as she kissed the top of his head. She slipped farther down and kissed his lips. Groggy blue eyes opened.

"Hi," she whispered. "How's my magnificent warrior this morning?"

Growling, he pulled her on top of him. "Hungry for my warrior vixen."

She giggled, making a poor attempt of fighting him off. "Does it ever stop?"

"I hope not." He flashed the smile that made her weak.

She caressed his cheek and kissed him again. "I hope not, too. However-"

"No. Not this morning."

She slipped from his clutches and rolled off the bed. "*However*, my lecherous demon, you have other important business this morning. It's time you had a heart-to-heart with Inferno."

He mimicked her signature eye roll and placed a pillow over his head. "After last night? The man wants my heart on a platter and my head on a pike. There is no reasoning with him."

She pulled at the pillow. "Come on, Dar. I can't have my two favorite men at odds. We have to be on the same..." She noticed something unusual on his chest. "I don't recall you having a tattoo."

He tossed the pillow aside and glanced down, touching the mark, a golden sun, its rays alive with the passion shared between them. "I didn't do it," he laughed, looking up at her. "This, *mo chuisle,* was all *your* doing." He nodded at her. "Look down."

"Huh?" she muttered, doing just that. "What the hell?"

Dar came up fast, grabbing her around the waist, rolling her body over his. "It proves we are one and belong together."

"I don't understand."

He traced the outline of the emblazoned sun on her chest. "I don't understand it, either. I have heard tales, but haven't seen it with my own eyes…until today. You have branded me as yours, and yours I shall always be."

Her eyes widened at a sudden realization. "Dar, did we have these last night? Could this be why Inferno was so furious? Cause he was bloody well pissed off before I turned."

"So much happened so fast, I didn't notice."

"Me, either, and afterward, well…" Her gaze softened. She felt a warmth rush through her, giving rise to an unquenchable desire. "We were…preoccupied."

Etain recognized the glint in his eye.

"Exactly what I was thinking." Dar claimed her mouth with his, setting her on fire. Breathless, her body melted as he tasted his way to stiff nipples, his hand conducting a thorough exploration over her skin and down between her thighs, eliciting a guttural moan. An alarm rang in a small part of her brain, warning her of…something. What? She couldn't remember. She was safe in his capable arms, under his delicious control. But… God, who cared? This time, she didn't mind giving in to him.

Holy hell, how could such… What's the word? I don't know. I don't… Oh god!

She clung to him, her eyes rolling back. Her heart felt like it was in her throat. She bit her bottom lip, unable to breathe. All she knew at this moment was pure ecstasy.

Once the glow subsided, Etain picked up her clothes, blowing out a disgusted breath. *I don't know if I can stand to wear these one more time.* She considered her options, donning the outfit for one last excursion. Having instructed Dar to find Inferno in the hopes of reconciliation, she went in search of Spirit, peeking in on Faux and, as suspected, found the mage. She hoped last night's events hadn't affected their relationship.

"*Bore da,* Spirit. How's she doing?"

"*Bore da.* Our little patient is much better. I think the poultice has finally drawn out the poison. We should have our feisty Faux back in no time."

Etain breathed a sigh of relief, pushing a few stray hairs from the sleeping girl's forehead. "Thank goodness. We needed some good news."

"That we did, lass."

She tentatively broached the subject of the previous night's events. "Spirit, I'm truly sorry for-"

"What's done is done. Although I saw it coming, I admit it was a shock. I hope you had the good sense not to lose your virginity under this roof." Her gaze demanded confirmation.

"Nowhere near," Etain admitted.

Relief showed on Spirit's face. "Small favors. Inferno's fuming." She offered a warm smile. "But the mark you share changes things…for me anyway. It doesn't mean he'll accept it."

"Hells bells," she muttered, helping Spirit smooth out the sheets on the bed as best they could. "I'm afraid I sent the lamb to meet the lion."

"How so, love?"

"Well…" She bit her bottom lip. "I told Dar to make nice with Inferno."

They held each other's gaze for a moment. The next, they erupted into laughter.

"Goddess of us all, lass. It'll be the fifth of November early this year."

Etain covered her mouth, hoping to muffle her laugh so as not to disturb the sleeping Faux. "Can you imagine the fireworks?"

Spirit shook her head. "That's a show I don't mind missing."

"True, but I hope they can come to some sort of resolution."

"They're men, love. They'll do whatever they're gonna do, whether we like it or not."

Etain shrugged. "Aside from that, I wanted to see if you'd help me with something."

"Did you now?"

The women stepped into the hallway.

"In case you haven't noticed, I've been wearing the same clothes forever and I can't practice in that beautiful outfit you gave me."

"I know how you love your leathers. Since I don't have anything to match 'em, I kept me mouth shut." The women headed in the direction of Spirit's bedroom. "What's running round in that head of yours?"

Excited to share her idea, she explained. "I have a closet full of clothes back home in the human realm. I thought I'd pop over, pick up a few items, and be back before Dar noticed." She placed a hand on Spirit's arm. "I was hoping you'd go with me."

"Hmmm." She stroked her chin, contemplating. "Faux's doing well, Inferno's busy with the building, and I've not been to your place. I could use a short break. Give me a minute to change."

"I'll meet you downstairs." She turned to go, but Spirit caught her by the arm.

"You stay right here. There's one thing we need to take care of before we go." Etain gave her a questioning look. "You'll see." She disappeared into her bedroom, reemerging a few moments later. "I know it's a quick trip, but leaving those two old roosters alone makes me nervous."

"Alone? Your whole clan's down there."

"Etain, I've only just been able to keep those two from killing each other." She turned toward the opposite end of the hall. "If last night wasn't bad enough, you should've seen the looks they gave Linq after you left the party. They looked ready to tear his head off." Spirit stopped.

A puzzled Etain waited, wondering if the wall before them bore any significance. Spirit winked and waved her hand, murmuring words Etain couldn't make out. A door appeared, opening to a flight of stairs.

"I never noticed this before," Etain said, peering up into the darkness.

"No reason to." Spirit motioned for her to follow. "This is my private room where I prepare most of me special blends and brews. I keep the door concealed so no one comes nosing about."

"Spirit?"

"Hmmm?" Coming to another door, she reached into her pocket and brought out a key to open the lock. Two dormer windows flooded a fair-sized room with light.

"You said *they*." Spirit opened one window, while Etain opened the other. "I assume you mean Dar and Inferno?" Etain wandered about the room, noting the rows of shelves on every wall, each one lined with an assortment of bottles, vials, and books. Hanging from the rafters and perfuming the air were bunches of drying herbs tied together with bits of string.

"Aye," Spirit said, choosing several bottles from the shelves, placing them on the table.

"Why would they turn on Linq? I thought he was a friend." Etain watched her blend several herbs together.

"Lass," she began, handing a small vial to Etain, "hold this. When I tell you to, pour it in, slowly. You know Inferno doesn't like anyone getting in his business, especially when he's angry, friend or no."

"Yeah, so?" Holding the vial ready, she waited as Spirit pounded and stirred, breaking the leaves down into a fine powder. She then split the mixture into two bowls.

"Linq was trying to keep the peace, but they were determined to have a go at each other." She widened her eyes. "And with the whole clan standing there a'watchin'."

"Why can't he just be happy for me?"

Spirit gave her a scathing look. "You listen to me, lassie, and listen good." Surprised, Etain stepped back. "Inferno is fierce in his loyalties and doesn't take kindly to others messin' with his family." The more she said, the stronger her accent became, the spatula in her hand as threatening as Etain's own crystal sword. "And in case ya hadn't noticed, missy, yer family. I can turn me eye knowing how things betwixt a man and woman be their concern, but Inferno sees ya as his sister… No, more like a daughter." The hand dropped to her side and she squared her shoulders, head high. "He doesn't like the way Dar treats ya, and I'm beginning to agree with him, especially after seeing what I saw last night."

Etain blinked.

Spirit pointed to the vial in her hand. "Pour that in this bowl after my third stir round." Picking up the bowl, she moved close to give Etain easier access. "Here's one, two, three. Pour it all in." She continued stirring until it turned into a paste. "Grab two of those small jars and place them in front of me. Bring the red string, too." Content with her mixture, she placed the bowl on the table. Twisting the cap off each small jar, she pulled Etain to her side. "This one is for Inferno, and that one's for Dar."

Spirit took two small plastic bags from her pocket. Each contained tufts of brown hair. One, *Dar* written across it, she handed to Etain, placing another that said *Inferno* in front of her. She winked. "I took liberties…just in case." She picked up another bottle and placed one rose petal next to each jar. "Here's a bit of amber, a piece of paper, and some red string. Now, do as I do and repeat the words I say, except you'll say Dar where I say Inferno. Aye?"

"Aye."

With a circle of protection invoked, she instructed Etain to draw a gingerbread-type doll on her paper and name it Dar. "Tell the paper doll you're disappointed in his actions against Inferno and he will not use his demon powers against him, no matter what. I'll do the same, but switch the names and substitute Alamir powers for demon." Each quietly spoke to their doll. Etain mimicked Spirit, scooping out a dab of the paste and spreading it over the doll. They then placed the amber, rose petals, and a pinch of the dry mixture into the jar as they commanded, "Dar/Inferno, I bind you from harming Inferno/Dar with your demon/Alamir powers."

They folded the dolls into a square and wrapped them with the red string. With each wrapping, they said, "Once around, securely bound. Now's the time for cooling down." Knotting the string three times, they placed the dolls in the jars and added a teaspoon of oil. "I place sacred oil all around you, about you, and below you to make your path slippery should you violate the Law of Rede."

Etain followed Spirit's lead, filled her jar three-quarters full of water, then walked to a refrigerator in the far corner of the room. The women placed their jars inside the freezer as they continued to chant. "Time to chill out. I place around you, Inferno/Dar, the crystal sphere of the Mother's Orb to hold you in a positive light. I ask the Lady to empower this spell and insure it's working to the best of all concerned. As I will it, so mote it be."

Spirit closed the freezer door. "Well done. The worst trouble they'll get into will be either their fists or the swords. Let's straighten up and be on our way." Putting away all evidence, they locked up, then made one more detour by Etain's room.

"We can leave from here." Strapping on *Nim*, Etain caught the concerned look on Spirit's face. "If I've learned anything from all the knocks Dar's given me, it's to be prepared." Standing in the middle of the room, they clasped hands. Blue electrical charges surrounded the women, and they disappeared.

14

A COUPLE OF JARVLEN

Etain and Spirit emerged within the walls of Etain's home. "You stay here while I clear the house."

Spirit took a seat. "I don't know why you're worried. You've been gone for a while. Who would come looking around here?"

Etain hollered back. "Gotta be sure." Walking into the living room, she gave the all clear. "I'm gonna run to my room and throw some things in a bag. Make yourself at home. It won't take long." She disappeared down the hallway.

Spirit roamed into the kitchen, rummaging through the cupboards, not finding much in the way of groceries. In the refrigerator, she discovered an out of date carton of milk. "Lass, do you never clean things out?" She poured the contents down the kitchen sink with one hand, holding her nose with the other. Bored with her exploration, she walked toward the living room with thoughts of rifling through Etain's music collection.

Coming into the room, she was surprised by a man, his back to her. She wondered how he'd known where to find them.

"Dar? What're you doi-" A foul laugh cut her words short. "Oh. It's you. Dar should've killed you whilst he had the chance."

"Come now. I thought the Welsh were a welcoming sort."

"I'm not Welsh."

"That explains it then." His hand flashed out, blasting her with a power ball, hurling her back into the kitchen. When she hit the wall, everything went dark.

Midir's black cloak lapped at his boots as he strolled down the hallway. He knew where to find her. He could feel the heat of her blood, as though it were his own. Glancing into each room along his way, he savored the simple, yet tasteful design of the home she had made for herself, giving him new insights into her psyche. Coming to the last door, he found her foraging through an open dresser drawer. He leaned against the doorjamb, entertained by the view of her ass.

"Hey, Spirit, would you mind checking the closet?" Etain waved a hand in the general direction, the other busy sorting through her things.

"Why, yes, I *would* mind." Midir grinned when she whirled around, happy he caught her off-guard. "I'm quite busy appreciating the view."

"Midir."

"Welcome home, little darlin'," he greeted in an uncharacteristic southern drawl.

"Where's Spirit?" She licked her lips.

"Poor girl is resting." His gaze roamed over her. "It will do her good."

"If she's hurt, you'll answer to me." Etain inched closer to the bed.

Midir drew his black sword. "I'm very much counting on it, milady. I plan on answering to you for many nights to come." He brandished the blade in her face, forcing her back against the dresser. "I have plans for us."

"Go away, Midir," she spat. "There's nothing here for you."

He came in close, dropping the sword to his side. "Women think they know what's best for a man," he said, inhaling her scent. "What I need…" Her breath was warm against his cheek, "and what I want…" He felt the radiant heat of her body, "have gone beyond anything you would understand." He grabbed a handful of her hair, jerking her head to look at him. "My want goes far beyond my need, but I'm confident you will fulfill both of them beyond my expectations." He savaged her mouth with his, further stimulated by the struggle in her eyes.

Midir pulled back, licking his lips. "You taste different." He spun around and walked to the other side of the room, muttering to himself. "I would know if he had."

Etain scrubbed at her mouth with the back of her hand. "All you know is force. You have no regard for free will."

He turned. "I am the king of free will, *mon petit*."

"Your own."

"Which is of the utmost importance, especially in this case," he said, a curious glint in his eye. "Why align yourself with him? He's done nothing but bring misery to your life."

"No, that would be *you*. Dar is my heart."

"Your *heart*?" His laugh was brutal. "It must be a black one indeed. There are things you don't know about him."

"There are things *you* don't know about *me*."

He moved to the four-poster bed and leaned against the column closest to *Nim'Na'Sharr*. "You've seen his demon side, haven't you? Felt the terror of watching him morph." He smiled, recognizing the slight change in her expression. "I bet you *didn't* know… He never sprouted wings until he shared blood with you." He waited a few moments to let the revelation sink in. "Even *I've* benefited from your little exchange." With that said, he removed his cloak, placing it on the bed. A pair of white leather wings extended from his back. He laughed at the horror in her eyes. "You see, *mon petit*, I know many things about you, things of which you have no knowledge, thanks to your coddling parents." Midir released his wings and put on the cloak. "But I will teach you. I've been planning this for a long time."

"I-I don't understand. A-as a child, he…" She thought hard, trying to remember the vision of Dar and Midir as boys. Dar had turned, killing that woman. But did he have wings? *I can't remember!*

"You let them die," Midir said, suddenly.

The words cut into her concentration, shattering her thoughts. "What?"

"You ran like a scared little girl," his voice, so similar to Dar's.

She held onto the dresser for support. "I…" Her thoughts tumbled, making her dizzy.

"Such a loving daughter, leaving them alone to die." A sly grin spread across his face. "You ran, and ran, and ran."

"How could you know?" Her thoughts spiraled, the past mixing with the present. "I was just a kid." *Could I have saved them? How?* Wretched eyes looked on a face so like Dar's, yet so different. *How does he know?*

"An excuse. You had power, even then."

"What?" She stared at him, eyes wide. "You *knew* me?"

"I remember the first day your mother brought you in. Your father was so proud, showing off his precious little empath. I felt it the moment you entered the room. Of course, your parents thought they knew how to play the game, thought they'd played me for a fool." She felt mesmerized by his gaze, swallowed up whole in their green depths. "I saw the potential in you. Such sensitivity and intelligence, not to mention your promised beauty." His twisted smile was more of a leer. "Which has been fulfilled many times over. Then, as if that weren't enough reason to acquire you, I came across the tale of a dragon warrior descended from Lyoness. A warrior with the promise to change everything."

Get it together, Etain. You know bullshit when you hear it. He's playing you.

The thought was enough to turn her fear into determination. Straightening her shoulders, she shifted her hips and raised her chin. "And you wonder why I chose Dar?"

Midir flashed a warning glare. "Your family was an obstacle easily removed."

"A demon killed my family."

"Zagan." The acid grin returned. "Quite the assassin." He eased himself down on the edge of the bed. "I hear Dar did him in."

Stop changing the game, damn you!

His voice was matter-of-fact. "Zagan was quick, clean, and professional. Unfortunately," he mused, "the job on your family wasn't so clean, but a couple of *jarvlen* fixed that." His casual air horrified her. "It was a means to an end. Strictly business."

Her arms fell to her sides, hands curling into fists. "The slaughter of my family was *business*?" The demon within yearned to lash out, her talons itching for release.

With a cavalier air, he rattled on. "Then there was that nasty business of Dar nearly slicing you in half." His smile, a tainted version of Dar's boyish grin, knocked the breath from her. "Let's be sensible about the whole affair. How could it have been him when he was too busy with his boy scout duties? What a gullible sod! His holier-than-thou attitude made it easy to phase in and lift the sword." In his excitement, he acted out the scene, ending with a javelin throw. "Never saw it coming." Her skin crawled, hearing his nearly maniacal laugh. "If that wall hadn't been there, who knows where you would have landed." He clapped his hands. "It was entertainment at its best."

Hearing the coldness in his voice, she couldn't believe his disregard for the precious lives he had destroyed. She sank to her knees, her vision blurred by tears.

"If you lived, I knew it would empower you. But Dar was there, wasn't he? A sucker for the down-and-out. He can't resist coming to the rescue. Never did I think he would share our blood." If possible, his dialogue became livelier as he walked to her and patted her on the head. "It was the boost needed to spark your powers into overdrive."

She suffered his words in pained silence.

"One of my favorites was when your... What do you call her? Your *sister?*" The man chuckled. "Think about it, *mon petit*. How can she be your sister when Dar is her sire?"

"No! Shut up, Midir! Shut up!"

He grabbed her by the chin, forcing her to look at him. "Surely you see it." He crouched down, green eyes piercing into hers. "Much as I hate to say it, the boy has style." He cocked his head. "Are you aware she carries his child? Yes, I see you are. *I* know because my sword vibrated from its life force." He caressed her cheek. "So smooth, so perfectly did her soft flesh part, taking in every inch."

She jerked away. "I can't believe you have any link to Dar."

Licking his lips, he straightened, walking back to the bed. "Where was I? Oh, yes, the day your *sister* mortally wounded you." He shook his head. "Etain, that was stupid. You're better than she is, yet you let her get the best of you. *Mon petit*, never be a doormat." A smile came to his lying lips. "On the bright side, it *did* lead you to becoming my Etain."

"I am *not* your Etain," she said, jaw clenched.

"Do you really think he's done with her?" He strode over to her, reached down with bruising speed, and yanked her up by her arm. "Hell, woman. Are you blind? Why do you think he keeps her around? If she's carrying his child, how long before you're discarded? I know my brother. He's not as honorable as he would have everyone believe. His loyalty will be with the mother of his child, not some vixen he's taken a fancy to."

"He loves me," she said, feeling like a child and, worse, sounding like one.

"He loves the chase. Once he's had you, he'll relegate you to guard duty…if he's smart. If not, he'll do away with you."

Again, her eyes moved to the bed. "He made the sword for me…to prove his love."

"Not another sword! The blackguard." He raised his hands in exasperation. "I've lost count of how many times he's used that one. You won't have it for long, *mon petit*. One morning, you will wake up and it will be gone, along with your lover. The sword is very effective in keeping his women compliant." His hot breath caressed her neck. "Now, I would make you my queen." Lustful lips trailed along her delicate skin. "Who do you think has taken care of you since you were set free?" Catching an earlobe in his teeth, he gingerly tugged, making her tremble.

She turned into his face. "Stop."

He traced a line down her neck with his finger, pulling the neckline of her shirt, exposing a soft shoulder. "Where's the dragon?"

She hadn't a clue what he was talking about, but said, "Replaced." His eyes followed hers to the ripped cloth just above her left breast. The shimmer enticed him to the exposed skin. As his hand neared the mark, a flash of golden fire flashed.

Eyes wide, he ripped the shirt from her body. "This can't be." Tattered pieces fell to the floor. "Stupid girl!"

"I told you I wasn't yours." She lashed out with a taloned hand, catching him across the chest.

He staggered back, surprised, but recovered quickly and came at her, tearing off his cloak. He slapped her, knocking her to her knees, and grabbed her by the throat. "I knew you tasted different." He dragged her onto the bed and straddled her hips. Dagger in hand, he traced the tip around the mark and along her ribs. "He had you in that shit castle of the Alamir, didn't he? The cursed protection spell kept it from me."

She spat in his face. "I will see you dead."

He slapped her again, splitting her lip. Curling her hand into a fist, she tried to hit him, but he pinned her arms against the bed.

"*I* am the one who made sure of your inheritance. Made sure everything your father owned was passed to you."

"You murdered my family!"

He pulled her arms down to her sides, holding them in place with his knees, then slapped her again. "How else would you have this house, your car, your life? Dar has done nothing but get in the way." She struggled to get free. His attack intensified until she lay unconscious, a fist to her jaw the deciding blow.

He pressed his body against her slack form. "I *will* have you, *mon petit*." Impertinent hands snaked over succulent flesh, raising gooseflesh on his arms. The mark over her left breast glowed in a threatening light. He forced himself to move away, trembling as he stood next to the bed. "Once we're in my realm, all this will be forgotten. I *will* remove that stain from your body." He smoothed his hair and straightened his clothes. "Since I can't have you at the moment, your little friend will do nicely. The power I take from her will be a welcome delight."

The green-eyed demon walked into the kitchen, expectant of his interlude with the mage, but the room was empty.

"Looking for me?" Spirit's voice dripped with contempt.

He whirled around, seeing a pulsating energy ball of green light in her hand. "I have a little present for you. Matches your bloody eyes." She released the ball and turned for a quick escape.

Midir dodged the blast by phasing out, immediately reappearing in her path. "Such impatience," he said, laughing at her shocked expression. "I love a forceful woman." With a slight move of his hand, he blasted her to the floor. "Let's see how forceful you are after I'm done with you."

———

With his first step, a surge of energy threw him back into the corner. He gazed up into the violet eyes of a demon, wings spread, talons at the ready. "You will not touch her."

He stared in amazed appreciation.

"Get out, Midir."

"Not without you." He turned his face to the heavens. "Thank you, Dar." He scrambled to his feet, drawing his sword. "As for you, my beauty…" He waved the blade in her face. "If you come to me, I'll forget about the mage. Otherwise, I fully intend to be satisfied, one way or another, before I leave."

"You won't get the chance." She lashed out, but Midir sidestepped just beyond the reach of her deadly talons.

A voice spoke to her, one she had never heard before.

Call to me, sweet lady. Dar has made me yours. Call to me. Let me be your vengeance.

Arm at her side, the talons retracted. "*Nim'Na'Sharr.*" The sword appeared in her hand, its crystal blade aglow with the same violet as Etain's eyes.

Midir held his black blade in front of him. "What is that?"

"You don't recognize it? Is this not *the* sword Dar bestows on all his ladies?" She took her stance, raising her blade. A shard of sunlight peeked through the curtains, glinting off the crystal blade, casting a rainbow of colors through the room. "She's quite lovely, don't you think?" Her wings arced up and snapped-in close to her body. "Were their wings as pretty as mine?" She whipped *Nim* through the air, slashing across and down, bringing her blade up, deflecting his attack. She ducked down and clipped his shins with the tip.

"You bitch!" he screamed, raising his sword. She countered with a graceful twist, bringing her body and sword up, meeting his fevered attempt. Just as quickly, she swiped the sword toward his midriff. Midir jumped back, looked down at his belly, and watched the fabric split, revealing a line of blood. "Leave with me, now."

"You came alone. You leave alone."

She moved to Spirit and offered a hand up, taking her eyes off her opponent. Midir hoisted his sword up. Spirit screamed, reacting with a freezing blast, staying his move in midair. Etain whirled around, *Nim* in the lead. The crystal crashed into his frozen blade, shattering the black blade. Unfortunately, as she turned, her shoulder clipped Spirit's jaw, knocking her into the corner.

Midir recovered before Etain, dropped the broken sword, and threw a left-handed power blast into the mage. Etain gasped, watching Spirit hit the wall again and slump to the floor. Midir grabbed his dirk, stabbing into the mark on Etain's chest. She blinked, not sure of what had happened. Spirit needed her help, but…

Dark spots clouded her vision. Midir kept fading in and out. *Is this a new trick?* She felt so strange. Midir stretched his arms out, catching her as her legs gave way. Someone called her name, but she couldn't respond.

Nim'Na'Sharr fell from her hand, its glow fading.

15

IN SEARCH OF A DEMON

Dar crawled out of bed and dressed, his mind mulling over Etain's request. "For you, my love, I will try to make peace with Inferno. Maybe the pigheaded fool will listen." Gazing out the window, he noticed the sun peeking over the horizon. "A red sunrise." He picked up his scabbard. "Blood will be spilled this day." He unsheathed the blade for a quick inspection. "Let's make sure it is not mine, *Ba'alzamon*." The blade returned to its sheath, he strapped it across his back and left the room. Reaching the kitchen door, he heard Inferno in conversation.

"I don't like it, boys. It's been too quiet."

Someone chuckled. "You love to whinge, mate. Enjoy the peace while we have it."

Dar recognized the voice.

"When me balls twitch, it means something's up, and they been twitchin' a lot lately."

Usually when Wolfe was around, there was also…

Elfin joined in the conversation. "I think it has more to do with what's been going on upstairs than the *Bok*."

"Or what hasn't," Wolfe chimed in. "Maybe we should have a chat with Spirit."

Dar sighed and pushed through the door. "Morning, gentlemen. Inferno, we need to talk."

Their smiles faded.

"That we do, demon, but it won't be with words." Hatred burned bright in the man's eyes. "Me blade has plenty to say."

What a difference a day makes.

Dar did his best to remain civil. "We should sit down and settle our differences in a peaceful manner." From the corner of his eye, he caught the movements of Wolfe and Elfin reaching for their dirks. He stepped back. "You disappoint me. I thought if it came down to this, you'd be man enough to fight me one-on-one."

"I don't need help to beat you," Inferno barked. "This is between me and the demon, boys." A devilish smile crossed his face. "Put the dogs in the kennel, then come watch me put Lord Darknight in his place."

"If that's how it has to be." Dar resolved himself to the chieftain's decision. "I'll be waiting at the shore." He wanted to take the fight away from the house to ensure the women would not hear the clash of blades. Exiting through the back door, he could not resist a final taunt. "If you have the balls to bring it." It felt good giving in to the darkness, if only for a tiny toe dip. He would like nothing better than to show this pain in the ass what pathetic really looked like.

Etain's request faintly echoed in his mind. Being the warrior he was, he rationalized with his conscience.

I offered terms. He set them. Negotiations done.

Wolfe and Elfin rushed off to spread news of the ensuing battle. It was a rare opportunity to watch two blade masters go at it. One being a Krymerian made it all the more special. The clan gathered at the castle wall overlooking the shore.

"Okay, boys," Wolfe said, taking a seat. "I say Inferno takes him down in five flat."

Elfin was the voice of reason. "Come on. Dar's a seasoned warrior. I'll give him longer than that. I say he'll last a half-hour, Inferno eventually taking the win."

Most agreed their chieftain was the better swordsman.

"I'll place a hundred Dar holds his own," Linq said, interrupting their game. "If you'd ever seen him in action, you wouldn't dismiss him so quickly. He'll last well past a half-hour."

The others laughed as Wolfe answered the elf. "It's obvious you've never seen Inferno fight. He charges in and does a fine job of breaking down his opponent."

"There are only two people I have encountered who can best me, and they're both down there." Linq held up a hand at the expected retorts. "I know Inferno is undefeated…within the Alamir." Hearing a warrior yell, their heads turned to the clash unfolding at the water's edge. "He's never faced a Krymerian with something to lose."

The rivals circled one another, sizing up their opponent. At exactly the same moment, the men charged, Inferno swinging his fists. A shirtless Dar ducked and heaved an uppercut Inferno blocked with ease. The Alamir came back with a right hook, meeting nothing but air.

The two carried on for over an hour. Winded, bruised, and bleeding, they separated.

"Ya think yer smart, don't ya, demon?" Inferno yelled. "Yer a blasted fool." His hand went to the hilt of his sword. "What ya think is love in her eyes is nothing more than pity." He slashed out at Dar's head.

The black blade of *Ba'alzamon* met Inferno's blade, jarring the Alamir to the bone. "You would be wise not to speak of things you know nothing about." Dar's voice was heavy with venom. "You have no idea what's in her heart." Jumping back, he reversed his grip on the hilt and came around in a swirling cyclone, swinging his fist at the same time.

Inferno blocked the sword, but the fist caught him on the side of the head. He stumbled to the side. "Bleedin' bastard! I'll have your heart."

Metal rang, neither gaining the upper hand. They charged again. Dar leaped over Inferno's head as he swung his sword in a downward chop, but the warrior landed off-kilter. Inferno's blade slashed down. Dar went with the bad landing, rolling on his back and coming to his feet, dodging the blow. Certain he had cleared the attack, a sudden stabbing pain in the chest told him differently. He dropped to a knee, glanced down, finding a line of oozing blood from one shoulder to the other.

Inferno didn't give him time to recoup. "Ya had no right to pass yer taint on to her." He laid a shallow gash across Dar's back, twisted, and jabbed out with his elbow, catching Dar on the left side of the face. "Ya see what happens when ya face someone with real experience? I'll be glad when yer dead and she's free of yer poison." Raising his sword, Inferno gasped, coughed, and staggered to the side. The tip of his sword fell into the dirt. He looked down at a nasty gash just below his ribs. "Yer faster than I give credit, devil. But it ain't enough to save yer life."

While the man bellowed his threats, Dar took a moment to check his injuries. The bloody gash was expected, but the hole in the mark he and Etain shared gave the warrior concern.

The bloody men, covered in sweat and dirt, dropped their blades and faced off. Dar swiped at his eyes, having to squint in order to focus on his blurry opponent. Inferno favored his left side, keeping one arm across his battered ribs. Each man raised a hand toward the other.

At the wall, Linq yelled, "Watch out! Power surge!" The air crackled with a magical charge. Everyone hit the dirt, waiting for the sonic boom that was sure to blast across the hillside.

"Any minute now," Wolfe whispered, hands over his ears.

Silence. There were no sounds of clashing swords, no grunts of effort, no barrage of insults. All they heard was their own excited breathing. Tentatively, each one raised a head, lowered their hands from their ears, and looked at each other. One by one, heads popped up from behind the wall.

Inferno and Dar stood several paces apart, puzzled expressions on their faces, each with a hand extended in front of him. Inferno conjured fireball after fireball, only to see each one sizzle and implode before he could release. Dar whipped the winds into a maelstrom of destruction that would spin like a fury for a moment, then wobble and fall like a top that had run out of momentum.

Dar lowered his hand, chuckling. "It appears we have been outmaneuvered by someone much wiser than either of us."

Inferno shook his head, lowering his hand. "Aye. Me wife knows us better than we do. Guess we'll have to sort this out the old-fashioned way." Pain was evident in his face as he bent over to regain his sword.

Dar had had enough. "Inferno, there is no need for this."

"I need to do this for me girl. She'll nigh be free until yer dead." He brought the blade up, struggling to move in with a series of slashes. "Her blood'll clear, and the stain on her chest'll fade. She can move on, start a new life."

Dar sidestepped Inferno's weary attempts, answering with a few glancing blows. The men continued until neither of them could stand or lift their blades.

Inferno stumbled back, his shirt drenched in blood and sweat, dropping his sword to his side. Dar sat hard in the dirt, looking every bit as haggard as his counterpart.

Inferno looked over at Dar. "As soon as I get me second wind, demon-"

Spirit, on her knees, suddenly appeared between the two. Her body trembled as she held up Etain's *Nim'Na'Sharr*.

"She's gone, Dar...by Midir's hand." She collapsed. The sword shifted from her grasp, standing tall in the dirt next to her prone form.

As Linq and the others rushed down the hillside, Inferno ran to his fallen wife, cradling her in his arms, gingerly touching her burnt clothing. "What's happened to ya, love?" he asked, brushing the hair from her face.

"We should get her to the house," Linq said.

"Aye."

His clansmen helped lift her, ensuring she was safe within Inferno's arms.

Elfin and Wolfe, who had gone for water, left the buckets at the wall and met the advancing group. Wolfe rushed ahead to open the front doors of the castle.

A bolt of lightning made several in the group jump. Elfin looked up at the darkening sky. "Where'd this come from?"

Linq eyed those around him. "Everyone get to the house."

"It's not safe out here, Linq," Elfin argued, ducking at the flash of another lightning strike.

"I'll be fine. Go!" The elf watched the others hurry away. Assured they were safely inside, he ventured to the wall, gazing out toward the estuary. Dar was there, on his knees. Linq had no answers as to how Spirit came to have Etain's sword, other than she had to have been with the girl.

He recognized the Krymerian's handiwork, understanding what such a gift from the big man meant. Dar had dared to love again. Linq hoped this wasn't the end but, at this point, he wasn't sure which way it would go. He was only certain of one thing. Dar would search for Etain and bring her back. Linq lowered his head, saying a prayer for the Krymerian lord and his lady.

In the lounge, Inferno laid his wife on the sofa. "A cool cloth and a blanket. Now!" he barked.

"Aye, sir," Zorn and another clansman disappeared to do his bidding.

"How is she, Inferno?" Wolfe asked, lurking behind his chieftain.

"Where's she been?" Elfin circled round to the other side of the sofa.

Inferno smoothed the hair from her face. "I don't know, boys." He caressed her lips with his thumb. "Wake up, love. I need you to talk to me." He lifted her hand to his heart. "*Os gwelwch yn dda fy cariad. Deffro* (Please, my love. Wake up)."

Zorn returned with a cloth in a bowl of cool water. BadMan spread a blanket over the sleeping Spirit. Inferno would not leave her side or accept anything to eat or drink. "Not until she opens her beautiful eyes and speaks to me."

The clan dispersed throughout the ground floor to await news of their fallen mistress. A few speculated on the absence of the Krymerian. Some considered him callus and hard-hearted for having not checked on Spirit's well-being. Others commented on the crystal sword they had seen in her hands. Many echoed the same questions Wolfe and Elfin had asked.

Zorn, Wolfe, and Elfin prepared a meal. Linq went upstairs to check on Faux, who remained asleep.

Later in the evening, Spirit's eyes fluttered open. She touched Inferno's bowed head. "You all right, love?"

His head snapped up, eyes round as saucers. "*Fy cariad* (My love), yer awake. *Sut wyt ti* (How are you)?" Tears glistened in his eyes as he caressed her cheek.

"A little banged up, but fine otherwise." Tears came to her eyes. "If it weren't for our lass, I'd be roggered and dead now. Me poor girl."

"*Tawel yn awr. Rydych yn gartref diogel* (Hush now. Yer home safe)." Inferno held her tight, letting her cry into his shoulder. Struggling to keep his own tears in check, they finally slid down his cheeks and into Spirit's soft brown hair. "It'll get sorted."

"Dar must be stark raving," she sobbed. "He'll go after his brother and we'll lose him, too." She pulled back, frantic, glancing around the room. "Don't let him go, love. It will be the end of him." Her gaze came back to her husband. "For Etain's sake, you must stop him."

"*Mi hardd feinir gwallt brownach* (Me beautiful brown-haired lass), ya know I have no sway over the man."

Linq, having overheard her last words, came into the room and kneeled next to Inferno. "He is already gone, milady."

As soon as Spirit appeared with *Nim'Na'Sharr* in her hands, Dar did not move or utter a sound. Left alone, he stared at the crystal sword, trying to make sense of what it meant. *Gone? How could it be?* Tears filled his eyes. *She cannot just be...gone.* He crawled to the blade, kneeling before the iconic symbol of his love. He reached out, but could not touch the sword. It would make it all too real. "Etain."

He had to touch it. He *must* touch it. He reached out once more. The memories of the blade would tell him everything. Holding *Nim'Na'Sharr* tight to his chest, he rocked back and forth, tears falling. His heart felt like a wound in his chest.

The sword was cold and, worst of all, silent.

"I have failed you, my love," Dar whispered in anguish. "Even my greatest creation could not protect you."

The happiness of the last few days, the warmth of their love, dissolved into a cold knot of hate.

"Midir."

His face went blank, void of emotion. *Nim'Na'Sharr* filled the sheath across his back.

Ba'alzmon spoke to him. *It is time to be the Fuer grissa ost drauka* (death bringer)*, to bring death to your dark half and any who stand in your way.*

Dar's hand clenched the hilt of the bloody sword. "Aye, it is time."

A transformed Dar appeared on a darker plane. The spawn at the gate seemed unaffected by the appearance of another demon. Midir had so many working for him, it was easy to lose track. However, on second glance, a spear halted the new one at the gate. "No permission, no enter."

The self-declared *Fuer grissa ost drauka* growled, grabbing the demon by the head. Dar's fingers curled, nails digging into the soft flesh. The pathetic creature screamed, struggling against his fierce grip. With a loud crack, the guard convulsed violently, yet his reaper continued squeezing until the skull burst with a sickening pop. Dar tossed the body aside, then shattered the gate with a mighty blast.

"Where are you, brother?" he called out. "Come face me now or, by all that is Kaos, I will tear this castle apart!"

Buer fledglings from the lowest demon class, their eyes glowing bright green, skin the color of filth, rolled from the castle gates on their five legs. The obvious leader spoke. "Master gone." He signaled for the others to form a tight circle around the invader. "You no leave…" He gave Dar a genuine smile, sounding rather pleased with the situation. "We kill."

A troop of two-legged horned demons joined them, forming an inner ring. They held round shields chest-high, casting an eerie sheen over the trespasser, the points of their spears aimed at his heart. The Buer demons fanned out, allowing another set of horned demons to form an outer ring. This group threw their spears to the ground and placed hands on their swords. A soft rhythmic chant began as the two circles slowly moved in opposite directions. They kept the circle tight, moving with Dar as he moved.

"Give me your master and no one need die."

A strangled sound came from the Buer demon. Judging by the gleam in its eye, Dar took it for laughter. "*We* give quick death...to you."

Dar's chest heaved, his jaw muscles flexing. The chanting increased in speed as the circles moved faster. Dar glared at the lead demon. "Give me your master."

"We many. You one. We win."

Dar laughed, hearing *Ba'alzamon's* whispered desire to be unleashed, longing for the taste of demon blood.

"You laugh?" The leader narrowed his eyes. "You understand dance of death, mongrel?"

Dar stripped off his shirt. "Let me show you a new step." The fury from his heart poured into the black blade. In return, the storm of the sword's thirst for blood thundered through him. The circles accelerated, the chanting becoming more feverish, their weapons whirling faster with each turn.

Heedless of the danger, he pulled the magic of *Ba'alzamon* into him, feeding his hate to the point of sickness. Taken over by the malevolent nature within the blade, his muscles flexed, glistening with sweat, yet he held the leash on the bloodlust, locating a quiet place of focus. He would need it to defeat this legion of death.

Be a feather, not a rock, a voice within him urged. *Unleash the Kaos.* At the center of the moving circles, he brought the gleaming black blade to his forehead.

"*Ba'alzamon,* be true this day."

In his stillness, he saw the first come from the left. *Float in the wind of the storm.* Dar spun with the attack. Letting the demon sweep past him, he coasted with the press of the charge, the magic of the sword guiding him. The attacker tumbled to the ground.

Instantly, another came in, twirling his spear. Dar spun as the assailant passed, splintering the shaft in two. The demon turned, raising the speared half of the broken shaft. Dar lashed out, slicing it in half again.

Another charged from behind. A foot to the chest threw the demon back. Dar struggled with the increasing need to release the death bringer. Dead demons would tell no tales and, right now, he needed information. Using the flat side of *Ba'alzamon*, he slipped through the pressing throng, striking the back of a head here, using a foot to trip an advance there. The faster they came, the faster he reacted, the magic of his sword feeding off their energy. Fluidly, he moved among the attackers, splintering spears when he could, trying to disarm them instead of killing. It was imperative he find out the whereabouts of his brother.

"Stop before it goes too far!"

Yelling at the demons was a mistake: the distraction allowed a spear to infiltrate his flowing defense. He felt the warmth of his own blood running down his side. Spinning his blade, *Ba'alzamon* whistled through the air, lopping off the hand attached to the spear. The resulting scream was female. Surprised, he looked back. Would it have made a difference had he known? No. They were as deadly as any male.

First blood fed the rage. The need to kill boiled up within him, making him thirsty for more. With great effort, he managed to master the fury. Dar glided like a phantom, conserving his energy as he moved. All the time, *Ba'alzamon* whispered for release.

The outer ring, which had continued circling as the inner one led the attack, stopped. With swords whirling, they assumed the advance. Those with spears stepped back as the outer ring came forward. Dar knew any hesitation on his part would prove fatal. Instead of waiting for their attack, he took the fight to them, shattering as many blades as possible.

Hot pain flashed through the flesh over his ribs. Although Dar did not see the blade, he moved by instinct, receiving only a shallow cut instead of a killing gash. *Ba'alzamon's* magic leapt to his defense. He could no longer contain the fury. It was time for the *Fuer grissa ost drauka*.

The night erupted in a warm mist of toxic blood. Only conscious of *Nim'Na'Sharr* in his left hand and *Ba'alzamon* in his right, primal screams filled the air as he sliced through the throng. Disembodied heads tumbled. Body parts flew. Blood sluiced over the ground. Horrors melded together into one continuous killing rampage.

No blade could touch him. He countered every strike as if he had seen it a thousand times before, knowing from which direction it would come and how to defend. Two came at him from opposite sides. *Nim* slit the throat of one, *Ba'alzamon* piercing the other's heart at the same time.

The slaughter continued until no more challenges met his blades. Rivulets of blood coursed down his body, dripping off the ends of his lowered weapons. Bits of demon flesh clung to him. Dar surveyed the carnage, torn between disappointment and satisfaction. There would be no exchange of information, but the bloodlust was quenched. Perhaps it was what he needed before facing his dark brother.

He turned at a slight movement behind him. A demon holding herself up with one hand, the other missing, staggered to her feet and pulled a knife from her belt. Dar remained deathlike in a cocoon of magic, watching her come for him. *Ba'alzamon*, singing its death song, whipped up, impaling her through the heart. Baring her blood-streaked fangs, her gaze locked with Dar's. She collapsed to the ground, her last breath gurgling away.

Dar stared at the female demon. He appreciated her final act of loyalty, no matter how misplaced. Their sacrifices would go unnoticed by Midir. He placed a boot on her chest, freed his blade, and stabbed both *Ba'alzamon* and *Nim'Na'Sharr* into the ground. He faced the black fortress.

"There's no one left to protect your miserable ass. Return her to me. Now."

Silence answered his demand. The fury rose inside, but he knew losing control again could prove fatal. His death would ensure Etain's path to a dark future, meaning the end of the Alamir and everything for which he had fought. Instead, he channeled the rage to strengthen his determination and returned Etain's crystal blade to the scabbard on his back. The black blade of death returned to its master's hand, ready for what may come. With a resolute stride, he entered the gates, not stopping until he was within the walls of the castle. He called for his brother. This time, he heard the scramble of the remaining demon minions fleeing to avoid Dar.

In the main hall, it occurred to him he was wasting valuable time. Rather than call out again, he turned his search within and reached out for Etain. Nothing. He reached out again for his incorrigible brother. His senses confirmed neither were in this realm.

Dar walked outside, faced the castle, and raised his hands. The fortress began to tremble and heave. Cracks spread through the stone façade, making the walls shift and crumble. Screams of those inside blended with the rumbles of the disintegrating building. Soon in ruins, rubble littered the ground, shrouded in a fog of dust.

The tormented reaper vanished.

Outside the door of his lost love's home, afraid to enter but fearing not to, Dar placed his hand on the knob. Never had an inanimate object provoked this much anxiety. He turned the handle and gave the door a little push, letting it open on its own.

Please be here... Tell me it's only a nightmare.

Inside, photographs on the mantle drew him into the room. One, in particular, caught his eye - Etain laughing with friends. Tears his vision as images of her face filled his mind. The love shared in their short time together, the laughter, their undeniable bond.

"I let my petty quarrels get in the way. Inferno is not the enemy."

He moved into the kitchen. Seeing the table overturned, he set it upright. His fight to remain strong proved futile. Hot tears streamed down his bloodstained face.

He trolled through the house, coming to her bedroom. The mussed bed raised the fear of what may have happened. Noticing the partially packed bag relieved him of that fear, and he rummaged through it. Shirts, undergarments... Nothing much of interest, except...

"What's this?" A glint of silver had him digging deeper. Just as he grabbed it, he dropped it back into the bag. "Ouch!" He licked the line of blood on his palm. A bit more cautious, he reached for the item again. Once brought into the light, he saw it was a journal. The unusual binding of silver seemed to shimmer at his touch. Inside, he found a name scrawled in a childish hand. Etain Rhys. Dar thumbed through the pages, but there were no further entries.

Then he spotted the torn shirt on the floor. The book forgotten, he picked up the leather scrap and breathed in her scent.

How far did you take it, Midir?

Visions of *Ba'alzamon* embedded through Midir's heart threatened to resurrect the bloodlust. Dar forced himself to walk back to the living room. This time, he saw the pool of blood in the center of the room. The light of his life extinguished at that spot. The *Fuer grissa ost drauka* sank to his knees, reduced to a sobbing child. He placed his hand over the mark he had shared with his love, finding some comfort that it remained with him, swearing he would never love another.

"How many times must the quenching of your thirst for blood be at the cost of my happiness?"

A sobering thought suddenly worked its way through his grief-muddled mind. He looked at his chest, noting the mark was directly over his heart. However, Etain's lay more to the left, extending down onto her breast, the tips of the flames dipping down to the pink tip.

Hope seeped into the void, shining a faint light. Coming to his feet, he returned to the bedroom, scooped up the half-packed bag, and returned to the living room. There, he gathered the broken fragments of Midir's sword, the twin to *Ba'alzamon* and was gone.

Later in the evening, everyone came together in the kitchen, listening to Spirit tell her story. Suddenly, she stopped and looked toward the hallway. "Someone's here…in the lounge."

When Inferno jumped to his feet, she grabbed his arm. "Go easy."

Wolfe, Elfin, and Linq followed close behind. They were left speechless at the sight that greeted them.

Standing in the middle of the room was Dar, covered in blood and gore, his face streaked with dirt and tears. "They would not give me what I asked for. Otherwise, it would not have come to this."

"Are you hurt?" Linq asked.

Dar's cold gaze landed on Inferno. "Where is Spirit? I must speak with her."

"Not with those blades in yer murdering hands. Answer the fucking question," Inferno blustered from the doorway.

Dar dropped the bag, patiently placing *Ba'alzamon* at his feet. "The bag is Etain's. Leave this blade where it lies. No one is to touch it. *No one.*" As he reached back for *Nim*, other hands in the room moved to their swords. Sensitive to the tension, he held the blade flat in both hands, extending it out in front of him. "Take this to Spirit. Only she can locate what is lost."

With no response from Inferno, Linq reached for the sword. Dar acknowledged the elf with a nod, then moved toward the door.

Inferno blocked his path. "Yer gonna answer me before ya leave this room, or ya won't be leaving at all."

Dar eyed the man and his men behind him. He turned to Linq. "Please, get the blade to Spirit. I will be along to explain." His steady gaze returned to those blocking his way. "It is not my blood. I went to Midir's castle in search of retribution…for Etain."

"Is he dead then?" Inferno asked, motioning to his clan to stand down.

"He was not there."

"From the looks of ya, I'd say he won't find much when he returns."

"It's urgent I speak with Spirit."

Inferno stepped aside, but followed him to the kitchen.

Dar found the mage rising from her chair. "Spirit, you must scry for Etain."

She backed away. "No. You keep away from me. She is gone. I saw her stabbed through the heart with me own eyes."

He stopped, caught off-guard by the fear in her eyes. He scrubbed at the dried blood on his chest, doing his best to will her into acceptance of a new perspective. "My brother would not have taken her body if she were dead. Look at the mark. It glows. It is faint, but it glows."

Her gaze went to the mark, the struggle to believe showing in her face. She came closer to Dar, a tentative hand stretching out, lightly touching his chest. She looked up into his eyes.

"Now, will you scry?" He motioned to Linq. "This blade is bound to her by blood." He slapped a swathe of old leather on the table.

"What is that?" she asked, accepting the sword.

"A map of realms," Linq said before Dar could answer. Inferno and his men completed the circle around the table, peering at the unusual map.

"It's like nothing I've seen before. Where did it come from?" she asked.

"Makes no difference from where it came. If she were in the Alamir realm, I would know. Our mark tells me she is alive, but nothing more. This map shows the realms above, below, and beside us. She is in one of those. Scry with the blade and you will find her." He reached out to her, but she stepped back. "Please, Spirit. I'm begging you." He sighed and let his hand fall to his side. "She is all that matters to me."

"I will try," she said, uncertainty in her face. "But you must wait outside."

"As you wish, milady. I have faith in you." At the door, he asked Inferno about his forge. The man offered to walk with him. "Thank you, but no. I need to be alone for a while. Sit with Spirit. She will need your support more than I."

With *Ba'alzamon* in hand, Dar made his way to the forge. He wasted no time in stoking the fire, infusing magic into the flames, making them burn hotter and brighter. Quickening the tempo of his words, the fire intensified into a blazing inferno. He placed the fragments of Midir's shattered sword into a smelting pot and set it over the flames. As the fragments melted, Dar lifted *Ba'alzamon*.

"I'm sorry for what I am about to do, my old friend. The time has come for you to be reborn. This union will increase your power and remove any sway Midir may have had over your brother." Using all his strength, he broke the blade from the hilt and slipped it into the pot, watching the black metal slowly merge with its twin.

Giving the two blades time to melt properly, Dar designed two new hilts. Once the concoction was ready, he removed the pot and poured the molten metal into three casts, two larger than the third. From the far wall, he chose two hammers...one heavy, one lighter. As the metal cooled, he prepared for the work to come, choosing several fine-tipped chisels and placing them close. He returned to the blocks of black metal. The first, heated to a bright red glow, he placed on the anvil and pounded, turning and folding the metal, molding it to his will.

He labored well into the morning hours, sweat rolling down his body, slowly washing away the gore. With each bang of the hammer, sparks flew as the blade took shape. Patiently working the material, a curve formed, broadening toward the tip. Satisfied, he placed the blade on the worktable, then retrieved the other block of black metal. As with the first, Dar worked with the material until it was the same size and similar balance. He stepped back to view the twin scimitars.

With lighter strikes, he rounded the last block of metal into a medallion in the shape of the sun. Using a fine-tipped chisel and the light hammer, he etched flames into the metal that matched the ones on his chest, then returned to the worktable. On the first blade, he etched a sun with rays running down its length. On the opposite side, he repeated the design. The other blade, which he decorated with burning flames, received the same attention to detail.

"Nice work," Linq said, standing at the door. Dar looked up, a smile on his face. "I think they would make even the most skilled weapons master envious. You *do* realize you've worked straight through two nights and a day?"

"Has the sun come up?" Dar asked, admiring his work.

Linq glanced over his shoulder. "Not quite yet."

"What gets you up this early?" Dar raised a brow. "Or did you pull the short straw?"

His question brought a grin to the elf's lips. "I've come to offer my assistance in the hunt."

"Your offer is well met. Thank you, Linq. But I do this one alone." Dar placed the medallion in a pocket. "I will not risk the death of another by my brother's hand. This will end with the death of either Midir or me." He picked up both swords. "I could use your help in another way."

"Since you won't allow me to travel with you, it's the least I can do."

"The blades must be named so they know their master and understand their duties," Dar explained as they walked toward the shore.

"From the fracas of the other day, I would think all that fairly clear." Linq grinned.

"Just do what needs doing, elf, and let me get to it."

Dar extended his right arm into the first rays of the sun. Dagger in hand, Linq cut into the Krymerian's forearm. Dar dragged the blade with sun etchings through the welling blood, lifted it up, and declared, "I name thee Day Star, Sun of Salvation, for the light of my life. Darkness shall flee from your light." He extended his left arm, allowing the elf to repeat the process. Dar dragged the second blade, etched with flames, through the blood, lifted it to the sun, and declared, "I name thee Burning Heart, Flame of Retribution. Darkness may flee, but it cannot hide from your cleansing fire." The blades shined in the early morning sun in acceptance of their commissions.

Dar lifted both scimitars to the sun, crossing them over his head. "Midir! Death is coming for you."

16

MON PETIT

T he air shimmered, opening a portal. Demon servants suddenly materialized as Midir entered his domain, Etain in his arms.

"Welcome home, milord," said his most trusted female servant, Lilith.

"Get me a sheet," he ordered, hurrying into the closest room. In the library, he rushed to a red velvet chaise, laying her down gently. "And bring cloths soaked in a solution of chamomile and lavender."

"Yes, master." She bowed, exiting the room.

Raum, his manservant, stepped forward.

"Have my bed freshened and turned down. Our guest will be recuperating there for the next few days."

"Yes, milord."

Lilith quickly returned with a sheet. "The solution is almost ready, sir." A simple nod acknowledged the information as he wrapped the sheet about the patient, leaving the wound exposed. Etain cried out in pain, but did not wake.

Midir spoke softly. "I'm sorry for the rough treatment, *mon petit*, but it is necessary." Pushing stray wisps of hair from her face, he leaned over and kissed her forehead. His finger traveled across her cheek and down to the mark, the ugly wound in its center. "The things you make me do to you."

Another minion arrived with several cloths and a basin of steaming liquid. "Shall I tend to her, master?" Lilith asked.

"Leave us."

She and the minion bowed and quietly left the room.

Dipping a cloth into the solution, he gently washed the wound, removing the dried blood. A small incision in his forearm allowed a healing flow of blood into the wound. It sizzled, emitting a thin trail of smoke as it penetrated the layers of tissue. She grabbed at her chest, emitting a low hiss of pain.

Sweat covered his brow, struggling to hold her still, but was encouraged by the reaction. "Release the demon. It will quicken the healing process."

As suddenly as she had awakened, she fell limp in his arms. Dabbing her face with a fresh cloth, he checked the wound and found it had sealed, leaving only a faint scar.

Aware of her loss of blood, he stripped off his shirt and dragged the blade across his shoulder, then pulled her close. "*Mon petit*, we must rebuild your strength. You are too weak to sustain the demon. Take mine to make you strong."

Her eyes fluttered open, roused by the scent of blood. Her lips curved in a slight smile and she kissed his cheek. "Dar. You always take care of me," she muttered, flicking out her tongue for a taste. In the next moment, her lips clamped onto the flow.

"Yes, *mon petit*. Take it all. It is an endless spring."

Her eyes opened to the long dark hair, glancing at the distinctive jaw and strong neckline. Something made her jerk back and look down at his chest. Her eyes traveled to his face. "No!"

Weakened, he collapsed to his knees. Violet eyes darted about the strange room. She turned her back, curling into a ball within her wings.

Having heard the screams, Raum rushed in. "Master, let me have Lilith get you something."

"Not necessary," he croaked. "She is amazing, is she not?"

"Yes, milord. Who is she?"

"She is my future wife. Let's see that half-wit brother of mine stop us now." He looked up at his manservant. "Leave us. My lady can provide everything I need to regain my strength."

"Keep your hands off me." Her voice was cold. "I will kill you before I marry you." Her wings retracted and disappeared.

Midir smiled, trailing a finger along her bare back. "You will change your mind, *mon petit*." He chanted a spell, coaxing her into a deep sleep. Rolling her onto her back, his fingertips traced over her perfect breasts, lingering over the mark. "This will be the first thing to go after we rid you of these disgusting rags."

After removing her boots and clothes, he wrapped the sheet around her before scooping her up into his arms. Lightheaded from his own loss of blood, he stumbled back a step, but recovered well enough to carry her upstairs to his bedroom. As instructed, the bed linens had been changed and turned down. Laying his prize on the bed, he sat on the edge. *To have her here...* It was almost too much to endure. He smoothed the hair around her angelic face and savored the sweet taste of her lips, as his hand roamed over her body, choosing to interpret her unconscious moan as one of pleasure.

"See, *mon petit*, you respond to me quite nicely." His tongue slinked along her neck. "I will teach you to appreciate the sweetness, as well as the darkness, of love."

She turned onto her side and curled into a fetal position. This only served to encourage his attentions. He rolled into the bed, spooning his body to hers, groping the curve of her hip, coming around to her belly, then cupping her breast. "You will be mine, *mon petit*," he panted, his obvious excitement straining for release. With great effort, he forced himself away, lifting the covers over her. "I must be patient," he whispered, adjusting his trousers. "We have plenty of time."

He reached for her delicate arm. Extending a single talon, he dragged it along the inside of her forearm. His head dipped, his tongue snaking out for a taste of the sweet nectar. A delightful burn lit up his mouth. Eager for more, his lips encased the incision. Drinking the salty elixir, he felt it scorching the back of his throat. A hiss escaped through his teeth as he withdrew.

"Perfection. I cannot afford to waste any more time. Your training will begin soon, *mon petit*. We will reprogram that beautiful brain." He tucked her arm under the covers. She was getting harder to resist, but he must not spoil his own plans. "By the time he finds this place, our welcoming party will be in ready and waiting."

Enjoying a huge stretch, Etain woke the next morning, refreshed and renewed. Her hand landed on a body tucked beneath the covers beside her. She rolled over, throwing an arm over her sleeping warrior, snuggling into Dar's warmth. "Good morning, sleepyhead. What does my irresistible master have in store for me today?"

He took her by the wrist and turned. Nose-to-nose, he said, "Today, you will learn the correct way to fight with your demon senses. For now, you will learn how to love like a demon."

"Midir." Memories of yesterday rushed in. Struggling to get free, her horror escalated when she found they were both naked. "What have you done? Get off me!"

He worked a knee between her legs. "*Mon petit*, you enflame my soul. Be my demon love. Turn for me as I make you mine."

"Stop with the *mon petit* crap." Her ivory talons extended, leaving trails of blood in their wake. "I am not yours and never will be." Her entire body heaved against his in a valiant attempt to push him off.

"Turn for me," he demanded, pushing her arms above her head.

The demon materialized, her wings digging into the mattress. A fully aroused Midir changed as well, his great white wings fanning out behind him. His broad smile revealed deadly fangs. "It has begun."

"It has not! You will let me go." Frustration made her gasp for air. She fought with everything she had, but nothing worked.

"Etain," he said in a malevolent whisper. "You took my blood willingly."

"No." But the look in his eyes told her it was the truth. "I-I thought you were Dar." With the confession, her demon blood cooled.

"Luckily for me, we look so much alike." He leaned in for a kiss, but she turned her head.

"Please, Midir. I can't bear this." She felt broken inside, as though she had betrayed her love for Dar and her family.

In an unusual moment of benevolence, he complied with her request. The effort of calming his blood reflected in his face.

"This one time, Etain. You will not find me so generous again." He rolled out of the bed and dressed, casting an occasional glance in her direction. Etain kept her head turned, the sight of him unbearable.

He paused at the door. "Think on this. Whether anything happened or not, he will assume the worst. Do you really think he'll want you back?"

She reached for a vase on the bedside table and hurled it at the door as it was closing. "Go to hell!" Throwing herself from the bed, she crawled, like a wild animal, to the open balcony doors, tears spilling down her cheeks. Beneath her were sheer cliffs ending at a shore of rocky crags. She would have to fly.

To where?

Not even a shimmer could save her. Without knowing her exact location, there was no hope of escape.

Her mind tumbled back to yesterday. "Oh god, Spirit. I'm so sorry." Sitting on the floor, she wrapped her arms around her legs, resting her head on her knees, crying for the loss of her dear friend.

In the stillness, she could hear Midir, downstairs barking orders. The sound of his voice made her skin crawl. "I *will* be free of you, then I can go home."

Looking about the room, she noticed another door. Rather than walk, she crawled across the floor and pushed it open. The room on the other side boasted a huge stone bath in its center. Coming to her feet, she bypassed the tub for the walk-in shower, setting the temperature as hot as her skin could handle.

I will avenge your death, sweet Spirit, along with those of my family. It may take time, but it will happen.

With the dregs of the day washed away, she turned off the water and was surprised to find Midir standing at the door. "Have I no privacy in this prison?" she asked, wrapping herself in an oversized towel.

"Nothing to do with you is secret from me," he said, watching her every move.

"So it seems." She dried her hair with another towel. His comment brought back an earlier conversation. Their eyes met in the mirror. "Is it true what you said about my inheritance?"

"I wanted to take care of you."

"Not murdering my family would've been a good start."

"No, that had to happen. Otherwise, you wouldn't be here today."

She felt the hairs on the back of her neck prickle. "Why? What's so special about me?"

"I will tell you in time." He leaned against the doorjamb, watching her in the mirror. "You'll find a brush and comb in the drawer to your right. I *will* tell you this. I underestimated the power of the orb, or perhaps it was you I underestimated. Either way, once you entered the Alamir, I lost you for a time."

"You are so full of shit, Midir. You're telling me you orchestrated it all...the murder, the orb, the change?" She rolled her eyes. "No one knows if they're Alamir until it happens."

Her words made him laugh. "Such eloquent language, *mon-*" She cut a stern look at him, "milady." He continued to smile. "My brother has said as much on repeated occasions. I shouldn't have mentioned it. You're not ready for the whole story, but you soon will be."

Etain worked the comb through the tangles in her hair. "Was Dar part of your plan, or was it just dumb luck?"

"A bit of both," he admitted. "I let you go, but you came back to me. It is proof we belong together."

"You kid yourself, Midir. This mark I share with Dar proves otherwise. Not even *you* can change that."

Raising an eyebrow, he shifted his weight. "It will change with his death. His power will become my power. His blood will become my blood. Then you will realize it is I to whom you are bound."

"You're insane."

"Perhaps. When Dar turns up here, which is inevitable, he'll have a special surprise waiting for him."

"I don't suppose you're gonna share that little tidbit, are you?"

"At the appropriate time, *mon petit*." He moved closer, twining a damp tendril around his finger. "Since you're feeling better, let's get to training."

She tried to pull away. "You have nothing to teach me." Etain thought she saw a glimmer in his eyes, but it disappeared almost as quickly as it had appeared.

The tendril became a handful of hair. "Your impudence does not bode well for your friends. I hear your mage left behind four beautiful children." Their eyes met in the mirror – hers filled with pain at the reminder of Spirit; his, a guarded threat. "Would you like to watch while I take them down one by one?"

Etain jabbed an elbow into his ribs, pushing him away. "You are despicable. If I have my way, you'll be dead before dark."

Midir coughed, holding his side. "If you do as I say, those brats will never know I exist."

Moments passed as she pondered the options. Deciding cooperation may be the best avenue, for now, she looked away. "Am I to be completely humiliated by training in the raw?"

"An enticing proposition, but no. I have prepared for your comfort." He jerked his head toward the bedroom, still gripping his side. "Everything you need is in the armoire."

Etain cut a wide path around him. Too focused on Midir, she'd not given much notice to what was in the room. A dressing table, sitting before a generous window, held beautiful bottles, jars, and various items for her hair. Beyond the dressing table... *How'd I miss that monstrous thing?* She appreciated the artistry of the carved doors, but it wasn't to her taste. Too masculine. She opened the armoire, finding an assortment of leathers on padded hangers.

Recovered from her assault, he smiled. "I didn't know your favorite color, so I had several made."

She eyed the array of colors. "Black is the only color for me now."

The smile disappeared from his face. "Then wear the black. I'll have more made. The others will be thrown out." He stormed to the door. "Get dressed and meet me in the courtyard."

She took her time, luxuriating in the suppleness of the leather, admiring her reflection in the mirror. "Nice fit." The man had spared no expense. *Too bad... You're wasting your time and money, bucko.* She gathered her damp hair back into a clip. "All I need from you is your death."

As soon as she stepped into the courtyard, she had to duck and roll to avoid the blade aimed at her neck. Hunched down, she assessed the perimeter as another came at her from the side. Rising up slightly, she spun to her right, extended a leg, and knocked the would-be assailant onto his demon ass. She grabbed his fallen sword and rolled again, coming to her feet in a crouched position. Two more demons charged in. She sidestepped the one to the left, raising her sword to block an attack from the right and cut under with a fist to his gut. Etain twisted away, the demon's dagger in her grasp. With a flick of the wrist, she stabbed the other in the shoulder as he breezed past. Parrying another onslaught, she ended with a drop down sidestep, knocking her opponent off-balance, and finished the job with a swift boot to his ass.

High on adrenaline and sword ready, she turned at the sound of footsteps.

Midir blocked her move with ease. "Impressive. You're a natural."

"Thank the gods. My life is complete." She lowered her blade, prepared to step past him.

"You're not done here," he said, offering her a tankard. "Refresh yourself. You have more work to do."

She eyed the drink. "If it brings us closer to your end, I'm happy to carry on. But if it involves Dar, I won't fight him." Thirst won over doubt.

"The death of my brother is a pleasure for me only. I train you for our conquest of the Alamir."

She peered over the edge of the mug. "Conquest of the Alamir?" She rolled her eyes. "You *have* lost it." He turned as she walked past. Instincts blazing, she swung back, the mug whizzing mere centimeters past his head. She curved over and back, deflecting his blow with her sword. "Face it, Midir. I'll never be with you, or *for* you."

He launched a brutal attack, each word he spoke accentuated with the strike of his blade, forcing her back, step after step.

"Why do you persistently deny a love that is…for you…and you alone?" His eyes glowed with a palpable evil. "He will use you and toss you aside like a worthless whore."

She growled through clenched teeth, bringing her blade down, pushing his to the ground. You like to think you know him, but you know nothing." Etain took the advantage, forcing him back to the outer wall. She moved in for the kill, but her vision suddenly blurred. Rather than run him through, she ran into him. She felt hands on her arms, giving her support. It was a struggle to lift her head, but she had to look into his face. Nothing made sense.

"Dar?" Midir pushed her off and slashed at her with his blade. She wobbled, barely able to stay on her feet, dropping her sword. "What're you doing?" she asked, her attention on his face, in spite of the blood trickling down her arm. He slashed the other one. "*What* are you doing?"

"Teaching you the difference between a master and amateur."

He lurched forward, angling his sword overhead. She stumbled, landing on her backside. His blade came sweeping down. Twisting at the last moment, she reached for her sword, deflecting his strike.

Hour after hour, he continued the onslaught, switching personas from Midir to Dar, then back to Midir. Occasionally, he allowed her a moment of rest, just long enough to quench her thirst with the potion he'd made especially for her. Then the assault would resume. Physically, he drove her to exhaustion. Mentally, he kept her off-balance. Emotionally, he aimed to destroy her completely.

His taunts were relentless…mocking her dead family, ridiculing her for willingly taking his blood, and expounding on her ignorance in siding with Dar. However, the taunts that cut her to the core were those about Dar no longer wanting her. They spoke to a primal fear. After all, it was Faux who carried his child, not her.

By the end of the day, traumatized and defeated, she collapsed at his feet, her heart broken.

Dar! screamed through her head.

Midir snapped his fingers, setting two servants in motion.

"Run a hot bath and leave her to soak. I'll be up soon."

They each placed a clawed hand under an armpit, hauling Etain from the yard and into the castle. In the bedroom, they dumped their burden on the floor and busied themselves with preparing the bath. Unbeknownst to them, their senseless chatter roused the sleeping warrior.

Damn…still alive.

With the preparations completed, they shuffled into the bedroom, neither of them noticing Etain awake and aware. One kneeled down, reaching for the buttons of her top, while the other worked on removing her boots. A well-placed fist against a soft demon jaw sent the first one sliding across the floor. The other received a resounding kick to the knee, bringing him down with a thud. Despite her objections, they picked themselves up and returned to their ministrations.

She batted at them with hands and still booted feet. "Leave me the hell alone! I don't need your help."

Flustered, the top demon bellowed, "We must place you in the bath as the master instructed. Let us do our job."

Etain pushed them off one more time and rolled to a crouch. "Keep your clammy paws off me."

"Miss…," one began, stepping forward. Watery eyes widened when Etain sprang forward. Two hard punches to his face and he was out. She turned to the other. With a look of terror, he ran to the door, screaming like a child, tripping over the threshold. He picked himself up, falling again when the body of his unconscious cohort collided into his back.

"Tell your master to go to hell." She slammed the door and threw the lock in place. Sinking to the floor, the pain crept in, reminding her of the brutal day. "He will not break me." She ran a hand through her hair. "Maybe a hot bath would help, master or no master."

Pushing her stiff body up, she trekked to the bath, stripping off her ruined leathers as she moved. Just as she eased herself down into the water, there was a bang on the bedroom door. She leaned back, wishing its magic could make all her aches and pains go away.

A moment later, another source of pain kicked the door open. She relaxed into the water, eyes closed. Aware of him looming over the bath, she dismissed him with a wave of a hand. "Go away, Midir. You've done enough damage today. I've had quite enough of your attempts to break me."

"I have two servants with broken bones who say otherwise." A shrug was her only response. He trailed a finger across her bare shoulder. "Your fighting today was flawless. Such graceful strength." She slid deeper to drown his voice out, but he pulled her up to face him. "Rest for now, lady. Tomorrow is a new day with new challenges. I have business outside the castle tonight, so I won't be joining you." He leaned in with a heated kiss. "But tomorrow evening will be ours." He left her to bathe in solitude.

"Good riddance," she said, scrubbing a hand across her mouth. A handy loofah made short work of the dirt and grime on her flesh, but no amount of scrubbing could remove the lingering sensation of his touch.

Wrapped in a towel, she walked back into the bedroom and

rummaged through the armoire. Amongst the clothes, she discovered a long purple silk robe, her favorite color, slipped it on, and ventured downstairs for a bite to eat.

Fortunately, no one seemed to be about. Happy to be left alone, she peeked into each room until she found the kitchen.

All the luxuries. I shouldn't be surprised.

The refrigerator offered a selection of sliced ham, cheese, and fruit. After filling a small plate, she found a selection of crystal glassware in a nearby cabinet. With plate in one hand and glass of water in the other, she made her way down the hall. Taking Midir at his word that she would not be disturbed, she chose to enjoy her simple meal in the library.

Setting her treats on a small table next to a beautiful red chaise, she sat down and relaxed back, closing her eyes. She stroked the soft velvet, thinking of how decadent it all felt.

Her eyes popped open, scanning the room in front of her. She listened for any noise. Hearing none, she reached for the glass of water, taking a sip, then rolled a piece of cheese into a slice of ham. Intrigued by the books, she ventured to the shelves for a closer look. Many of the volumes were duplicates of those she'd seen in Dar's library. Again, she was struck by how alike these two men were, yet so different. *If I'd met Midir first...* She shuddered, not daring to complete the thought.

One heavily gilded spine caught her eye. Thankful for the distraction, she shoved the rest of the ham into her mouth as she needed both hands to remove it from the shelf, and carried it to the chaise. Opening the cover, she breathed in the smell of old paper, caressing the delicate pages. The title page was several leaves in with "VonNeshta" illuminated in gold leaf.

Thumbing past names and drawings of VonNeshta ancestors, she found portraits of two young, seemingly innocent boys. One was fair-haired with blue eyes, the other dark-haired and green-eyed. Memories of the visions she'd seen after a blooding with Dar told her these faces belonged to the brothers. She smiled, tracing a finger over Dar's baby face.

So handsome, even then…and blonde.

The next pages were paintings of a man and a woman, who were undoubtedly their parents. Dar had his father's eyes. Midir was the image of their mother. Even his hair was the same as hers…long, dark, and thick.

She realized then that Dar had never said much about his mother, wondering what the story was between them. When he told her of the slaughter of his family, he'd not mentioned his mother. She presumed the lady must have died when the boys were young.

The next page held pictures of a honey blonde woman with two small children, a girl and a boy. "Alexia," she whispered, admiring her beauty. "These must be Victoria and Henrí. What a beautiful family, Dar."

Turning the pages, she thought it odd Midir would

keep a family album. "You murder them all, yet keep their pictures? Creepy."

Toward the end of the book, the entries changed to familiar names and modern photographs. Etain's mouth dropped open, seeing a portrait of her mom, dad, and brother. Her hand trembled, caressing their faces. It must have been taken before her birth. Her brother, Robert, looked no more than two years old. They all looked so young. Tears formed, falling down her cheeks, splattering on the protective film over the photos.

On the next page were photos of her and her brother. Not portraits or family pictures. These were covert. Taken without their knowledge or consent, and long before her family's deaths. The remainder of the album consisted of Etain and Robert at various ages. It made her skin crawl.

Coming to the last page, the red eyes of a flame-haired young man stared at her. It was as though he could see into her and knew her thoughts. She slammed the book closed, tightened the sash of her robe, and left the room.

"Thank you for standing witness, Linq. You are a good friend. For that, I am most grateful."

"Something tells me it's just the beginning."

Dar placed a hand on his shoulder. "If I had family, I would not ask this of you. Should I fall in the fight with Midir, I wish you to usher my soul to its eternal resting place. It would be a great honor if you would sing of my deeds and my death."

"I am honored by your request, High Lord, but you're a better warrior than Midir. You'll be back."

Dar chuckled, touched by his friend's vote of confidence. "I'll do my best not to let you down."

Returning to the house, they made their way to Spirit. "Milady, have you found anything?"

"Nothing." She sounded as dejected as she looked. "I don't believe we will. I told you. I saw her stabbed in the heart with me own two eyes."

"And I told you she is alive."

"I've searched in every corner with not so much as a glimmer. There's nothing left of her in this realm."

"Spirit, do not concentrate on the Alamir realm. She's not here." His patience showed signs of wear. "Midir has taken her to another. That is why I gave you the map. You must search above and below. Do not stop until you find her."

"Dar." Inferno's voice served as a warning. "Ya best watch how ya talk to me wife, or that crystal skin-pricker won't be the only sword with blood on it."

"Someone around here has to be strong. I know she lives. If you won't say what must be said then I will." He pushed past Inferno toward Spirit and crouched down to look her in the eye. "Spirit, you know I speak the truth, don't you? See with your heart, not your eyes."

"Dar, you don't understand-" Inferno started.

"I understand better than you can imagine." His attention returned to Spirit. "Here. This may help." Dar took hold of the sword and ran his hand along its sharp edge, smearing his blood on the blade. "Much to my disgust, I share the same blood as my brother. Etain is linked to both of us through it. Follow the trail it provides and you will find my heart." He sat across from the bewildered mage, watching intently as she began once more.

Not fully recovered from her ordeal, Spirit's chants grew weaker by the hour and Inferno's patience wore ever thinner. Just as he was ready to put a stop to the farce, the blade began to give off a bright white glow. Eyes wide, Spirit looked at Dar. At the same time, a voice, full of anguish, shattered his thoughts, rocking him to the depths of his soul.

Dar and Spirit spoke as one. "I know where she is."

17

SUCKER PUNCH

It could be said that Freeblood was angry and wanted answers. It could also be said the *Bok'Na'Ra* were not nice people, but that would be subtle by comparison, and much less relevant. Anxious to be on his way, Freeblood stepped out of a pub somewhere in the southern Australian sector. The changes in his life since meeting the blonde girl had been nothing short of mind-blowing. Gifted with an unnatural speed now, he had developed new strength in body and mind. His vocabulary was constantly expanding with words and ideas he always thought as make-believe…Alamir, *Bok'Na'Ra*, swords, magic. Then there was the blood thing. *And the blue gem.*

It had appeared one night while at a wild ass concert in Japan, embedded in the palm of his hand, pulsing to the beat of the music. That was the night he met the strangest dude yet. At first, he thought it a gimmick, a costume for the concert, but soon learned the man was more real than he imagined. Aside from his diabolical ideas and freakishly red skin, he taught Freeblood how to manipulate the blue gem. Unfortunately, that was all he did. Freeblood was again left with a head full of unanswered questions.

He wasn't exactly sure where he was going. His inner compass kept pointing him west, no matter what the blonde nag in his head said. However, he found if he didn't concentrate too hard on his direction, he could veer in a westerly fashion without causing himself too much discomfort. By making a dash up through Asia, moving in a zig-zag formation, it wasn't long before he landed in Germany. Upon reaching Berlin, he grabbed a drink from a dockworker in a local bar and downed it. He had picked up a few names during his journey, such as Dar and Inferno. He knew they had something to do with the UWS clan, but wasn't certain which of them would give him answers. Letting out a loud belch, he resumed his sprint over the continent, ready to demand answers from a certain blonde.

In no time, a great castle loomed before him. The heat in his veins was not as strong today, but something about this place drew him in. Walking through the gates, he headed to the front door, lifted the massive knocker, and let it bang against the cast iron strike plate. Getting no response, he did it again. There were people here. He could hear their muffled voices on the other side of the door. He turned the knob. Unchallenged, Freeblood stepped inside.

"Oh, yeah. This is the place."

"Who the hell do you think you are?" A man with wild hair, not much older than himself, asked, his hand going to the hilt of his sword. "You can't just walk in here."

"I guess the door knocker's just for looks, huh?"

"Who are you?" The man stalked toward him.

"Freeblood. You?"

"This is a private residence."

"Hence why I knocked." He shook his head, sensing the futility of the current conversation. "I'm looking for a girl. Etain, I think her name-"

"You know Etain?"

"I know I didn't stutter." He darted behind the man and moonwalked past him. "I have questions. She has answers."

Freeblood heard footsteps behind him.

"Found your way back, I see."

He turned, looking up at the biggest man he'd ever seen, dressed in black leathers, sporting two serious blades on his back, plus a fancy one on his hip. "No thanks to Etain. Do you know her?"

The big man looked past Freeblood at the wild-haired one. "I've heard the name."

Is that a grin on his face? Did I say something funny?

A blonde elf walked up, taking the funny man's attention away. "Linq, we found her."

Freeblood scowled as another came along.

"When do we leave?" This one was shorter, had brown hair, and had human ears. He cast a questioning look at Freeblood.

"As soon as you tell Spirit," said the big one.

"Ack, she already knows I'll be-"

Freeblood jumped back as the big man swung his fist, knocking the new guy out cold.

"Freeblood, help me lay him on the couch."

"What?" *How the hell does he know my name?* "Uh… Oh, yeah." Wary of these strange men, he thought it prudent to play along until he found out where to find Etain.

"That was extreme," the elf said.

"Extreme measures for an extreme man. You know he wouldn't stay behind otherwise." The big man shot Freeblood a steely look. "We've met, but I haven't the time to explain. You stay here until we get back, and do *not* cause trouble."

"When? I'm pretty sure I'd remember someone like you, and I don't remember *ever* meeting you. I want to see Etain."

Crazy hair ran interference, dropping an arm across his shoulders. "Freeblood… Is that your name?"

"Yeah. You gonna tell me where she is?"

"Let me introduce myself. I am Wolfe. Have you sworn to a clan yet?"

Nursing a sore jaw, and pissed as hell, Inferno spotted five riders headed toward Laugharne flying a banner emblazoned with a sword, its hilt the image of a dragon's wings, tail curled down the blade.

Fucking hell.

"We have company, love."

Spirit joined him at the window. "Goddess of us all. What now?"

"I'll go have a nosey. Maybe I can get rid of 'em." He looked over at Freeblood. "Keep yer arse in here and don't get in the way." He pecked Spirit on the cheek and went outside, followed by Felix and Ruby.

Seeing Inferno, the riders stopped. A stern woman of average height spoke. "Where is Dar?" Pale hair and dark leathers accentuated her glaring grey eyes.

"Aren't we Mary Sunshine today? Who the hell's askin'?" He bloody well knew the reputation of each one, but was damned if he'd give them the satisfaction of letting them know it.

"Surely you recognize the LOKI banner. We are the High Council and have come to collect our chieftain," answered Pyro, Commander of the Blood Warriors faction of the clan, and the only man in the group.

Although not fond of the demon lord, something about this group rubbed Inferno in an even worse way. "LOKI. It's been a long time. Must be serious to have the five of ya leave yer cozy castle and come this far."

The blonde woman huffed. "We have clan business that doesn't concern UWS. Stop wasting our time and tell us where he is."

Inferno scratched his chin. "Well, see, there's the problem. The fact yer standing in front of the UWS chieftain on UWS land *makes* it our business. Now, if ya'd like to get off yer high horses, maybe we could have a civil conversation."

Swee, the healer of the clan, gave him a sheepish smile. He remembered the small, brunette woman dressed in green-leather armor as one of the more reasonable members. "Apologies, Inferno. We meant no disrespect."

He eyed the rest of the group, knowing the apology came from her alone. He'd love to have a go at the tossers, get them in the dirt and show 'em a thing or two. He looked back at the castle, seeing his beautiful wife standing in their new bay window, and thought again.

"The man's not here. I don't know when or if he'll be back." He crossed his arms over his chest. "Family business, ya see."

A look passed among them. "He has no family," Pyro said. "Tell us where he is and we'll leave you in peace."

"He'll be back when his business with his brother is done." Inferno spread his feet farther apart, ready to argue his point. "If ya insist on being bullheaded idiots, the lot of ya can cool your heels down at the shore. Or…if ya can behave as noble Alamir, then ya can come wait in me lounge."

Swee spoke on behalf of the others. "The long trip has made us forget our manners." She looked to the formidable woman glaring at Inferno. "Savage, we aren't going to get any information by bullying our way in. I'm sure Dar will be back soon, then we can be on our way." Savage glanced at Pyro, who nodded. Swee smiled at Inferno. "We'll behave as best we can, milord."

Midir entered the wasteland realm…flat, dry, and grey. Had there ever been plant life on this plane, it had long since withered and died. His destination loomed in the distance, blurred by the windblown sand biting into his skin. Gathering his cloak close, he battled against the wind to approach a set of massive gates.

The walls of the castle became more distinct as he neared, their color such a deep red that it appeared black. Its gates loomed like dark sentinels, impervious to the wild stirrings of the land. He gained access through a smaller door set within the gate. Without a word, a guard dressed in black led him inside. Midir could not tell if the body was demon, *Bok*, or something other. Left alone in the main hall, he removed his cloak, his attention turning to the assortment of weapons displayed around the room.

"Do we have a problem?" asked a tall, red-skinned demon impeccably dressed in suit and tie.

"What a ridiculous question."

"We agreed there would be no contact until she turned." Flames, serving as hair, burned white-hot, revealing his disapproval.

"About that..." Midir continued admiring the collection. "I want you to hold off a while longer." He turned at the "hmph" from the demon. "Perhaps you've forgotten how it is with her. She cannot be coerced."

"Have you become distracted, Midir?" There was a smirk on the blood-red lips.

"Merely determined. She is the crux of our success. Once she is ours, we can proceed with the stones."

"How are we to know when she is ours?"

Midir grinned. "A test."

A raised brow showed his interest. "Something I would enjoy?"

"You will stay put." Midir, no longer amused by the conversation, pointed a finger in the demon's face. "She's on the edge. Knowledge of you could push her in the wrong direction. We're almost there. Do *not* fuck it up."

"We're in far more danger of *you* fucking it up...Father. Even if we meet, she wouldn't know me. Remember why we do this, and keep your eyes off her pretty little ass."

Etain woke to an overcast morning and a brisk breeze blowing through the balcony doors. Shivering, she padded across the room, closed the doors, and went to stoke up a fire. Once warm enough to function, she opened the armoire, staring at new wardrobe. The black from the day before were history, so she chose the darkest ones she could find – a blue as deep as Dar's eyes. Her fingers caressed the soft leather, her thoughts drifting to another place. With a shake of her head, she shook off the urge to cry.

"I *will* find a way to get back to you."

After dressing, she stopped by the kitchen for a quick bite. Lilith handed her a tankard of the same drink as the day before. Having felt no further effects after her first encounter with the mixture, she downed it, then headed toward the door. Determined to beat whatever challenges Midir had in store for her today, she thought, *Pay attention, Etain. When the opportunity shows itself, you be ready to take it.*

Memories of yesterday's attack put her on guard. The door had been open then. Today it was closed. The handle turned easily enough, but the door proved heavier than she'd thought. Planting her feet, she tugged for all she was worth, grunting with the effort. Opening it halfway, she waited for the sounds of attack. No bodies lurched into the entry, no war cries, nothing. She peeked into the courtyard. Finding it empty, she placed both hands on the face of the massive door and pushed with all her might. The creaking wood slammed against the wall, sending a loud boom throughout the castle, sufficient warning for anyone who may be lying in wait.

Although she couldn't see him, her senses told her Midir was near. Constantly vigilant, she inched along the wall toward a rolling rack of swords. Choosing her weapon, she worked through a few exercises, loosening her muscles. A few practice jabs ended with her in the center of the yard.

A tingle ran up her spine.

"Etain."

She turned and stepped back, aiming the sword at his heart. "This is your last game at my expense. Today will see you dead."

"I've come to take you home."

"Ah, a new tactic." Her laugh was cold. "Another promise to tear out my heart and break me down. I won't fall like yesterday."

"Fall? Are you hurt? Let me check," he said, holding out his hand.

"Like you care." She took another step back, whirled around, and replaced the blade at his chest. "I'm ready for anything you dish out."

"I would hope so. It's because I care that we trained so hard."

Crimson wings arced over her head, the glow in her eyes intense. "Which one are you today? The Dar who ran me through, then shared his tainted blood to bind me to him forever?" The tip of the sword slashed up, leaving a gash across his cheek. He staggered back just as she made a play for his midsection. "Or the Dar who took my sister to bed?" Rolling her shoulders, she pulled her sword close. "Or perhaps you'll have the balls to show your own face. It would make watching you die all the sweeter."

She circled around him, forcing him to defend himself. He put Burning Heart to work, deflecting her jabs.

"As if that weren't enough, you incestuous bastard, you give her a child." She stopped in front of him. "But the demon demanded more, didn't he? The sacrifice of innocence…*my* innocence, my heart, my soul. What are your plans for me now, *Dar*? Am I to stand aside and watch you raise your child with her, or am I a liability to be eliminated like so many others in your past?"

"I don't understand, *mo chuisle*."

"Do not call me that! Only Dar can say those words to me. Not you." Violet orbs transformed into a deadly stare of light. "*Never* you, Midir, murdering bastard." Her sword came crashing down.

Dar dove to the side and rolled, coming into a crouch, Burning Heart and Day Star crossed over his head. "Etain," he yelled. "I *am* Dar!"

"You are a liar. I would know if you were him. I feel no love from you."

Shifting his weight, Dar came up and kicked her in the stomach, knocking her back a few steps. He threw his blades to the ground. "I will not fight you."

"You *will* fight me. I will have my revenge for my father, my mother, and for Dar's family, too, while I'm at it."

"Killing *me* will not give you the satisfaction you seek. But if you truly do not feel my love, my life isn't worth living." Her eyes were their true demon violet, but encased within a green glow. "I will not live without you."

"Then don't."

As she drew her sword back, he held up a hand. "Will you honor me with one last request?"

"What?"

He removed *Nim'Na'Sharr* from the scabbard on his hip and offered her the hilt. "If my life is to end this day, I would rather be destroyed by the two creations I hold most dear. Forged from my family's history - you, from my blood, and *Nim'Na'Sharr,* from my love for you." She shifted the demon sword to her left hand, using the tip to push him back a step. With her right hand, she reached for the crystal blade. "And…" He drew her gaze back to him, "I ask you wear this medallion. It and the sword belong together…with you." She bowed her head and allowed him to place the medallion around her neck. "Your cry told me where to find you," he whispered and stepped back.

"What did you say?" The medallion turned crimson, the blade of *Nim'Na'Sharr* following suit.

"I was at Laugharne, waiting for Spirit to find you. When you screamed my name, I knew where to go."

"Liar. Spirit is dead." She tossed the demon blade aside, taking hold of *Nim* with both hands. "I saw what you did. Another life taken without mercy. Did you think I'd forgotten?"

Dar noticed the green in her eyes fading as the medallion burned brighter, drawing the evil into itself. "Etain, you *have* forgotten." She raised a brow. "You have forgotten *Nim* cannot be handled by evil. Were I Midir…"

Crimson faded into pink, then pure white. Simultaneously, white light flashed over her body, turning her eyes a penetrating ice blue, changing her hair and wings white. *Nim'Na'Sharr* changed with her. Its runes glowed, a brilliant white light bursting from the crystal blade. Etain's head snapped back, her arms extended out. The purifying light cleansed her body, mind, and spirit of Midir's influence. Once the light dissipated, she collapsed to her knees, head lowered.

Dar held his ground, waiting.

After several minutes, she lifted her head, locking her gaze with his. "Nice trick, Midir."

He was taken aback. How could his plan not have worked? The light was damn near spiritual. It should have burned everything…

She came to her feet. Without moving her head, her eyes slid to the left, to the right, then back to him. Dar blinked, hoping he saw what he thought were signals intended for him. With both hands on the hilt of *Nim*, she raised the blade.

"Duck!"

Dar dropped down, grabbing Burning Heart and Day Star as Etain slashed over his head. Her move was so close, the air stirred his hair. Spinning out of his crouch, a fine mist of blood sprayed over his body as he slashed up at one demon, blocking another's attack. Clawed hands were hacked off and demon hearts pierced. Etain was busy with her own troop of demons, her blade turning each one to dust.

Clipped by a lucky punch, a distracted Dar fell to one knee. Etain raced to his side, slicing the demon into oblivion, its dusty remains whirling in the wind. Smiling, she offered her hand. "You had me worried for a minute."

"I had *you* worried?" He smiled, happy to see she was his Etain once again.

The warriors stood back-to-back, taking on the next onslaught of demons. Eventually, they parted, but kept each other in sight. Another band of demons came out of nowhere, concentrating on Dar, splitting the duo farther apart. He lost sight of Etain in the bedlam.

A booming voice suddenly brought everything to a halt. "Dar! I have something to show you, brother." The sea of demons parted, giving Dar full view of Midir holding Etain by the hair. Glaring across the courtyard, he forced her to kneel, his dirk at her throat. "I always regretted that you missed my performance with Alexia and the children." Blood trickled down her neck. "But seeing your face as I drain the life from this one will more than make up for my disappointment."

Dar dropped his swords. "I'm the one you want. Fight me, man-to-man. Leave her out of this."

"What I *want* is to see you suffer. The pain in your eyes will make my victory all the sweeter."

"Midir..." His voice rang with warning.

Midir yanked her head back. "Watch this, Dar." He repositioned the dagger, his intent clear.

Etain's hand shot up, driving a dagger through his forearm. Surprised by the attack, he dropped the blade. She rolled to the side and called to *Nim*. The faithful sword immediately appeared in her hand. As she moved, Dar grabbed both his blades, running through the opening of demons. He jumped into a somersault, sailing over the few blocking his way, and landed in front of Midir.

A dangerous smile lifted the corners of his mouth. "Make me suffer now, brother."

18

VELNOXTICA

Dar's gaze penetrated Midir to the depths of his black soul. "Show me," he snarled, Day Star flashing forward, leaving a shallow gash across his left shoulder. Burning Heart opened another cut across Midir's right shoulder. "You have taken everything I've ever loved, but not this time, brother. Not this time. This life you will not destroy." He followed his brother's retreating steps, Day Star in the lead.

Midir answered his strikes. "You have no life with this one." His sword slid past Dar's block and scored a hit, leaving a cut across his neck. "You can feel it in her blood. Whatever bond you had weakens by the minute. You should know she has willingly taken my blood." He came at him with an overhead swing.

Dar blocked his move. "You lie. She would nev-"

"But she did." Midir held his sword close, giving his poisoned words time to work. "She's ready to be mine."

Dar then realized the game played at his expense. *Just moments ago, this dark force was ready to sacrifice her just to see him suffer.* He dropped his swords and looked over at Etain. "Let's test that theory."

Across the yard, Etain bit her bottom lip, watching as Midir's sword sliced into Dar, who went down to a knee. "No!" *Nim'Na'Sharr* went into action, killing demons in her bid to get to him. There were far too many to make much headway, but she continued to fight regardless.

Midir leaned down, glaring into his brother's face. "I will take her while your corpse grows cold and the crows feed on your flesh. She will bear me many sons."

"Which is it, Midir? Wife or victim?" Dar struggled to restrain the beast within. "If you asked her, I think she'd say they are the same. See for yourself. She fights for me." His voice ended in a roar as Burning Heart sliced deep across Midir's chest. The injured warrior dragged himself to his feet, blood rolling down his leg. "I will see the both of us dead before I allow her to be tainted by you." With renewed strength, he launched a fresh volley of blows.

They exchanged blow for blow, each taking numerous hits. Out of the blue, Midir asked, "How is your daughter?"

Dar withdrew a few steps. "Victoria is dead. You murdered her."

Midir laughed. "You really believe she was *your* daughter?" He brandished his sword. "That's the past. I'm talking about the here and now. The little demon girl. Who would've thought the righteous Dar of Krymeria would fuck his own daughter?" Midir laughed. "And leave her pregnant?"

"She isn't…" He refused to take the bait. "How do you know of the child?"

"On the lakeshore, when we battled last, I felt the presence of another life. One that wasn't there when I first met her." He eyed his brother. "It will bring back sweet memories, destroying your latest attempt to build a family. You remember your first family, don't you? I peeled the flesh from their small bodies, one agonizing strip at a time, while they begged for their lives. Their cries were music to my ears." He backed away a few more steps. "Once you are dead, Etain will stand by my side, then I will rip your whore and her unborn bastard apart."

Images from the past mixed with those of the present. Dar's control over the beast slipped a notch. "You...will... not...touch...them," rumbled from deep in his chest. "You will not destroy the life of another innocent."

The rage burst forth, annihilating Dar's slender thread of control. Instead of the bloodlust, a golden glow emanated through his skin, growing brighter and brighter, as if the very sun itself burned within him. "*No more!*"

Midir sprinted away, disappearing through the open door.

Day Star blazed with golden fire. Burning Heart burned with flames of crimson.

"The air reeks with your fear. Come out, come out, wherever you are," he said, slicing along the wall in a methodical cadence as he worked his way closer to his cowering brother. "Come out and play with your new master. His name is Death."

Although Etain had never seen Dar in this state, she had heard enough stories about his white light, his solar flare ultimá, to realize what was happening. The ground trembled. Windows exploded outwards, covering the ground with shards of glass. She frantically hacked her way through the demon horde standing between her and safety, diving behind the remains of a partial wall for protection.

She shivered, seeing the melted edges of the stone wall. "Holy hell."

Having heard Dar's proclamation to his brother, she raised up, peering over the wall. There wasn't a demon in sight and what little vegetation had existed was now ash. The destruction left her overwhelmed.

Dar's glowing swords caught her eye. *Nim'Na'Sharr*, linked by the blood to her creator, as well as her mistress, spoke of the mighty weapons. *They are his newest creations. Day Star, which he named for the sun and salvation of his heart. His love for you is true, mistress. The other is Burning Heart, the flaming retribution he seeks against those who have taken innocent lives.*

A loud yelp from across the yard ended the conversation. Dar had obviously located his brother. He stalked toward a deformed iron door melted by the power emanating from him.

A voice from behind made him stop.

"Not now, Etain."

"I can think of no better time." Having shared blood, she knew more about him than anyone, knew the things most important to him. "You mean to kill him," she stated, knowing his answer. She walked around to face him.

"We're wasting time." He looked over her shoulder at the melted doorway.

Her eyes went to the blade etched in flames. "Flame of Retribution? Is that how you want this to play out?"

His gaze snapped back to her, his expression one of grim surprise so intense, it made her jump. She cleared her throat and nodded toward her own blade. "*Nim* told me of your new swords." He glanced at the crystal in her hand. His expression remained grim, but he understood. *Good.*

"Killing Midir, to stop him from doing more harm, is a good thing." She leaned forward, bringing her face close to his. "But to kill him in retribution of your own loss, to prove yourself against him, or to satisfy your hate is not." He cocked his head, ready to rebuke what she said, but she didn't give him the chance. "You have been terribly wronged but will Midir's death change those wrongs?" Dar was silent. "Stop for a minute and think. His death won't undo what he's done or bring back your family."

"You're a fine one to talk. Tell me you weren't satisfied seeing the head of your family's assassin separated from his neck."

"If I denied it, you'd know it was a lie. Aye, it felt good to know he would never kill again. But it wasn't me who wielded the sword, was it? You did it for me. To keep me safe. To make sure I *felt* safe. You did that for love.

"Killing Midir for revenge will only complete his evil by twisting the good in you to darkness. If you fight with hate in your heart, he will win and you will die. If the goodness in you dies, I will die. Faux will die. The child will die. Everything you've fought for will die."

He felt like he had been slapped, but he knew it was true. Leaning back, he saw Etain as he had never seen her before. Here stood this woman, seemingly young and inexperienced, laying bare his very core with her words.

"Be true to yourself, my love," she whispered. "Your heart must be pure to defeat your brother. This must be done for the safeguard of innocence, not the evil of revenge." Smoothing his brow with her fingertips, she took his face into her hands. "I love you, Dar. You are my life. Do not let the darkness of your brother steal your light."

Those three words meant more to him than anything else. The tension eased from his muscles. He had to forget about revenge and release the hate in his heart. Midir was his dark side and must be accepted without reservation. It was essential he engage in the spirit of justice, not revenge.

"Thank you," he said.

"With that said..." She stepped back. "You owe me a life."

"How so?" Where was she going with this?

"The assassin who butchered my family."

"Aye. What about him?"

"Midir sent him." She gripped his arm, her gaze boring into his. "Midir murdered my family. His life is mine."

Dar pulled from her grasp. "He is my brother, *my* responsibility."

"You had your chance. *I* will end him."

"What was the talk about virtue, about taking his life for the right reasons?"

"*That* was saving your soul."

"Is your soul not worth saving?"

"Killing him *will* save mine, and free you from having to kill your brother. Let me do this for you...and for me."

He took a step closer to the door where Midir had fled. "I once told you it would take the strength of a demon to kill him."

She lifted her chin. "I am a demon."

"With a lot to learn. You cannot beat him, Etain. He is too strong."

The look on her face cut him to the core. When she spun around, disappearing through the door, his sympathy flashed into anger. "*Goddamn it.*" He dashed after her and his brother.

Along the way, he encountered small pockets of demons, easily overcoming their attempts to kill him. Neither Etain nor Midir had shown themselves Sensing their locations, he found a modicum of solace knowing they were moving in opposite directions. He moved deeper into the tunnels beneath the castle, following corridor after corridor, staving off the fear that, at some point, his lady would cross paths with his brother before he could catch up to either of them.

Turning a corner, he came upon a throng of demons, their long spears jabbing at his face. Dar managed to take one of the lead demons down, but the press of those behind pushed him back. Giving ground, he fought off their thrusts. When an opportunity showed itself, he was quick to take it.

A distinctive odor, strong enough to overpower the stench of the demons, rolled through the passageway. A syrupy, sweet reek that rekindled memories of Krymeria, the world of his birth. Some noble families had kept such creatures as a show of strength, monstrous beasts that exuded that unmistakable smell. Velnoxtica, lumpy masses of rag-like, sticky tendrils that engulfed and dissolved anything that came into contact with it. One drop of the mucus from the fleshy center would eat through skin and bone within seconds.

Aware of what lay in wait, Dar increased the fervor of his fight, mentally kicking himself for letting these maggots herd him so easily. A sudden flutter on his back made him glance over his shoulder. The Velnoxtica, barely ten feet away, was already reaching out with its sticky fingers. His twin blades weaved through the demons, spinning and cutting in as magnificent a dance as he had ever performed. The demons' bravery boosted by the sight of the creature, surged forward, unaffected by Dar's flashing scimitars. Many had to be hit several times before even acknowledging the first blow. There were simply too many for the warrior to hold his ground. The flicking tendrils stretching their full length, searching for their next meal, felt their way toward him. He had no room to maneuver. The spears would either run him through or force him into the creature. Eyes bright, his burst of laughter startled the demons. He'd be damned if a demon would end his life. Dar spun on his heels, diving into the mass of the Velnoxtica.

Etain pulled up short, staring at the dark hole where Dar had disappeared. She didn't know what he faced, but she'd seen the grotesque tendrils reaching for him. And the smell... *Bloody hell!* Holding her breath, she watched the demons back away and disappear down another corridor. She listened to Dar's struggle and waited. A minute or so later, she gasped for air, running a hand through her hair.

Come on, Dar. Please come out. She bit her bottom lip, her heart in her throat. "Please, my love," she whispered.

Just as she decided to go after him, the sound of footsteps made her retreat into the shadows. Midir came into view, a smirk on his face.

"And so you die," he said, sheathing his sword. "The risks I took getting you here to prove whose life was the lie. To show you the emotions you hold onto so dearly have no place in the heart of a true warrior. If Father were here, he'd finally understand who is the better son. At least our struggle is over." He laughed. "I thought you almost my equal. Never would I have fallen into such a trap."

Etain swiped away her tears, reached for her dagger, and lunged at the man. "You aren't far behind him, fucker."

Midir turned in time, leaning back and over, avoiding the deadly arc of her blade. Going with the move, he slid past her, grabbing her around the waist and getting hold of her wrist. "Lady Etain. Perfect timing." He squeezed until she dropped the blade. "Alone at last."

"You make me sick," she said, struggling against his grip. "Dar!"

"He won't be saving anyone anymore. Say your farewells, milady."

"No! Let me go! Dar! Dar!" Tears blurred her vision. She felt sick to her stomach, her heart about to explode. She had to get to him. He couldn't be dead. She would know. She would feel the loss.

No matter how hard she fought, Midir held tight.

"Let's leave the Velnoxtica to its dinner."

"Fuck...off!" Using the force of her wings, she pushed against Midir, his grip loosening when he hit the rock wall. Twisting from his grasp, her talons extended, slashing down, raking him from cheek to belly. "You won't live to see another day," she said, her other set of talons ready to strike.

Midir barrelled into her, transitioning into his demon form. His great wings far exceeded the span of Etain's, engulfing her completely. "I will...and so will you."

Trapped within his embrace, Etain could do no more than move her head. She stilled and, hard as it was, allowed his face to come close to hers. His breath against her skin, the condescending leer in his eyes, his smirk... It was too much. She lashed out with her teeth.

He snapped back, his grin erased. "Taming you will be a pleasure."

"I'll kill myself first."

In spite of his struggles to hold the wildcat, Midir laughed. "Begging for bondage so soon? You are a delight."

"Stop!" she screamed. "Let me go!"

His laughter echoed off the walls as he dragged her down the corridor. "I will never let you go, Lady Etain. You are mine."

19

FALLEN

Hearing footsteps, Midir slowed his pace, tightened his grip on Etain, and waited.

"Is that fear I smell?" she asked, making another attempt at freedom.

He gave her a lopsided grin. "Merely anticipation, milady."

A soldier in full armor, followed by men clad similarly, appeared from an opposite corridor. "Milord, are you well?"

"Lieutenant Cromorth. Yes, we…" He stole a glance at Etain, "are fine. We have fulfilled our objective and the prize is ours."

Cromorth bowed his head. "Shall we sweep the remaining corridors, milord?"

"No need. The threat has been eliminated. You and the men take the night off. Enjoy yourselves."

"Yes, milord." With a salute, he and his men disappeared down the tunnel.

"Dar isn't dead."

"Let it go, Etain. I won. He's gone. The sooner you accept that fact, the easier it will be."

"Nothing's gonna be easy for you, especially me." She gave him a hard push. "I can walk on my own."

"Until we're clear of these tunnels, you're stuck to me."

She expressed her disgust with a snort. "Afraid I'll rescue him from whatever monster you've set on him?"

"Not likely. Velnoxtica don't leave remains. You'd only be risking yourself."

She slapped him. "Asshole."

He gritted his teeth. "You have no idea. But keep it up and I will leave no doubts." He squeezed her arm, making her yelp, and pushed her ahead of him. "Let's go. This day has made me weary."

After a few steps, she stopped, smirked, and continued walking.

"Confident, are we?" he asked.

She shrugged. "I don't have anything to do with this. It's whatever Midir wants."

"From your point of view, I'm sure it looks that way. I told your father I would take care of you, and I have."

"Great job, killing everyone I've ever loved."

"Not everyone… There's still that Alamir chieftain and his brats."

Anticipating her violent reaction, Midir slammed into her, pinning her against the rock wall. "You and I, we have history. It's time you learned the orchestration of your-"

"This obsession with me is sickening. I was just a girl. No one special. I was happy! Why? Why would you tell my father such a thing? How long had you planned their murders? What history have we ever had?"

He felt the hairs on the back of his neck rise. The cold steel against his throat told him it was too late.

"We don't give a damn about your lies," Dar said, his lips close to Midir's ear. "Let her go, then we will end this farce we call brotherhood."

A nervous smile crossed Midir's face. "Well done, brother. Not many have survived the drool of the Velnoxtica."

Midir pressed his body into Etain's for a brief moment, then gave her a hard push. She stumbled out of the line of fire just as he swung around with his saber, followed by a dagger jab. Dar twirled out of the way and turned, slashing down with his own sword. Saber and scimitar locked hilts, bringing the combatants face-to-face.

Dar heaved up, pushing his evil sibling back. "It's not so hard if you know where to aim."

Midir rolled with the momentum from Dar's shove, but stepped on a stone, losing his footing. Although he tried to catch himself, he slipped to one knee. Dar was on him with both blades.

Midir reacted equally fast, his head and shoulders bobbing as he tried to get back to his feet. Unfortunately for Dar, his assault left him too close to the wall to move. He attempted to ease back as Midir straightened.

"I had hoped our sweet Etain would come around to my way of thinking, see you for what you really are. How is it you invoke such loyalty from *both* women?"

"Love is something you will never understand."

"You've forgotten what it means to be Krymerian, protecting useless Alamir parasites, lowering yourself to their level." Midir lunged forward. "You give your power to a woman who has no need for it." His tongue was sharp. "She will drain everything you are and leave you to rot."

Dar blocked, accepting the words with a smile. "You are a contradiction. One minute, you fight to possess her; the next, you threaten her life. What does it matter to you?"

An austere glow lit in Midir's eyes. "All our lives, everything has been for you. The legacy, the kingdom, the honor, and you lost it all."

Dar pushed him back. "Our futures were taken from us by your thirst for revenge. What does any of it have to do with Etain?"

"*I* found her long before you became aware of the human realm or the Alamir. *I* watched her grow. *I* saw her potential. *I* engineered her initiation into the Alamir for the very power you refuse to harness for yourself. Control of such power requires a strength and finesse of which you have no concept."

Dar moved toward his brother, his jaw firm in the knowledge of what he must do. "Whatever power she may have is hers. You will not take control of it."

Midir advanced with equal confidence. "Come and die then." He growled as he carried out the next attack, whipping the saber toward Dar's neck, thrusting low with the dagger. Dar barely had time to raise one blade and lower the other, pushing the dagger aside. Midir continued to pummel him, Dar deflecting as best he could, suffering several cuts.

"First blood is mine," Midir crowed, sliding a finger down the blade for a taste of the red stain.

"Last blood counts for more," Dar countered, pressing on with a cool head despite the sweat trickling down his back. He cut at Midir from impossible angles, blood stains telling on his shirt. Dar recognized the boiling anger in his brother and sought to exploit it. He leaned to the left, cutting back with a right thrust, his left close behind. Midir diverted the attack with a sweeping blow, grinning at Dar's apparent mistake. His dagger struck through the opening toward Dar's heart. As the blade came in, Dar cocked back his head then slammed into Midir's nose before he could pierce his heart. The dagger and saber clanged against the floor. Midir yelled and grabbed his face, grimacing in pain as he stumbled back.

"Your hate weakens your ability," Dar said, stepping forward.

"You haven't won yet."

"Brother, you lost a long time ago."

Midir displayed a contemptuous smile, spun on his heels, dipping down to retrieve his blades, and took flight down a passageway. Dar was quick to pursue, leaving Etain alone.

Etain watched them disappear into the darkness, listening to their footsteps fade. She had listened to the exchange between the brothers, too stunned to interrupt.

The question for her was whether to follow or leave them to it. Her instincts reminded her of Midir's constant lies. It was highly probable another ambush lay in wait for Dar, but would her presence help or would it only serve to distract him from what needed doing? She remembered the fight at the Laugharne shore. Midir had shown no mercy to either Faux or his brother. Given the chance, he intended to end Dar's life in any way he could, which she could not allow.

Her decision made, she turned toward the dark tunnel they had run down just moments earlier. Hearing footsteps coming toward her, she paused. Could Midir have circled back? It was possible. Angered by the prospect of his plan to ambush Dar from behind, she turned, *Nim* raised, prepared to strike.

She froze.

It was not Midir…or Dar. Since becoming Alamir, she had seen many unusual beings, but this was not anything she had ever seen before. Her mind whirled, trying to make sense of what she saw. The breath caught in her throat and her head throbbed, making her light-headed. An hallucination was the only way she could explain this spectacle. She guessed it to be about six-two with eyes of black burning coals beneath a mane of pulsating flames. His skin had the sheen of fresh blood, but she soon realized that was not the case. The color was consistent and smooth with no apparent splatters that would indicate a recent killing. Well-formed muscles across a broad chest and shoulders tapered down into a set of painfully perfect abs. The muscles in his arms flexed as he sheathed the sword in his hand.

So, she thought, *I'm not considered a threat.*

Etain brought up her sword, aiming the point toward the abomination, knees soft, body alert to any sudden move. His burning gaze took her in from head to toe, leaving behind a sense of violation. Strange and threatening as he was, she held her ground, much to his amusement. One demon behind him made a move to pass the flame-headed leader. The red-skinned man's arm shot up, dagger in hand, striking the demon in the midriff, followed by a brutal stab up just below the chin. The offender gurgled in surprise and fell. A miniscule cock of the leader's head set the others into a retreat. He flashed a macabre smile of sharpened teeth, laughed, and took his leave. Etain's eyes widened seeing the ridge along his back.

She blinked several times, keeping watch on the hole into which he had gone. *Surely, that's not the end of it.* After several minutes, it became obvious she had been left alone. Letting out a breath, she sheathed her blade.

Why is he so familiar? She remembered the photograph in Midir's album. *What does he have to do with all this?*

The echoes of swords clashing drifted through the tunnel, reminding her of another demon with a solitary thought in mind. Dar's death. She ran her hands through her hair and stared into the darkness one last time to ensure no one was there. Satisfied she wouldn't have to defend her flank, she turned and dashed down the tunnel that would take her to Dar.

What had been dark stillness exploded into motion at the shine of flashing blades. Ambushed by Midir, Dar was just able to twist back from the angle of the blow. However, he lost his footing and staggered forward. He felt a burn across his shoulder blades, followed by a wetness soaking into his shirt and running down his back. He turned, his back to the wall. Midir came at him with another furious attack, both knowing he had only moments before the shock wore off. Dar steadied himself quickly enough to defend the initial assault. Their blades locked. The brothers eyeballed one another, their faces only inches apart.

"Now you pay for your crimes, Midir."

A wild, exhilarated look brightened Midir's eyes, his lips curling into a perverse grin. He spat in Dar's eyes.

The shock broke Dar's concentration and he drew back. It was only a split second, but even that was too long. Dar jerked his head to the side, trying to clear his vision. Midir brought his blade down toward his head.

Etain exploded out of the darkness, jumping onto Midir's back. She wrapped an arm around his neck, her talons extended, poised to strike. He stumbled. Using the momentum, he propelled backward into the wall.

Hearing the breath whoosh out of her, Dar wiped his eyes with his sleeve. "No, Etain!"

Before she could recover, Midir dropped his blade and grabbed the dagger in his belt. With a twisted grin, his mad and fevered eyes burned into those of his brother. Considerably stronger than his attacker, he pulled her arm down from his neck. In a flash, the dagger stabbed into the blue leather-clad arm and deep into the white skin beneath, slicing her from elbow to wrist. Blood sprayed over his face.

"No!" Dar screamed.

Midir laughed. "Mores the pity. We could have ruled the world."

Dar's next move came more from instinct than calculation. Dropping his blades, he tucked his foot under him, pushed against the wall and lunged. At the same time, he spoke healing words he hoped she would understand. "*Mo chuisle! Beannaigh an fhuil gur féidir do sheirbhíseach a chur ar ais. Líon isteach an soitheach leis an saol, a thabhairt ar ais chugam.*"

Dar flung one foot behind Midir's ankle, pulling him away from Etain, her blood spurting with every heartbeat. "*Líon isteach cuid soitheach leis an saol, thabhairt ar ais chugam!*"

Midir toppled to the floor, losing his dagger in the process, but had enough forethought to twist and force Dar beneath him. "You can't save her."

Dar forced himself to focus on his brother rather than Etain. "Either way, she will be free of you." The dagger inches away, the men grappled, neither able to make purchase. Swinging out, Dar punched his brother in the face, giving himself the advantage he needed. Dagger in hand, Dar drove the tip into his brother's ribs, scraping past bone, straight into the black heart.

Midir's eyes widened for a brief moment. Flashing a bloody smile, he said, "Death is not the end for us, brother. As long as you live…" He grimaced, trying to catch a breath. "I will be with you." Dar watched the green eyes glaze over as Midir exhaled his last breath.

"May you finally find peace."

Dar pushed him away and rolled to his feet. Midir's dark spirit rose from the broken form, lingering, as though saying farewell to its former vessel, then circled the brother of light, in wait of his quiet invitation. With wings fanned wall to wall, Dar breathed in the ethereal remains of his dark half. Waged in an eternal way, the slithering darkness moved throughout his body, clashing with the light flowing within his veins. His body vibrated with the rise and fall of flesh where the two engaged. His eyes rolled and his head jerked back, a painful howl coursing throughout the passageways.

White talons faded in and out, slowly changing into the hands of his Krymerian form. The final step of his metamorphosis stretched his height to eight feet. His transformation complete, a pure white light shot from his eyes, disintegrating Midir's body. Dar collapsed to the floor on hands and knees, gasping for air.

A soft moan from the darkness brought him back to his senses. "Etain." He fumbled his way to her. As gently as possible, he rolled her over and ripped away the leather, exposing the nasty gash.

"I…heard…the…words," she whispered and licked her lips. "And…I…remembered…" Her eyes closed.

"You did well, milady."

Although the healing chant had saved her life, she wasn't strong enough to complete the process. He cut into his arm with a single talon and shared his blood with this precious woman, whispering the words he'd screamed to her only moments ago. "You will not die this day. We have a life to live together."

Her body reacted in a way he never expected. The bare skin of her wings had grown snow white crimson tipped feathers. Her height grew to seven feet tall. Ice blue eyes fluttered open as her hair returned to luscious silver.

"Dar?" Her voice was little more than a croak. "Is that you?"

"Aye, *mo chuisle*," he said, awestruck by her altered state, but oblivious to his own.

"You're okay?"

"Aye."

She clutched at him. "Midir…"

"You need never fear him again. He is dead."

"I wanted to be the hero," she said, relaxing in his arms. "To be *your* savior, like you've been for me so many times. I'm sorry-"

He placed a finger to her lips. "My precious lady, you *are* my hero. Although you may not see it, you have saved me on countless occasions. I am forever indebted to you."

Her look of doubt turned to concern. "You look different," she said, touching his face. "Your eyes…and hair. What's happened?"

He looked himself over, noting the change in his wings. From the corner of his eye, he saw the strands of blonde hair. "I have become the true High Lord of Kaos." He appraised the changes in her. "And you are my High Lady of Kaos."

"High Lady?"

He helped her sit up. "I am as surprised as you. I knew things would change with Midir's death, but not to this degree, or that it would affect you, as well. Together, we will restore a race as old as time."

"Surprised is putting it mildly." She disentangled herself from his arms. "Thank you for the save." She noticed the change in her own wings, ruffling the feathers. "Life with you is certainly interesting. It'll take some getting used to." She gave him a sideways glance. "As for restoring a race, well… We'll have a nice long chat…later."

"I know this is overwhelming. You go ahead to Inferno's, put a smile on Spirit's face. She's not had an easy time of it, believing you dead. There are things I need to finish here." He helped her to her feet.

Her gaze fell on the pile of ashes. "Midir?"

He lifted her chin. "Go back to Laugharne. I give you my word. I will not be long."

"I will be waiting, my love." She held his gaze for a long, loving moment, then ran a hand through her hair, biting her bottom lip.

"What's wrong?"

"I have no idea where we are. Give me a boost?"

"Apologies, *mo chuisle*." He opened a portal with the wave of a hand. Placing a soft kiss on his lips, she stepped through and was gone.

Etain's kiss warm on his lips, Dar returned to Midir's ashes. The anger and hate still burned in Dar's heart, but with his passing, the edges began to soften. He knew they would eventually fade into nothing more than distant memories. In all the time he had planned, schemed, and fought for this day, it had been his belief that were he fortunate enough to be the victor in this bizarre battle, he would feel a sense of satisfaction, of accomplishment.

I thought I would feel whole again. I told Etain we were. I believe we are, but saying the words are not the same as feeling it in your bones.

Strangely enough, he felt a loss, as though something were missing. It made no sense to him. From the moment the priests gave him breath as a separate entity, he and Midir had been at odds. Never did they agree on anything.

He tormented me his entire life. Yet I mourn his passing.

Midir had shown Dar how a life lived in jealousy, coveting things not meant for him, could turn an already black heart into a lifeless, loveless force of pure evil. Now that his essence had reunited with Dar's, he prayed he would not repeat his mistakes.

A magical incantation opened a portal to his home realm, Krymeria. He laid his brother's ashes to rest in the rich Krymerian soil away from the VonNeshta mausoleum. There were no special honors. The lightweight saber, so recently wielded with every intention of ending his brother's life, became his headstone.

302

Dar wished him Godspeed on his way to whatever afterlife awaited him, hoping he would find peace. There were no regrets for the taking of his life. Dar's only regret was that he had lost yet another member of his family, a fellow Krymerian, a brother. Dar VonNeshta had truly become the last of his kind.

Dar and Etain survived his dark brother, Midir.
Or so they thought…

DreamReaper
Blood of Kaos Series Book II

Coming Winter 2018

ABOUT THE AUTHOR

After marrying her special someone, Nesa decided life was too short to spend it all in just one place. Instead of him moving to Texas (her home), Nesa moved to Manchester, England (his home). Since then life has been an adventure and has had a positive influence on her and her writing.

The things you learn when you experience another culture!

Nesa is a "learn as you go" kind of gal, which can be challenging, especially when it comes to writing. Although it took a backseat to raising her three children, and work, the desire to write never died. Now that her kids are grown, she can indulge in her fantastical stories.

You can find Nesa Miller here:

- Website: https://ladyofkaos.com/
- Amazon: My Book
- Facebook: https://www.facebook.com/AuthorNesaMiller
- Facebook Alamir Page:
- https://www.facebook.com/theAlamir/
- Twitter: @LadyofKaos
- Goodreads: https://www.goodreads.com/LadyofKaos

92325169R00190

Made in the USA
Lexington, KY
02 July 2018